Popi's Place

A novel by Rainelle Saunders

"I was transported into the world of Popi's Place. It was so good, it left me wanting more!!!"

-- *Craig Cochran, DreamWorks Animation*

"The story of six friends sharing love, friendship and secrets, and how the lives of these women are tangled up, messed up and in need of the soul searching which will allow them to be the people they are meant to be. Popi's Place...where truth and faith transcends and illuminates the female spirit in this first, moving novel by Rainelle Saunders."

--*Tara Sullivan, CEO, Creative Creations*

"Rainelle Saunders' Popi's Place captivates from sentence one. Can you say juicy? Say it twice – juicy, juicy. Written with humor, eloquence, grittiness, and sophistication, the tapestry of distinctly complex characters is masterfully and vividly woven – shocking you one moment, intriguing you the next and cracking you up the next. Popi's Place is packed with surprises and pulls on every emotion."

--*Stacey Johnson-Whaley, Film Producer*

"When you can visualize the setting and what each person looks like, then you know the picture has been painted with detailed strokes, and that is how Popi's Place is painted. You want to turn each page to have more and more revealed."

--*Jeannine Fisher, Jeannine Fisher Casting*

"A delicious mix....was quickly sucked into each character and I wanted more, more, and some more. A fantastic read from a first time author!"

--*Yolanda J., Owner, A Tart To Remember*

Glover Lane Press
Publishers Since January 2000
4570 Van Nuys Blvd., Suite 573
Sherman Oaks, CA 91403
www.gloverlanepress.webs.com

ISBN-13: 978-0615838670
ISBN-10: 0615838677

Cover Design by Azaan Kamau
Cover Photo by Donald Starks Photography

Also note that this work contains sexual themes, objectionable language and behavior which may offend some readers.

The Mission of Glover Lane Press is to Uplift, Empower, Elevate the Masses and Provide American Jobs. Every book published by Glover Lane Press and its many imprints, is printed and manufactured in the United States of America, ensuring and maintaining American employment.

Acknowledgements

I want to extend my thanks and undying gratitude: to all of my friends from “the Nuke”; to my “sista” in Harlem, who had a vision many years ago that has kept my light burning so that I will never give up, and who provided a haven during the first year of writing this novel; for all of the “colored girls” who have inspired me on this journey; to everyone who heeded the call with their time and talents when needed; to those who came in and out of my life to bestow valuable lessons; to friends and family whose faith in me helped me to get here and wouldn’t let anything stop me; and last but never least, God, Goddess and all of my “angels on the other side” for the inspiration, the life and the unconditional love.

Prologue

Los Angeles, July 15, 2006

How does it feel to be dead? That's what the beautiful, blond woman lying on her own living room floor wanted to know, because she wasn't sure if she was dead or alive. How could she tell? Everything in her body was numb, and although there was a muted humming that remained constant in her ears, she couldn't hear any specific sounds. But her mind was racing.

Where was the high-pitched yapping from that annoying dog across the hall? He was small enough to fit in somebody's purse, but he made enough noise to give everyone in the building a splitting headache.

And what about the chunky brat whose mother let him ride his damn tricycle up and down the hallway while her fat ass watched soap operas and reality shows? Was it really important to know who Erica's eighteenth husband was going to be? And was watching continuous reruns of bimbo housewives with too much money, too much time on their hands, and no common sense, going to make her a good mother? The only time that lazy woman paid attention to the poor kid was when she yelled at him during the commercials.

And what about the noisy gay guys from the apartment upstairs? They routinely banged each other on Saturday afternoons while listening to old Jody Watley albums. It's Saturday, she thought. So where were they? There were no sounds. No sounds at all, except for the strange hum.

The woman was sprawled out on the newly waxed, hardwood floor in a very awkward way, her long, blond hair spread haphazardly over her swollen face. She tried really hard to move some part, any part, of her body, but couldn't make that happen. She wasn't even able to open her eyes. She was totally helpless and confused. Nothing in her brain seemed to be responding properly. She didn't even feel any pain.

All of a sudden, a familiar sensation washed over her body from deep inside of her. She was so cold. But how could that be? It was Los Angeles in the middle of July and her apartment had been unbearably hot for three days. She was working that old ass air conditioner overtime and it had suddenly stopped running. As usual, she had to constantly harass Alex, her Armenian landlord, in order for him to come and take a look at it. Apparently, every appliance in the building had broken down at the same time.

Finally, Alex had shown up the day before. He still hadn't fixed the air conditioner, though. Said he needed to get some kind of part. So, in reality, her apartment should still be feeling like a sauna. Instead, she felt like she was lying on a block of ice inside of a butcher's freezer. Maybe she wasn't in her apartment at all. Maybe she really *was* in a freezer. Yikes!

Something was very wrong. She had to be dreaming. She would have pinched herself, but that would have required her to move a muscle. She was seriously unable to make that happen, so she finally came to realize that her mind and her thoughts were the only things that she had at her disposal.

Once again, she had to wonder if she was dead. Then she had the strangest thought about her underwear. What was it that her grandmother liked to say? You must have on clean underwear in case you get run over by a car and your dress ends up around your waist. Well, if that actually happened, they'd be lucky to find her with any underwear on at all. In which case, upon the news, her grandmother would immediately drop dead from embarrassment.

She had to concentrate on waking up, because, if she wasn't really dead, then she sure as hell had to get herself out of this nightmare. Think, think, think. Alright, so she was having a dream about freezing to death and going crazy. Or she was dreaming that she was already dead and freezing in the morgue. Shit! Maybe she was one of those people who was mistaken for dead, but actually was aware of their surroundings and now she was going to be buried alive. But wouldn't they have to do an autopsy first? Damn, this dream really sucked. She tried to remember what she had eaten that day. Aha! That's it. No more Indian food for her.

Suddenly, true panic began to set in and she was screaming inside of her head as she remembered what had happened earlier.

***

It was the biggest night of her life. All of the drama of the past few weeks was dying down and she was finally getting a chance to prove that she had what it took to be a star. And when that moment came, she wanted to look fabulous, so she had a multitude of dresses and assorted accessories laid across her bed.

"Should I be sexy, sophisticated or shocking?" she asked herself out loud. She was going to be a trendsetter. And it didn't hurt that she actually had talent, but since when had a lack of talent ever stopped someone from making it in the music business?

There had been a sound at the door. That must be the landlord, she thought. Thank God that he had finally shown up to fix the air conditioner. She was in her bedroom, but had left the front door open for him when he said he was on his way over. The temperature was in the triple digits and she couldn't even put her makeup on without stopping every two minutes to stick her face in front of a fan. That didn't do much good, though. She had three large fans that were whipping warm air around.

"Well, Alex, it's about damn time," she said as she entered the living room, carrying several dresses. But, the person standing there wasn't her landlord. It was someone she had not planned to ever see again. She was face to face with someone she loved. A black woman, someone she hadn't seen in a while, but who was like a sister to her. A woman who was holding a gun that was aimed right at her. She was shocked, but managed to put a smile on her face.

"Wow," she said calmly. "I wasn't expecting to see you. I didn't even know you were back. What are you doing here?"

"Don't fuck wit me, trick. I think you know exactly why I'm here," the gun-yielding woman said.

"You missed me?" the beautiful blond asked, attempting a little humor. But the other woman was not in a lighthearted mood, so she decided to address the issue at hand. “What are you doing with a gun?”

“I think you know that, too.”

“Sweetie, a lot has happened since the last time I saw you.

I know you must be upset. Can we talk about it?”

“There’s nothing to talk about,” the black woman said.

“I came to settle a score.”

“C’mon now. You sound like a fucking movie character. Give me a hug or somethin’.”

The blond woman made a move toward her estranged loved one, but that only caused the woman to tighten her grip on the gun, showing that she meant business.

“Don’t come any closer or I swear I’ll splatter your white ass all over this nice, shiny floor.”

Afraid, the blond put her hands in the air and slowly backed away.

“Okay, but you really need to put that gun down. This isn’t right. You love me. You’re not really gonna shoot me.”

The other woman’s eyes held no love or compassion, just hatred and vengeance. “You don’t know what the hell I’ll do.”

“He isn’t worth it,” the blond woman said.

“You think this is about some nigga you fucked?” the other woman laughed. “Oh, wait a minute. That’s right.” She was eerily nonchalant as she slowly moved closer to the blond. “That nigga was mine.”

Then she pulled the trigger.

Book One

~~~~~~~~~~

CHAPTER 1

Snookie 6:45 pm

Snookie Watson was a young black woman on a mission. In her little Ford Escort, she felt like a racecar driver as she sped up La Brea Avenue on her way to Hollywood. She glanced down at the dashboard clock, which read 6:45, and stepped on the gas. It was Saturday night, the time that Snookie usually looked forward to all week. Everything was supposed to be wonderful in Snookie's world because she was on her way to Popi's Place, her favorite nightspot.

However, life had been very cruel to Snookie these past couple of months. Between the man drama and the friend drama, her fucked up job had actually taken a back seat for a change. No matter how much she wanted to feel like a classy lady, her bad judgment and her big mouth always got her into trouble and showed off her ghetto mentality. Her friend Portia said that there was nothing wrong with being ghetto. Ignorance was the problem. Snookie's recent actions had come close to doing some major damage to her freedom and she was just getting over that. Now, some new shit had put her in a foul mood for the past several days.

The air conditioner in Snookie's car was barely working, so she rolled down her window. It was late July, but there was a nice breeze that evening and feeling the wind on her face was beginning to make her feel better. Besides, hanging out at Popi's Place with her five best girlfriends was always the highlight of her week.

Snookie was trying desperately to hold onto the good feelings that being at Popi's Place always gave her. Popi's Place was her sanctuary, the place where she could forget about her ordinary life and hang out with extraordinary people. Snookie and her girlfriends had shared many good memories there, but all good
~~~~~~~~~~

things must come to an end, and this past month had felt like the end of something good.

Snookie looked at the clock again, just as an old lady driving a 1959 Chevy in front of her stopped suddenly at the yellow light. Snookie looked up just in the nick of time. She slammed on her brakes, honked her horn loudly and yelled out the window. "Stupid bitch! What's wrong with you? Take that old piece o' shit car off the road."

By her calculations, she should already have been at Popi's Place sipping on her first Long Island Iced Tea, but she had to get her braids redone and it took all day. Her black braids were impossibly long and intertwined with lollipop red. And her scalp was on fire because, as Snookie said, "The bitch pulls too damn tight".

It was almost seven o'clock and Snookie pushed the gas pedal a little bit harder and ran a red light making the left onto Melrose Avenue. Normally, Snookie arrived no later than six-thirty to secure a table for herself and her girlfriends. The other ladies would arrive sporadically throughout the night. Snookie was too cheap to valet park, so she managed to find a decent spot on the street every week by getting there minutes after the doors were opened. But tonight, unexpectedly, Snookie saw that there were at least a dozen cars waiting to valet park. She cruised past her regular spots and found them already occupied. She had to circle the block again. Now she was getting pissed off, and that was never a good thing for Snookie.

"What the fuck is goin' on?" she muttered, as she passed Popi's Place for the third time. "I'm gonna end up parkin' a mile away."

Snookie couldn't help but notice that the line of people waiting to get in extended out the front door and down the block. All kinds of folks liked to hang out at Popi's Place; black, white, and everything in between. And tonight it appeared that everyone had come to party at the best little R&B/jazz spot in Hollywood.

Snookie finally found a spot nine blocks away from the club. She grabbed her small, red purse, which matched the red mini-dress that she was wearing. She even had the nerve to be wearing red shoes. She knew that she looked hot. Not that she'd ever been a great beauty or even considered pretty. She had big ears and when she smiled, she looked like a rabbit, but she was tall and thin. That had to be worth something in this town. It was Hollywood, after all. Besides, her mocha brown skin looked great in red.

Ten years ago, Snookie could never have worn a dress like this. She was from Mobile, Alabama and the old folks back home would have cringed if she ever stepped out of the house wearing a bright red dress, never mind one that showed off her long, skinny legs. The old ladies in the neighborhood that Snookie grew up in still believed that only harlots and home-wreckers wore red dresses out in public. Snookie couldn't help but have a naughty thought about her hometown neighbors.

"Old Mrs. Durham would drop dead if she could see me now," Snookie snickered, as she checked her face in the rearview mirror. "Oh, hell! The old fart already dropped dead. But I bet she'd roll over in her Alabama grave, if her ass wasn't so fat."

Snookie wasn't going to let anyone dictate her life or tell her what to do ever again. She was in charge and that was the way it was going to stay.

After a final check to make sure that she had make-up, money and breath spray in her red purse; Snookie put on a pair of dark sunglasses and carefully got out of the car, trying not to wrinkle her dress. She took a quick glance at her watch and began trotting towards Popi's Place. Snookie hated to wear high heels, but she traded her tennis shoes and flats for a pair of very uncomfortable, pointy-toed, red stilettos with six-inch heels.

"Shit, I ain't gonna be able to keep this up for nine blocks."

She wasn't watching where her feet were going, and so it was only a matter of time before she tripped over a stretch of broken sidewalk.

"Dammit!" Snookie grunted, as she stopped for a moment to check her shoes. She looked up to the heavens. "Break my neck, why don't ya?"

She was beginning to sweat, so she slowed down to a fast walk.

"What the hell do I pay taxes for?" she yelled out loud. "It's not bad enough that these raggedy ass streets tear up my car? Now there's fucking potholes in the sidewalk?"

Needless to say, this little evening hike was putting Snookie right back into a bad mood. After six blocks, she had to stop for a moment to catch her breath. She felt jittery and was having what she imagined were hot flashes of some kind. She was walking as though hot lava was licking at her feet.

"My feet are gonna fall right off," she thought, as she approached the final block.

CHAPTER 2

Aurora 6:50 pm

Aurora Duncan was sitting in the back of a limousine, stuck in traffic with thousands of other people trying to get out of Los Angeles International Airport. Her driver, Mark Sullivan, had been patiently waiting for her when she arrived two hours late. As Aurora walked out of the terminal, he couldn't help but notice how messy she appeared. Her hair was normally flawless and she always looked fresh in her designer clothes and high-heeled shoes, even when she had been traveling, which was often. However, at that moment, she looked like she had been in this same suit for three days. She had passed over the handle of her luggage to Mark without a word. He simply smiled and opened the door for her as he realized that it was going to be a long ride.

And it was. Aurora still hadn't said a word to Mark. She hadn't cracked so much as a smirk in his direction. He looked at her in his rear view mirror and also noticed that she looked stressed out and tired. The dark circles under her beautiful, amber eyes made her look like she hadn't slept in days. Aurora laid her head back for a few moments. She couldn't wait to get out of her suit and be comfortable. Her company business had taken her all over the East Coast this past week. Today alone she had been in several airports, anxious to get back to important personal business.

It was amazing that she had been able to concentrate on her work lately. She had so many things to deal with in her personal life, things that had devastated her, but she was a professional. Somehow, she had been able to function on autopilot. Not anywhere near her normal level of excellence, but just enough to get by.

Now that she was back, she had to fight hard to hold onto her sanity. Things that she had found out in the last twenty-four hours had driven her to the brink of desperation, and while she had been holding her feelings in for the sake of work, now she felt like her brain was going to burst. She couldn't think straight. She didn't know what she would do in that state of mind, but she didn't care anymore. She was going to set herself free, even if she had to sacrifice everyone else in order to do it.

Aurora made a call, listened for several seconds and ended the call, frustrated. "What the hell? Somebody better answer the damn phone."

She dialed and hung up several more times.

"That bastard!"

Aurora wanted to strangle someone at that moment, but took a deep breath instead and pushed the intercom to talk to Mark, who responded immediately. "Yes?"

"Can you get me home sometime tonight?"

Not waiting for a response, Aurora poured herself a glass of Cristal champagne which was chilling on ice. She thought about her New York trip, where she was checking out new hip-hop artists for Tazora Records. She was an executive vice-president who liked to be hands-on. That was one of the reasons for Aurora's success in the music business. However, Aurora Duncan was not a typical music executive. She was extremely beautiful and very intelligent, which was a lethal combination in the male-dominated hip-hop world. She used both assets to her advantage and always came out a winner, except when it came to her personal life. Beauty and intelligence didn't mean a damn thing in that vast wasteland.

She lowered the divider this time to speak directly to Mark.

"What the hell is the problem, Mark?"

"Sorry, Aurora. It's Saturday night. What can I say?"

"Aurora?" she asked, indignantly.

"I mean, *Miss Duncan*."

Mark was amused. He was familiar with this particular mood. It happened every time she found out her boyfriend was cheating on her.

"You are my employee, Mark. Did you forget that?"

"No, Miss Duncan. Traffic is a bitch right now, but if you just sit back and enjoy that bubbly I brought for you, we'll be in Redondo Beach in no time."

Mark smiled his most charming smile as he watched her carefully in the rear view mirror. She was so agitated that he couldn't help but push a few of her lovely buttons.

"You sure you don't want me to take you straight to Popi's Place?" he asked.

"Do I look like I want to be seen in public right now?"

"You look beautiful," he said as Aurora began making another call. "How about after you go home to change?" he asked.

"I have more important business to take care of."

"What?" Mark was shocked. "You're not hangin' out wit your girls tonight? What's up wit that? It's Sinful Saturday."

"What did I just say?"

Aurora disconnected the call and looked at her watch. She realized that it was after 7pm. Snookie had been blowing up her phone for two days. She was expected to show up at Popi's Place, but there was no way she could think about that now. The ladies would just have to wait. First, she had to go see a man about some bullshit.

"I feel like dancing," Mark said, interrupting her thoughts. "I might just have to stop by and get my groove on wit you and your girls."

"Shut up!" Aurora snapped. "I'm not interested in your damn social life."

"Oooh, you came back with that New York attitude. I like that. Anything I can do to help?"

"You can drive, Mark. Just fucking drive, can you do that?"

Aurora raised the divider as Mark watched her in the rearview mirror. Their eyes met a moment before the divider closed.

By the time she finished her second glass of champagne, the limo pulled up in front of her beautiful townhouse in Redondo Beach. Mark rushed out to open her door and reached out his hand to help her out of the car. She jumped out, ignoring his hand, and ran up the front steps as Mark retrieved her bags from the trunk.

"Where would you like me to put these?" he asked, entering.

Without turning around, she snapped, "Just set them down somewhere."

Mark set the bags down by the door and stood watching her. She stopped at the bottom of the staircase without turning. "What do you *want*?"

"Am I off the clock now?" he asked.

Aurora turned to him with a charming smile. "Listen, Mark, I'm sorry if I've been snippy tonight. I'm a little uptight, that's all."

Mark seductively walked towards her with an equally charming smile.

"No worries. I've got the cure for what ails you, remember?" he reached out and brushed a lock of hair out of her face.

Aurora's smile disappeared. "No thank you, Mark. That's not the cure I need tonight. It's been a long trip and I really can't wait to take a bath."

"You know I'd be happy to help you with that," he said, hopefully.

"I've got it from here," she said, not amused. "Lock the door behind you."

Mark looked regretful. "Alright, then. Enjoy your evening and drive carefully."

"I will," she said, running upstairs.

"Drink some coffee."

"Goodnight, Mark."

Aurora rushed to her bedroom to check her home phone. There was a message from her mother in Chicago, reminding her to fly home next month for her sister, Sharon's birthday party. There were three messages from Snookie, begging her to come to Popi's Place as soon as her plane landed. She erased them all and dialed a number. Again, she waited and then slammed the phone down in frustration. She sat on the bed to remove her shoes and managed to fling one across the room, narrowly missing the beautiful African carving that she received as a present from her friend, Debbie.

Aurora jumped up and began rummaging through her closet for something. Finally, she found what she was looking for and tossed it into her purse. She caught a glimpse of herself in her full-length mirror. She was shocked by her appearance, but made no attempt to do anything about it. She wished that she had the time or the inclination to jump into a hot shower where she could try to wash away all thoughts of the man whom she had given her heart to, and the woman that he was screwing.

Minutes later, Aurora was in her BMW sports car, racing north on the 405 Freeway. She dialed a number on her cell phone. After an annoying number of rings, the sound of extremely loud rap music filled her ears as a familiar voice answered.

"Riptide Recording."

"Hey, Stevie, it's Aurora," she yelled. "Damn, it's loud over there."

Stevie was one of the engineers at the recording studio. He quickly sat up in his chair, turned down the volume on the console slightly, and tried to sound cheerful. He passed a blunt to one of the two musicians who were sitting with him. All three were watching the action going on in the vocal booth.

"Hey, boo. You back in LA?"

"Don't call me that," Aurora shouted. "You *know* I hate that!"

"Sorry, boo. What's shakin' baby girl? How was New York?"

"Crowded, asshole," she replied. "Is Krome there?"

"You check out the new songs, yet?" Stevie asked.

Aurora was impatient. "Yes, now stop wasting my time. Where's Krome?"

Krome Bumpa, the number one rapper/producer on the Tazora Records label, was half-naked in the dark vocal booth with a sexy, white woman. He had her pinned up against a wall and was running his dark, chocolate hands through her long, blond hair.

"He ain't here," said Stevie.

"He's not answering his cell and I've been calling the studio for an hour. What the hell's goin' on?"

Krome had the blond mounted on top of him as he penetrated her.

"We're workin' over here, woman," said Stevie, watching the show.

"Sounds like you're fucking around," said Aurora.

"Not me, baby," said Stevie. "I'm serious as a mortician. Ha ha! Anyway, Krome had to get deep into something. He'll be coming any minute now."

One of the musicians began choking on the smoke as he laughed at Stevie, who snatched the blunt back and managed to respond between drags.

"I'm sorry, beautiful. Krome's in a serious meeting. Want me to give him a message or somethin'?"

Aurora began to merge onto the 10 Freeway.

"I'm on my way over and there's one blond bitch that better not be there."

"I'll tell Krome that you called," said Stevie, nonchalantly.

"You do that!" she screamed. "Unless you want to witness a motherfuckin' murder tonight."

She disconnected the call and stepped on the gas.

CHAPTER 3

Debbie 6:55 pm

Debbie Marshall hadn't said a word in over an hour, and neither had the man on the other side of the curtain. She hadn't even seen him, yet. She had been quietly sitting in this comfy leather loveseat, awaiting further instruction. She looked at her watch.

"Damn," she thought.

When she first arrived, there was smooth jazz playing on the stereo and the door had been left ajar. She tentatively peeked into the studio, then entered slowly and walked around looking as though she had never been in there before.

"Oh, my God," she whispered. "Am I in the right studio?"

The dark, solid furniture had been replaced with softer, more stylish sofas and chairs. Colorful artwork and accent pieces were all around, replacing the bare walls and corners. On a table next to the door was a note, instructing her to take a seat, enjoy the music, and help herself to the refreshments.

She couldn't help but to pause in front of a large mirror with a beautiful, hand-carved wooden frame. She allowed herself to enjoy the reflection of her naturally curly hair gently framing her lovely brown face. She looked like a young Lola Falana.

"He's being awfully mysterious," she mumbled, adjusting a couple of curls.

Debbie spotted a little bar with an uncorked bottle of red wine, and a plate of fruit, crackers and cheese. She went straight for one of the wine glasses and began pouring.

"Lawrence? Are you here?" she called out.

"Is that the beautiful Debbie Marshall?" His deep, sexy voice resonated from behind a heavy curtain that separated his workspace from his living space.

"It is I," she responded cheerfully.

"Help yourself to a glass of merlot."

"Already there," she said. "So, what's with the extreme studio makeover?"

"You like?"

Debbie looked around and spotted an African sculpture. She shook her head, amused, as she sipped her wine.

"I see you finally found the perfect spot for the piece I bought you. I was afraid it would stay forever in the back of your closet."

"It finally grew on me," he said, chuckling.

"So, when can I see you, Mr. Desmond?" she asked. "Patience isn't my virtue."

"Just relax," he said. "You've already waited several weeks."

She plopped herself into a banana yellow loveseat that she had never seen before.

"Okay, Mr. Desmond. One minute."

That minute had turned into an hour as Debbie found herself so relaxed that she lost track of time. She needed to relax because there was a whole lot of secretive shit going on in her life. Her friends were all mad at each other and she didn't know why. She had a few ideas, but she couldn't believe her own crazy mind. For now, she was going to enjoy the moment and try to figure out the secret behind the curtain.

Debbie became alert again as Earth Wind & Fire caressed her in surround sound with their beautiful classic, *Head to the Sky*. Crossing her long, lovely legs, Debbie took a sip of the rich merlot and patiently waited for this fascinating man to come around the corner. She knew not to rush him. She knew how sensitive some creative people could be. He had to reveal himself at the right moment, and in his own time.

As Debbie sank further into the plush leather, she thought about how often she had been in this space, admiring the man who lived and worked here.

"Many more times than I should have, no doubt," she whispered to herself.

The studio had been tastefully redecorated. Lawrence was challenged when it came to color. Dark solids usually dominated every bit of space. Very masculine, but a little boring for her taste. Even though the décor did reflect the man, Debbie didn't find him boring at all. Dark and solid, yes. Masculine, absolutely. But, boring, no.

As Debbie looked around the studio tonight, however, several exotic and colorful paintings adorned the walls. Sculptures from Africa were tastefully placed around the room on custom-made tree trunk tables. Each piece was unique and beautiful. Everything in this place was designed to be pleasing to the eye.

Enough was enough. Debbie resisted the urge to yank that curtain back and tell him to get over himself already. Undoubtedly, he wouldn't appreciate her unsolicited opinions. But, it wouldn't be the first time. She tended to speak her mind. Debbie couldn't decide if she was more excited to see him, or whatever he'd been hiding from her. He had made such a secret production out of this evening, she felt that she should just continue to drink her wine and enjoy the solitude.

She glanced at her watch again. It was after seven o'clock and she was supposed to be on her way to Popi's Place for a special reunion party that she would be attending with her friends later tonight. Portia had made her promise that she would show up and Snookie must have left three or four messages. She never broke a promise to her friends, but she didn't say what time she would get there, so she would get there, eventually.

At the moment, she could care less about the party. She was much too absorbed in anticipation of the surprise that awaited her. It must be something pretty wonderful for him to take all this time to prepare for it. As a matter of fact, he had been working on this project for weeks. He had been very unavailable to her. But, that was the way she wanted it, so she couldn't complain.

Debbie could hear his smooth voice quietly humming along with the music. She closed her eyes and pictured the way that his lips moved when he was totally concentrating. She began to daydream about how those lips would feel on hers. Suddenly, a deep, silky voice broke through the image.

"So, my young protégé, come and see what has kept my undivided attention for the past six weeks."

Startled out of her thoughts, Debbie opened her eyes, quickly regained her composure and looked at her watch.

"Six weeks and seventy-five minutes, to be exact," she said.

Lawrence Desmond, hot, sexy and twenty years her senior, was standing over her. "But, no one's counting, right?"

He reached out a hand to help her out of the chair. Electricity ran through her fingertips as she gently placed her long, slender fingers into the palm of his strong, masculine hand. As she rose, she once again made note of how tall and handsome he was. But, what the hell was he wearing? What happened to the stuffy suit?

Dressed in loose-fitting, white linen, drawstring pants, his dark skin glowed in a gold, linen shirt. The collar was open, exposing a very sexy gold chain at his throat. He looked like he had just stepped off the pages of a sexy, island magazine.

"So, I finally get to see your new designs? Is that why I'm here?"

"You tell me. Why are you here?" he teased. "My wit or sense of style?"

"You are a very frustrating person, you know that?"

As Debbie tried her best to look perturbed, Lawrence flashed that picture perfect smile and all pretenses faded away. He gently stroked her face.

"You look absolutely radiant," he crooned.

"Thank you, Lawrence."

"Close your eyes," he said.

Debbie complied, not sure what to expect. He still had her by the hand and finally led her around to the other side. He dropped her hand and swept his arms in a grand gesture.

"Alright, it's time," he said, excitedly. "Open your eyes and tell me what you think about my latest creations. I imagine that you will have an opinion."

Debbie opened her eyes and saw the line of nine well-dressed mannequins, each displaying a beautifully designed man's suit. Lawrence appeared to calm down as he watched her. She walked along the wall, carefully examining each beautiful piece. She really liked the designs, but she had to suppress a giggle. Finally, she found her voice.

"Hmmm. The colors are daring. Vibrant and bold. The lines and detailing are very interesting. A whole new look, totally unexpected."

"That's very polite of you," he said. "What do you really think?"

He smiled and continued to watch her carefully as she continued her scrutiny of the colorful pieces.

"I'm amazed that you would come up with this line," she continued. "You're usually a much more conservative designer. And, trust me, your conservatism is the only thing keeping these suits from screaming out 'Pimps R Us'."

Lawrence laughed out loud and playfully shook his finger.

"You're a terrible person."

"And I'm about to be even worse," Debbie said as she stepped back and got a good look at him. "*What* are you wearing?"

Lawrence modeled his new look and moved a little closer.

"You are welcome to examine it for quality," he said.

"No thank you," Debbie said, turning back to the collection.

"I've decided to be a little more adventurous," he said proudly. "I guess I took it to heart when you said that I was uptight, and that it showed in my designs, so I decided to team up with your favorite rapper, the one you and your girlfriends love to hate."

"Oh, Lord! Did I push you that far? I said that you could afford to loosen up a bit," Debbie said, feeling a little embarrassed. "I didn't mean to be offensive."

Lawrence moved closer to her, stepping up beside her and making her take in a breath of his cologne. She tentatively moved away so that she could turn to face him. God, I'm actually blushing, she thought, as she tried to sound normal.

"I was just saying that you have lots of talent and I thought you could expand your ideas and be a little more…"

"Creative?" he whispered. "I got that."

He moved close to her again. This time she didn't even flinch.

"It's actually what inspired me," he said. "Your bluntness. Your boldness. Two of the many things I like about you."

"I was just being honest."

"Honesty. That's good. Tell me more. I can handle it."

"I think your designs are great. I love the new clothes, your new look, everything. You will certainly shock everyone. Look at you. You look…so…so…comfortable."

A little too comfortable, she thought, as he moved into her personal space. Debbie couldn't take it. Lawrence was too sexy for her to be alone with him. She had promised herself that she wouldn't see him anymore, but here she was. She had always made excuses to be with him and had always been able to keep her cool around him.

And then it happened. Once. The unthinkable. After that, she forced herself to keep her distance. After unsuccessfully pursuing her for weeks, he backed off, until yesterday when he called and she dropped everything. This was crazy and it had to stop.

Debbie stepped back. "I think I'd better go."

"You waited all this time and now you're just going to run off?"

"I have to be at Popi's Place, and you obviously need a cold shower."

"You don't bite your tongue, do you?" he laughed.

"That would hurt."

Debbie turned to leave and Lawrence gently turned her toward him.

"Debbie, I won't hurt you," he said sincerely.

He pulled her into his arms and kissed her passionately. After a long moment, he pulled away, stunned and embarrassed by his actions. He released her and stepped back.

"I apologize, Debbie. I shouldn't have been that adventurous."

"No, you shouldn't have, Lawrence. What would your wife say?"

He was devastated.

"I love Anita," he replied. "And she doesn't deserve to be hurt, but Debbie, my sweet, sweet Debbie. What am I going to do about you?"

He reached for her again and she slipped away.

"Lawrence, we agreed."

"I know. I'm sorry. What should I do? You tell me, I'll gladly oblige."

"Coming here was a big mistake," Debbie said, as she quickly headed around the corner towards the door. Lawrence immediately ran after her.

"Please don't go!"

The look in his eyes was so pleading that Debbie just wanted to fold herself into his arms and never leave. Why did he have to look so damn good when he was begging? A man should be very unattractive in this sad, pathetic state. She took a deep breath and hoped that she would be strong enough for both of them.

"Look, you know that I'm attracted to you and we do have a strong connection, but if we're gonna see each other at all, then we're gonna need to stay in the 'friendly place'. You know what I mean?"

"Alright, Debbie, I surrender to whatever you say. You've been a good friend. I respect you and I respect your opinions. I really appreciate someone like you in my life."

"Someone like me?" she smirked.

"Okay. You. I appreciate *you.*"

"And I need someone I can trust," she said seriously. "I trust *you*, Lawrence."

"That means a lot, so you've got me."

"Good," she said. "Then, we're cool."

"I guess I want you in my life more than in my bed."

"That's because it's your only option," she reminded him.

"Exactly." They both laughed and the tension was broken.

Debbie began to relax. "It was really, really good, though," she said, sighing.

"Best I ever had," he smiled.

"Wow." She was otherwise speechless.

"I love you, Debbie," he said, meaning it with all his heart.

She allowed Lawrence to take her into his embrace and they enjoyed a wonderful moment of real love. Neither one of them saw Anita Desmond, whose heartbroken eyes were watching in disbelief from the unclosed door.

CHAPTER 4

Candy 7:00 pm

Candy Martin was the only black woman enjoying "weekend happy hour" in the predominately white Dovetail Bar, but that was never a problem for her. She preferred it that way. She loved white men and only white men. And the richer, the better.

She liked to identify herself as the little chocolate drop in a world of vanilla. There were a couple of black men, but as usual, they were breaking their necks to get to the white women. They paid her no attention at all. Her friend, Snookie, told her that it's because they can smell the white boys on her. She thought it had more to do with her being too intimidating. She was a smart, young, dark-skinned beauty who was not shy.

There was a contradiction in Candy Martin. She always tried to speak proper English, even around her girlfriends, and she also didn't curse. But she also had her freaky side. Candy loved to wear provocative clothes because it drove the men wild. At the moment, she was in her element, surrounded by a group of horny, white executive types. She was dressed in a silky, white blouse that showed off a little too much of her ample cleavage and clung to her large, pointy nipples. Her black, leather skirt was so short that any man in the place could tell you that she wasn't wearing any panties. Her long, dark legs were smoothly waxed, and her strappy, gold stilettos showed off her perfectly pedicured toes.

While Candy laughed it up with several of her admirers, one brave young man weaved his way through the crowd and settled close beside her at the bar. She could feel him staring at her, so she swiveled her stool around to face him. She crossed her legs and allowed her ankle to rub against his leg. He looked like he was barely out of college.

"Hey, handsome, if you take a picture, it'll last longer."

Embarrassed, he turned a shade of red and cleared his throat.

"Sorry," he said. "I guess I was staring."

"I guess you were," she quipped. "May I help you?"

"You look really hot tonight," he said.

Candy leaned in to touch his face, rubbing against him with her breasts.

"You are so sweet," she whispered. "What's your name?"

The young man turned even redder.

"Matthew Dockmeyer. I'm a stockbroker at Marigold. Can I buy you a drink?"

"I have a drink."

He looked disappointed and turned away.

"Okay, Mr. Stockbroker," Candy laughed. "Don't give up so easily."

He quickly turned back in anticipation. She looked directly into his eyes.

"You can buy my next glass of champagne," she cooed.

"Okay, cool," he said excitedly.

As he turned to get the bartender's attention, Candy's cell phone rang. She smiled and slipped off the stool, giving the two gentlemen at the table beside the bar an eyeful.

"Excuse me, gentlemen," she purred.

Candy headed to the back of the restaurant, where she could talk privately.

"Hello?... Hey, girl… I'm still at happy hour… Are the other ladies going to be there?... Okay, don't worry, I'll be there. I may be a little late, though…yes, yes, yes, I know how important tonight is for all of us… I'll see you later."

That darn Snookie sure could get on her last nerve. Candy wished that she could be nice and numb by the time she had to deal with those friends of hers. Deep down she knew that she shouldn't be anywhere near a bar, but she wasn't prepared to deprive herself of anything that would make her feel better. She had been a very bad girl these past few weeks and she had little faith that a reunion at Popi's Place was going fix a damn thing, but she had to try. She was responsible for a good part of the drama, and for the fact that they had all been disconnected from each other lately. The least she could do was show up. If everyone else was willing to forgive and forget, why wouldn't she do her part? But she had to indulge once more before she had to give up everything.

"Heaven knows I need a little extra help," she thought.

Candy decided to stop in the ladies room before heading back to the bar. If she was going to face those other women at Popi's Place later, she needed some reinforcement. Two attractive brunettes gave her curious looks when she entered. A drunken redhead was rinsing her mouth out in the sink. There were three stalls. Two of them appeared to be occupied.

She looked at the women and said, "Anyone waiting?"

"I am," one of the brunettes muttered.

"So, what's wrong with that one?" she asked, pointing at the open stall.

The drunken redhead managed to speak.

"That one is a little messy. I was just in there, if you get my drift."

While Candy waited, she couldn't help but reflect on her life as of late. Her mind wouldn't allow her to stop thinking about her mistakes. She had done some things that she was not very proud of. She had made choices that could have ruined her life and the lives of several people that she loved. She was determined to make things right, but she was far from being perfect. She was going to enjoy herself tonight, no matter what. Besides, there were only so many changes a person could make in a week.

Candy checked her lipstick in the mirror, and as soon as a stall was available, she hurried in, opened her Louis Vuitton purse, pulled out a little, glass vial and snorted some of the best cocaine she'd ever had. As Candy slowly sauntered back to the bar, the men in the crowded room seemed to part like the Red Sea to let her pass through. She was happy to see that she hadn't lost her "white boy mojo". Matthew Dockmeyer had a bottle of champagne on ice waiting for her when she arrived. She looked mildly impressed.

"Oooh, a whole bottle, I see."

"Thought I might join you for a glass or two."

"Thank you, Mr. Stockbroker."

As she scooted back onto her stool, her blouse opened just wide enough to give him a full peak at one of her dark, pointy nipples. He grinned broadly as he poured her a glass of champagne, which fizzed over the top of her glass and onto the bar. He quickly grabbed some napkins to soak up the mess.

"Oops," she said, enjoying his discomfort.

"I'm a little excited, I guess."

"That's alright. I understand." Candy moved closer. "What's your name again?"

CHAPTER 5

Portia 7:05 pm

Portia Taylor-Adams was a big woman who was not afraid to look in the mirror. As a matter of fact, as she stood in her bedroom, posing in front of her full-length mirror, she was thinking that she could still turn a head or two. She had big hair, overdone makeup, and the long, sculpted nails that nobody could imagine were of any practical use, but you sure couldn't tell her that she wasn't "the shit".

Portia's two great passions were shopping for expensive clothes and eating at great restaurants. Bags from her recent shopping spree were spread all over her bed. She made good money working for a prominent plastic surgeon in Beverly Hills and she liked to keep her money in the community by eating and shopping as often as possible.

Portia's husband, Chuck, was downstairs in the kitchen rushing around. Once again, he had misplaced his car keys. He was tall and nicely dressed in a casual pair of khaki pants, which he filled out nicely in the front and the back. He wore a well-fitted knit shirt that showed off how well he took care of his body. He was young and muscular, with a ready smile and great skin.

Chuck stopped for a moment at the kitchen counter and lifted the foil from a huge pan of fried chicken. He took out a chicken wing and tried to eat it without getting anything on his clothes as he walked to the bottom of the staircase. "Hey, baby," he yelled. "Are my keys up there?"

As he waited for a response, he turned and spotted the keys on a table in the living room.

"Never mind, honey. I got 'em. See you at Popi's Place later."

"You better come up here and give me some sugar," Portia responded.

Chuck ran up the stairs and gave her a juicy smack on the lips. Portia pulled back quickly.

"Your lips are greasy," she said with a frown.

"Your chicken is greasy," Chuck shot back.

"I spent all day frying that chicken."

"No, you spent all day shopping. You spent about an hour frying that chicken."

"And?" inquired Portia, with her hands on her ample hips.

"No problem, baby. You're greasy and I eat you all the time."

Portia popped him on the head. "Get on out of here, boy. Try not to get too drunk before I get to Popi's."

"Alright, baby. I love you."

"Love you, too."

Chuck kissed her again and ran back down the steps.

Portia looked out of her bedroom window and watched her husband for a few minutes as he got into his Mustang and drove away. She was a lot happier today than she had been in months. She was thankful for that because things hadn't been all that lovey-dovey between Portia and Chuck lately. As a matter of fact, they had been separated for a few weeks and he had just moved back into the house a few days ago. They had put themselves through some serious drama, made peace and created major life changes. Portia tended to blame herself, but Chuck was no angel, either. They both had to admit their mistakes.

Portia had been feeling very insecure in her marriage during the past year. Things bothered her now that had never bothered her before. Like the fact that she was several years older than Chuck. Age had never been an issue. She loved the youthful enthusiasm in him that some would have called immaturity.

Portia and Chuck had a good sex life. He wanted it all the time and she rarely had a reason to turn him down. He loved her voluptuous body and she felt good about herself. But it only took a few simple things in the past few months to unravel those good feelings. Things that rocked Portia's confidence and caused her to push Chuck away. There were times when she felt that nothing would be able to make her feel good again. But here she was, on Saturday night, getting ready to party.

"Those skinny bitches better look out, cause I'm back," she laughed.

Portia checked the time and saw that she was going to be fashionably late. It didn't really matter. She would never be the first one there because nobody could beat Snookie Watson to Popi's Place. The cheap bitch refused to valet park her car. Portia giggled at the thought that Snookie wasn't going to know what to do with herself if they all stopped showing up on Saturday nights from now on. Portia, on the other hand, would have plenty to keep her busy after tonight. That's why she wanted to look extra good.

Tonight was going to be a special night. They were all going to face some demons tonight and Portia was determined to live it up. Who knows when she would get another chance to party hard with her best friends? She was closing a huge chapter of her life. As she chose the perfect purse and the perfect shoes to match her perfect outfit, she examined herself in the mirror one last time.

"Perfect," she said out loud with a satisfied smile.

Portia grabbed her keys and jumped into her Mercedes. Things were never going to be the same and she couldn't wait to get started on her new life.

CHAPTER 6

Melissa 7:10 pm

Melissa Murdock was feeling like the golden child. She had waited all of her life to get her big break. And now, here she was, on the night before she was going to sign her big record deal. Her five best girlfriends didn't know about it yet. She had carefully guarded her secret, and now she couldn't wait to tell them. Unfortunately, that wasn't the only secret that Melissa was keeping.

It had been weeks since she'd spent quality time with her friends. They had their regular Saturday nights at Popi's Place over the years, but she had been missing in action lately. She had spent the past few weeks trying to forget how much she had sacrificed to be in this enviable position. She had a record company executive interested in signing her to a major contract. And not just any executive, either. She had Palmer Whitmore, a music industry legend, eating out of her pretty, little hands. She was the golden haired diva with the creamy white skin and the chocolaty velvet voice. Men could not resist her and women wanted to be her.

Melissa had been shopping for the past week. She had to have the right outfit to express herself. The right dress, the right shoes, everything. She liked to take fashion chances. She had an amazing body and eclectic taste. Sometimes she was bohemian, sometimes rocker girl. She looked great in a formal gown, and could rock a pair of torn-up jeans like nobody's business. Melissa liked to go against the trends. As a matter of fact, she rarely paid any attention to what the trends were.

One day she wanted to have her designer friend, Debbie Marshall, work on a clothing line with her. Then she would be setting her own trends. That's what superstars did, and Melissa Murdock couldn't wait to become a star. She glanced at the clock and took a deep breath.

"Don't they hire people to do this shit?" she quipped, as she tossed aside another choice. Who was she kidding, though? She would probably insist on doing her own shopping anyway. She just wanted the studio to foot the bill.

One thing that Melissa knew for sure: she was an original. She had worked really hard and she had done things that she never would have imagined, but she was going to make it big. She had used and been used. She had hurt and been hurt. She had paid, and now she was going to make somebody else pay.

If everything went according to plan, she would be able to wash away the past and build a whole new life for herself. She just hoped that her friends would give her the support and love that she needed to make a fresh start. She knew that it would be asking a lot, but nobody was perfect, and she had certainly put up with a whole lot of everybody else's crap over the years. It was time for them to give her a break. Hell, they should be grateful that she was willing to share her good fortune with them. The way that they had been acting lately, she could see herself dumping them for some of those stars who were of her caliber. Real divas. She could learn a thing or two from some of those chicks.

There were so many things that Melissa hadn't been able to share with her friends recently. The five women had been going through a lot of personal dramas with each other, and she had her usual difficulties coping with the pressure of believing in herself as an artist, and not just using her beauty to get what she wanted.

The other ladies had no idea that she was going to be making her big debut at Popi's Place tonight. There had been a lot of difficult times in her relationships these past weeks. She wasn't the type of person who shared everything. Not even with her best friends. But this time she had a secret that could destroy everything; her friendships and her career. She had taken a lot of chances and it had paid off. However, as with most sacrifices, a price had to be paid. She just hoped that it had been worth it.

Tonight was going to be amazing. For once, she decided that she was going to enjoy every minute of the career that she always dreamed about. She finally had her shit together, and had something to be proud of, and she would be damned if she was going to blow it this time. She didn't care how much it cost her.

CHAPTER 7

Popi's Place 7:15 pm

Popi's Place had thrived as a great hangout for more than sixty years. This Hollywood landmark had provided live R&B and jazz seven nights a week to loyal regulars and a continuous sprinkle of cool celebrities. As a matter of fact, three of the ten owners were celebrities themselves.

The regulars came during the week to enjoy the socializing at the bar, the great European cuisine, and more drama than a daytime soap opera. Celebrities came to see and be seen in an atmosphere that was a mix of class and naughty fun. On a normal weekday, it didn't cost a thing to walk through the popular doors, but on the weekends, the owners liked to charge a cover just to walk into the bar. However, Snookie Watson and her friends rarely paid.

As she finally reached the club, Snookie bypassed the long line and was shocked by the actual size of the crowd. Limousines lined the street and there was organized chaos at the front door. A short, round man whom she'd never seen before was acting as a bouncer. She realized that in order to cut this line, she was going to have to put out a little extra effort. These people looked like they were about to get some free shit. Or maybe, like her, they just couldn't wait to get a damn drink.

Snookie stuck out her chest, adjusted her sunglasses, and approached the front door as if she owned the place. As she tried to bully her way to the front of the line, she accidentally bumped into the huge hips of a black woman in a silver, sequined dress who was also pushing her way towards the front door.

The woman snarled, "Hey, you scrawny bitch. Where the hell do you think you're going?"

Snookie swung her long braids around to face the woman. "Who are you calling scrawny?"

"Just wait your turn like everybody else," replied the woman. "I been waitin' here for a half hour and you ain't gonna just come up in here and jump in front of me."

"Well, excuse the hell outta me, bubblicious," Snookie replied.

She thought "hippo hips" looked like a shiny, Las Vegas billboard in that silver dress and decided to keep the peace or she might never make it inside. She couldn't forget that she had paid full price for the hot, little designer dress that she was wearing, and Snookie never paid full price for anything. So, after a quick flashback of how fabulous she looked, Snookie took a deep breath.

"Did they advertise in the paper or somethin'?" Snookie smiled a phony smile and quickly slipped between two well-dressed white men in line ahead of her.

"Hey, thanks for holding my place, guys," she said as she suddenly turned her heel over, almost falling into one of the men, who caught her.

"Hey, are you alright?" he asked.

Snookie looked at him, embarrassed. "I'm fine."

"God don't like ugly," the woman behind her muttered under her breath.

Snookie replied, "He must have figured that out after he made you."

Then she turned to the man, who was still holding her up. "Thank you. I'm so clumsy sometimes," she said, smiling.

Snookie leaned over, exposing some cleavage, to whisper in the bouncer's ear. She may not have been the prettiest girl in town, but she knew how to use what she had.

"I'm with him," she purred, "but I need to use the little girl's room immediately. I'm sure you understand."

The bouncer hesitated and Snookie quickly slipped past him and turned back to smile at the well-dressed man before she strutted through the front door. As Snookie bypassed the ladies' bathroom, which was just inside the front door, a tall, redheaded woman came out, almost running her over.

"Oh, I'm so sorry," said the woman. "I'm just trying to get back inside the club. It's a madhouse in here tonight."

"No problem," Snookie said, "I'm right behind you."

Popi's Place was divided into three main areas. There was a large bar area, where the regulars liked to hang out. There was a restaurant area, filled with tables and booths, for people who wanted to enjoy the music and still carry on conversations while they ate. And there was the clubroom, where guests could be up close and personal with the live music and test their moves on the dance floor. Dinner was served in there as well, and folks paid a little extra money to be in there.

There was a long line of people standing along the narrow, dimly lit hallway. Most of them were gazing at the dark, red walls, impressed by the photo gallery of jazz musicians. Many of these great artists, like Lionel Hampton, Dizzy Gillespie and Buddy Rich, had actually graced the stage in the restaurant's clubroom. Portraits of others like Count Basie, Louis Armstrong, Billie Holliday, and Duke Ellington were simply treasures to behold. Snookie felt a moment of sadness, knowing that an era of her life here might be coming to an end.

As Snookie snapped out of her fog, she realized that she had lost sight of the tall redhead, so she continued to slowly push and squeeze her way past the throng, much to the irritation of the people she passed. Finally, she ended up behind a huge man at the end of the hallway, which was the entrance to the bar. The doorway was blocked off with a red, velvet rope. Roxanne, the lovely, blond hostess with the plastered-on smile, was standing behind a little podium, collecting money and trying to keep the antsy crowd under control by allowing them to enter one or two at a time.

Snookie tried to peek around the huge man who was directly in front of her. It was hard for her to see anything in the dark hallway, because she still hadn't taken her sunglasses off. She saw Roxanne unhook the rope to let a couple of people into the bar as the redhead stepped up and said, "I was in the ladies room, remember?"

"Of course," replied Roxanne, "You were smart to make an early reservation." As Roxanne snapped the rope behind her, the redhead said, "You got that right. Thanks."

Snookie tried to work herself around the huge man, who handed Roxanne his money. He turned his head towards Snookie without seeing her. "Hey, what's your problem, lady?" he asked.

"Put some steam in it, big guy," she said, bumping him from behind.

Roxanne opened the rope to let him in. "Thank you, sir. Have a nice evening."

He said, "I should get a free drink with this, you know."

"Of course, you should," replied Roxanne. "Too bad I don't own the place."

As the man began to move, Snookie bumped him again, trying to slip in behind him. The man turned around this time. "Are you blind?" he growled.

Seeing Snookie with her dark shades on, he immediately felt bad. "Oh, sorry lady." He stepped past Roxanne into the club.

"I'm not blind, moron," Snookie said as she moved forward. "Hey, Roxanne."

Roxanne quickly hooked the rope back into place.

"What are you doing?" Snookie snapped. "Let me in."

"Excuse me, that'll be twenty dollars, please." Roxanne said, smiling.

Shocked, Snookie looked at Roxanne like she had horns coming out of her head. "I don't think so," Snookie said, indignantly. "I have a table."

A young white couple, who were next in line to pay, moved a little closer. The young woman cleared her throat impatiently, and then spoke to Roxanne in a squeaky voice, "Excuse me, but I believe *we're* next."

The young man added, "We were behind the fat guy. She came outta nowhere."

"Apparently," said Roxanne.

Snookie ignored them. "Roxanne, don't you remember me?"

The young man snapped his fingers at Roxanne. "Hello? Anybody home? Can we get in, please? Here's our money."

"Of course, sir," replied Roxanne, taking the money. "I'm very sorry for the delay."

Roxanne unhooked the rope to let the couple in. Before stepping into the club, the young woman turned to Snookie with a superior air. "Sweetie, it's just easier to pay the money."

Snookie felt the heat rising in her face and imagined that her brown cheeks had turned red. "I'm Snookie Watson, bitch!"

"Okay, Miss Bitch." Roxanne said calmly. "That'll be twenty dollars."

Snookie had another vision of knocking the mess out of somebody, but then closed her eyes for a moment as the calm returned.

"Oh, you funny. Girl, you lucky I paid full price for this dress."

Snookie was so proud of her self-restraint. This "turning the other cheek" shit wasn't easy. She looked around to see a lot of irritated people in the line behind her and realized that there could be a mutiny any second.

"Where's Jacques?" Snookie asked, grinding her teeth. "I can't believe this shit. I've been coming here every Saturday night for years and I don't pay. I *never* pay. And I sure as hell ain't gonna pay tonight. You been working here for what, two months already? And you can't remember me? Chantal always remembered me."

"Maybe your hair is longer this week," replied Roxanne, sweetly.

"Oh no, you didn't go *there*!"

"I'm just trying to do my job."

"It's your job to remember me. I always have a table in the clubroom and I don't pay at the door. Okay?"

Roxanne's calm was impenetrable. Then in her sweetest Valley girl twang, she said, "Okay, I apologize, but if you want to… like…be recognized, then maybe you shouldn't… like…wear sunglasses at night. Now, let me check the reservation book. Is that Cookie with a C?"

"It's *Snookie*, you dimwit!" She was about to bust a vein.

Roxanne, who seemed to be about as smart as a bottle cap, managed to keep her pearly white smile intact.

"Whatever you say, ma'am."

Snookie was now convinced that there was a conspiracy going on to get her into Anger Management classes.

At that moment, Jacques, the French maitre'd, walked up behind Roxanne. Jacques was jovial, and often pretentious, but he never lost his cool. He was really good at his job.

"Bon soir, Mademoiselle Snookie," he said as he unhooked the rope, bowed slightly, and gallantly gestured for Snookie to enter.

"Thank God!"

Snookie sauntered past Roxanne, shooting poisoned darts with her eyes. Of course, Roxanne couldn't even see her eyes behind the dark shades and took the next people in line without missing a beat.

"Miss Snookie. How are you, my dear?" Jacques continued. "You look positively lovely tonight."

"I'm pissed off right now, if you wanna know the truth, but if you get me my favorite table, I'll forget about that bimbo at the front door."

"Forgive me. Roxanne is still learning. Please follow me immediately. I've had to fight off rabid wolves to save you a great table. It's a good thing that you called. It's been a while since you've all been together on Saturday night."

"I miss having a nice table. What's going on in here?"

"Annual fundraiser for Popi's charity."

The sound of smooth jazz caressing the air through the perfectly placed speakers was already calming Snookie as she followed Jacques through the crowded bar. The restaurant tables were just beginning to fill up. They made their way into the clubroom with Snookie swinging her braids around annoyingly. She actually popped a couple of people with the long ropes of hair as she passed.

"Is it extra dark in here?" Snookie mumbled, peeking over her sunglasses. "I can't see shit with these things on."

The clubroom was sparse as Jacques led Snookie to a large booth, situated in a nice corner, not too close to the bandstand. The band was still setting up. Jacques turned to Snookie and gestured for her to slide in.

"Thanks, Frenchie," she said.

"I hope that everything is satisfactory tonight. I apologize for any inconvenience at the front door. Your first Long Island Iced Tea is coming momentarily and it's on the house."

Snookie managed a humble smile. "Thank you, Jacques."

Jacques had been running Popi's Place with precision for many years. Most of his special treatment and benefits were reserved for the regulars and celebrities, but if you weren't one of those, you could slip a twenty or two into his palm and that just might get you a little favor.

Snookie and her girlfriends were considered special customers and always got seated at the finest booth in the clubroom, unless a celebrity showed up, which got them bumped to a nearby table. Not the best table, but still a good table.

Snookie's friends spent a lot of money in Popi's Place. They were beautiful, sexy, and financially secure. Snookie was cheap, almost always broke, and secretly felt like the ugly one of the group. She noticed that even her friend with the great big ass got more attention from men, who flocked around them, buying food and drinks. The women rarely had to fully pay their own tabs, and they tipped very well.

Snookie's friends had important contacts, which made her feel important. And Snookie liked to feel important, so she took these Saturday nights very seriously, insisting that all of the ladies show up no matter what time they got there. Only sickness, death, or out of town business let them off the hook. Snookie could get loud and obnoxious at times, so her friends did their best to show up every week to avoid her tirades. They were an odd combination, these six women, and people often wondered what kept them together.

As Snookie's Long Island Iced Tea was delivered, she was a little preoccupied by the whereabouts of her five friends. Of all people, she was the one who had pulled them all back together after several weeks of intense drama. They had finally all agreed to get back together at their favorite place, after not being there for the past three weeks. That had never happened before. It was as though the whole world had gone crazy.

Snookie took a deep breath and prayed a silent prayer. It was still too early to tell, but there was no guarantee that any of them would show up tonight. It had been that kind of a week. This was perhaps the last night of their friendship.

Snookie's first sip turned into a huge gulp. Have mercy!

Book Two

CHAPTER 8

Snookie

"Snookie?" the librarian asked in a snooty tone. "What kind of a name is that?"

"It's the name my mama gave me."

"Well, I don't believe that's the name that your mother gave you. That sounds like a nickname. May I see your birth certificate?"

"I'm just tryin' to take out a daggone book," Snookie replied, a little louder. "Why I got to have my birthin' papers?"

The librarian lowered her voice to a whisper.

"I just need to confirm your legal name before I issue you a library card. That's the way it works here, young lady."

"I didn't see you axe lily-white Molly Miller for her birthin' papers. Why you got to see mines?" Snookie began to talk even louder.

"Young lady, please tone your voice down. You are in a library."

"Well, it feels like a freakin' prison."

"Do I need to call security?" she said, reaching for the phone.

"You need to take the stick up out yo' ass."

Snookie's sister, Shawna, pulled her away from the counter.

"C'mon, Snookie. She gonna call the rent-a-cop on you." The two of them ran out of the door, laughing.

"Wait a minute!" Snookie squealed. "I didn't get my books!"

"You a crazy girl, Snookie."

Snookie and Shawna were only a year apart in age. Snookie was ten and Shawna was nine. They had different fathers. Their mother, Jessie Mae, was only twenty-six and had been pregnant for the past eleven years until she finally had her tubes tied. Snookie's father was unknown and her nine brothers and sisters were from two other fathers. They were all a year apart, down to a 9-month old, and lived with Jessie Mae and her current husband in a run-down, three-bedroom house in Mobile, Alabama.

Snookie was the oldest and the loudest. Her mother was loud, too, and always seemed to be unhappy. Jessie Mae sat on the couch most of the day watching television and had the children fending for themselves. Snookie and Shawna ended up doing most of the cooking and cleaning. With all the mouths she had to feed, you'd think that Jessie Mae would work harder, but instead, she had her husband, Vincent, working his fingers to the bone to provide for her and her ten children.

Snookie was more of a mother to her siblings than Jessie Mae ever was. With all of the six younger brothers and three younger sisters ultimately looking to her for care, Snookie had to make a lot of noise in order to get their attention and make them listen to her. Most of the time, she didn't mind, because she loved her mother and wanted to help out. Snookie knew that she was the reason that Jessie Mae had lived a difficult life for all these years. At least that's what she had been told ever since she could remember.

Jessie Mae liked to play the martyr and constantly made Snookie feel responsible for everything that went wrong in her life. Since Snookie was the first child, she was the beginning of all of Jessie Mae's problems. Snookie was only ten years old and there was no reason in the world that she should have had to bear the burden of Jessie Mae's bad choices in life. Yet, she bore it.

***

Jessie Mae Franklin was a fast little girl, grown beyond her years. Her mother, Dorothy, owned a whorehouse in New Orleans and had always let her run around with the "Birds" in the house. They treated her like a little sister, let her hang out in their rooms when they weren't working, and never discussed their business. Jessie Mae played innocent, watched them carefully and stayed out of their way. The Birds all thought that Jessie Mae was cute, but none of them really paid her much attention. It was all about the Birds. They were always pretty, pampered and half-dressed.

Olive, who was one of Dorothy's best girls, seemed to care about her. Jessie Mae thought that she was the most beautiful woman she'd ever seen. Olive was Creole and had the longest eyelashes on the planet. She was the only Bird who never wore false eyelashes. Jessie Mae hung out in her room the most.

"Olive, I wanna be just like you when I grow up."

"Sugar, that's probably the last thing that Miss Dorothy would want to hear. You been hangin' around us Birds too long."

"One day, I'll be pretty and then I'll get lots of attention, too."

"Jessie Mae, you have a pretty face and lovely brown skin, but you're still young and have plenty of time to grow up and decide what you want to do with your life."

"I already know," said Jessie Mae, as she admired herself in the mirror.

Olive couldn't help but laugh as she looked at Jessie Mae. She liked to tease her about her boyish figure. "Well, girl, you better hurry up and grow you some titties," she said. "That's the only way you gonna get any attention around here."

Jessie Mae really loved the big, old house that they lived in. It had four floors, lots of beautiful rooms and many hiding places that no one knew about. Jessie Mae spent lots of time roaming around that house at night when she was supposed to be asleep and often saw the Birds having sex. She was very aware of what to do with a boy. The first time that she let a boy touch her private parts, she was five years old. He was six.

Jessie Mae liked to be the center of attention, especially with the opposite sex. The neighborhood kids knew her as "the little easy". She would bring the neighborhood boys down the street behind Old Man Johnson's garage and let them feel up under her skirt. She continued this kind of behavior all the way into high school.

It wasn't a surprise to anyone else in town, but Dorothy Franklin had the nerve to be shocked when her fifteen-year-old daughter, Jessie Mae, managed to get herself pregnant. For someone who was in the sex business, Dorothy sure didn't have a clue about what her own daughter was up to. Olive was the one who told her.

"I think you better check on Jessie Mae," she said. "She's been spending a lot of extra time in the bathroom every morning. Sounds like she can't keep nothin' down."

Dorothy took Jessie Mae to the same gynecologist where she sent her girls. Jessie Mae was definitely having a baby. She was already in her third month. Dorothy felt like a fool and didn't know how to react to this news. Neither she nor Jessie Mae spoke a word to each other all through the long car ride home. As soon as they got back to the house, Dorothy finally turned to face her daughter.

"How the hell did you get pregnant?" Dorothy asked.

"The usual way," Jessie Mae responded, smirking.

Dorothy smacked Jessie Mae hard, knocking the smirk right off her face.

"What you hit me for?" Jessie Mae asked, shocked.

"You wanna answer me, gal?" Dorothy wasn't playing. "Who the hell you been messin' around wit?"

"I don't know," Jessie Mae responded.

Dorothy smacked her again.

"Stop hittin' me!" she screamed.

"I'll slap you white if you don't answer me," Dorothy said, fuming. "Now, tell me who the father is."

Jessie Mae was crying. She had never seen her mother this angry, at least not since that wild night three years ago, a night that Jessie Mae would never forget.

Dorothy Franklin had the best whorehouse in town. It was appropriately called "The Gilded Cage". She had a reputation in New Orleans for having the most exotic girls. Black girls who looked white, for men who were color struck, but wanted the flavor. She had the really dark girls, who were there for the slave fantasies that she found common among her white clients. She had a couple of rare Birds who were actually white, but wanted to be fucked by black men. She even had girls who would perform unusual sex acts and fantasies in a special room that she called "the red hot room".

Dorothy was a tough lady who knew how to make money. She ran a clean house and was willing to provide just about anything for the pleasure of men. She understood that she needed to have something a little different than what was being offered by the other houses. She was known for having the most erotic atmosphere and providing free shows in the lounge while the clients waited for their Birds to be ready.

When Jessie Mae was only twelve years old, there was an incident in the house. The night wasn't particularly different than any other when it began. The lounge had a nice fire going in the fireplace and the light from the amber lamps made the room glow with a flattering gold tone. As usual, some of the girls were walking around in revealing lingerie passing out free drinks. The men waiting in the lounge were teased and flirted with by these sexy girls. The young ladies looked almost ethereal as their skin glistened in that amber light: angels in a whorehouse.

It was also the night Olive landed on Dorothy's doorstep, and it was a night to remember. It was raining like cats and dogs outside, but inside the house it was warm and cozy. It was packed that night. All of Dorothy's best customers were in town at the same time. It's a good thing her best Birds were all healthy. There had been a bug going around for two weeks and three of the girls had just recently recovered.

Jessie Mae was supposed to be in bed asleep, but was feeling a little naughty that night and wanted to see what was going on in the red-hot room, so she checked the reservation book and decided to sneak into the room and hide under the bed until the client arrived. Dorothy kept all of the rooms spotless. Not a speck of dust could be found anywhere. Not on the furniture, not on the floors, and not even under the beds.

Jessie Mae didn't recognize the code name of the client coming in tonight. The names in the book were always coded, and only Dorothy knew the clients' real names, but she never wrote those details down. Dorothy was able to keep track of everything in her head. For the money that she charged her clients, they definitely paid for anonymity.

Jessie Mae had almost fallen asleep waiting for the special client to enter the red-hot room. In the meantime, Cassie, a petite brunette, entered the room and waited on the bed. Finally, there was a forceful knock on the door and Cassie got up to open it.

Black Buck Bill, as the girls knew him, was an intimidating figure. He was 6'4", in his late 40's, and had the tight build of a football quarterback. He was not a bad looking guy, either. He had nice, smooth brown skin and well-manicured hands. The girls all liked him because he was a gentleman and liked his sex straight up.

This was the very first time that he had requested the red-hot room. Everyone was curious to know what his fantasy would be. Jessie Mae had heard that Cassie would be taking care of him. She was a special Bird who only worked when Dorothy requested her. Whatever she did, it drove men crazy, because they always came back for more.

That night Cassie was wearing a cheerleading outfit, complete with pom poms. The second that Cassie locked the door behind her, Black Buck Bill was getting ready. He stayed on the other side of the room watching her for a long minute.

"Sit down," he said, gesturing to the large armchair next to her. She sat down and waited. He walked over to her, reached into his pocket and pulled out a cherry lollipop, which he unwrapped and stuck into her slightly open mouth.

As Cassie licked and sucked on the sweet stick, Black Buck Bill removed his jacket and backed away. Then he instructed Cassie to slowly open her legs. She allowed her toes to rise as she parted her knees. The clean, white panties that she wore were staring back at Black Buck Bill, as he pulled down his pants and allowed his raging hard-on to spring free from his boxer shorts.

Next, he rubbed himself and got down on his knees. He crawled across the room and planted his face into Cassie's crotch. He worked his tongue around the edges of her white panties until his tongue found its target. After a minute, he grabbed her by her waist and hoisted her up so that her face was close to his face, and then proceeded to kiss her deeply. Cassie wrapped her legs around him. He manhandled Cassie a little bit, which wasn't difficult, because she was only five feet tall. She was eighteen, had a pre-teenaged girl's body, and a grown woman's seductiveness.

Then he backed off and sat on the floor a few feet away.

That's when something caught his attention, the slight movement of something that was under the bed. He leaned over, looked under the bed and found twelve-year-old Jessie Mae hiding. He went to reach for her leg, but she was able to scramble away. He grabbed the edge of the bed and moved it halfway across the floor. Jesse Mae lay exposed in her flannel nightgown, which was hiked up to her naked thighs. She made no move to cover herself. As a matter of fact, she confidently allowed her knees to part as she gave Black Buck Bill a clear view of her virgin vagina. He grabbed Jessie Mae off the floor, lifted her in the air and flung her onto the bed. She was out of breath from the excitement.

Cassie hadn't moved. She watched the whole thing as if it were on a movie screen. As she watched Jessie Mae pull the nightgown over her head, she knew that something crazy was about to happen. Black Buck Bill gestured for Cassie to come over to the bed. As she approached, he stuck one of his huge fingers into Jessie Mae's wet vagina. She squealed, loving it. Then he grabbed Cassie by the back of her neck and forced her head down. She immediately took his swollen member into her mouth.

After that, everything happened quickly. Someone busted in the door. There was screaming and the sound of bone crushing as two goons, wielding baseball bats, proceeded to beat Black Buck Bill into a bloody pulp. Standing in the middle of the chaos was Dorothy Franklin, orchestrating the whole thing. Her eyes were blazing with fury and Jessie Mae would have sworn that her mother was possessed by the devil. Dorothy found Cassie trying to slip out of the room, snatched her by the hair and slapped the shit out of her, causing her lip and nose to bleed. Then she grabbed Jessie Mae by the arm, tossed her the nightgown and pushed her out the door.

"Go to your room and don't move until I come to get you," Dorothy hissed.

Black Buck Bill was almost unconscious when the two goons threw him out the back door into the pouring rain onto a heap of trashcans in the alley. Dorothy followed to make sure that someone cleaned up the trail of blood left behind. She stood on the porch to see what they had done with Black Buck Bill and that's when she spotted a girl in the alley with huge, pitiful eyes. Dorothy looked at her intently before she called out to her.

"Hey, gal," she said. "Come here."

The girl was drenched. She had on a thin, sleeveless dress and sandals.

"Whatchu doin' hangin' around behind my house?"

"Maxie sent me," said the girl, her teeth chattering.

Dorothy looked around. She still didn't see any sign of Black Buck Bill. She gestured to the girl.

"What's your name?"

"Olive ."

"Well, Miss Olive, you ain't gonna be no good to me if you got pneumonia. Come on in here and get some warm clothes on."

The girl smiled gratefully and ran up the steps through the back door. Dorothy gave the alley one last glance before walking inside and locking the door behind her. After showing Olive around and introducing her to the girls, Dorothy went to confront Jesse Mae, who was in her bedroom, cowering in fear.

"What the hell did you think that you were doin' tonight?" asked Dorothy, as she entered Jesse Mae's bedroom, slamming the door.

"I…I'm sorry…" Jesse Mae stuttered.

"Didn't I tell you that the workrooms are off limits?"

"Yes, ma'am."

"Do you wanna be a whore?"

Jesse Mae wasn't sure what to say. She kind of did. She thought the Birds were elegant and beautiful. They got to wear all kinds of fancy clothes and they got lots of money and attention from men. Sounded like a good life to her. But the look on her mother's face suggested that saying yes wasn't a good thing. She took a chance.

"I wanna be just like you, Momma."

Dorothy's eyes were on fire, but when she stared her daughter down, she saw that Jesse Mae looked so innocent.

"Don't let me catch you in any of the workrooms again. Next time, I will hurt you. Understand me, gal?"

"Yes, ma'am."

Jessie Mae had a fleeting thought as she went back to her room. How did her mother know that she was in that room? They sure as hell didn't beat him to a pulp over a fantasy that he had paid for. How did Dorothy and her goons get there so fast? Maybe that special room had a secret peephole, too. Just a thought.

***

That night, three years ago, Jessie Mae escaped Dorothy's complete wrath, but this time there was no escaping. Being a grandmother was not in Dorothy's plan at this time in her life and this was not what she wanted for her only daughter. Jessie Mae was still rubbing her cheek after her mother slapped her for the second time.

"You got two seconds to answer my question," Dorothy Mae said. "Who is the father of your damn baby?"

"Momma, I really don't know," she cried. "I been messin' wit three guys."

"What three guys?"

"Just some boys who were passing through town during Mardis Gras."

"Did you bother to get any of their names?"

"No. I was with a group of friends just having fun."

"Does it sound like it's gonna be fun now, Jessie Mae?"

Jessie Mae put her head down. "No, ma'am."

"I can't believe you're a goddamn whore!" Dorothy yelled.

"I live in a goddamn whorehouse!" Jessie Mae countered.

"How dare you talk to me like that?"

"Well, it's true," Jessie Mae said, getting a little bolder. "How did you expect me to turn out? It's what you taught me."

"Did you get paid?"

"No."

"Then you're a *stupid* whore and you didn't learn a damn thing from me. Now get the fuck out of my house."

CHAPTER 9

Aurora

Baxter Duncan was drunk and in rare form as he burst through the front door and confronted his wife, Camille. "Where the hell is she?" he roared.

"Shhh," she replied. "She cried herself to sleep. You scared her half to death."

He proceeded to trample muddy boots over the carpet where Camille was vacuuming, still cleaning up a big mess that he had made a few hours earlier.

"Dammit, Baxter. Don't you have enough sense to take your boots off first? I guess you don't see me with this damn vacuum cleaner in the middle of the floor."

"Why the hell are you vacuuming at ten o'clock at night?"

"I just love to vacuum," she snapped sarcastically. "Didn't you know that?"

He slapped her hard across her face. "Shut your smart ass mouth. Where is she, Camille?" he roared, heading to the staircase. "Aurora!"

"You bastard." Camille was seething. "Don't you dare go near my daughter in that condition."

"*Your* daughter?" Baxter turned around menacingly and walked toward Camille. "You trying to tell me if I can see my daughter or not?"

"Go sleep it off, Baxter," she said.

"I'll beat the shit outta both of ya," he shouted, stumbling back in her direction.

Camille had grabbed a baseball bat from behind the couch and was holding it in swinging position. "I mean it. Put your hands on me or my daughter again and I'll crack your skull wide open."

Baxter stopped in his tracks, but enhanced his angry scowl. After several seconds, he turned and walked into the kitchen. Camille stood looking at him for a long time. Once again she wondered why she was still there, in that house, with that man. One day she was going to snap and when she did, one of them was going to end up dead.

It was the beginning of spring and the snowfalls had finally subsided. A harsh, Chicago winter was about to bid goodbye for the season. Camille Kennedy and her two best friends, Vicky and Linda, were skipping school today. It was only a half-day anyway. Teachers' conference.

Camille was a tall, exotic, caramel-skinned beauty with long, wavy hair and amber eyes, courtesy of her Puerto Rican mother and Jamaican father. Her parents, Jonathan and Maria Kennedy, were upper middle class, had a solid marriage and made a good, easy life for their only child.

Jonathan Kennedy was a Jamaican immigrant who had moved to Chicago with his grandmother, Sofia, when he was five years old. Sofia came to town to take over her brother's businesses after he suffered a stroke. They lived on the rugged South Side, and even though his grandmother worked hard running a hair salon and a Jamaican food restaurant, she was able to keep a tight rein on her precious grandson as he grew into a young man. Jonathan Kennedy was going to be somebody important one day.

Sofia's greatest business success was the expansion of the salon into a full-service beauty shop, which she initiated on her own, selling exotic hair care and beauty products. She became very good at combining excellent products with her own special brand of island beauty secrets. She loved to help women feel better.

Even though he was a young teenager, Sofia began to teach Jonathan how to appreciate women of quality. Jonathan learned his lessons well and made an extra effort to show that he appreciated at least one woman, a special young woman by the name of Maria Vega. Maria's mother, Carmen, had been a customer of Sofia's for many years and often brought her daughter along to the salon, especially now that Maria was old enough to wear a little makeup and get beauty tips.

Jonathan enjoyed watching his grandmother work. She was smart and very patient. He was a quick learner and liked it when Sofia asked him to hang around and help her out with her beauty parties. She would throw a little event once a month to bring in new business and fortify her relationships with her current clients. Jonathan was charming and helpful, and got to flirt with the older women, who thought he was cute. But he always had his eye on Mrs. Vega's daughter.

One summer when they were both eighteen, Jonathan and Maria ran into each other at an outdoor concert. They began hanging out together. It didn't take long for them to fall in love. They were the perfect couple. They had the same dreams and goals and they set out to make them happen. One of Jonathan's goals was to have his own business, which was assured once Sofia had taken him as an apprentice and taught him everything he needed to know. By the time he was twenty-two he was running all of her businesses and had expanded into selling men's and women's fragrances, and health products. He was a natural.

Jonathan bought Maria a beautiful diamond ring and promised her the world. They couldn't wait to get married and start a family. Sofia threw the couple a huge, Puerto Rican wedding. Maria got pregnant immediately and they were blessed with a lovely, wild-haired child. They named her Camille.

Camille was sweetly spoiled by her maternal grandmother and paternal great-grandmother. Carmen Vega taught her how to speak Spanish. Sofia, whose father was originally from Martinique, taught Camille how to speak French. Camille was the apple of their eye, and they all showered her with beautiful things. But after a short bout with aggressive lung cancer, Sofia died when Camille was only eight years old. She left everything to her grandson Jonathan and his family.

There was never a shortage of love from Camille's parents. Jonathan and Maria loved each other deeply and they loved her unconditionally. Sometimes she appreciated them for being good parents, but sometimes she took everything for granted. All in all, Camille had a good heart, was an excellent student, and didn't give them too much trouble. That's how she managed to stay out of private school. Camille loved going to public high school with her best friends. They all lived in nice houses a few blocks from school, which made it difficult to skip classes unless they went out of the neighborhood. That's what the girls were doing today, skipping school. Camille, Vicky and Linda were like the Three Musketeers since they were little girls.

Vicky Reese was cute and chubby. She was short, light-skinned and liked to smoke cigarettes almost as much as she liked to eat. Being a smoker hadn't curbed her appetite one bit. With her funky cornrows and thick, gold-rimmed glasses, she was a stark contrast to Camille. Vicky was the youngest in a family where she had six brothers and sisters who were much older than she was. They protected her from outsiders like she was weak, but within her family she was tough and always fought for respect.

Vicky's parents were older than the Kennedys. They were older than most of the other parents. They were in their sixties and had raised a brood, so they were tired. They didn't keep up with Vicky too much. She was able to pull a lot of stuff over on them, but she wasn't really bad. Besides, those older siblings kept her in line. Even though they no longer lived at home, they seemed to always know when she was up to something.

Linda Bell was different from either of her two friends. She was tall and slim, with creamy dark skin, and had a head of wild hair, courtesy of her Indian father, which she wore in a huge Afro. She had older siblings, too, but hers still lived at home. Her older brother sold pot and her older sister had two children out of wedlock. Both parents worked hard, but Mr. Bell was hardly ever at home and Mrs. Bell was oblivious to most of what went on in her own house, even when she was there.

The three seniors met around the corner from Hunter High School and began their day of hooky. First, they had to stop at a little convenience store under the el train station to pick up cigarettes. After that, they headed across town to their favorite White Castle to grab some food. While the girls downed several cheeseburgers, fries and shakes, they discussed fashion, sports and, of course, boys.

None of the girls were seriously dating at that time, and none of them were virgins. Linda was the quiet one, but she was an athlete and really liked to compete with the boys. She ran track and liked to play basketball and tennis. She was secretly messing with one of the boys on the basketball team and also one of the boys on the track team.

Vicky was into hating all boys at the moment. She had her heart broken the year before. She was dating an older boy who got her pregnant. When she told him about it, he got very upset, because he had recently found out that another girl at another high school was also pregnant at the same time. Vicky couldn't deal with the humiliation or the pain. She had an abortion and vowed to never fall in love again.

Camille had recently broken up with her boyfriend of a year and a half. His name was Jeremy. He was fine as they come, and they looked good together, but he turned out to be a real jerk. After a year of hanging out with him, she finally thought she loved him, so she lost her virginity to him. He had bugged her about it for the entire time and then after they finally had sex, he seemed to lose his interest in her. He had constantly taken her for granted, and was lazy about going to school. Ever. He smoked pot all the time and was messing with other girls, too.

Vicky was a serious cigarette smoker, but Camille only liked to puff without inhaling, because she thought she looked good smoking. Linda used to be a light smoker, but these days she stayed away from cigarettes, alcohol, or anything else that would interfere with her continuing reign as the female track star of Hunter High.

While they enjoyed their White Castle feast, the girls continued to gossip about everybody and everything that they could think of. Vicky enjoyed her cigarette and Camille sat there puffing away. Vicky had been slyly watching Camille as they lit up the second round of cigarettes and began smoking. There was Camille, just blowing smoke like nobody's business. She had the flicks and the flickers down pat, but not the slightest bit of smoke was penetrating her virgin throat. Vicky couldn't take it anymore.

"Girl, you ain't really smokin' that cig," she said. "And I'm tired of you fakin' the funk and wastin' a good smoke."

"What do you mean?" asked Camille. "I'm smokin' it."

"You don't know what the hell you're doin'. Watch me," Vicky said as she pulled deeply on the cigarette. As the smoke filled her mouth, she sucked it into her throat and lungs, slowly releasing it into the air in little, round puffs. She smiled confidently at Camille.

"That's how you inhale a cigarette," she said.

"I can do that."

Camille attempted to repeat the deep inhalation of her friend. Within seconds, she was choking. Linda slapped her on the back.

"You alright, Camille?" she asked. "Vicky, what did you have to go and do that for? You know she's a lightweight."

After several minutes, the choking fit subsided. Camille grabbed her purse, jumped up from the table and headed to the ladies room, which was occupied. She leaned against the wall, broke out in a cold sweat and turned an interesting shade of green. She managed to pull her beautiful mane into a sloppy ponytail as she slid down the wall and was seated on the floor of White Castle, looking pitiful.

Linda was at the table admonishing Vicky.

"Why can't you just leave her alone? If she wants to puff, let her puff. She's just trying to look cool."

"Shut up, Linda," snapped Vicky. "You'd still be smoking, too, if it didn't cut precious seconds off your running time."

"Exactly," said Linda. "It wasn't good for me, and you're the one who told me to stop, so why do you want to get Camille started down that nasty ass road?"

"I taught her a lesson, didn't I?" Vicky grinned. "I bet she won't be thinkin' she's so cute anymore."

"Is that how you treat your best friend?" Linda asked.

"You know I love that girl," said Vicky. "Camille's got a lot goin' on. She's a hot mama with a slammin' body, gorgeous face, and hair to die for, but sometimes she's such a goody two shoes. I'm just trying to help her grow some balls."

"She doesn't need any balls," said Linda. "But I can see that you do."

"Touché, bitch."

Camille was still on the floor, miserable. Finally, a woman came out of the bathroom with her small child. Camille rushed in and locked the door behind her. She had difficulty breathing and thought she might throw up, but nothing came, just dryness. Eventually, she was able to breathe normally, splash some cold water on her face, and return to the table. Camille reached into her purse and tossed her entire three packs of cigarettes into Vicky's lap.

"That's it. I quit," she said. "I don't want to ever see another cigarette in my life."

Vicky and Linda began laughing. Camille could only shake her head.

***

Baxter Duncan was a good-looking saxophone player with his own band. The musicians were all seniors in high school and played locally around Chicago. They were very popular with the teen crowd as well as some colleges. Baxter was very talented on his horn and could also make young ladies swoon with his soulful voice. He was very sexy and could have any number of young, hot girls at his beck and call, but his eye was on Camille Kennedy and she was the one who wouldn't give him the time of day.

When junior year began, Baxter transferred to Hunter High because his mother moved him and his three younger brothers from the projects on the South Side to another projects closer to Camille's neighborhood. He was already known around town and was popular, so he had no problem socializing at Hunter High. His only problem was that he had too many girlfriends. He had one at his old school, one at Hunter, and one who was a singer who had graduated the year before.

Baxter first saw Camille at a basketball game. He really wanted to meet her, but he had one of his girls with him. Whenever he saw Camille alone at school, he tried to speak, but she barely acknowledged him. Not in a rude way, though, just uninterested. Other times, she was hanging out with her boyfriend, Jeremy.

Baxter had his hands full, but he still had to have more. There was something so sexy about Camille. She also had an innocence that he recognized. She didn't know how truly beautiful she was. She had a ready laugh and wasn't trying to be anything special. She simply was. That was hard for a guy like Baxter to resist. For any guy to resist.

In the meantime, Camille was very aware of Baxter. She saw him and his dimples coming a mile away. Ever since that first year, she knew that he was interested, but she also knew that he was a player, and although he was attractive, she didn't want to fall into that trap. She was beginning to get fed up with Jeremy, but she loved him and wasn't going to cheat on him. She had to keep her distance from Baxter Duncan.

When Baxter and Camille were both seniors they shared homeroom and history class together. He had been biding his time. He could see how devoted she was to Jeremy, even though the dude didn't seem to deserve her. Baxter's big plan was to try and be her friend, and then maybe she would start to like him. That was a challenge, because they couldn't be more different.

Camille Kennedy was a smart, playful girl who spoke three languages. Baxter Duncan was a musician with a dark soul. Camille had two loving parents who owned several businesses and had a home in a nice neighborhood. Baxter had a hard-working mother trying to raise him and his three brothers alone in the projects. Camille walked a few blocks from her house to school. He had to take a bus. She had a boyfriend. He was still juggling a couple of girls here and there. There was nothing on the surface to make him think that he and Camille should be together, but that did not deter him from believing in his master plan.

Then, right before Christmas, Camille found a letter in one of Jeremy's books that convinced her Jeremy was talking to a girl out of town. She confronted him in the lobby after school and he confessed, swearing that he had only been talking. However, he admitted lying about his whereabouts some of those times that he had stood her up. He thought that coming clean with her would make it all go away.

Camille was furious. She tried to walk away, but Jeremy grabbed her arm and begged for her forgiveness. Jeremy was used to getting away with his indiscretions and thought that he could easily make everything better.

"Hit me, Camille," he said.

"What?"

"Just hit me and get it over with. It'll make us even, okay?"

"No, it won't."

"If you get the anger out, then you can forgive me, right?"

"Are you crazy? I'm not going to hit you. I'll either forgive you or I won't."

Baxter simply wouldn't stop goading her. Camille was very frustrated and needed to lash out at something, so in the middle of the school lobby, in front of a small group of students, with Jeremy carrying on like a fool, she hauled off and slapped him. Hard. Even though he was asking for it, he was still stunned by the intensity of her anger. So was she. That was the beginning of the end.

A couple of months later, Camille had a birthday party at Linda's house. Linda's family was away and she had the house to herself. It was snowing like crazy that night, but it didn't stop a large group of teens from making it to the party.

Camille and Jeremy were still seeing each other, but things were not the same anymore. As a matter of fact, he hadn't even shown up for her party. Camille tried to act like it didn't bother her. She was determined to have a good time with or without him.

Baxter Duncan arrived at the party solo. Camille seemed genuinely happy to see him, but after a quick greeting, she ran off. He assumed that she was with her boyfriend, so he ate some food and enjoyed the flirtations of the other young women at the party. He really only wanted to spend time with Camille, but every time he spotted her, she was talking with her friends. After a while, he realized that Jeremy wasn't there, so he went on a mission. He eventually found her sitting alone in one of the bedrooms with her head down. She seemed really lonely. He squatted in front of her.

"Hey, birthday girl," Baxter whispered charmingly. "Would you mind smiling, please?"

"Why?" she asked, not moving.

"Well, it's dark in here and I heard that your smile can light up an entire room."

She looked up at him, and then he flashed his sexy dimples. She appreciated his efforts and managed a little smirk.

"Did you get that out of a book or something?"

He looked into her sad, beautiful eyes and his heart damn near skipped right out of his chest. This was more than a conquest. He wanted this girl bad.

"You know that you deserve someone better than Jeremy," he said.

"Oh, really?" she asked. "Someone devoted to his girls the way that you are?"

"I've never made any promises or commitments to anybody. They know what they're getting into. Nobody's getting hurt. We all know the score."

"Then why didn't you bring them all with you tonight?"

"Tonight, it's all about you."

Baxter pulled out a little present from his pocket. He looked embarrassed.

"Here, I got you a little something."

"Wow. That's so sweet. Thank you."

"Open it later," he smiled.

Those damn dimples again, she thought.

"Okay," she said, looking pleased.

Baxter couldn't take his eyes away from her. Then the moment passed and the sadness returned to her beautiful eyes. In that vulnerable moment, Baxter stood up and reached out his hand to her. She let him raise her to her feet.

"Dance with me."

She immediately melted into his arms as they did a slow grind to the sound of The Chi-Lites singing *Oh, Girl*. Then he looked into her eyes, which he thought were the color of cream soda. He loved cream soda, and he loved Camille Kennedy. He leaned over, kissed her cheek and tasted the salty remnants of tears that had fallen earlier. He immediately moved his lips across her face, took her in his arms, and kissed her lips for a few precious seconds. She didn't resist, but he reluctantly let her go when her friends started calling her to come and do the birthday cake.

"Happy Birthday, Camille," he said sweetly.

For the rest of the night, Camille avoided Baxter until he finally left. Even though she seemed to be enjoying her birthday without Jeremy, a few of her male friends decided to go looking for him. They found him at the local pool hall, drinking. They dragged him to the party, which was embarrassing for Camille. She had endured enough and broke up with Jeremy the very next day.

Camille was going to enjoy her single status again. She was too young to be tied down anyway. This was their last year of high school. It should be all about fun and figuring out where to go to college. As a matter of fact, she had been offered several scholarships and was leaning towards going to UCLA.

Over a month after the party, Camille was still avoiding Baxter. He had been pretty good about giving her space. He didn't give her any special attention at school and she didn't initiate any conversation. Camille knew that she was attracted to Baxter, but she was afraid to let herself be hurt again. When he kissed her at the party, she knew that she was in trouble, but figured that she would try to hold out as long as possible.

Baxter knew that Camille wasn't seeing Jeremy anymore, but he didn't want her still thinking about her ex-boyfriend while he was trying to get her attention. For the first couple of weeks after the party, she still seemed to be sad, but gradually, he saw her blossoming again. She even began to smile and laugh with her friends again. However, she still tried to avoid his gaze when he walked into class every day and winked at her.

Then, one Friday afternoon after the smoking debacle with Vicky and Linda, Camille was sitting at the front of her history class taking notes from the blackboard. Baxter entered right after the bell rang and slipped Camille a flyer on his way to a seat in the back. Mr. Barris, the history teacher, had his back to the class, but apparently had eyes in the back of his head.

"Mr. Duncan, you are late," he said as he turned toward the class.

"It wasn't me, Mr. Barris. It was the lovely Camille Kennedy running up in here after the bell like she owns the place."

The students chuckled as Camille rolled her eyes. Mr. Barris wasn't very strict. However, he didn't take any mess from his students.

"Perhaps you would both like to visit with me after school."

Baxter stood up and said, "We'd love to, sir."

Mr. Barris was not amused. "Sit down, Mr. Duncan. I would not subject this lovely young lady to spending any more time with you than is absolutely necessary."

This time Camille joined in with the laughter as Baxter bowed to his classmates.

"With all due respect," Baxter said. "Every moment with Miss Kennedy is absolutely necessary, sir." He smiled and sat back down.

"Try to control your hormones until after class, Mr. Duncan."

Mr. Barris turned back to the blackboard as Camille blushed. She picked up the flyer and Baxter had written a note inviting her to his band's show later that night. She looked at him quickly. He wasn't sure what her reaction was, but he smiled broadly in anticipation. She smiled a little smile. That was enough to encourage him.

He couldn't wait for class to be over, so when the bell finally rang, he raced up behind Camille, who had grabbed her jacket and hurried out the door first, as usual. This time he wasn't going to let her go without a fight.

"Hey, Camille. Why you runnin' away from me, girl?" he asked.

"Didn't know I was supposed to be waiting on you," she replied innocently, trying to put on her jacket and balance her books. He immediately tried to assist her, but she shrugged off his help and continued to move as he kept up with her.

"You got my note, right?"

"So?"

"Oh, okay. I see what game you wanna play."

"You're the game player, Mr. Duncan. What do you want me there for? Don't you have a fan club or something that can come to clap for you?"

He gently grabbed her arm. "Will you please stop for a minute?"

She stopped. "Since you said please."

Baxter threw her his most engaging smile, which she could no longer ignore.

"I really want you to come to the show tonight and be my special guest. You haven't heard my new band. We're really good."

"Sorry, your minute is up and I can't come. I'm busy tonight," she responded with a charming smile of her own.

"Bring your friends with you," he said.

"Maybe next time."

Damn, why did he have to be so cute? That was all Camille could think about. She liked his dimples and the way that his eyes seemed to light up when he smiled, which seemed to be a lot more often lately. If anyone had asked, he would have said that he smiled only for her. He was damn near irresistible and he knew it.

As Camille walked away, she was trying to decide what she was going to wear that night. She resisted the urge to look back. She had to get home and call her girls as soon as possible. Forget about their plans to go to the movies tonight. This would be a much more memorable evening. Linda was going to get her mother's car, so Camille was praying that her crazy friend wouldn't do anything to ruin it.

"Where is this place, anyway?" Camille thought.

Camille pulled out the flyer, which she had put inside her history book. She wondered how late she could stay out without getting into trouble. Maybe she better spend the night at Linda's. She walked a little faster. She had a lot of plans to make.

Baxter watched Camille and wondered what she'd be wearing to the show that night. Oh, yeah. He had no doubt that she would be there. He headed to the bus stop wondering what it would take to make Camille Kennedy his number one girl.

CHAPTER 10

Debbie

The golden sunlight beamed through the bedroom window, bringing a warm breeze to the late April air. There was something special about Harlem, NY in the springtime. Little Debbie Marshall was playing alone in her room, humming a happy tune. It was a small room, but everything was kept neatly in its place. Her little canopied bed sat on one side of the room. The pink and white bedspread was very feminine, bordered in lace, and the decorative pillows had colorful flowers that had been embroidered by hand. The other side of the room was covered with several shelves, where Debbie kept her books, family photos and her prized dolls.

The frilly, pink curtains on the little window were blowing gently, giving the room even more of a feminine touch. Definitely girly. The little dolls that had Debbie's undivided attention were old and dirty, as though they had been used a thousand times, but they were all dressed up in colorful fabrics, making them appear to be fresh and new. Each doll was being placed in a specific position at a little table. It was important to her that everything be just right. She was preparing for a special tea party with her favorite possessions. As she placed the dolls, her father's voice broke her reverie.

"Debbie, do you hear me calling you?"

She jumped and turned around, surprised to see him standing in the doorway. "I'm sorry, Daddy. I was singing to myself."

Michael Marshall looked at the dolls around the table, and then looked at his daughter with an intense pain in his eyes. It was a look that Debbie had gotten used to seeing, but it always had the power to make her sad.

"Come eat your lunch," he said, quickly walking away.

Debbie got up and followed her father into the kitchen, where he had prepared two frozen TV dinners in the microwave. As much as Debbie hated eating the same old fried chicken, mashed potatoes and corn that came in these little plastic trays, she cherished the time that she spent at the table with her father. He didn't talk much these days, but something about his mere presence still made her feel safe.

Michael was a big man. Tall and strong. At least that's the way he used to be. These days he seemed to be more of a shell. He didn't even seem as tall. The weight of his pain shrunk him down to an almost unrecognizable version of his former self.

"Did you wash your hands? Michael asked.

"Sorry, Daddy. I'll be right back."

Debbie headed to the bathroom. Michael immediately walked over to the freezer, where he retrieved a half empty bottle of vodka. He took a long swallow, poured himself a full glass and returned the bottle to its icy home. Then he got a carton of milk from the refrigerator and poured a glass for Debbie. When he went to put the milk back, he couldn't resist taking another swig from the bottle of vodka in the freezer. Debbie watched her father do this familiar dance as she returned to the table, smiling.

"Okay, Daddy. I'm ready, now."

Michael sat down, picked up his fork and began to eat.

Debbie whispered, "We didn't pray."

He put his fork down without looking up. Debbie lowered her head.

"Thank you, God, for giving us this food. Please bless my Daddy for taking such good care of me and please give Mommy our love and tell her that Daddy misses her very much."

Holding back a tear that was constantly prepared to fall, Michael picked up his fork again and proceeded to eat in silence. Debbie knew that this day would be extremely difficult for him, but it was a rare Saturday that she spent with him instead of her grandparents, and even though they never talked about it, today was a very important day for her. It was April 20th, and it was her birthday.

***

Valerie Goodwin and Michael Marshall were high school sweethearts living and loving in the heart of Harlem. They were perfect together, the envy of all their friends. Valerie had the body of a sex goddess and the heart of an angel. She was 5'7" with a classically beautiful face and short, curly hair. People used to tell her that she looked like Dorothy Dandridge. Michael was a handsome, popular football jock with a winning personality. He was 6'3", had a great physique, was slightly bow-legged and had a huge afro. Before Valerie came along, Michael had seven or eight girls that he dated regularly.

Michael fell hard the first time that he laid eyes on Valerie Goodwin in homeroom on the first day of senior year. Valerie and her family had just moved to Harlem from White Plains, NY. She walked into the classroom with a quietly confident air, and the world stood still for Michael. Somehow, through the fog, he knew that his hound dog days were over.

It took Michael a good six weeks to convince Valerie to go out with him. She hadn't planned to get tied down to the first guy who came along, but it was immediately clear to her that the first guy just happened to be the best guy. She saw how the girls all wanted to drop their panties at the very sight of him, but there was no point in her getting into that line. If he wanted her, he was not only going to have to work hard to get her, but he would have to be prepared to make sacrifices to keep her.

He brought her flowers from his mother's garden, offered to carry her books and did all of the corny things that he could think of to get her attention. He need not have worried. He had her full attention from day one.

"Michael, why are you wasting your time with me?" she asked one day, when he was walking her home. "You can have any girl in school."

"Girl, don't play with me. If I wasn't here, you know there would be two hundred other knuckleheads over here trying to get your number. I've just got them all convinced that it's a done deal, so they ain't even trying."

"Oh, really?" Valerie laughed at his boldness. "So, you mean if I didn't let you walk me home, I might be able to finally get a date with the quarterback?"

"You like Jessie?" he asked, with true concern and disbelief.

"Maybe," she replied, really enjoying his discomfort.

He thought about it for a moment.

"Oh, hell no. That's not gonna happen."

Michael stopped, grabbed her by the arm, spun her around close to him and kissed her deeply. She didn't resist. He released her so that he could speak.

"You're my girl, okay?"

"Okay."

Michael Marshall's parents were hard working, middle class black folks who attended church regularly. Mr. Marshall was a postman in Harlem for twenty years and Mrs. Marshall owned and operated a formal dress shop. They doted on their only son and supported his football career while stressing the importance of an education. Growing up over the years, Michael was a good son who didn't give them too much trouble. He was polite and caring, with a good sense of humor. That made him a favorite of the young girls. His father was proud of that, but his mother was slightly concerned.

"He's a little too charming for his own good. One of these days he's going to get some poor girl in trouble, and you know what I mean."

Valerie knew about all the girls Michael used to run around with, but he swore that none of them were serious and most were just flirtations. It was all about her now. She believed in what they had, so she trusted him to take care of his business and let the others go. It was one of the things that he found so amazing about her. She never pressured him, never even mentioned his former antics with "half the girls in school".

For the entire senior year, Valerie and Michael were the perfect couple. Valerie was such a kind, unpretentious girl, that it was hard for anyone not to like her. The other girls that Michael had dated didn't even try to compete. They all wanted to be her. They also felt that she had somehow come out of nowhere and snagged one of the most popular guys at Harlem High, but fate is fate. What was a girl to do? Once they got to know her, most of the girls at school had no problem being her friend. She had that special quality. One minute they wanted to kick her ass, the next minute, they wanted to go out for pizza.

Except for this one girl named Anna Booth. There's always one. Anna could just as easily have ripped the long eyelashes out of Valerie's eyelids. The other girls were smart and knew that what they had with Michael was a good time, at best. They were pretty sure that the other fish in the sea would be available to them.

Anna, on the other hand, wasn't the most attractive girl, but she was really smart. As far as dating went, Michael thought that she was too short and a little too chubby for his taste, but since she would do anything for him, including some of his homework, he had let her hang around. He thought she was cute, but mainly, she was just always available. There were times, however, when he felt a little guilty about having her in his posse, because he didn't really like her that much. Felt she was a little too needy.

Valerie had tried to be friendly with Anna before she and Michael ever got together. The three of them were in some of the same classes, but Anna didn't care to make friends with other girls. Valerie realized that she wasn't going to make everybody happy, so she just tried to stay out of Anna's way. Anna didn't make that easy. She was a troubled young girl looking for a little love. She just picked the wrong method with the wrong guy at the wrong time.

Michael tried to let Anna down easily, and hoped that she would go away gently into the night, but she was not going to be kicked to the curb without a fight. Anna found it very difficult to accept the inevitable and had somehow convinced herself that Michael would choose her one day over all the other girls. It's why she slept with him. It's why she put up with being one of many. It was all for the dream.

Well, that dream turned into a nightmare for Anna the minute that Valerie Goodwin came to Harlem. Anna kept trying to throw herself at Michael and he tried to be cool about it, but eventually he had to make it clear that he was no longer fooling around. He was a one-woman man and that woman was Valerie Goodwin.

One week later, Anna Booth jumped in front of a subway train at the 110th St. station. Most of the students took it all in stride, but Valerie was devastated. She had never known a person her own age who had died. She expressed this to Michael.

"It's sad, but you gotta toughen up, baby. You livin' in Harlem now and people die here every day from somethin'. We got to all learn how to move on."

"Are you really that heartless?" she asked.

"I'm not heartless. I just don't care that much, so I'm not gonna think about it."

"But she did it because of you, Michael. That doesn't bother you?"

"No, Val. She did it to herself. Something was wrong with her and she focused on me, but I wasn't the problem."

"You used her, Michael," Valerie said, gently. "She had feelings for you. You said you didn't like her as a person, but you were willing to have sex with her. You have to accept that much responsibility before you can dismiss it."

"I'll think about it," he said, quietly.

"You'll have to, if you want to be with me. I can't tolerate a coward."

"Damn, girl," Michael said. "Go easy on me."

It was a challenge for him, but with Valerie's help, Michael eventually made peace with Anna's suicide. She even went with him to see Anna's parents, who graciously let him off the hook. Apparently, Anna had been going through emotional ups and downs for years and was often prescribed medication that she hated to take.

The Booths were in mourning over their daughter, but they made it clear that there was no blame being laid at Michael's feet. However, Anna's father did take him aside to give him a bit of fatherly advice.

"That's a lovely girl you've got there, Michael," he said. "I can tell that you really care about her. I always wished that Anna could've found a nice boy. The friends she attracted didn't give a damn about her."

Michael saw the pain in the man's eyes.

"I'm so sorry, Mr. Booth," he said. "Please forgive me."

Michael waited a long minute before Mr. Booth was able to speak again, and then the older man put an arm around his shoulder.

"Treat that young lady and all of the women in your life with respect. You're a young man now. Act like a man."

After that, Valerie and Michael spent all of their spare time together. Valerie even tried out for the cheerleading squad to be closer to Michael during football season. She helped him to keep up with his grades and he made sure that they had lots of social fun, despite the fact that Valerie insisted on remaining a virgin.

"If you want me to continue being your girlfriend, then that's the way it's going to be," she stated innocently. "Otherwise, I wish you all the happiness in the world with one of those other girls."

Although he appeared to be exasperated, he wouldn't have dreamed of having it any other way. Valerie Goodwin was his future wife and the mother of his future children, so where was he going to go?

The Marshalls never really met any of the girls Michael dated, so when he first asked if he could bring Valerie over for Sunday dinner, they knew that she must be something special. She was. They both fell in love with her. They could see the subtle change in Michael, and now they knew the reason why. He had become a little more serious about his future.

The Goodwins were a bit more apprehensive after meeting Michael for the first time. Valerie's parents were both educators and wanted to make sure that their little girl had the same opportunity to go to college that they had. They wanted her to get her degree and have a successful career. They also knew that Valerie wanted to follow in their footsteps and initially they took her relationship with Michael lightly.

"We need to talk to her about this boyfriend of hers," Mrs. Goodwin told her husband. "I don't like it."

"Don't worry about Valerie. It's just puppy love."

"You haven't seen her the way that I have lately. It's deeper than puppy love. It's her *first* love. You know what kind of a distraction that kind of love can be. To a young, innocent girl like Valerie, it's the most important thing in the world."

Mr. Goodwin still wasn't fazed. He pulled his wife into his arms because that always made her calm down and feel safe.

"No harm, sweetheart. Don't worry. Our baby is a smart girl. She'll be over that smooth talker any day now."

"The way that I got over you?" she said with a doubtful smirk.

Mr. Goodwin thought about that for a few seconds.

"You're right," he said. "Tonight we lock her up in her room for the next ten years."

They chuckled lovingly and Mr. Goodwin held his wife tighter as they remembered how strong that kind of love could be. The Goodwins were soon to discover that it really was much more than puppy love. Although they tried to convince their daughter not to get so serious about Michael, even they could see that the two young people were in love. Eventually, Michael was able to win them over with his charm. By the time Valerie sewed the last bead on her prom dress, it was pretty much assumed that the two would end up getting married.

Valerie was the light of Michael's life and he treated her like the precious jewel that she was. He supported her college ambitions, even though it would mean them being apart. She decided to stay home in New York and go to NYU; he got a scholarship to play football at Howard. That meant a lot of traveling between the two schools.

Valerie was a talented seamstress who made most of her own clothes. She earned extra money by designing dresses and selling them to her friends and the young women she met at school. She and Michael talked and wrote to each other constantly. Most of their school breaks were spent together in NYC or in Washington, DC. Nothing would stop them from being together.

Michael Marshall was as popular at Howard as he was in Harlem. It didn't hurt his reputation that he scored several winning touchdowns in his first season and became a hero among his team members. He was getting stronger, more handsome, and the ladies loved him. Howard University was like a smorgasbord of black beauty. What the hell was he going to do? This wasn't high school and Valerie wasn't with him every minute.

Michael was a big flirt and had a great time hanging out with his friends. The fact that he was devoted to Valerie made him all the more desirable to the young ladies. They all wanted a real man and Michael was definitely becoming a real man. He was trying really hard to wait for Valerie. Of course, he wished he could convince her to take their relationship to the next level. Before her, he had gotten used to having sex regularly and it was starting to get to him that he had abstained for so long. He was tired of 'tooting his own horn', so to speak.

John Becker, one of his teammates and best friend, was renting a yacht and taking the team on a cruise after the school year was over. They had made it to a semi-final championship in their division, so they had a lot to celebrate.

John was a nice-looking guy with cute freckles on his pleasant face. He had a slim build and was from a prominent black family in Maryland. All of the men in his family from three generations back had gone to Howard. His grandfather had recently died and left him a small inheritance. One of John's dreams was to sail on a luxury yacht.

Michael wanted Valerie to be there, but she had another commitment. Their time had been really challenged lately because she was working on deadlines with her designs and going to classes full-time. Michael understood, of course, but it became more difficult for him when he couldn't see her as often as before.

John told the guys that they could invite guests, if they chose. He was also bringing some of his family along: two brothers, a sister, and two cousins. It was going to be a big boat. The guys teased Michael about deciding to come solo. Several of the guys offered to set him up with a date, but he declined.

"Do I look like I need help getting a date?" he asked.

Of course, they all knew that he could have had any one of the lovely ladies on campus, if he chose, but they had all met Valerie and so it was really hard for any of them to seriously debate him on the issue. She was one beautiful woman, inside and out.

Washington, DC was clear and sunny on the morning of the sail. Michael stepped onto the pier looking like a rich playboy dressed in white linen, which looked really good against his smooth, brown skin. He decided to just look forward to a relaxing time with his teammates. They were going to have plenty of food and drinks, and a live band. It was going to be a real celebration.

At least half of the players brought dates. Not girlfriends, just dates. This was the kind of event that they knew not to bring their significant others to. No need in having any reports going back to the home front. They all understood the importance of discretion. The guys who didn't bring women along decided to have a guys outing. They were a little late getting started because John was waiting for his family, who had run into some traffic. Finally, he spotted them on their way down the ramp.

"I'll be right back guys," John said. "Then we can take this party on the ocean."

John approached his two brothers, who were accompanied by three young women. As they came closer, the guys gathered at the rail to watch the approaching group. John's sister looked just like him, light-skinned with lots of freckles. She was a big girl, but her weight was packed into a nice frame.

However, what really had everyone's attention were the two cousins. They were identical twins and were stunning. They looked like models with their shoulder length curly hair blowing in the wind. They were both about 5'10" with cocoa brown skin. They had small, perky breasts and the kind of behind that you could almost sit a soda can on top of. One sister was wearing a blue, one-piece cutout bathing suit and tight shorts. The other one had on a white pleated miniskirt. The slightest breeze revealed the bright yellow bikini bottom that matched the sexy top, which barely covered her breasts.

John hugged them all and led them down to the boat, where his friends were acting like schoolboys. Michael, however, was grounded where he stood, mesmerized by the sight. As he watched the others rush to greet the newcomers, he didn't realize that John had broken from the group and was leading the twin in the yellow bikini by the hand and right in his direction.

"Hey, Michael," called John. "Come here and meet your number one fan."

Snapping out of his fog, Michael walked over to John and looked into the most beautiful eyes he had ever seen. He was surprised by how amazing they were and how they seemed to look right through him. They were naturally gold with a hint of amber. Almost impossibly human, more feline than anything.

"Bom dia, Michael," purred the cat, with a melodic accent.

"Hi," said Michael, feeling like an idiot.

"This is my cousin, Yaritza," said John. "She and her sister are visiting here from Brazil."

"I am wanting to meet you," said Yaritza, taking his face in her hands. "John always send us picture and tape of your game. I think you are so handsome."

She kissed him gently and sweetly on both cheeks. He could feel her warm breath as she brushed her cheek alongside his. The blood rushed to his head. Both heads, as a matter of fact.

"Thank you," he said, blushing.

"Are you going to keep him all by yourself, Yaritza?" asked her twin as she walked up and slipped her arm through Michael's.

"I can only do what he allows me to do," Yaritza replied, giving Michael an intense stare. "This is my sister, Iliana."

"Okay, Marshall," said Kenny, one of his teammates. "You gotta share."

"Come on, everybody," said John, laughing. "Food and drinks on the deck."

That yacht trip was one of the most difficult times of Michael's life. He had the twins vying for his attention: two hot, Brazilian bombshells who didn't mind letting him know what they would be willing to do with him. Some of the other women, hot as they were, seemed to be a little intimidated by the twins. After all, those bitches were from Brazil. You don't get more exotic than that.

Within an hour, the twins were topless on the deck, letting the guys do tequila shots off their bodies. Michael, who was only human, sucked and licked those beautiful bodies with more enthusiasm than anybody else.

Whatever else happened that night disappeared in a drunken haze. Michael woke up naked in a Potomac River motel in bed with the twins and one of the girls who was supposed to be with Kenny. Hung over and disgusted, Michael grabbed his clothes from the floor and snuck out of the room before anyone could see him. He did his best to never talk about that night again, but he carried the guilt with him every time he had to look into Valerie's trusting eyes.

The following school year, Michael came home to Harlem for the Christmas holiday. The day after he arrived, he went to Valerie's father to ask for her hand in marriage. Being a sucker for tradition, Mr. Goodwin didn't waste any time giving his permission. He knew what his daughter wanted and trusted Michael to take good care of his baby. So, with her parent's blessing, Michael presented Valerie with a modest diamond ring and she barely got a good look at it before she was in his arms, crying.

Wedding plans went into full swing as Valerie and her parents tried to figure out a budget. The Goodwins offered to handle the big expenses. Michael's parents insisted on helping, too. The couple agreed to wait until after graduation, still over two years away. Valerie figured they would need that much time to plan the wedding of her dreams.

On Christmas Eve, Valerie surprised Michael with a small gift of his own. Sitting in her car along Central Park, he opened his gift with anticipation.

"I told you not to get me anything, girl."

"You won't want to turn this gift down, Michael."

Inside a little box, he was puzzled to find a room key to the Waldorf Astoria. "Michael," she said, gently. "I want you to make love to me for the first time. Tonight."

Speechless, he simply took her into his arms and held her tight. Valerie wasn't necessarily saving herself for marriage, but she was saving herself for a real commitment. Now that she had her ring, she decided that it was time to give her whole self to Michael.

After a few moments, he released her and looked into her eyes.

"Baby, are you sure?"

"If you knew how much it cost me to rent that room for two nights during Christmas, we'd be there right now."

"Then, let's go, baby! Let's go!"

Two years later, they both graduated and Michael moved back to Harlem. He got a desk job at Chase Manhattan Bank and rented a small, two-bedroom apartment above his mother's dress shop. Valerie got a job teaching at a local elementary school. They were preparing to make a good life together and were deeply in love.

At the end of the summer, the lovebirds tied the knot. The wedding was well planned and went off without a hitch. The weather on that day was beautiful. Both sets of parents were proud and happy, despite the cost, and the newlyweds were ecstatic. Of course, the bride made her own gown, simple and elegant in creamy, white satin. Over two hundred friends, family and co-workers joined them on their special day.

"The sky's the limit, baby," Michael said, as he held Valerie close to him on their wedding night. "I'm going to make you a very happy woman."

"I can't imagine being much happier than I am right now, Michael. What are you going to do to top this?"

"Just give me time, Mrs. Marshall. Just give me time."

After spending their honeymoon in the Bahamas, Valerie moved into the apartment with Michael and began to turn it into a home. She decorated slowly and deliberately, shopping at thrift stores for interesting pieces, which she refurbished and painted. Michael didn't care, as long as she was happy.

After six months, she found out that they were going to have a baby. She wanted Michael to be the first to know, but had to find just the right way to tell him. She decided to wait two weeks until his birthday. It was amazing how she was able to keep it to herself for so long. Several times she almost let the cat out of the bag. The night of his birthday, she took him to dinner and gave him a large, beautifully wrapped gift.

"Hurry up, Michael!" Her excitement was contagious.

He laughed. "I'm destroying this fancy paper as fast as I can."

As Michael opened the package with anticipation, Valerie beamed at the man she loved. He finally uncovered a huge box of disposable diapers.

"What the hell…?"

It took him a minute to realize the significance, but as he looked over at his beautiful wife, it almost appeared as if she was glowing…really glowing. He threw the box of diapers up into the air, narrowly missing a passing waiter with a tray of drinks. He hurried around the table to pull Valerie from her chair and swing her around.

"We're having a baby!" he shouted. "This beautiful woman is going to be the mother of my child. Hallelujah!!!"

The restaurant erupted into applause as the other diners couldn't help but get caught up in Michael's excitement. At that moment he had never been more happy or more in love. His life was complete. He quickly paid the bill and they rushed to share the news with the new grandparents.

Valerie's pregnancy wasn't easy on her from the beginning. She had three intense months of morning sickness and intense cramping in her legs. By her fifth month, her doctor ordered strict bed rest, so she took an early maternity leave. That was fine with her, because it was winter and New York was very cold that year. The entire family rallied around to help take care of her and, finally, by her seventh month, she was able to relax a little and enjoy her pregnancy.

Eventually, they found out that they were having a little girl and Valerie was excited about the thought of being able to dress her up like a baby doll. The two grandmothers took turns coming over with catalogs to help Valerie shop for baby furniture, and Valerie insisted on making some of the baby clothes herself.

In her eighth month, Valerie had almost completed the nursery. She decorated the room in a very girly pink, right down to the ruffled curtains that she made. On one of the shelves were enough dolls to fill a toy store. Now, all they had to do was wait for the baby to come, which was going to be early May.

Michael worked very hard at the bank, training to be a loan officer. Valerie occupied her time reading and singing to the baby in her womb. One April morning, two weeks before her due date, Valerie began to have severe pains. She tried to ride it out, but finally called downstairs to her mother-in-law, who was at the dress shop. Sure that the baby was on its way, Mrs. Marshall rushed upstairs to get Valerie and take her to the hospital. She called Michael at work and asked him to meet them there.

Within an hour, Michael, his parents and Valerie's parents were gathered in the waiting room, waiting to hear some news. After what seemed like an eternity, the doctors finally reported that the baby was in distress and that they would have to perform a C-section. The family was assured that it was a routine decision, under the circumstances, and that they were doing what was necessary to prevent further complications. Finally, the 7lb. 6oz. baby girl was brought into the world. Mother and daughter were fine and everyone was relieved.

The new grandparents fawned at the little darling from the nursery window, while Michael stayed by his wife's side. Valerie was weak, but managed a smile when she opened her eyes and saw her husband standing there. Michael held her hand.

"Welcome back, Sunshine."

An hour later, Michael watched Valerie as she held their new daughter. He fell in love with her all over again. He didn't think that he could love anyone as much as he loved his wife, and now he found his heart opening up on a whole new level with the love that he felt for his baby girl. Valerie tried to stay awake, but kept drifting in and out of consciousness. The nurses took the baby back to the nursery. Michael continued to stay by Valerie's side for hours until his mother forced him to go home and get some sleep.

"You have the rest of your life to look after them," she said. "A few more days and you can bring both of them home."

That day never came. During the C-section surgery, Valerie had developed a blood clot. Somehow, the doctors were not able to monitor it sufficiently. She died eighteen hours after Deborah Lynn Marshall came into the world, which sent Michael into a tailspin from which he never fully recovered.

CHAPTER 11

Candy

Katie Martin was fifteen, but looked older. She and her mother, Gwen, lived in a tiny, one-bedroom house in a run-down area of Camden, South Carolina. They weren't exactly poor, but as Gwen liked to remind her, "we got a cash flow disease, and until you graduate and get you a job, you gonna have to suffer wit the symptoms."

Katie hated their little house. "It always stinks in here," she complained to Gwen. "Every time you cook chit'lins, I can smell it three blocks away."

In this town the older black people could remember how the rich, white Northern families used to migrate there during the winter. Camden was known as a great horse town for those who could afford the equestrian activities. Gwen grew up in a time when white folks expected black folks to step off to the side when they passed each other on the sidewalk. Gwen never did get with that program.

On her way to school, Gwen and her friends encountered that situation with the young white kids one time too many. One day she began holding her ground. She often bumped those white kids right into the street. After a while, they did their best to avoid her. Gwen was tough then and she was tough now.

Gwen and her daughter had been living in Camden for the past thirteen years on their own. Katie's father was a traveling salesman who never wanted children. He tried to be there for Gwen and Katie in the beginning, but freedom kept beckoning him, so he went away one day when Katie was still a baby and never came back. He sent a letter and some money and hadn't been heard from since. It just wasn't the life that he wanted.

Gwen never wanted to have children, either, but she stuck it out. She had several jobs over the years and started out trying to be a decent mother. Even though money was always tight, she would cook, clean and even make clothes for Katie. After a few years, things began to change. Gwen felt that she needed to have a life.

When Katie was about nine, she noticed that her mother was staying out late drinking, sometimes leaving her alone all night. Gwen stayed drunk most of the time and hadn't really taken care of Katie since she lost her last job three years before.

Gwen had a job at the local grocery store, but she was suspected of stealing, and although they couldn't prove it, they were prepared to fire her. Gwen got wind of it, and the day before her boss was going to release her, she "accidentally" fell during her shift, injuring her back and earning her a disability check. It was barely enough to cover their expenses, but it allowed Gwen to sit on her ass and drink all day.

As Katie got older, she became fed up with her mother. With their tiny house and only one bedroom, Katie never had any privacy and rarely felt comfortable at home. She slept on the living room couch and had to keep her clothes in a collection of cardboard boxes. Gwen didn't hang out at the bars anymore, now she had men at the house all hours of the day and night. Katie couldn't help but notice gifts popping up: small appliances, food, jewelry, and music. Never anything too expensive, just stuff that they could use.

Gwen insisted that she had sacrificed a lot and deserved to have nice things. So, as long as these men were willing to supply those things, Katie needed to mind her own business. That didn't stop Katie from expressing herself. She was disturbed by these activities and tried to discuss it with her mother, which caused them to fight constantly.

"This is *my* house and if you don't like the way I run things in *my* house, you can get the hell out," Gwen said.

"I'm only thirteen!" cried Katie.

"Then shut the fuck up!"

Eventually, Katie stopped complaining and stayed away as much as possible. Being in school was better than dealing with Gwen and the drama. She wasn't a half bad student. She was just restless and bored. Besides, she didn't like the way those men looked at her when she was around the house. There was something sleazy about them.

Katie had developed early and by the time she was fifteen, she had the large breasts and hips of a grown woman. She wasn't conventionally pretty in the face, but had beautiful, dark brown skin; clear of the teenaged acne that plagued other girls her age.

Katie liked to hang around with "the outsiders", who were a little older. They were neglected girls, like her, who were basically unsupervised at home and did pretty much what they pleased. And what pleased Katie Martin the most was jumping into Patty Carter's Chevy Nova every Saturday night with a bunch of her girls and driving thirty miles away to party with the coolest black folks around, at a club called The Cave.

The Cave was an old farmhouse that the owner turned into an underground hot spot. Young people came from miles around to listen to the hottest R&B music and hook up with each other. There was no alcohol for sale at The Cave, but they were allowed to bring their own, and because ID's weren't checked too closely, under-aged kids like Katie, who looked older, could get away with fake ID's.

Katie loved to dance and flirt with the older boys. She also loved to smoke Salem cigarettes. Her girlfriends would drink and even have sex, but they watched out for her like she was a little sister and made sure that she didn't get into too much trouble.

One Saturday night, she and her girlfriends were celebrating Katie's 16th birthday. Katie wanted to feel grown up, so the girls gave her a little slack and didn't keep such a careful watch on her. They were all having a great time until Patty Carter had too much to drink and got sick. Since Katie was having so much fun celebrating her birthday, the other girls took Patty outside to attend to her, leaving Katie on her own.

A group of boys was making sure that Katie had a good time. She drank until she couldn't see straight and danced until her clothes came off. Katie wanted to be someone else that night. She wanted to be loved and desired. So, in a dark, backroom, feeling like a woman, Katie Martin lost her virginity to a drunken stranger and five of his friends. She wasn't too drunk to remember that.

By the time Katie's friends found her two hours later, she was lying alone on a couch in the backroom, almost unconscious. The other girls assumed that she had simply gotten drunk and passed out. She swore that she couldn't remember a thing. There was no way that she could tell them that she had willingly had sex with six drunken boys in the backroom of their favorite spot on her birthday. Her friends would have felt responsible and Katie actually cared, so she never said a word to anyone. Not even after she found out that she was pregnant.

Patty was the first one to get suspicious. She presented her theory to the others, but none of Katie's friends could believe it.

"Innocent Katie?" they asked. "How?"

When her friends confronted her with their suspicions, Katie lied. She told them that she had been having a secret affair with a married, traveling salesman that she met in town. She told them how the man reminded her of her father, whom Katie didn't actually remember, but she had one old picture that she cherished. Katie was very convincing, and amazingly, everyone believed her. She also told them that she had been planning to run away with this married man, until the shit hit the fan.

"You see… um…what happened was…his wife found out about us, so he backed out. Now, I'm stuck wit a baby."

One night, before Gwen got too drunk, Katie repeated her successful tale and told Gwen about the baby. Her mother simply looked at her and shook her head.

"I knew I'd be hearin' them words one day," Gwen said. "You turned out just the way I thought you would, gal. Makin' me a granny 'fore my time."

Katie just looked back at her mother. Then Gwen said, almost as an afterthought, "That'll get us another check, ya know."

Katie stopped drinking and stayed away from The Cave. She never wanted to see those guys again. She even quit school. Her friends still came around for a while during her pregnancy, but since Katie didn't hang out anymore, most of them drifted away. Patty was the only one who stuck by her and that was just fine with Katie. She only cared about getting ready for the baby.

One day, Katie went into the hall closet and pulled out a used sewing machine that her mother had received from one of her "gentlemen callers". Gwen used to sew on it when Katie was younger, but now she was usually too drunk or too busy to do much of anything except run around behind some man. However, in a few of her sober moments, she gave Katie enough instruction to get her started. After a couple of months, Katie was able to make a few simple things for the baby.

The situation at home was now reversed again. Gwen wasn't getting much male attention these days. Her drinking had taken a toll on her looks, and with Katie always at home reminding her that she was about to become a grandmother, Gwen began feeling the pressure of having no real life of her own, so now she spent a lot of time away.

It was a hot, summer night in Camden when Katie Martin gave birth to a baby girl who came into the world screaming like a wild animal. It seemed only fitting, because it was on a wild night that the little darling was conceived. Katie didn't even know what the father looked like, since it could have been any one of the six young men that she had sex with in the backroom of The Cave that night. Well, not quite any one of them. Katie knew exactly which one of those young men was the father of her baby. It was the dark one, the one who was black as coal. She knew that because her baby girl came out the same shade, the color of semi-sweet chocolate. Katie named her Candy.

CHAPTER 12

Portia

"Wait up, Dana," pleaded Portia as she huffed and puffed.

"Walk faster, Portia!" said Dana.

The two teenagers were on an excursion. It was Sunday afternoon and they were bored. They started out at the MGM on the Las Vegas Strip and decided to walk over to the Rio, which was a short distance off the strip, not far if you were in a car.

"It's too far," Portia protested.

Dana was frustrated. "Don't be such a baby. It's right over there."

"Yeah, right over there on the other side of the interstate."

"C'mon, Portia."

The girls walked through a field, climbed a hill, and came to a hole in the fence where locals knew you could climb through to cross I-15, which would take them closer to their destination. They had been walking for twenty minutes and finally arrived at a mini mall. Portia was out of breath.

"I have to go to the bathroom, Dana."

"Stop lying. You just don't wanna keep going."

"I'm not lying. Let's call a cab."

Dana sucked her teeth, stomped into an electronics store and walked up to the man at the counter. "Excuse me, sir."

"Can I help you?" he snarled, barely looking at her.

"We need to call a cab to get to the Rio."

"Sorry, young lady. There's a pay phone outside."

"Well, then call 911," said Portia, plopping to the floor. "You choose, cause I'm not moving."

***

Henry and Alice West felt like the luckiest parents in all of Washington, DC. While a lot of parents in their circle had to bury their sons during these lasts months of the Vietnam War, they were attending their son Darryl's graduation from Howard Medical School. Their two older daughters were with them. Kelly and Katrina were twins, beautiful, talented and spoiled. Darryl's fiancée, Ophelia, and her parents were there, too. It was a beautiful day and the campus was buzzing with activity.

"Our son looks so handsome," Alice said, beaming proudly.

"Yes, he does," agreed Henry, his voice breaking.

Henry reached out to take his wife's hand, and when she turned to look at him, Alice was surprised to see a little tear in his eye as he watched his son receive his diploma. Darryl was the baby and the only boy, so there was a special pride that Henry felt, knowing that he had done his best and gotten all of his children through college.

There was a great deal of gratitude that Henry West felt for the opportunities which allowed him to provide a decent living for his family. He helped his son to achieve his lifelong dream of becoming a doctor. Henry knew that his heart was bursting, and he was sure that if Alice wasn't standing there beside him, strong and supportive as always, he might just pass out from the bliss.

It's true that Darryl West always wanted to be a doctor. The first time he ever banged his knees, watched them bleed, and studied how carefully and lovingly his mother took care of him, he wondered what it would be like to help people that way. His mother had been a candy striper at a local hospital before she married his father and always spoke very highly of the doctors and nurses. It made a great impression on young Darryl. He knew what he wanted to do for the rest of his life and who he wanted to spend it with.

The object of Darryl's affection had always been his petite next-door neighbor, Ophelia Allen. The two of them had loved each other since kindergarten. They grew up in a nice, middle class neighborhood in the nation's capitol. Life was good.

Jonas and Laurie Allen doted on Ophelia, their only child. She had pretty, brown eyes and a bubbly personality, but sweet as she was, she expected to be treated like a princess. Lucky for her, Darryl West fancied himself a prince, so things between them worked out fine. Both families lived in well kept, brick row houses.

Mr. West and Mr. Allen both worked for the government and their wives stayed home to raise the children.

Darryl's twin sisters, Kelly and Katrina, were two years older, but everyone thought that they were younger because Darryl was such a big boy. Husky is the word that was used to describe him. He was also taller than most of the boys in his class and he loved his mother's cooking. His favorite meal was meatloaf with mashed potatoes, green beans, macaroni and cheese, and Pillsbury crescent rolls. If there was a sweet potato pie in there somewhere, he was in heaven. His friends often teased him, calling him "Green Giant" because of his size and the fact that he was one of the few kids in the neighborhood who loved to eat all types of vegetables.

Even though he was twice her size, Ophelia Allen was very protective of her friend, Darryl. They had known each other for as long as they could remember and had played together as toddlers. On their first day of kindergarten, their mothers walked them to school together. Ophelia was happily holding her mother's hand, while Darryl was trying everything in his power to resist Alice's attempts to hold his.

"I don't wanna hold your hand, Mommy," Darryl said as he clutched his Superman lunchbox.

"You don't?" Alice asked. "Since when?"

"I'm a big boy now," he responded.

Ophelia gave him her sweetest look and said, "I'm holding *my* Mommy's hand, Darryl. Here, you can hold my other hand." She extended her tiny hand and passed her mother the Barbie lunchbox she carried.

"Okay, I'll get in the middle," he suggested. "Come on, Mommy."

Alice giggled as she watched her baby showing off his independence. He happily grabbed her hand and then turned to Ophelia, who was still waiting with her hand out.

Darryl and Ophelia both swore that it was at that very moment when they felt the connection which would take them all the way to adulthood. Some things were just meant to be, and their friends and family never questioned the relationship between them. Their birthdays were even two weeks apart, so they insisted on combining their parties every year. It was just assumed that they would spend their lives together.

The only other person who Darryl spent as much time with was his best friend, Kenny Taylor. Kenny lived down the street and was very happy to share his friend with the prettiest girl in town. As a matter of fact, they were called The Inseparable Trio, and from the time they were all in first grade together, proceeded to live up to their name.

Kenny Taylor's family moved on the block when he was six. His father was a decorated, career Army man and his mother was a professor. He was the new kid on the block and, like Ophelia, had no siblings, so he was a prime candidate for her kindness. She was a very intuitive little girl and knew that even though Kenny was a good looking kid, he was an outsider and still was going to need a friend. Kenny was attracted to her smile and her contagious giggle. It didn't take long for him to have his first childhood crush. For Ophelia, he was the brother she always wanted.

When Ophelia first spotted the moving van in front of the old Jefferson house, she pleaded with her mother for them to be the first ones on the block to invite Kenny and his family over for dinner. No problem. Laurie Allen's job was to make her little girl happy, so Jonas and Laurie Allen hosted a dinner party for the Taylors and invited the Wests to come as well. Ophelia would never have excluded Darryl. It was already understood.

Ophelia brought Kenny into her circle and he quickly realized that Darryl and Ophelia were especially close, but they all became fast friends. It was no secret how Kenny felt about her, and he always teased Darryl.

"You're my best buddy, but you're lucky I didn't meet her first." That was Kenny's mantra, and it made the two of them laugh.

As they got older, the trio explored various interests together. They liked nature and spent lots of time outdoors collecting all sorts of flowers and insects. However, they always released whatever they captured, mostly on Ophelia's insistence. None of them really wanted to do any harm to the harmless.

A week before their tenth birthday party, Darryl and Ophelia spent an afternoon catching and releasing butterflies, and he expressed his desire to be a doctor.

"It's the only thing I want to be when I grow up."

"I think that's a great idea, Darryl," Ophelia said, smiling. "Doctors are very successful, aren't they?"

"If they're good doctors."

"That goes without saying, Darryl," she said, confidently. "You'll be the best."

"We'll live in a really big house and have lots and lots of kids," he stated.

"You forgot something, Darryl."

"Like what?" he asked.

Ophelia turned to look at him, but didn't say a word. It was all in her eyes. Even this nine-year-old girl had mastered "the look" already. The one that said, "Boy, please."

"Alright, alright," he laughed. "The really big wedding comes first."

Ophelia was satisfied. "And a dog," she added. "Don't forget the dog."

Darryl smiled a knowing smile.

The birthday party for Darryl and Ophelia was a neighborhood highlight. The Allens always went over the top for their daughter. There were over fifty children there with plenty of chaperones spread between the West's backyard and the Allen's backyard. There was lots of food, games and activities. Dressed as a prince and princess, Darryl and Ophelia were dancing to their favorite songs. Kenny, who had become very outgoing over the years, was doing card tricks for a small group of kids.

It was finally time for the presents to be opened. Ophelia received many nice gifts. Lots of girly clothes, dolls and games. Darryl received a new bicycle, a toy doctor's bag with a first aid kit, and lots of books. While the last of Ophelia's gifts was being unwrapped, Darryl disappeared for a few minutes. When he returned, he presented Ophelia with his special gift for her tenth birthday; a beautiful, black cocker spaniel that she immediately named Pebbles. He had saved his allowance for an entire year and with her parent's permission, and a little help from his own parents, bought her the puppy.

"This is the best present I've ever had!" she squealed.

After giving the puppy a loving embrace, Ophelia jumped up and gave Darryl a big kiss on the lips, shocking him and everyone else. That was the first kiss, the one to seal the deal. All four parents looked at each other and shook their heads, chuckling. The unspoken message was that they were destined to be family, although they hoped that it would be many years before it officially happened. Nonetheless, that little lip lock was the second crucial moment of their relationship, one that Darryl and Ophelia would talk about for years afterward.

Kenny's presents were also appreciated. He had gifted hands and liked to make things. He carved several wooden animal pieces for Darryl, and made beautiful doll carvings for Ophelia out of Ivory Soap bars. He presented them at the end of the birthday party. Ophelia gave him a huge hug and a kiss on the cheek. He received an equally warm hug from his best friend, Darryl. Kenny was pleased with himself, knowing how much his two best friends appreciated his thoughtful gifts, but it was the smile on Ophelia's face that made his heart warm. He once again fell for the girl he couldn't have.

By the time The Inseparable Trio went to high school, Darryl West had discovered football. He was still big, but had grown into his body much better and became a pretty good wide receiver. It was his good hands which made him an asset to the team. That's why it was so devastating to him when he got tackled during a game and injured his left hand. He soon realized that despite his large size, he could really be hurt out there. Getting knocked down by a bunch of boys even bigger than him was no fun. During the time he had to let his finger heal, he thought about the future. Football could definitely put an end to his big dreams of being Dr. West. No way was he going to let that happen. He would never want to disappoint his true love.

Darryl and Ophelia were an enviable couple all through high school, supporting each other in every way. Things weren't always perfect, though. Like most good friends, they told each other the truth and pissed each other off. But they stayed together. They loved and respected each other. The plan never wavered. The prince and princess worked hard to make sure that their kingdom was built on solid ground.

The biggest debate that they had was about when to have sex. Ophelia was actually the one who wanted to lose her virginity. Darryl was willing to hold out for marriage. They did a lot of making out, but had good heads on their shoulders. They talked everything out and weren't going to do anything foolish. One night before high school graduation, they were lying together on Darryl's bed. He had convinced her once more that they should stick to their agreement.

"We have big plans, baby," he said. "I just don't want us to have any regrets."

"I know," Ophelia said. "We have our whole lives together, right?"

"Right," he assured her with a big hug. "Everything will come in time."

Kenny Taylor was tall, light-skinned, and had a big afro. He was considered "fine" and had finally discovered that there were a whole lot of pretty high school girls who wanted to give him their undivided attention, especially since he was on the track team and in fantastic physical shape. He was quick to jump at the opportunities and eventually stopped pining over Ophelia. He was smart, too, excelling in math and the sciences. It was English that he had a little problem with. That's where Ophelia was very helpful. She got Kenny through the toughest English tests, and he helped her and Darryl with the things that he could do well.

It was no surprise when Kenny decided that he was going to be a doctor, too. Darryl was thrilled that his friend would be going to medical school. Now he just had to convince Kenny to go with him to Howard University. Of course, Ophelia wanted to go there, too. They could all stay in Washington, DC.

The three friends, Darryl, Ophelia and Kenny, went to Howard University and enjoyed every minute. It was a lot of hard work, but they were up to the task. While the happy couple was buckling down and planning a future together, Kenny was a little bit wild. He watched his best friends enjoy a solid relationship for most of his life, but he didn't feel as though that was the life for him. He couldn't see himself settling down any time soon. The girls he dated were beautiful and fun, and most seemed ready to snap him up as a husband, but he realized that he was bored easily. They didn't stimulate him the way that he needed to be stimulated. And it wasn't about sex. Sex was easy. It was an elusive quality that these young women seemed to be lacking. There was always something about them that wasn't good enough, and it really wasn't fair to them. It wasn't their fault that they couldn't live up to his perfect woman. They weren't Ophelia Allen and they couldn't be her if they tried.

It was a curse for Kenny that the woman who fulfilled all of his qualifications, and gave him unconditional love and support, was never going to be more than a friend. He had always known that and had buried his feelings of lust and desire for her a long time ago. He had to do that in order to be what she needed him to be. He was a good man. He knew his place and was happy in it. He would never have done anything to hurt either one of them. He loved Darryl, too. They were bonded like brothers, for life.

At the end of their senior year of college, Darryl West threw a huge party at a local club, invited all of their friends and family, and presented his lady love with a beautiful diamond ring. Darryl and Ophelia were officially engaged and no one was happier for them than Kenny Taylor. He hadn't yet found the woman of his dreams, but he was surely happy that his two favorite people were taking the next step in their future.

By then, Ophelia had won the battle; she and Darryl moved into a small apartment together and consummated their relationship. There wasn't a lot of fanfare. They were both virgins, so they approached first-time sex with the same mild enthusiasm as their other ventures. Curiosity mixed with practicality. They used birth control faithfully to make sure that there were no accidents to prevent them from fulfilling their dreams. Darryl was determined to be a doctor and Ophelia was going to be a teacher. There was no doubt they were very much in love and were going to make beautiful babies someday.

But, in the meantime, they were in college full-time and had side jobs in order to put away extra money for the wedding. The plan was to get married right after Darryl's graduation from medical school. They loved being in their hometown with the support of their families, so it was only natural that they continue on at Howard, where Darryl and Kenny went to the Medical School and Ophelia studied for her Master's in Education.

***

Then, after several grueling years, it was a month away from Howard University Medical School's big graduation day. Life was good and the wedding plans were in full force, with plenty of help from Laurie Allen and Alice West. Then, for no apparent reason, Ophelia seemed to be buckling under the pressure. Her mother was the first to notice that she wasn't her usual, bubbly self and appeared to be distracted. Ophelia hid it well, especially when her mother questioned her. But, she really needed to talk to Darryl.

A couple of nights later, she planned a nice dinner for Darryl and had the table beautifully set when he arrived home from his night job.

"Wow, this is nice, baby. What's the occasion?" he asked, smiling.

"I thought you deserved something a little special."

Suddenly, it was time for the graduation ceremony, and on this beautiful day, all of the families were there to watch Darryl West and Kenny Taylor graduate from Howard University Medical School. Darryl was on his way to fulfilling his lifelong dream of becoming a doctor. He specialized in General Medicine, while Kenny realized that he would make an excellent surgeon.

At the end of the ceremony, Darryl was standing with a group of friends when a woman began walking across the lawn, approaching with a strange look on her face.

"Oh, fuck!" exclaimed Craig Jones, who was standing next to Darryl.

In the next few seconds, time seemed to stand still. Before anyone knew what had happened, the young woman had pulled out a pistol and opened fire on the group, hitting Craig in his left wrist and right thigh as the other guys ran for cover. Several of the future doctors quickly tended to Craig, who was yelling and cursing like a madman.

Kenny, who was nearby when the gunshots rang out, tackled the young woman to the ground and a second man managed to grab the gun from her hand. Minutes later, security police had her in custody. When Kenny turned to look for Darryl, he couldn't believe his eyes. His best friend was lying silently on the ground, lifeless, surrounded by his shocked family and an inconsolable Ophelia, who had to be pried away from her dead lover by three grown men before she passed out from the emotional pain. Her parents and a paramedic tended to her.

Barely able to move his legs, Kenny slowly made his way over to the small group. He didn't want to look, but he couldn't stay away. When he reached the spot where his best friend lay, he fell to his knees and broke down. The bullet had pierced Darryl through the heart, exactly where Kenny was experiencing his pain.

Darryl's father, who was barely able to understand what had happened, was the first one to help Kenny to his feet and give him a supportive embrace. They cried in each other's arms for several minutes. Alice West, who wanted to be strong for her family, remained calm and was able to answer some questions when the police arrived, but she was several seconds from a nervous breakdown herself.

"Thank God that we were all together," Alice stated calmly, as her son's covered body was being wheeled away on a gurney.

Kelly and Katrina went to embrace their mother, whose thin veil of composure evaporated with the outpouring of love from her beautiful twins. Alice West could control her emotions no longer. The reality of her situation hit her so hard that every cell in her body was screaming for an explanation. Why had this happened to her son? What had he done to this woman to make her want to kill him?

The only answer to be found was no consolation at all. Darryl was simply in the wrong place at the wrong time. How cliché was that? He just happened to be standing next to Craig, who was her target. Craig was a friend of Darryl's who had been dating the young woman, but had recently dumped her for a white woman. Lord knows, to a black woman in Washington, D.C., that might be a legitimate reason for losing your damn mind, but to shoot up innocent people?

It was several weeks before things began to calm down. The Wests had a lovely funeral for Darryl. Alice was holding up a lot better than her husband, who had to be medicated. Ophelia and her parents dealt with the wedding and eventually they were able to get some of their money back. But that wasn't the biggest issue. Ophelia had a secret that she had to deal with and she didn't know what to do about it. She went to the only person who could help her with the answer.

Ophelia hadn't seen Kenny since the funeral, although he had tried to reach out several times. She just wasn't ready to accept that the Trio no longer existed. But now, here they were, having coffee and cake on the little terrace outside of her apartment. Kenny sat silently and let her speak when she was ready.

"I'm pregnant," she blurted out before she could think of what to say.

Kenny was speechless. He looked into her eyes for several seconds and then fell to his knees in front of her. She came onto the floor with him and they held each other for a long time. Finally, he found his voicc.

"Did he know?" Kenny asked.

"Yes," she admitted. "We had talked about having an abortion. We were trying so hard not to mess up. It just happened."

"Oh, my God!" Kenny cried. "Does anybody else know?"

"No. We weren't going to say anything."

"Ophelia…"

"I know, I know. I have to tell Henry and Alice."

"Not if you're still planning to get rid of it."

Ophelia loved Kenny like a big brother. If anyone could help her to get through this, it would be him. Like the loyal friend that he was, Kenny was with her every step of the way, and when she finally decided to keep the baby, a part of Darryl that was left behind, Kenny offered to marry her and give her baby a father. She refused at first, but prayed hard for the right answer, and she knew what

Darryl would want for her. He would approve of this union if he knew he couldn't be here himself.

Kenny Taylor married Ophelia Allen in a simple ceremony one month after Darryl's funeral. To friends and family, it was a blessing in the face of tragedy. To outsiders, it would never be understood, so neither family felt the need to explain.

"Let the naysayers have their gossip," Kenny stated. "We have something more precious in our lives."

Kenny came from a military family: his father was a career Army man, a lieutenant colonel with an exemplary record. Kenny himself was well known to be a man of great integrity. He might not have seen it coming in his life, but Kenny Taylor turned out to be an excellent husband and father. He and Ophelia began marriage with a mutual love and respect for one another. Kenny was very patient and waited for Ophelia to come to him as a wife, which she did six months after her daughter, Portia, was born.

CHAPTER 13

Melissa

"White girl, white girl, white girl!" The four black girls were chanting as they surrounded Melissa, who was holding her ground. She really was a little too tired to fight, but she was thinking that if they came any closer she was going to have to show them what happens when a fifteen-year-old white girl gets ghetto on their asses.

"Here we go again," thought Melissa as she looked into those silly black faces. These girls were all from this upscale black neighborhood. They weren't tough. They just wished that they were tough. They only picked on her to harass because they thought she was just some dumb, white girl. She knew that she needed to get out of this scramble fast, so she ran up to the biggest girl in the bunch, tackled her to the ground and began to pummel her in the head.

The other girls encouraged the fight as the two girls rolled around in the dirt, but refused to jump in because they didn't want to insult their friend, who prided herself on fighting her own battles. However, as Melissa began to get the best of the big girl, one of the other girls jumped in and tried to hold Melissa down. Melissa was tough. "Damn. I haven't even unpacked my suitcase, yet," she thought as she threw a punch that backed the second girl off. Where the hell were her cousins?

Every summer, Melissa came from Dallas, Texas to visit her black relatives in Los Angeles, the Murdocks. Her father was James Jr., or Junior, as he was commonly known. He didn't live in LA, but a lot of her folks did. There was Mama Susie and James Sr., her grandparents; her aunts, Becka and Ruth; Becka's husband, Pete, and her cousins, Eleanor, Johnny and Leslie. They all welcomed her. These were her Daddy's people and they didn't seem to mind at all that she looked just like her pretty, white mother.

Susie Murdock, the family matriarch, was a big, caramel skinned woman who hailed from North Carolina. Everyone called her Mama Susie. She was 5'9" and weighed about 300 lbs., but she didn't look fat. Just big-boned. At least that's what the folks back in Charlotte used to say.

In contrast, her husband, James, was a diminutive man, almost frail-looking. But one look into his eyes and you knew that he was not weak. Those eyes told the story of a man who had seen a whole lot in his lifetime. There was also a kindness there. He was Creole, from Louisiana. He could relate to his granddaughter, Melissa. He understood his people's preoccupation with skin color. He was raised to believe that being lighter was better. However, he married a woman who barely passed the paper bag test.

Susie and James Murdock had been married for almost forty years and had three children, Becka, Ruth, and the baby, who was Melissa's father, James, Jr. They had made a good life for their family. The five-bedroom house they owned was large, even by LA standards. It was in an area called Washington Square, which was a private, gated neighborhood off Crenshaw Blvd., right down the street from the part of town that the Crips and the Bloods called home. The houses in their private community were big, well kept, and mostly black-owned.

James, Sr. was a sound engineer who worked for the movie industry, one of the few blacks who worked in the business consistently. Susie had a successful catering business for years, but retired early so she could renovate the house and spend more time with the family.

Becka was the oldest of the Murdock children. She was tall, like her mother, but worked out several times a week. She was also an excellent cook who didn't eat too much of her own food. She was married to Pete Foster, a bank executive. He was dark-skinned and muscular. They were the parents of Eleanor and Johnny.

Becka had a great head for business and had worked for her mother's catering company since she graduated from college. She had recently taken over the business. Becka was taking the company to another level by using James' studio connections. "Nothing like a little healthy nepotism to keep things flowing," she thought. White folks did it all the time in that business. Becka was determined to be successful. She wanted to open a restaurant of her own someday.

Ruth was the next in line. She was short like her father, but she was fat. No other way to put it. She ate everything in sight, trying to comfort herself over the bad choices she had made. She married a man she barely knew when she was eighteen. He ran off with his secretary a year later while she was pregnant with her daughter, Leslie. Ruth and her daughter had to move in with her parents and they had been there ever since.

James Jr. was the baby, the one who was the most spoiled. Junior was very light-skinned like his father with a thick head of wavy brown hair and gray eyes. He went to college on a music scholarship, formed a singing group with his friends, and ran around with a lot of women. He tended to favor the darker girls, and he took them in all shapes, sizes and colors, as long as they were sistas. Junior loved him some black women.

Junior Murdock was a ladies' man, tall and handsome. When he was a senior at Los Angeles High School, he was the captain of the basketball team, keyboard player for the school jazz band, and star of the yearly musical. He remembered being mesmerized by the musicals when Becka was in the chorus. He loved to sing, and even though he thought the school productions were kind of corny, Junior would be the first one to admit how much he enjoyed all of the attention. He appreciated how much the girls loved to see him strutting around onstage. He couldn't disappoint his fans.

Growing up in Los Angeles, Junior could have been a movie star if he wanted to. He had good looks, brains, talent and charisma. James Sr. knew the stars and took Junior to the set with him many times when he was working on a film project. Junior once read a scene with Sidney Poitier, who complimented him on his acting potential. Thanks to his father, Junior attended parties and premiers at the various studios where he met stars like Danny Glover, Al Pacino, Bill Cosby, and Ruby Dee, who thought he would look good on film. Susie was excited and thought that her son could be famous one day.

Unfortunately, Junior felt that the long, tedious hours of filmmaking made for a boring life. He liked to move and shake and be seen, so despite a little motherly pressure from Susie, he let his parents know that if he was going to do any acting, it would be on stage, live, up close and personal.

In the meantime, he wanted to pursue his music, so when he was offered a scholarship to attend UCLA, he accepted. That was something that he was really looking forward to, but first he was going to have a blowout graduation party. After all, he was going to be starting his summer job three days later.

James, Sr. rented out a mansion for his son's party. Any 17–20-year-old in Los Angeles worth knowing was there. Becka catered the amazing food, using Mama Susie's finest recipes. Junior and his father took care of the guest list, which included the finest girls, the best athletes, the most talented musicians, and the cream of black Hollywood. That party was the talk of the town for years afterward.

One evening in July, Junior was leaning against a car in front of his job at Wilson's Beauty Supply on Crenshaw Blvd. The store had been closed for about two hours. He and his friend, Gary, had finished with their work about thirty minutes before.

Gary Wilson was Junior's best friend and fellow basketball player. He was tall and skinny with a strange sense of humor. He wasn't as good-looking as Junior, but the girls seemed to like him because he was funny. Gary's family lived down the street from the Murdocks. His father owned a chain of hair salons and beauty supply shops. During the summers, Gary and Junior worked part-time in the salons helping to clean up. That way they were able to make a little money and stay out of trouble.

Leaning on the car with Junior was a sexy young lady. He had no idea what her name was, but he could tell you that she had a big, beautiful behind squeezed into a pair of tiny, red shorts. She was close to him, running her fingers through his wavy hair.

"You sure this ain't no perm?" she asked, smacking her gum.

"Naw, baby," he answered, grinning. "This is the real deal."

Junior had been waiting for Corinne, one of his girlfriends, to pick him up, but she was late and Gary had gone down the street to Fatburger to get something to eat. In the meantime, Junior was talking to the girl with no name. She was a tall girl who had nice breasts and a small waist, but it was her backside that got all of the attention. It jutted out into a perfect bubble. Even women had to look and say, "Damn". This girl had a behind that made her look beautiful, even if she looked like a booger bear. Junior wasn't really sure what her face looked like, because she was more than happy to turn around and show him her assets as she flirted with him.

Suddenly, Corrine pulled up in her yellow Gremlin and immediately jumped out of the car. She was dark brown with a short, sexy haircut. Junior loved his dark-skinned girls.

"Who's that big ass bitch?" Corinne asked with one hand on her hip and the other one aimed at the girl, who was switching hard as she walked away. Junior licked his lips and never took his eyes off the nameless booty.

"Doesn't matter. I'm with you now," he replied sincerely.

"Really?" she snapped her fingers in front of his eyes.

Junior looked at Corinne, who was not amused, and tried to put his arms around her. She wasn't having it. "Don't touch me!"

"Aw, c'mon now, baby," he said sweetly.

"Why were you talking to her, Junior?"

Corinne was a girl from the hood. She was always looking for something to pick a fight about. Junior didn't mind, though. He liked his girls a little on the rough side. That way he could play a little rough back.

"You know you can't stay mad at me, girl, so you might as well forgive me now."

"And what if I don't?" Corinne looked him in his eyes.

"Then you'll be standing here mad by yourself," he chuckled, "and I'll be chasing that big ass that just went down the street."

"I can't stand you," she said as she tried to hit Junior in his head, but he easily intercepted her, causing her to hit herself.

"Ouch, that hurt," she cried, rubbing her chin.

"See, Corinne, you play too much."

"Whatever you say, Junior. It's your world, right?"

Gary walked up eating a messy hamburger wrapped in paper. "Yo, yo, yo!" he said, stepping between them.

"Excuse me!" Corinne snapped.

"You're excused," Gary said as he continued to chomp on his burger.

"What the hell do you want, Gary?" asked Corinne.

"Oh, were you two in the middle of something?"

"Nosy ass. Go mind your own business."

Corinne tried to knock the burger from Gary's hand, but only managed to spill ketchup from the messy paper all over her sandals.

"Shit."

Gary held onto his sandwich and shook his head at Corinne.

"Good."

As she tried to swipe at Gary again, Junior pinned her arms behind her. "Cut it out. What's the matter with you, Corinne?"

"Let me go, Junior."

While Junior had her pinned helplessly, Gary shoved the paper-wrapped burger toward her mouth.

"You should've just asked me if you wanted a bite," he said, smearing ketchup all over her face and chin. The burger landed on the ground. Gary threw his hands up.

"See what you made me do? You owe me a burger, girl."

Corinne struggled even harder to get out of Junior's grasp. She screamed, "I'm gonna kick your ass, Gary!"

"Stop moving around, Corinne," Junior laughed. "You're gonna hurt yourself."

"No, but I'm gonna hurt *him*. Then, I'm gonna hurt *you*."

Junior looked at Gary. "That wasn't cool, man. You owe her an apology."

"You right, Junior," Gary said, sincerely. "I'm a bad boy."

"I'm gonna kill somebody if you don't let me go," Corinne screamed.

Junior put a hand over her mouth as a couple of older men stepped out of the liquor store to look around. They weren't at all surprised to see who was making the commotion and went back inside, mumbling about young people.

"You got the old men ready to call the cops." said Junior.

"I'm done. You stayin' here with the wicked witch?"

"Naw, man. We're cool. You ready to go?"

"I'll meet you at the spot in ten minutes," said Gary. "What about *her*, man? She's about to bite your hand off."

"I got her, but you better get outta here." said Junior.

"Oooh, I'm so scared," Gary laughed as he skipped backwards down the street.

Corinne, who was beyond pissed, struggled until Junior let her go. She tried to punch him again, but couldn't get a good hit and twisted her wrist.

"Ow!" she squealed.

"Stop being so predictable. You alright?"

"You made me hurt myself, Junior."

"You ain't hurt. Stop cryin'," he said as he walked away. "Later."

Corinne tried to jump on Junior's back. He sidestepped to avoid her and she tripped and bumped her hip on a parked car. She winced in pain, but Junior didn't care. In a split second, his face went from playful to deadly. "You wanna test me, girl?"

She could see that he was no longer amused.

"You are one cold son of a bitch."

He turned and walked away again.

"Fuck you, Junior Murdock!" Corinne screamed behind him.

"Maybe later." He strutted off down the street to catch up with Gary.

After that, he stopped spending so much time with Corinne, which made her crazy. She tried to be around him, but turned into more of a stalker than a girlfriend. She constantly called him and tried to be wherever he was. It was annoying to him, especially because he was going to be attending college in the fall. At least that was the plan.

Junior eventually got rid of Corinne and decided to stay single and unattached for a very long time. He went to UCLA on the music scholarship, and then got involved with some actors who persuaded him to try his hand at doing musical theatre. He had a chance to work on a couple of good shows and got bitten by the acting bug. Or perhaps he got bitten by the hot, young girls who flocked to see him every time he performed.

One thing was for sure. Junior Murdock was destined to be a star. He breezed through college and graduated with a degree that he had no use for. All he knew was that it was time to take a serious look at a career on stage. He was ripe and ready for the world and was sure that the world was ready for him, too. Now, if he could only get his parents to take him seriously. Susie and James still wanted him to be a high yellow Sidney Poitier. He actually heard his mother say that. What could he do but laugh? Anyway, it was time for the next step.

"Broadway, here I come!"

Book Three

CHAPTER 14

Snookie

Being kicked out of her mother's house was devastating to Jessie Mae. She loved her wild life in The Gilded Cage. She would certainly miss the freedom she enjoyed being around the Birds, and being around all of the sexual excitement. Was she supposed to have avoided all that? Her mother was being totally unreasonable. How could Dorothy raise her daughter in a whorehouse and expect her to be an innocent virgin? But in Dorothy's world, her daughter was expected to be perfect, unaffected by her surroundings. She was supposed to learn how to be an entrepreneur, not a working girl.

Jessie Mae had to pack her things and take a bus to Mobile, Alabama, where her Aunt Patricia lived. Patricia McClain was Dorothy's older sister, a churchgoing math teacher who was married, but couldn't have any children of her own. She was more than happy to take care of Jessie Mae and her baby. Dorothy sent Patricia some money to help her out, but otherwise wanted nothing to do with her promiscuous daughter.

When Jessie Mae first arrived, she was quiet and shy. She had only met her Aunt Patricia a couple of times when she was a little girl, but she remembered liking her very much. Even though Patricia attended church regularly, she was a stylish woman who was very non-judgmental, even about her sister Dorothy.

Patricia's husband, Vincent, was another story. He was not a very pleasant man. He was a little short, not in bad shape, and wouldn't have been a bad looking guy if it weren't for the permanent scowl. He seemed to be judging her with every look. He didn't say very much, but when he did each word was filled with hidden resentment. It didn't take her long to figure out that he didn't want her there. She knew immediately that she would have to handle the situation very carefully. If she couldn't stay there in Mobile, then she had nowhere else to go.

"I don't think Uncle Vincent likes me very much," Jessie Mae told her aunt one night after Vincent left for work.

"Oh, don't pay him any mind, gal. He's just used to having the house to himself during the day, that's all. He likes to watch TV in the den, so you can be in there until 3:00. After that just make sure to stay out of his way. The TV in your room is small, but it gets good reception, so you won't miss any of your favorite shows."

Since Vincent worked at night, Jessie Mae was often alone with him during the day. She tried to be very quiet when he was asleep and she offered to cook so that he would have a meal waiting for him when he got up in the afternoon. Patricia didn't do much cooking at all, so she was glad to have Jessie Mae take a little bit of that pressure off of her, and every extra effort that Jessie Mae put forth was appreciated.

One afternoon Jessie Mae had on a pretty red sundress that Patricia had given her. She loved how it flowed, even though it was a little too big. The straps kept slipping off her shoulders. Even pregnant, she wasn't gaining much weight and was still thin. However, her breasts were beginning to fill out a little.

Jessie Mae was busy cleaning up in the den when Vincent, who was still in his bathrobe, as usual, stopped in the doorway to watch her. She didn't have on a bra and one time when she bent over, her right breast was totally exposed for several seconds until she realized that Vincent was watching. She quickly pulled the straps up.

"Oh, Uncle Vincent. Sorry, I didn't hear you come in. I'm gonna be outta your way in a flash."

"No, no. Take your time. My program won't be on for another ten minutes. I'll just chat wit ya while you work."

Chat? He wanted to chat? Right then and there she realized something that she already knew. A man is a man. Uncle or no uncle. For ten minutes, she dusted around that den and gave him a peep show. Miraculously, he was nice to her and couldn't keep a stupid grin off his face. He even thanked her when she brought him a sandwich.

"Come here, gal. Lemme me give ya a lil' kiss on the cheek to show ya how much I appreciate ya helpin' out roun' here." As she bent down, he held her arm down and had a view of her beautiful, swelling breasts up close. When she looked down, she could see his erection poking out of the opening in his pajama bottoms. Lord have mercy! Being pregnant was making her horny. She was actually getting excited.

Every day after that, Jessie Mae was cleaning up some mess that Vincent had left in the den when he came from work at 2:00 in the morning. The next afternoon, she would be in there cleaning thirty minutes before Vincent's show came on, and he seemed to be waking up a few minutes earlier each day to come and watch her work. Once he came into the den, he couldn't stop talking.

He seemed content to get aroused and go into his room to finish himself off. He never tried to go any further with her and so the two of them continued the sexy routine each day without Patricia suspecting a thing. She was just happy that Vincent had finally loosened up and began to treat her niece like family.

On Sundays, Patricia insisted on taking Jessie Mae to church with her. It was a small church with a handsome minister and a good choir, so Jessie Mae didn't mind too much. It was really the only thing that Patricia demanded from her, so she went without protest. She just hated how hot it got in there sometimes. Those paper fans just didn't do the trick. The church could use a good air conditioner, she thought.

However, Jessie Mae was getting lazy and was tired of cleaning up after Vincent's horny ass. One day, she finished early and was sitting on the sofa across from his favorite chair. She had on a short housedress and had her legs propped up on the couch. She knew that once he sat down, he would have a clear view of her crotch. Up to her old tricks, she made sure that he had a chance to see her lovely blue lace panties.

"You finish your work already?" he asked as he plopped into his favorite chair. Within seconds, his erection was in full bloom.

"Yeah, but I get tired a lot quicker now than before. Seems like there's more to do every day an' the baby been kickin' a lot."

"Oh...well...I guess I could help out some by not makin' such a mess."

"Really? You think you could?" she asked in her innocent voice.

"Sure I could. Why not?" he said, his mind racing. "Long as you promise to sit in here and rest after ya git done."

"Okay, Uncle Vincent. I can do that."

"Good girl."

Life became better for everyone, although Patricia wondered why Vincent was more amorous in the bedroom lately. She assumed that he was under less stress now that there was someone to help her out with the housework and she wasn't nagging him about his messiness.

For Jessie Mae, life became even easier and eventually she gave birth to her first child. She named her Snookie.

"What kinda name is that for a child?" asked Patricia.

"I dunno," replied Jessie Mae. "She just looks like a Snookie."

"Alright."

Patricia was very supportive of everything that Jessie Mae did. She probably overcompensated a little because she knew how hard her sister Dorothy had been. She wanted Jessie Mae to feel loved and protected. Vincent was more practical. When Patricia and Jessie Mae brought the baby home, Patricia went looking for her husband and found him in the garage digging through old boxes.

"What the heck are you doin' in here, honey? You're whippin' up a buncha dust, ya know that?"

"Ya'll come home wit the baby?" he asked, not looking up.

"Yes...but what...?"

"Her name still Snookie?"

"Yes, honey."

"Well then I'm lookin' for my boxin' gloves. That kid's gonna need to know how to fight with a name like that."

"Oh, Vincent...you need to stop," she giggled.

"I'm serious."

Jessie Mae never stopped being a fast girl. Months after Snookie was born, she wanted to get out into the streets. She left Patricia to take care of little Snookie as soon as the woman walked through the front door from working all day. Then Jessie Mae would immediately be running out. One day, Patricia decided to confront her.

"Jessie Mae, what are you gonna do now? You can't run the streets every night."

"I'm too young to be tied down," she said. "You're old. You know what to do."

"First of all, I don't appreciate being called old, but you're right. You are too young and Snookie needs to be looked after. If you're not going to do it, then I will, but you need to get you a little job or somethin' so you can help out wit the bills."

"Are you kidding me?" Jessie Mae was shocked. Her free ride was over.

"No, I'm not kidding, Jessie Mae," said Patricia firmly. "If you can hang out doing whatever you do, you can look for a job."

"But Uncle Vincent makes plenty of money."

"Honey, you might have my husband wrapped around your little finger, but he's always gonna side with me. Do not take my kindness for weakness. We took you in when you had nowhere to go. It's time to pay your dues. We love you, but now that the baby's here, you need to support yourself and her. We're here to help you, that's all."

Jessie Mae just couldn't behave herself. Instead of getting a job, she began messing with a neighborhood hustler named Nicky Bond, who was eighteen. He wasn't a bad person, but Patricia knew his family and didn't approve, which only made Jessie Mae more eager to be with him. Nicky always had cash and Jessie Mae made sure that he gave some of that money to her.

Vincent, at his wife's insistence, was about to put his foot down and confront Nicky about staying away from his niece, when Jessie Mae gave them the awful news that she was pregnant again.

Vincent did have his talk, but now it was about how Nicky needed to help support his baby.

At first, Nicky tried to do the right thing and got a job at a local car wash. He and Jessie Mae seemed to be getting along fine and Nicky was very attentive to her. He worked his job six days a week and stopped by to see her almost every night. Since Jessie Mae appeared to be happy and Nicky seemed to be trying, Patricia began to soften up a bit.

Several months later, Jessie Mae gave birth to another girl who she named Shawna. Shortly after, Nicky lost his job and went back to hustling with a friend of his. He and Jessie Mae continued their relationship, got a small apartment together and had somewhat of a family life, although it wasn't the life she wanted. They would fight over money and she would kick him out. He'd stay away for awhile, come back with lots of cash, and she would be happy again. This went on for the next several years. By the time she was twenty-one, Jessie Mae had given birth to three more kids, Joe, Leesa, and Sam, but that's when life got even more difficult.

In a very short time, Nicky became the local weed and coke man with a steady stream of criminal types hanging around, so Jessie Mae and the children stayed with Patricia and Vincent, who realized that the children needed love and attention that they weren't getting from either of their parents. They were willing to take on the role of loving caretakers and did most of the work of raising the kids. Patricia still insisted on Jessie Mae going to church on Sundays, so now they took the kids, too.

If not for Vincent and Patricia, Snookie and her siblings would have suffered the wrath of Jessie Mae all day, every day. Whenever they were left alone with their mother, she would get upset, and she seemed to take it out on Snookie the most. If Snookie asked questions, she would be spanked. Hard. So she learned to stay out of her mother's way.

If there were any two people on the planet who shouldn't have been parents, Jessie Mae and Nicky were definitely on the list. They fought most of the time when they were together, but managed to have a lot of sex. The saddest thing was that Jessie Mae blamed her kids, especially Snookie, for ruining her life, and didn't mind telling her that every chance she got. Snookie was only five, who knows what it did to her psyche.

"It's all your fault that I'm in this mess, you little bastard," Jessie Mae said to Snookie one day. "I coulda had a good life. I coulda been a Bird."

Snookie always wondered what kind of bird her mother wanted to be. Maybe she could be a bird, too. Then she could fly away to someplace where mother birds took care of their baby birds. Where they loved them, fed them, kissed them and kept them safe. Maybe there would be a daddy bird there, too. A strong protector. That's what Snookie dreamed about.

While Jessie Mae was pregnant with her fifth child, life changed for the worse, again. First, Nicky got involved with some shady characters and ended up shot and killed in a botched liquor store holdup. That left all of Jessie Mae's children without fathers.

Then three months after baby Sam was born, Patricia had a heart attack and passed out during Sunday church service. She was rushed to the hospital by ambulance, but died shortly after. The family was devastated.

Vincent called Dorothy to tell her about her sister's death. They offered each other condolences and he said he would contact her with the funeral arrangements, but she made no mention about coming to Mobile. She never even asked about her daughter, so he didn't mention Jessie Mae, either. As far as he knew, Jessie Mae never talked about her mother, and Patricia had told him that any time she tried to keep Dorothy updated, she refused to hear anything about her daughter. Dorothy Franklin was a tough woman who could apparently hold a grudge with a viselike grip. Vincent kept his mouth shut because he didn't want to do anything to hurt Jessie Mae any further.

At the funeral, Dorothy showed up, but didn't speak to anyone, including her daughter. She came and went, unrecognized, by sitting in the back of the church. By the time that Vincent spotted the lone woman standing 100 feet away from everyone else at the gravesite and realized who she was, she had dashed away.

"I think your momma was here, Jessie Mae," Vincent said when they were back home. Several friends and neighbors had stopped by to bring food and show support.

"Really? What makes you think that?" she asked.

"I thought I saw her at the cemetery. She was in the back, but when I looked at her she dashed off 'fore I could git close enough to say anything."

"Well, she didn't wanna see me, so…who cares?"

Jessie Mae's children were too young to really understand what death was about. They got through the process pretty well, but Snookie took it hard because Patricia had always given her extra attention, knowing how much Jessie Mae resented her.

"Where's Auntie Patty?" Snookie asked constantly.

Jessie Mae had no patience. "She went to heaven. I tol' you that already. She ain't comin' back. Now stop askin' me."

Snookie just ran off and cried. After a few weeks went by, which was a long time for a five-year-old, she realized that her momma was right. Her favorite person in the whole world was not coming back.

Vincent had loved his wife, who had taken good care of him over the years, and since Jessie Mae had come into their lives, he realized that he and Patricia had grown even closer, especially when it came to sex. All he had to do was fantasize about Jessie Mae's ripe body, which had been in a pregnant state for most of the past five years, and he was ready to go. In his heart, he felt content that he had given Patricia a lot of attention in recent years, even if it was illicitly inspired.

As for Jessie Mae, she realized that she was going to be stuck with her children and would have to raise them on her own. That didn't put her in the best mood. She was snippy and irritable for weeks. The only thing that made her feel better was the fact that Vincent had no intention of throwing her out. Financially they would be fine. Vincent received the benefits of his wife's life insurance policy. As a matter of fact, Patricia had a nice savings that she left to Jessie Mae and the children.

Late one night, while Vincent was still at work and after the other kids were asleep, Jessie Mae came down to the den to watch television while she was breast-feeding baby Sam. They both fell asleep on the couch. Vincent came in and saw her lying there topless in a pair of tight shorts. He went over, picked up the baby and took him up to his crib. Then he took a shower. When Jessie Mae woke up, Vincent, wearing only a towel, was kneeling on the floor beside her, caressing her swollen breasts.

"Oh!" she said as he backed off. "Hey, where's Sam?"

"I put him to bed."

"What are you doing?" she asked. He answered by kissing her deeply. He had aroused her and she didn't resist.

"I need to make love to you," he said, voice husky with lust.

"Alright," she responded.

Vincent scooped her up and carried her up to his bed.

Six months later, though it caused a bit of a scandal, Vincent married Jessie Mae in a small civil ceremony. She was three months pregnant at the time. Since Snookie and four of her siblings had no father in their lives, Vincent gave all of them his last name. Snookie McClain was a good name.

Together Jessie Mae and Vincent had five more children. She was pregnant every year for the next five years. A few months after Jessie Mae reached her twenty-sixth birthday, she gave birth to her final baby and had her tubes tied.

For the next five years, Jessie Mae McClain became a bitter, ungrateful alcoholic. She rarely let Vincent touch her anymore. She just yelled and complained about everything and made him work harder and harder to give her the material things that she wanted. She was home with the kids all day and barely lifted a finger to do anything.

The five older kids were in school, so it was just Jessie Mae with the young ones at home all day. God knows how they managed to survive.

Sam, the oldest boy, who was now eight years old, stayed out in the yard most of the time after school, which left Snookie and Shawna in charge of the household. When Snookie and Shawna got home, the pressure of taking care of everything fell on them. They were still just little girls themselves, but they had to do a lot of the work. When they got home from school, they had to clean the house, change diapers, and play with the smaller children. Jessie Mae cooked dinner most of the time, because Vincent had to have a decent meal if he was going to stay strong and get to work every day, but for the kids, fast food and pizza was a regular lunch.

Jessie Mae couldn't even be bothered to answer questions from the children. They were naturally curious about things and asked the simple questions that most kids did. However, if the little ones went to their mother and wanted to know something, Jessie Mae would snap at them and say, "I'm tired of answering these silly ass questions. I already told Snookie and Shawna all this stuff years ago. If they didn't pass it on to ya, then you just shit outta luck."

Vincent still attended church on Sundays. He was basically a good man who really cared about the children and tried to maintain some balance. The older children weren't his, but he tried to be a good father to them all. They were receptive to his efforts and loved him. He even took the time to explain to the younger ones why the sky was blue and why rain was wet.

Jessie Mae refused to go to church since her Aunt Patricia died, but she let Vincent take Snookie, Shawna, and Sam with him. He really enjoyed their time together. They were getting older and needed him. He was able to give the children some kind of normalcy and they could ask as many questions as they wanted to without being yelled at. He would sometimes stop by the ice cream parlor after church to buy them a treat, and they agreed that they shouldn't tell their mother. He really had no idea how much the children dealt with being around her all day.

Every now and then, some of the more charitable members of the church would stop by their house to offer assistance, but Jessie Mae hated them being in her business. She was so unpleasant to them, that eventually they stopped coming by altogether.

According to Jessie Mae, Snookie had stolen her childhood and was the reason she never did anything special with her life. At least that's what ten-year-old Snookie was led to believe. Now Jessie Mae was determined to return the favor. At a time when Snookie just wanted to be a child and have fun, she had to play big sister and substitute mother to her nine younger brothers and sisters.

Jessie Mae, on the other hand, wanted to forget about her nine children so she could play. And playing games is what she did best.

While Vincent was busy working two jobs to take care of his family, his young wife was entertaining men in their bedroom. Jessie Mae would have Snookie watching most of the younger children outside. She even stooped so low as to give the two babies milk laced with Scotch, to put them to sleep. These little trysts happened at least twice a week, yet Vincent and the children were clueless, except for Snookie, who might not have understood exactly what her mother was doing, but she instinctively knew that it was something wrong and something that she was too young to know.

Whenever Snookie and her sister, Shawna, got a chance to get away and just be kids, they went crazy. Snookie seemed to have developed her mother's wild streak and because she had to grow up fast, she acted like an old soul.

"You a crazy girl, Snookie," Shawna said as they ran home from the library one afternoon. "That lady was stuck-up."

"She gimme grief 'bout my name," said Snookie. "Who she think she is?"

"You gonna help momma cook tonight?"

"Don't I always?"

"You think that lady's still there?"

"Course, she is, Shawna." Snookie said. "Why you think we get to play today?"

"Let's stop at the store an' git some candy."

Jessie Mae McClain had enjoyed her scandalous behavior for almost a year, but her day of reckoning had come. One afternoon a neighbor woman named Olean Brown came by to get her eight-year-old twin boys who were playing with Snookie and her siblings in the backyard. As she passed the kitchen window, she saw a half-naked man strutting up to Jessie Mae's refrigerator to get a beer.

Later that day, Olean called Jessie Mae and made a big stink. She threatened to tell Vincent about his wife's little adulterous play dates unless Jessie Mae agreed to change her ways. Jessie Mae didn't bother to deny anything. She simply listened.

"I'm gonna be watchin' you wit hawk eyes, gal," Olean said. "I'll be poppin' in for tea a coupla times a week. You'll never know when, but if my kids are there playin' wit your kids, then you better be watchin' 'em."

"I will," Jessie Mae said contritely.

"Patricia McClain was a good friend to me for many years and even though my husband and I don't get to see much of him anymore, Vincent is a good friend, too. I would hate to be the one to hurt him with this information."

"I don't wanna hurt Vincent, either."

"Good, cause he's a good man and you don't deserve him."

"You're right," Jessie Mae said, and she meant it.

"Now, I know that Patricia would have wanted him to be happy and for some godforsaken reason, he chose you. But I'll be damned if I'm gonna sit by and let you run all over him. Have I made myself clear?"

"Yes, ma'am," Jessie Mae replied.

"Good, then we understand each other. Please tell Vincent that we said hello."

"Sure."

"Goodnight, Jessie Mae."

"Goodnight, Olean."

After that day, Snookie and Shawna had a lot more free time. Snookie still had to be the big sister and help out a lot with the kids and the chores, but she found herself having a lot of fun, too. Because she had always been angry with her mother, and carried her attitude with her most of the time, she wasn't the most popular girl in school. She got into a lot of fights, mostly because she had inherited her mother's big mouth. She always said what was on her mind and that didn't go over well with the neighborhood kids.

Snookie was getting tall and her legs were skinny. She was funny looking and didn't seem like she could hurt a fly, but that was a mistake that a lot of the bullies made. What she *could* do was pack a punch. When it came to protecting herself or her siblings, Snookie threw down with the best of them. She had no problem fighting dirty, either.

Quite often, Olean's twins, Toby and Tremaine, came over to play in the backyard with Snookie's brother, Sam. The twins were eight years old, like Sam, but they were much bigger than he was.

Even so, Sam was tough. The boys liked to fight each other and took turns being the referee. Snookie kept an eye on their activities, and as long as they fought fair, she didn't bother them.

One day, while the boys were playing catch, Toby got hit in the head with the ball because he wasn't paying attention. He ran up to Sam and aggressively pushed him up against the tool shed. Sam jumped on him and they wrestled to the ground. Instead of being the peacemaker, Tremaine joined in and began to hit Sam while Toby had him pinned on the ground.

Snookie was doing the dishes and happened to look out the kitchen window. She saw the twins ganging up on Sam and immediately became furious. She ran out the backyard and grabbed the garden hose, which she turned on full blast. She ran up and aimed it directly at Tremaine, who backed off quickly.

"Go home!" she yelled, and immediately turned the hose on Toby, who ran off while Sam moved safely behind Snookie. Tremaine finally followed his brother out the yard and Sam went to turn the water off.

"Thanks, Snookie."

"Get your behind in the house."

Snookie lost her childhood taking care of her many siblings. Jessie Mae was not a good mother, but she did a little bit better after the threat by Olean. At least she stopped screwing men for lunch and stayed home to take care of her children. Unfortunately, it was too late for Snookie. She no longer believed in childish things, but she was still a child. Life was going to be challenging for a skinny, buck-toothed, black girl who had lost faith in the world that was supposed to keep her safe.

CHAPTER 15

Aurora

The crowd at the Oasis in Chicago was excited to hear their favorite band. The Soul Bandits played a blend of R&B, funk and fusion. The first set was played to get the crowd warmed up and dancing. There were a lot of Baxter Duncan's friends from school and a nice mix of older twenty-somethings. He kept his eye on the front door, even though there were several young women vying for his attention. During the first break, Baxter was drinking a Coke, wiping sweat from his forehead and accepting compliments from a couple of eager coeds. The crowd was enjoying music from the DJ.

When Baxter looked up, the only thing he saw was a vision of loveliness moving through the crowd. It was Camille Kennedy, who was wearing a flowing, cream-colored, knit dress that moved with her body and complimented her beautiful skin. She looked like one of those models in a shampoo commercial, moving in slow motion. Her long, dark hair was slightly curled, bouncing to the music as she tossed it over her shoulder. Males and females alike admired her beauty. Camille led the way, followed closely by Vicky and Linda, who looked pretty hot in their own right. The girls were slowly making their way to the front of the club.

"My God," Baxter thought, sweating again.

He was mesmerized. Camille caught every nuance of his behavior and silently enjoyed his discomfort. Mr. Cool was losing it, which was exactly the desired effect she had planned. No goody two shoes in this crew. It was going to be a fun night.

Forgetting all about the coeds, Baxter stepped directly into Camille's path, but before he could speak, Vicky stepped up. She was a solid foot shorter than Baxter, but she had a strong presence.

"Close your mouth, playboy," she said.

Baxter shot Vicky a nasty look, recovered and smiled at Camille. Be nice to the friends, he thought, and managed to say, "You all look lovely tonight."

The girls all murmured their thanks.

"I'm really glad you ladies could make it. No trouble getting in, right?" he asked.

Camille looked him directly in the eye.

"It's as though they were expecting us," she smiled.

Baxter never broke eye contact with Camille. "Good."

He took her by the hand and tried to separate her momentarily from her posse. Then one of the band members came to give him the five-minute warning.

Linda inquired, "Did we miss anything?"

"One set, but we have two more. You all are my guests. What can I get for you?"

Camille had to give Baxter credit. The boy had major skills on those horns. He played alto sax, soprano sax, flute, and piccolo. When he sang, his voice was like silk. Baxter wowed the audience with classics like *Reasons* by Earth, Wind & Fire, and *Mr. Magic* by Grover Washington, Jr. By midnight, Camille was sure he had stolen her heart.

A few weeks later, no one else existed for her. Baxter and Camille became inseparable. He waited for her after each class to walk her to her next class. He waited to meet her for lunch, and was there again after school. They went to the Hunter High basketball games sometimes, but most times he was at his guitar player's house. Jackie had the biggest garage, so that's where the band spent their time rehearsing. In the beginning, Baxter even let Camille join him at band practice.

One night, Baxter had a show at a local club. Camille wanted to come, but he convinced her not to because it was supposed to be a private party hosted by a group of white college students and he didn't want Camille to feel out of place. She wouldn't have been able to invite her girlfriends, so she agreed to stay at home.

Baxter was a very sexy guy and when he performed, the young women went crazy. This particular night, a pretty, young white girl caught his eye. She had on a tight, red mini-dress and she made it clear by her eye contact and body language that he could have her on the spot. Baxter wasn't doing anything to discourage the girl's attention.

At the end of the show, Baxter and his band mates spent time talking with their admirers, but he was surprised the girl in the red dress hadn't stayed around. He thought she was a sure thing. Even though he and Camille spent a lot of time together, she hadn't had sex with him yet. That didn't stop him from having all the sex he could handle.

As the crowd thinned out, he walked to the side of the stage to pack up his horns. That's when the white girl in the red dress sashayed up to him with her perky breasts.

"I guess I should have taken a ticket," she said in a high-pitched voice. "Hi, I'm Julie Carson."

"What's up?" he responded, barely looking up.

"I just wanted to say that I think you are really talented."

"Thank you."

"I love soul music and there's nothing sexier to me than a saxophone player."

"Is that right?" he asked as he finally looked at her. The little dress fit her body like a glove. She didn't have much of a behind, but her body was tight.

"I think it has something to do with your hands," she continued. "Let me see."

Before he could respond, she grabbed one of his hands and started to caress it. She held it close to her chest as she did this and he could feel her breast under his hand.

"And you play with such passion and feeling. Your fingers just look so hot running up and down the keys."

"You think so?" Baxter was getting excited.

"The whole time you were playing, I imagined these fingers running up and down my body."

Now she had his hand close to her crotch. She didn't seem to care if anyone saw them, but the way she worked it, no one could tell what they were doing. Suddenly, she had his hand between her legs and his fingers dripping with her juices.

"I have a bottle of vodka in my car," she smiled. "Would you like to come and have a drink with me?"

That night, the white girl in the red dress got exactly what she wanted: a good fuck from a sexy, black saxophone player.

Baxter gave it to her good for twenty minutes in the back seat of her car. They were both dripping with sweat when they were finished.

"That was fantastic, Baxter," Julie said. "Will you call me?"

"I have a girlfriend," he responded nonchalantly.

"Then have *her* call me," she grinned devilishly. He didn't respond. "So, when's your next show?"

"Don't know."

"Then I guess I'll have to book your band myself."

Julie reached between the front seats and grabbed a piece of paper and a pen.

"Write down the number of the person I should talk to."

Baxter smiled a charming smile and wrote down his number.

"Here," he said, opening the car door. "I gotta go."

"Thanks, Baxter Duncan," said Julie. "I'll see you soon."

Eventually, Baxter talked Camille into coming to his house one day when he had a day off from band practice. His mother wasn't home and she knew that he was tired of waiting for sex. It's not like she was a virgin or anything, but she just wanted to take her time after being jerked around by Jeremy. She still wasn't sure that Baxter had waited for her. Other girls just seemed too easy for him to come by.

Baxter was a charming guy and he convinced Camille that she was the one worth waiting for. So, that afternoon in Baxter's bedroom, Camille gave herself willingly to the boy she couldn't resist. After that, every time his mother was at work, he would sneak Camille up to his room and they would have sex until one of them had to go.

This went on for weeks. Camille was happy and thought she and Baxter were in love. If anyone else had observed their relationship, they might have said that Baxter was obsessed with Camille. He definitely didn't leave enough time for anyone else to spend time with her. That included her best friends. And when she did do things with them, which was now on rare occasions, she would want to rush home, and then would have to sit around waiting for Baxter to call.

Baxter also began talking about California. If Camille was going to Los Angeles to attend school, then he needed to find a way to be there, too. Maybe the whole band would be willing to move to Hollywood. It sure would be a nice change from the harsh Chicago winters. Baxter talked about it all the time and Camille was so happy. She almost told him that she would change her mind about going to UCLA if he couldn't come to LA, too. She never mentioned that to him, though, because she didn't want to get his hopes up. She knew that there was no way that she could explain to her parents how her college decisions were being determined by a high school boyfriend.

One day, when Camille went to band rehearsal with Baxter, he accused her of flirting with the other band members, so from that time on, she would have to wait at home after school until he called her. Then his rehearsal times began to get later and later and he became unpredictable. Oftentimes, he would be busy doing other things, which would make her crazy, because he never told her what those things were. Even her parents noticed that she was home a lot more. Her mother was concerned.

One evening, Maria baked some fresh cookies and brought a plate of them up to Camille's room, where she found her daughter moping.

"Look what I have," said Maria, waving the plate under Camille's nose.

"Thank you, Mommy."

Camille might have been a little depressed, but she wasn't about to pass up Maria's homemade cookies.

"Let's talk, sweetheart."

"I don't feel like talking," Camille said as she grabbed for a cookie. Maria moved the plate out of her reach.

"Mommy!" she cried.

Maria let her take a cookie. "Chica, I haven't seen Vicky and Linda around lately. Did you girls have a disagreement or something?"

Camille replied, "No, of course not, Mommy."

"You don't throw away your friends for no reason."

"I'm not throwing anybody away."

"Well, don't be letting that Duncan boy take up all of your time. Those boys will come and go, but your girlfriends are always there for you."

"I know, Mommy."

"He can come over here sometimes, you know. He can show us a little respect."

Eventually, Camille had to admit to herself that she had given all of her free time to Baxter. She was basically at his side the minute he snapped his fingers. She couldn't explain her feelings. It wasn't like her to neglect her family and friends. As a matter of fact, she would have been the first to criticize Linda or Vicky if they acted the same way.

After Camille missed several of Linda's important track meets, Vicky called an emergency sleepover. Camille was hesitant at first, but they were getting pissed off at her lack of availability lately, so she agreed to spend the night. Linda offered to come pick them up in her mother's car. She picked Vicky up first, and then honked twice as she pulled up in front of Camille's house. Camille bounced down the front walk like old times, with an innocent smile.

"What's happening?" she asked as she hopped into the car.

The three girls stopped at their favorite pizza place, picked up a couple of pies, some pop, and cigarettes. Linda drove them back to her house, where they paraded into the den to begin their night. She even had some beer in the fridge. None of them had yet mentioned the fact that it had been over a month since they had gotten together for a social night. They used to do this a few times a week, especially on the weekends. That was before Baxter. Vicky and Linda had been patient long enough. It was time to talk.

"So," began Linda, "you got a new life now, huh?"

"Look, guys, I know that I've been busy…"

"Screw all that, Camille," said Vicky. "We are your girls. You flaked out on our plans for the last three weeks so you could be with that nigga…"

"Fine ass nigga," added Camille, trying to lighten things up.

"Who gives a fuck?" Vicky continued. "You missed the last few track meets, which our girl won, by the way."

Linda was immediately feeling guilty about Vicky being so hard on Camille. She looked at Camille and smiled sweetly.

"It's okay," Linda said.

Vicky wouldn't let up.

"No, it's not okay. Don't be punkin' out, Linda. We talked about this for days."

Camille was sincerely regretful. The three of them had been through thick and thin and she didn't want to hurt them, but she assumed that they would understand. She was truly in love for the first time. Her relationship with Jeremy was nothing compared to this love she felt for Baxter. None of them had experienced this intensity in a relationship. Camille needed to make them understand. Love trumped friendship.

"You're my girls. I don't have to be there twenty-four seven to still be down."

"But you need to be wit homeboy every damn minute, right?" Vicky asked.

"That's different and you know it," said Camille.

"I know this dude got you all turned out and shit. What's up wit that?"

"We're concerned, that's all," added Linda. "We really miss you, Camille."

"Fine, let's talk," Camille finally agreed.

"Why are you lettin' that boy run you?" Vicky asked, not pulling any punches. "You used to be the one who lectured us about 'losing ourselves' in a relationship."

"My time with him is just so limited," Camille said. "I want to make sure that I can keep him. You see all those girls hanging around him at the club."

"So what?" asked Linda. "If they can get him, they can keep him. Whatchu want him for if he's a dog? You already had that shit wit Jeremy."

"You're right," agreed Camille.

They made a pact to spend time together and not let Baxter come between them, but Camille wondered how he would react. She didn't want to upset him by changing. It hadn't occurred to her that it was the same thing that she did to her friends without a second thought. Camille decided that she would be loyal to the girls and wean Baxter off slowly.

The first order of business was to go shopping for prom dresses together the following Saturday. After all, prom was only weeks away.

Camille had only vaguely discussed prom night with Baxter. His band received the most votes by the prom committee and was booked to play, so that was the only thing on his mind. This might actually be a perfect time to let him take care of his business while she spent some time taking care of hers. She waited until the end of the week.

"Thank God it's Friday," Camille thought, leaving her last class of the day.

As usual, Baxter was waiting for Camille at the back of the football field. Camille had decided to wait until the last minute to tell Baxter about her shopping plans the next day. The two of them had made tentative plans to get together before his band practice on Saturday afternoon.

This would be the first time that she ever made a decision to do something with her friends rather than to be with him, but she was sure he would understand. How many times had he cancelled their plans at the last minute? How often had she waited by the phone after he promised to call and never did?

Camille felt that she was really doing him a favor, giving him more time to study. He had been under a little pressure lately. He was very close to failing history and not being able to graduate. For some reason, he couldn't concentrate in that class because he was too busy keeping an eye on her. He constantly watched her to make sure she wasn't talking to other boys in class. It made her feel loved.

She crossed the football field and approached him with a smile. "Guess what?" she asked excitedly.

"What?" he asked as he wrapped his arm around her neck possessively.

"Tomorrow I'm shopping with the girls to find the sexiest prom dress ever."

"How you gonna make plans with them when you already have plans with me?" Baxter laughed, but was less than thrilled.

"But my plans with you weren't definite," said Camille.

"No, Camille," he said, letting her go roughly. "I need you with me tomorrow."

"You have band practice. Prom is almost here and I need to buy a dress."

"Who the hell are you trying to impress?" he roared. "Just wear something that you already have."

Camille couldn't believe her ears. This was the epitome of high school social events and she'd been waiting for this a long time.

"Are you kidding me? It's for the prom. I don't have anything to wear. Besides, I haven't hung out with Vicky and Linda in weeks."

"You were just with them the other night."

"Damn, are you my boyfriend or my father?" Camille yelled.

The words were barely out of her mouth when Baxter smacked her face so hard that she was positive she saw stars, and immediately rubbed her cheek, horrified. There were a couple of students walking across the field in the distance. They had no idea what was going on.

"What the hell did you hit me for?" she asked with tears in her eyes.

"Does your father hit you like that?" he asked, hovering over her, menacingly.

"N..n..no…of course not."

"Then I'm not your damn Daddy. Understand?"

After a few seconds of shock, Camille backed slowly away from Baxter, then turned and began running toward the students on the other side of the football field.

"Come back here right now, Camille," he yelled after her. "CAMILLE!"

Baxter made no attempt to chase after her and she kept on running from him and didn't stop until she arrived home. She went straight to bed and told her mother that her stomach hurt and she didn't feel like eating or doing anything but sleeping. She was going to unplug the phone in her room and if her friends called, any of them, she would talk to them in the morning.

Vicky and Linda were concerned when they didn't hear from Camille and couldn't reach her on Friday night. They knew to check in with her to make sure she hadn't changed her mind. Heaven knows that girl had not been thinking straight for weeks. Mrs. Kennedy told them that Camille came home from school not feeling well and was going to call them back in the morning. They would just have to wait.

Camille was in such a state of shock that she couldn't wrap her brain around the fact that Baxter Duncan, this wonderful boy she loved, had an evil twin. For a moment she remembered the day that Jeremy provoked her into slapping him. Karma was a bitch! But then she realized that it was a totally different situation.

Baxter had actually hit her. This was a man who was supposed to love her. It broke her heart and she couldn't stop crying. No one had ever hit her before. Her parents didn't even spank her when she was a child. At least she didn't remember if they did. They always talked to her like she had some sense as long as she acted like she had some sense. She was a good girl in a bad situation. She cried herself to sleep.

Next morning, Baxter showed up with flowers and a box of chocolates. Camille went outside to talk so her parents wouldn't start asking questions.

"I'm so sorry, Camille," Baxter said regretfully.

"I don't understand how you could hurt me," she said sadly. "I thought you loved me."

"I've been under a lot of stress and I know that's no excuse, but you make me crazy sometimes."

"I don't mean to." She was almost in tears again. "I'm sorry."

"I know," he said, knowing that he'd made his point. He gave her his most charming smile and her heart melted. "Do you forgive me?"

"Don't ever scare me like that again, Baxter."

"I love you. I'll never do anything like that again. I promise." He gave her a big hug and walked away. Then he turned to say, "Have fun shopping, okay?"

Camille couldn't avoid her mother as she brought the gifts into the house. "What's the occasion?" Mrs. Kennedy asked.

"Baxter and I had a little disagreement yesterday. I guess this means that I won."

Camille smiled confidently as she put the flowers into a vase and took them into her room. She could never tell anyone about Baxter hitting her. Not even her friends. Knowing Vicky, she would go after him with a tire iron and ruin everything.

By the time the girls caught up with Camille on Saturday morning, she was bubbly and fine, looking forward to going shopping. They went to several stores and enjoyed trying on the beautiful clothes. In one of the stores, they encountered a group of white girls from their school. Tiffany Carson, who was in Camille's math class, was there with her older sister, who was helping her to pick out a dress.

"Hi, Camille."

"Hi, Tiffany."

"You all are looking for dresses at the last minute, too, I see."

"Yeah, I guess so," said Camille. "Looks like there are plenty left, though."

"Can't wait to see your boyfriend's band play."

"I know. I'm pretty excited."

"You won't get too much dancing in, though. Not with him playing all night."

"Everybody wanted them, so I'm willing to make the sacrifice." Camille smiled.

"The Soul Bandits are the best, right? I heard they won the vote unanimously."

Tiffany's sister, overhearing part of their conversation, walked over.

"Tiff, you never told me the Soul Bandits were going to be playing at your prom."

"I didn't even know that you knew who they were," said Tiffany.

"Well, that saxophone player that I've been messing around with is in the band."

Tiffany quickly grabbed her sister by the arm. "Come on, Julie, let's go. I'm not finding anything here."

Vicky walked over to Julie quickly. "You're fucking Baxter Duncan?"

"Best sex I've ever had," replied Julie as Tiffany dragged her towards the door. Tiffany turned to Camille and mouthed "I'm sorry" as they left the store. Camille was stunned, her eyes tearing.

"That son of a bitch!" snarled Vicky.

Linda walked over with a beautiful peach colored gown.

"Now, Camille, tell me you won't be the hottest of the hot in this one."

Camille turned to look at the dress. "It's pretty."

"What's wrong, Camille?" asked Linda, concerned.

"Nothing. Come on, I'm going to go try it on."

Camille took the dress and headed to the dressing room. Linda, confused, looked at Vicky for clarification.

"Go help her out. I'll tell you later."

For the next three weeks, Camille daydreamed about the prom and how beautiful she was going to look in that peach gown that Linda found for her. It was a beautiful shade that accented her bronze skin. She never mentioned what Tiffany's sister said about sleeping with Baxter. Camille wanted everything to go smoothly. If she confronted him, he would only deny it. Then, he would undoubtedly turn things around on her somehow and get angry with her for questioning him in the first place.

Now, the big night was finally here. Baxter had been very pleasant during the time leading up to the prom. He even made plans for them to stay in a hotel for the night. A lot of the couples were doing that. Camille told her parents that there was a huge after party and then they were all going out to have breakfast. She wouldn't be back until early the next morning. They didn't give her a hard time. After all, it was prom night.

By the time Baxter picked her up, Camille looked like a princess. She, Vicky and Linda had all gone to the beauty salon to have their hair done. Camille had hers straightened. She loved her naturally curly hair, but wanted to try something different for her prom. They even went to Macy's and had their makeup done. They all felt like movie stars by the time they arrived at the dance. Soul Bandits played amazingly well and Camille was proud to be the girl in the front row.

Camille hung out with Vicky, Linda and their dates. During the night, Baxter stopped by their table when the band took their breaks, but he refused to dance with Camille, claiming that he needed to save his energy. She tried to understand and downplayed his attitude when her friends began to make comments.

"He's a jerk," said Vicky, holding no punches.

"He's working, Vicky," defended Camille. "Give him a break."

"No, that's *your* job."

Linda cut in, "Stop it, you two. Let's just have a good time."

Finally, the band played their final song, Earth, Wind & Fire's *Reasons*. As Baxter sang, he took the microphone and walked off the stage to sing directly to Camille, who was watching from the dance floor. He danced with her for a full minute while he sang. That gesture melted her heart once again and drew a bit of envy from all of the young ladies who wished that they were in her shoes. Baxter may have been sleeping around with a lot of girls, but he made it clear that Camille was the only one he claimed.

For the rest of prom night, Camille and her friends had a memorable time. There was a large group of them who partied all night and went to breakfast at a 24-hour diner in the morning before heading home satisfied.

Jonathan and Maria Kennedy were in bed, both pretending to be asleep, when Camille tipped in at 6:00am, but they were not asleep and knew the exact moment that her key hit the door. Twenty minutes later, Maria slipped out of bed, peeked into her daughter's room and found her sprawled across her bed, still in her prom dress. Satisfied that Camille was in one piece, Maria covered her daughter with a blanket and went happily back to her bedroom, where she quietly slipped back into bed with her husband.

"She alright?" Jonathan asked, turning over to hug her.

"She's fine," Maria responded, kissing him. "Let's finally get some sleep."

Next came graduation. Jonathan and Maria Kennedy were so proud of their beautiful daughter. Camille, Vicky and Linda enjoyed the end of one part of their lives and the beginning of a new, exciting phase. They would be on their own very soon.

Linda won a track scholarship to the University of Illinois, Vicky was going to Central State in Ohio, and Camille had decided to take the scholarship at UCLA. Life was about to get very strange, with all of them going their separate ways. They realized that the summer was going to be their last opportunity to really let their hair down and have some fun before they had to buckle down to the serious business of college life.

The rest of June was fun for the graduates. Baxter's band played often and the girls had fun dancing at the parties, shopping for new clothes and meeting new people. One morning, Camille was nauseous and couldn't get out of bed. She cancelled a shopping spree with Vicky and Linda, who came by to check on her. They sat in chairs while Camille sat on the side of her bed, still in her pajamas.

"I can't believe that you gave up a chance to go downtown with us," Linda said. "You must really be sick."

"I must've eaten something bad," Camille offered.

"I think you need to take a pregnancy test," blurted Vicky.

Camille looked at her like she had grown horns. "What?"

"I am very serious, Camille," Vicky continued. "Sounds like morning sickness to me. I've been around my pregnant sisters for years and you sound just like them when they found out."

"Damn, Camille," said Linda. "Vicky could be right. I remember when my sister was pregnant, too. She had morning sickness with both of her kids."

"When's the last time you had your period?" asked Linda.

"I don't know. I don't keep track of that stuff."

"That stuff?" Vicky asked. "Damn, Camille. It's your body, not a project."

Linda was hesitant, "Camille, you missed your pills a few times, remember?"

"Oh, hell," Camille said, falling back.. "How can I go to UCLA if I'm pregnant?"

The next day, the girls all went to Planned Parenthood, where it was confirmed. Camille was indeed pregnant. Her friends were shocked and disappointed, but they vowed to support whatever decisions she made.

Now that she was sure, she had to tell Baxter. He would know what to do.

"I'll give you the money," he said.

"I'm not getting rid of our baby, Baxter."

Jonathan and Maria Kennedy spent several days trying to talk their daughter out of ruining her life. They had never had this much conflict with Camille before. She was always a smart, considerate and ambitious girl. Now, she was determined to give up UCLA and stay in Chicago to be close to Baxter and have their baby. They didn't want her to have a baby at this point in her life, but they didn't like the options, either.

Everyone was upset and Camille didn't know what to think anymore. Her parents didn't approve of Baxter, but certainly didn't want their precious daughter to be a single mother. They wanted her to realize that she was too young for any of this responsibility and that perhaps she should consider giving the baby up for adoption. They even suggested that they might be willing to help raise the baby while she went away to school. They would do anything to keep her from throwing her life away for that Duncan boy.

Camille's parents didn't know about the physical abuse, but there was something about Baxter's attitude that they didn't like. They were sure that she was making a big mistake. However, by the end of the week, Camille was determined to be Baxter's wife.

The Kennedys had never turned their back on their daughter before, but for Jonathan, that was the last straw. He refused to pay for a wedding. Worse than that, he refused to support her in any way. She would have to move out. Jonathan wouldn't even speak to her. Maria backed her husband completely, except for cutting off communication. She and Camille sat in the kitchen on the day Camille was moving the last of her stuff to Baxter's house. Fresh baked cookies and warm milk was the way that Maria showed her love when they had difficult discussions.

"You want to act like a grown woman, Camille, so you must live with the consequences," Maria said. "You can't expect us to be happy about all of this. It's not what we have been working for."

"I can't believe that you and Daddy are being so stubborn."

"Lo siento, mija," Maria said regretfully. "You gave up your right to be walked down the aisle when you broke your father's heart."

Baxter Duncan and Camille Kennedy got married a week later in a small civil ceremony. Maria tried to talk Jonathan into going, but in the end only Vicky, Linda, Baxter's mother, and a couple of Baxter's band members attended. After they left City Hall, there was a backyard barbecue thrown by Jackie, Baxter's guitar player. A large group of the band's supporters stopped by the house to celebrate with them. The newlyweds spent the night at a local motel and then moved in with Baxter's mother the next day.

A few weeks later, the newlyweds found a small apartment on the South Side and began their life together. Baxter and his band got really busy and continued to be the talk of the town. Soul Bandits went into full swing and played at a lot of local clubs in and around Chicago. They had gigs booked for the rest of the summer.

By fall, Baxter had a day job at a local factory and Camille was left home alone getting ready for the baby. It didn't take long for problems to arise. Camille didn't see much of her new husband. The band rehearsed or had gigs every night of the week. Baxter constantly stayed out well past the time that his gigs ended. When he did come home, he smelled like perfume. With his history of bedding other girls, Camille was suspicious. She wanted to come to some shows. She missed watching him perform, but also needed to keep an eye on him, but he wouldn't let her since she was pregnant.

"You don't need to be around all that cigarette smoke," he insisted. "It's not good for you or the baby."

Camille couldn't argue with that logic, but she knew that he was fooling around. She just didn't want to upset him. He would only tell her that she was imagining things. That's exactly what Vicky said he would do. She was right.

“When men are cheating and you call them on it, they usually go straight to the crazy defense,” she would say. “It’s you, you’re crazy.”

Married life with Baxter wasn’t all that it was cracked up to be. Camille was lonely. Her best friends had gone off to college, so they mainly kept in contact through letters. They were both doing great. Linda was at the University of Illinois, so she wasn’t too far away, and Vicky called her at least once a week in addition to the letters. They were both having fun, enjoying their freedom. Camille began to wonder what life would have been like for her if she had gone to Los Angeles, but those thoughts weren’t healthy for her because it was too late for that and it made her sad to think about it.

Camille still had a rocky relationship with her parents, and although her mother called to check on her periodically, the conversations were strained and mostly about how Camille was taking care of herself. She was too proud to confess to her mother that there were problems. With all of the warnings that her parents had given, she had a hard time admitting that they might be right. Camille and Baxter argued almost every night when he got home. They were both frustrated. He hadn’t changed his lifestyle at all. With her, he seemed to be angry all the time, but when he talked about his shows, he was animated and excited. He used to be that way with her, but now everything had changed.

Under pressure, Baxter went with Camille when she had her ultrasound and they found out that they were having a girl. She couldn’t contain her happiness. He couldn’t contain his indifference. He barely participated in coming up with a name.

“You got any ideas, honey?” she asked, trying desperately to include him.

“Whatever you want, Camille.”

The prospect of being a father didn’t seem to make him happy. That shouldn’t have surprised her since he didn’t want the baby in the first place, but she was hoping that the reality of seeing a picture of the baby inside of her would snap him out of his attitude and make him see a positive future for them as a family. That’s what she prayed for.

As Chicago got cold, Camille spent most of her time at home alone. By mid-December, she was bored to death and ready for the baby, who wasn't due until January. She looked forward to seeing Vicky and Linda, who were both headed home for the holidays.

On Christmas Eve, Vicky and Linda surprised Camille by showing up with a pizza and lots of presents. They had an impromptu baby shower. She was thankful for them because Baxter's band was out of town. Her mother wanted her to come to their house, but Camille didn't want to hear her father rant about the mistakes that she'd made. While the three friends were laughing at one of Vicky's stories, Camille suddenly felt cramps. Minutes later, her water broke and they were on their way to the hospital.

Aurora Giselle Kennedy Duncan came into the world three weeks prematurely on Christmas Eve. Baxter was playing at a club in Gary, Indiana that night, but her girls were there to get her to the hospital and stay with her through seven hours of labor. By the time Baxter got finished with his gig and answered his page, it was very late, and he was over an hour away, so when he got back to Chicago he decided not to go to the hospital.

The next morning, when Baxter arrived at the door of Camille's hospital room, her parents were already there at her bedside cooing over their new granddaughter. Jonathan, who was holding the baby, looked up and spotted the reluctant father.

"Well, boy, it's about time," he said. "You better get in here and introduce yourself to this little angel of yours."

Baxter came into the room and gave Camille a kiss. "You okay?"

"Yeah, I'm okay. I'm glad you finally made it."

Baxter turned to look at his new baby. "Wow, she's so little."

"Here," said Jonathan.

The proud grandfather handed the baby to Baxter and patted him on the back. Baxter carefully took little Aurora into his arms and was left speechless.

"She's perfect, isn't she?" Baxter asked, still mesmerized.

"We're going to have to find the three of you a bigger apartment."

Jonathan Kennedy had apparently forgotten about their differences, at least for now. They were all in love with Aurora. Camille was so excited when they were able to take her home, but was also terrified at how Baxter was going to adjust to being a father.

CHAPTER 16

Debbie

Michael Marshall finished his dinner in silence as young Debbie tried to amuse him with anecdotes from her weekend with Grandma and Grandpa Marshall. They had taken her to Six Flags Great Adventure in New Jersey. It was a pre-birthday present. With her grandparents, she didn't have to hold back her joy at celebrating her birthday. They were able to separate her birth from the tragedy that accompanied it.

In the six years since Valerie's death, the entire family, on both sides, had a rough time. They had all taken Valerie's death hard, but they also realized that the new baby needed a healthy, happy family. Both of the grandmothers stepped in to help out in the first few months after Michael brought little Debbie home.

However, Michael wanted to learn how to take care of his daughter. He did fine for a while, and then slowly, almost imperceptibly, retreated into another world. It's a miracle that Debbie thrived. The only things that allowed him to go on were taking care of her every day and crawling into a bottle of vodka every night. He performed both of those functions with very little emotion. There wasn't room for anything else in his life.

Naturally, Valerie's parents were devastated by her death, but even they managed to continue on. Little Debbie was the one thing that kept them all together. She was a bright child who showed an amazing resemblance to her mother, physically and creatively. She loved to play dress-up and constantly designed little clothes for her dolls. The same dolls that Valerie had decorated her room with. As a matter of fact, nothing much had changed in that room for more than six years. Despite the advice from his parents and the Goodwins, Michael refused to change Debbie's room. That was the place that Valerie spent most of her time before going into labor. Somehow, those pink ruffled curtains that Valerie made with her own hands gave him some kind of warped peace of mind. They also caused him great spiritual pain.

Debbie learned to accept how special the dolls were and it's the reason she played with them constantly. She always hoped that it would bring her closer to her father. It never happened. Michael couldn't even bear to look into his daughter's face; that beautiful little face with the big brown eyes that looked just like Valerie's. Something deep inside of Michael convinced him that he hadn't deserved Valerie, and therefore didn't deserve their daughter.

Michael managed to get to the bank each day, take Debbie to and from school, and make it through the routine of surviving. To the outside world, he simply appeared to be sad, understandably so, and no one caught on that he was drinking himself into numbness each night. Debbie was the only one who saw his nightly ritual, but her instincts told her that she couldn't share this information with anyone. She didn't want to lose her Daddy, even if he only appeared to be a shell of a man most of the time. Although Debbie continued to live with her father, she pretty much raised herself at home. As a matter of fact, there were times when his young daughter appeared to be taking care of him.

On most weekends, Debbie's loving grandparents took over. The four of them shared her by taking her on alternate weekends. The Marshalls were Baptists who went to church every Sunday and brought Debbie with them whenever it was their turn to have her. Debbie went to Sunday school and learned all of the things one learns. The Marshalls wanted her to have Jesus in her life. Their son no longer seemed to believe in anything, including God. His faith had been shattered, so it was up to her grandparents to insure that Debbie had a relationship with the Lord.

The Goodwins were Methodists who didn't go to church every Sunday, but they tried to maintain a spiritual foundation for their granddaughter. They showed her how to be a good person by living what they believed. They were often turned off by some of the church politics, but enjoyed the sermons.

As Debbie got older, she noticed a bit of hypocrisy amongst both of the congregations. The Baptists were talking bad about the Methodists and the Methodists were talking about the Baptists. This confused her as a young girl because she attended both churches and couldn't really understand the differences between them. They both seemed to be mostly concerned about who was wearing what.

Debbie really enjoyed the weekends with her grandparents, but even they couldn't make up for the absence of her father's attention. She knew that Michael loved her, but somewhere in her young mind, she was sure that her existence was the cause of all of his problems. If his family knew how he treated her, emotionally neglecting her, they would have considered his behavior to be abusive. He wasn't abusive, not physically. He was just down and out. Depressed and defeated. However, the lack of affection caused a major emotional void in Debbie that she would attempt to fill for the rest of her life.

One day, when Debbie was nine years old, Michael unexpectedly announced that he was leaving the bank. No one really understood why.

"I need a change," he said. "We'll be just fine."

Michael took on odd jobs to pay the bills, but seemed to have lost his direction. His parents were worried about him. They tried to question Debbie, but she was only a child and couldn't tell them what they really needed to know. One night, while Debbie was at the Goodwins, Michael's father unexpectedly came to his place and found him drunk.

"This is how you're taking care of Debbie?" he asked. "You need help, son."

Mr. Marshall stayed with Michael all night, forcing him to talk while he sobered up. Michael finally faced the fact that his drinking was out of control and that he needed to clean up his act for his daughter's sake. He even admitted that deep down he probably blamed Debbie for Valerie's death.

"Valerie would be ashamed of you, Michael."

Those words stung Michael deep in his soul. "Daddy, when I look at that little girl, all I see is my life going away and I see the reason why I never want to love again."

His father looked at him with sadness and put his hands on Michael's shoulders.

"God took Valerie away from you, son. That was his will. Debbie was the gift he left in her place. Look what you've done with his gift."

That was a revelation for Michael. The truth of what he had been putting his young daughter through broke his heart. All Debbie wanted was to be loved. For the first time in a long time, Michael allowed himself to feel his grief. He collapsed into his father's arms and let those tears that he had held back for so long, burst forth.

After that night, Michael stopped drinking, but despite his father's advice, he refused to get professional help, insisting that he could do everything on his own.

"You're not Superman, Michael."

"Let me try, Dad. I know I can do this."

Michael began running to get his body back into shape. He spent a little more time with Debbie, and even tried getting back into the real world by dating on the weekends, while Debbie was with her grandparents. She began to see that her father was doing a little better. Michael still wasn't the most affectionate man in the world, but he seemed to be working really hard to get back to a normal life. Even this little change in Michael made Debbie very happy.

One day, Michael took Debbie down to lower Manhattan to the garment district to buy her some fabrics to sew with. She pulled Michael all over to pick out patterns and look at all of the pretty materials. He was amused for a while, and then suddenly became distracted. He called one of the salesgirls over to them.

"Help my daughter with this stuff. I'll be right back."

"Of course, sir. What's your name, honey?"

"Where are you going, Daddy?" Debbie asked, concerned.

He left the store without another word. Debbie showed the salesgirl the fabrics that she wanted and how much she needed. Then she took her items to the register and waited. After a few moments, she wandered over to the front of the store and peeked out the door. Michael was a couple of doors down in a confrontation with a man and a woman. He was grabbing the woman's arm and she was resisting. The man tried to intervene, but Michael looked like a wild man, so the man backed off. A lanky, young security guard from a nearby jewelry store was making his way over to the commotion.

"Hey, what's going on over there?" he asked with authority.

"This don't have nothin' to do with you, man," Michael roared. "Stay out of it."

"Is this man bothering you?" the guard asked the woman.

Debbie was afraid her father would be taken away.

"DADDY!" she yelled.

They all looked over and saw Debbie crying in the doorway of the fabric store. The woman looked back at Michael, and then she looked at the guard. The man with her began to speak, but she cut him off.

"No, everything's fine. Just a little misunderstanding, right, Michael?"

"You know what, brother?" Michael was disgusted. "You can have her."

As Michael walked away, Debbie ran up to hug him. He pushed her away from him, grabbed her by the arm and rushed her past the fabric store. "Let's go," he said.

"Wait, Daddy! What about my fabrics?"

Inevitably, the good times were over and before Debbie knew it, Michael had turned back into a zombie father, drinking and withdrawing from day-to-day life. She did, too. Although Debbie liked being in school, she didn't really socialize much with her classmates. She was shy and spent a lot of time avoiding group activities. Teachers considered her bright, but felt that she didn't really apply herself. She spent most of her time sketching, designing and sewing. She also liked to take old clothes, add something to them and make them like new. She didn't seem to be interested in too much else.

***

Years passed, and as Debbie got older she found it harder to concentrate in school and often barely passed into the next grade. She also learned that getting good grades did not impress Michael.

Her grandparents showed support, but Michael never seemed to be proud of her, no matter what she did.

Debbie had one good friend named Madeline Clayton. Debbie was ten when the Claytons moved into the apartment next door and it changed her life. She had spent a lot of time alone over the years so when Madeline arrived Debbie had someone her own age to play with. They were kindred spirits. Madeline had been lonely, too. She was the baby in her family, her closest sibling being an older, married sister who lived in the Bronx. Debbie often went with Madeline to spend the weekends there. Madeline also came to spend weekends with her at her grandparents' homes.

Madeline was a free spirit who hated school, but liked to call herself an uninspired genius. She was tall and thin. Debbie used her as a mannequin for a lot of her designs and encouraged her to be a model. They were alike in many ways and supported each other through the good times and the tough times.

Michael tried to get his life together again and stopped drinking when Debbie was twelve. Whatever bond he could have forged with her was long gone. They lived under the same roof with no real connection. She didn't feel like he was her family. He went to work, she went to school; she cooked and cleaned, ate dinner in her room and left his food on the stove. That was the life of a young lady who desperately missed having a mother, and a widowed husband who desperately missed his wife. Debbie's grandparents were still there for her, but that wasn't enough. There was a hole in her heart that couldn't be filled by anyone but her father.

Right before Debbie entered high school, Mr. Goodwin, her maternal grandfather, died of complications due to pneumonia. At the age of fourteen, she attended her first funeral. It was difficult for everyone. Michael should have been in a position to help Debbie through the loss, but his own grief still crippled him emotionally and he could only give the barest of support to his mother-in-law and his daughter. Once again, the Marshalls stepped in and took over the role of family strength for them all.

Grandma Goodwin had sisters and brothers who lived out of state. A large group of her family came from out of town for her husband's funeral. She wasn't going to be alone. Grandma

Goodwin wanted to keep her house, but her family insisted that she go to Baltimore to live with one of her brothers. So, she reluctantly sold her house and moved to Maryland a couple of months later. The Goodwins had always been good to Debbie. They had done everything they could to give her the love she so desperately needed, and she loved them, too. She realized how much she would miss them both. Debbie cried a lot of tears that year.

High school was a turning point for Debbie's social life. She rarely wore makeup and didn't fuss too much with her hair. Most of the time she kept neat cornrows and braids which hung past her shoulders. She was becoming a very beautiful young woman with a young woman's body. She was going to be a goddess like her mother, but she was unaware of the effect it had on boys her age. To her, boys were practically nonexistent. She found them immature, and treated the ones who admired her like little brothers.

Debbie Marshall and Madeline Clayton were thick as thieves. They had very few other girlfriends but the ones they hung around with also had dysfunctional families. Debbie tried to stay out of trouble and was able to get decent grades, but neither she nor her friends were living up to their potential.

After a major disagreement with Grandpa Marshall, Debbie had emancipated herself from going to church. She didn't like the people and was frustrated by the lack of answers to the questions she had. "Because the Bible says so" was not a satisfactory answer to every single question. One Sunday, she just protested one time too many and Mr. Marshall got upset.

"How come you can't be more like those little Kendricks girls? They come to church every Sunday. They dress nice and always enjoy being with their parents. I don't know why you can't be like them."

Unfortunately for Mr. Marshall, he had just compared her to two of the worst girls in the whole school. They did drugs, had sex with boys, lied, stole, cheated on tests when they weren't skipping school altogether, and were apparently wonderful examples of what a good Christian should be. Amazingly, all was forgiven as long as they showed up in church every week in their Sunday best.

"Grandpa Marshall, I don't wanna go to your church anymore. To you, that makes me a bad person. But, I'm not a bad person. I'm a good girl who doesn't give you or Grandma Marshall much grief. I get decent grades now and I haven't been in any trouble in school. But you throw Jenna and Mona Kendricks up in my face as examples of good Christians? You have no idea what those girls are really like and I'm not gonna be the one to rat them out, so I guess I'm just gonna have to go to hell."

"You watch your language, young lady. Do not disrespect me in my home."

"I apologize." Debbie was contrite.

Mr. Marshall took a deep breath. "I'm not going to fight you anymore. You do what you feel is right. Your grandmother and I have given you a good start. We know that you're a good girl and you're old enough to decide what you want to do. You don't have to come with us anymore if you don't want to. We still love you, Debbie."

Ah, the blessing of unconditional love: a rare and beautiful blessing. When you grow up with it, you tend to take it for granted, never understanding how you will live the rest of your life craving it.

"Thank you, Grandpa." She kissed him and stayed home by herself that Sunday.

That was a little triumph for Debbie, but maybe wasn't the best decision for keeping her busy and focused on positive things. Now, instead of spending the weekends with her family, she spent a lot of weekends hanging out with her friends: friends who weren't as bad as the Kendricks girls, but who were restless and uninspired nonetheless. That was a recipe for trouble. And trouble is exactly what was in store for Debbie Marshall.

CHAPTER 17

Candy

The Martins had a simple life in Camden, South Carolina. Katie doted on her baby and tried to be a better mother to Candy than the one she had. Gwen tried to help out, but all she really did was make Katie feel bad by constantly badgering her.

"How could you fuck a African?" Gwen asked with disdain. "Now, look what you ended up with. A little lump of coal wit a big ass head."

"Don't talk about her that way," Katie said. "She's my daughter and your granddaughter, like it or not."

But Katie realized that it wouldn't do any good. Her mother was just expressing the attitudes of people in their town and throughout the South who were still ashamed of their history and didn't want any reminders of the fact that they used to be slaves. Looking like an African would surely pop those thoughts into someone's head. It's not like there weren't dark-skinned blacks in Camden, but they sure as hell had a hard time living in peace. Katie would have to protect Candy from the cruel, color-obsessed world.

"I wasn't loved by my momma, but you will be loved by yours," Katie whispered into her daughter's ear.

As the years went by, Katie tried to make Candy feel special. Her intentions were good, but they often had the opposite effect. Candy was not considered to be a pretty child because of her dark skin. She actually had a strikingly attractive face, but because the other black kids in the neighborhood couldn't overlook her darkness, they said she looked like a little monkey. Katie would try to make her daughter feel better.

"Candy, baby, you got your looks from your daddy. You know what that means don't ya? That's considered to be good luck, you hear me?"

Gwen was downright mean. Candy's drunken grandmother constantly teased her about her big head, and when it came to her hair, even her mother's words were hurtful. Katie broke many combs over the years because Candy's hair was very thick. Nappy didn't quite cover the description. Katie tried to be funny, but she was insensitive.

"When you were a baby, I would turn you upside down to wash the pots and pans," she told Candy. "Your hair was so rough I used your head as a Brillo pad."

Then Katie would laugh, which would make Candy feel terrible. But Katie assured her that they would get that hair straight somehow. Candy couldn't wait for that day and got her mind set that she would be willing to change her hair, at all costs.

Katie would use the hot comb, but Candy hated that. It became an all day chore with her mother constantly burning her ears and her forehead with the damn thing. However, that did not deter Candy one bit. Then one day, Candy saw an ad for a permanent relaxer. Katie insisted that Candy was too young, but it sure would make her life easier. Candy pestered her until she finally gave in. Candy was nine years old.

Unfortunately, it wasn't strong enough. Katie applied the relaxer to Candy's hair every four weeks and it barely took. The chemicals eventually fried her hair until she had bald patches in her scalp. With all the drama of a stage actress, Candy threw herself across her bed screaming, "Now, I'm black, ugly and bald. What kind of life is ahead of me?"

When Candy was eleven, Katie and Gwen felt that she needed some fixin'. The school Candy went to was mostly black, but she never fit in. She kept getting into fights. The other kids called her names like tar baby, skillet, and eight ball. Imagine that.

"They're black, too," she told herself. "So what's the problem?"

She couldn't even get relief at home. Almost every day of her life, she got the same message; that she just wasn't good enough.

"If yo' black ass is ever gonna get a man, you better learn how to walk, talk and fuck like a proper lady," said Gwen with her grandmotherly advice.

Katie added insult to injury. "Your only salvation is in finding a white man."

"That's right, gal," Gwen vigorously nodded. "Listen to your Momma. Put some cream in that Zulu coffee. You wouldn't want your kids to suffer like you did."

"With a white man, those babies will be caramel, mocha or white chocolate, I guarantee," Katie continued.

Candy couldn't believe those two. What was this obsession with sweets?

***

It was late September and the weather was still hot enough to make Candy sweat. She had on a new, yellow dress, which she hated, and was walking as slow as she could without being late. It was only the second week in her new school and she had already been in trouble twice with her homeroom teacher, Mrs. Forester.

Candy was a little nervous about being around all these white kids, so she had been taking her time getting to school each day. Her mother fought to get her transferred from her old school to Grover Cleveland Junior High, where she was one of only twelve blacks, because she had so much trouble with the black kids at her neighborhood school.

Katie said, "Those kids are jealous because you are pure black. African black."

Candy didn't know about all that, but she knew that she was definitely too black to be wearing that sunshine yellow dress. In a continuing effort to make a lady out of her, Katie had started making her wear dresses to school. And the lighter, the better.

"Pastels bring out the color of your skin," Katie insisted.

Now that was the kind of shit that kept Candy fighting at the old school. The black kids accused her of being prissy and trying to be better than everybody else. Could it have something to do with the fact that she also had to attend Miss Kelsey's Charm School every Saturday? In any case, Candy promised that she wouldn't fight anymore.

Katie still received a government check, but she had also been sewing, baking and doing hair on the side. She put all of her extra money away for Candy and didn't let Gwen get anywhere near it. She knew her mother would have spent it all on alcohol: the same alcohol that had Gwen looking old before her time. As a matter of fact, Gwen still had men coming around, but now they didn't spend so much money buying her gifts. They just took her out to the pool halls to eat, drink and gamble. As much as Katie hated it, she couldn't control her mother. She just tried hard to make a better life for Candy.

Katie knew her mother didn't appreciate her for wanting the finer things in life. She loved reading fashion magazines, because those skinny white girls seemed to have a wonderful life. They had beautiful clothes and expensive jewelry. She wanted them for herself and definitely wanted them for her daughter.

"Listen, baby. Even though we're poor, we don't have to be low class."

So, all of a sudden, Candy had to be around a lot of white kids for the first time in her life and she wasn't too thrilled. They didn't seem to be appreciating her either. Things weren't exactly working out as her mother had planned. As Candy anxiously approached the playground, she saw that the children were still playing outside.

"Good," she thought, "I'm on time."

As she slowly walked into the schoolyard, the other children looked at her, but didn't acknowledge her. She tried to make eye contact and smile, but these white kids just wanted to look at her with blank stares. She began to feel like a zoo attraction. If all these little pasty faces started throwing peanuts, the scene would have been complete.

It had been two weeks and she had yet to make any friends. Maybe today would be different, she thought. If she could just get through the day, she'd be fine. Suddenly, a large splash of water hit her in the face, stopping her dead in her tracks. She screamed as she wiped her face and watched the wet patch on the front of her new dress grow larger and larger. A squeaky voice piped up beside her.

"Does the black wash off?"

Candy turned around to see Nancy Jansen standing there with an empty pail in her hand and a satisfied smirk on her face while several other children were laughing uncontrollably. Nancy was her physical opposite, with her pale, white skin and long, blond hair. At that moment, twelve-year-old Candy didn't know whether to slap the little bitch until her face turned red, or run away and hide. Candy decided to slap her, but before she could get her arm in motion, Mrs. Forester grabbed her.

"Is this the way you come to school, Miss Martin?" she asked, her beady eyes glaring.

"No, ma'am," said Candy, holding back her tears.

Mrs. Forester was the meanest teacher at Grover Cleveland. From the first day of school, Candy learned that arguing her case with Mrs. Forester was a waste of time. The woman had no patience. She was a mean, white woman with the pinched up face, who always appeared to be in some kind of pain. Candy was sure that Mrs. Forester was a witch. The West Coast kind: wicked. She even looked like a witch. She had a huge mole next to her nose that made it hard to look at her face too long. Candy had a moment when she wished that the pail of water had hit Mrs. Forester and melted her into a pile of smoke.

Mrs. Forester pushed Candy toward the school door.

"Don't we have rules about eating and drinking before class?" she sneered. "Get yourself to the bathroom."

Candy looked at Mrs. Forester and decided that she was afraid of the old bat. She hadn't had one kind thing to say to her all week. Candy simply lowered her head.

"Yes, ma'am," she replied.

When she looked up again, Mrs. Forester had walked away, along with the other children, who had found something more interesting to do. Except for Nancy Jansen, who had discarded the pail and was standing nearby, managing to have the most innocent look on her little, milky face. Needless to say, this was going to be a long year.

One Saturday afternoon while most of the children were playing in the schoolyard or swimming at the local YMCA, Candy was on her way to Miss Kelsey's to learn how to be a proper, Southern lady. She knew the drill. She had to be smarter and better groomed than the other girls, and even make her own money, because her looks would never get her a husband.

Candy, looking very prim and proper in her white dress, white bonnet and white gloves, was trying desperately to stay cool as she walked faster and faster down the street. The white bonnet protected her from the sun, and even though it only accentuated her dark skin, she had already gotten the idea that she better not get any darker.

As Candy walked past the neighborhood basketball court, she stopped for a moment to watch the boys show off their skills. That was the only place that she had ever felt comfortable. Last summer, she was right out there with the boys, getting dirty and scraping her knees. She was a good player, so they treated her like one of them. As a matter of fact, Candy was often mistaken for one of the boys, but she didn't care. The boys weren't required to be pretty.

Of course, Katie was determined not to let that happen to her daughter anymore. Candy, with her newfound image, including a collection of good wigs, continued on her way until she approached the front of a little, blue house with a big, blue sign that read MISS KELSEY'S CHARM SCHOOL.

Miss Kelsey often reminded Katie that, "Candy wasn't born pretty, and I can't teach the child how to be pretty, but at least she won't behave like a little savage."

After many faithful years with Miss Kelsey, you couldn't tell Candy Martin that she wasn't something special. She had the proper talk, proper walk, and the proper attitude to make her stand out in a crowd, which wasn't hard for Candy to do, because she was still the blackest thing in town.

CHAPTER 18

Portia

Kenny Taylor always tried to do the right thing when it came to Ophelia. Life in Washington, D.C. wasn't easy for the young couple after the tragic death of Darryl West, but they were doing their very best. Immediately after Portia was born, Kenny adopted her and cared for both of them with unconditional love and patience. Once Ophelia was ready to have a real marriage, he was able to express himself to her fully.

"I can't believe how much I've missed this kind of intimacy," she told him while lying in his arms after making love to him for the first time.

"We've had a lot of intimacy," he grinned, stroking her face. "That was more like an explosion, like a tidal wave of…"

"Alright, tiger," she interrupted. "That's enough. You're embarrassing me."

"You weren't embarrassed when your eyes were rolling up into your head."

"Kenny!" she squealed, playfully smacking his chest.

"It's just you and me here, babe," he said. "I love that you were so uninhibited."

Kenny had learned a few tricks while he was in his wild phase. He made their physical love an overwhelming experience for Ophelia. She had loved Darryl deeply and profoundly, and hadn't imagined herself with any other man. But Kenny had awakened something new and exciting in her. She felt that they could have a life together without diminishing her love for Darryl. She would always love Darryl, but she had to make a new future for their precious daughter, Portia.

Ophelia sat up, turned on the lamp beside her, and looked deeply into his eyes.

"Thank you, Kenny. Thank you for loving me and for loving our daughter."

"It's my honor, sweetheart. And it's only the beginning."

***

Kenny moved his new family into a townhouse in SW while he did his internship and residency at Georgetown. Life was good and time was able to heal a lot of the hurt. Darryl's parents, Ophelia's parents and Kenny's parents were all excellent grandparents and little Portia grew up knowing that she was special.

Portia loved her parents very much. From as far back as she could remember, they had told her the truth about Darryl, her biological father, and she knew that she was conceived out of a great love, and that Kenny had chosen to be her father. He was a wonderful husband and father and they enjoyed life as a family.

When Portia was two years old, Kenny followed in his father's footsteps and joined the Army as a Medic. As a result, Portia and Ophelia were often able to travel with him. They even spent a few years in Southeast Asia and Portia learned about other cultures and developed an appreciation for different types of food. Portia loved to eat and as she entered her elementary school years, it was obvious that she had inherited her biological father's genes. She was already bigger and taller than most of the other third graders, just like Darryl was when he was her age. She was teased, but not too many times. Portia felt good about herself and if any kid tried to say something to make her feel bad, she gave them a good reason to think twice the next time.

When Kenny thought it would be a better choice for his family, Ophelia and Portia returned to Washington, DC and moved into a nice apartment blocks away from where Ophelia grew up, to be close to Ophelia's parents and the Wests. Ophelia liked exposing Portia to the world, but she agreed that as Portia got older, it was better for her to have a stable home and friends who didn't change every couple of years.

One winter, when Portia was thirteen, Ophelia became very sick. She had been walking around feeling bad for a week, coughing and having trouble breathing. Laurie Allen insisted that her daughter go to the hospital, but even though Ophelia was married to a doctor, she wasn't one to run to a doctor for every little thing, so she sucked it up and insisted that she had a bad cold and just needed some rest. She lied down on the couch one afternoon after bringing Portia home from school.

"Sweetheart, call Grandma Laurie and ask her to come over and bring some more chicken soup."

"Are you going to be alright, Mommy?"

"Of course, baby."

Laurie Allen came over to fix dinner for her best girls and decided to spend the night. She helped Portia with her homework, did a little housekeeping and allowed Ophelia to sleep, which wasn't easy, because her symptoms kept her tossing and turning.

In the morning, Laurie called her husband and told him to come over for breakfast and take Portia to school while she tended to their daughter. Jonas was more than happy to help. There was nothing worse for a man than to feel helpless when it came to the needs of his family, so he came right over. Besides, Portia loved her Grandpa Jonas and she felt like a princess when he brought her to school in his big Mercedes. He always let her ride in the back and insisted that she wait until he opened her door for her.

"This is how you should always be treated, Portia," he said as he helped her out of the car with her backpack. "Like a lady."

"Thanks, Grandpa," she smiled. "See you later."

"I'll be here when you get out," he said, as she ran off.

When Jonas returned home, he found a message on the answering machine. Laurie was on her way to the hospital with Ophelia. She wanted him to meet them at the emergency room. After he had left with Portia, Laurie had gone to check on Ophelia. Her daughter could barely get out of bed to go to the bathroom without help. Her breathing was shallow, she had a high fever, and when she began coughing up blood, she realized how sick she really was, so she gave in and allowed her mother to take her to the hospital, where she was immediately admitted.

Ophelia was diagnosed with a severe case of bacterial pneumonia, complicated with sepsis. She had to be put on a ventilator to help her breathe. Kenny flew in from Thailand to be by his wife's side when he was told that her condition was critical. Ophelia remained in intensive care for a week while the doctors tried to treat the infection which was endangering her life. Kenny consulted with the medical team and was satisfied that they were doing everything possible to save Ophelia's life.

Jonas and Laurie took turns between going to the hospital and taking care of Portia. They didn't want to upset their granddaughter's life too much. She was allowed to see her mother a couple of times, but it made her very upset because Ophelia wasn't aware of her presence most of the time. Kenny didn't want his daughter to worry, but he realized that Ophelia was seriously ill and not improving. He tried to answer Portia's questions.

"Is Mommy going to die?" she asked him one afternoon after a short visit with Ophelia, who was getting weaker and weaker.

"I don't know, baby. I know she's fighting really hard."

Ophelia Taylor did fight really hard for almost a month, and then she couldn't fight anymore. The family came to say goodbye as she gave her last breath. She died with her family all around her. Kenny was trying to be strong for his daughter, but he was barely holding it together. He stepped out into the hospital corridor so that Ophelia's parents could have a moment with her. Portia followed.

"It's going to be alright, Daddy."

"Oh, baby," he cried, pulling her into a tight embrace. "She loved you so much."

"She loved all of us, Daddy. And she wasn't afraid."

"I know, baby," he said. "She was very brave."

"We all have to go someday. That's what Mommy said. The important thing is to be ready. To not have any regrets."

"Really?" he asked, surprised. "You talked to your mother about dying?"

"I'm not a baby. We talked about a lot of important things all the time. She said that when I die, I get to meet my other daddy."

"That's some kind of crazy conversation that you two had."

Portia shrugged and looked at Kenny sincerely.

"She didn't want me to be afraid."

Kenny hugged Portia with all of his might. He felt helpless because he was a doctor, but in the end he couldn't save his own wife. So now it was Portia who comforted and helped her father through his grief. They helped each other.

After the funeral, Portia moved in with the Allens. It helped them with their grief to be able to care for her. After a family conference with all concerned parties, Kenny and the three sets of grandparents decided that it was time for him to settle down with his daughter. When he completed his last tour overseas, he was offered an opportunity to go to Las Vegas, Nevada to start a medical business with another doctor whom he had befriended in the Army. He talked it over with Portia, who was very excited about the prospect of going to a new, exciting city. It was going to be another year before they could make the move, so Portia was able to spend lots of time with her grandparents.

Jonas and Laurie Allen had friends, Max and Julia Turner, who had retired to Henderson, Nevada, which was outside of Las Vegas. Max was a drummer who had always loved the flash of Las Vegas. Things there had changed dramatically over the years. During World War II, Max's father had moved his family from Sacramento, California to Las Vegas when he went to work in the magnesium plant. There was a lot of prejudice back then and only a few jobs available for black people. Max and his family survived. They understood how things worked in Sin City, and now Max and his wife were happy to share that knowledge with their friends.

The Turners had a granddaughter who was close to Portia's age. The Allens visited the Turners once a year, but Portia had never been with them, so they decided to take her with them during her Christmas break. The Turner's son, Scott, had moved back to Las Vegas after graduating from college three years before to be close to his parents. He had a wife, two young sons and a daughter, Dana, who was anxious to meet Portia.

The Turners hosted a variety of activities during the Allens' visit to Nevada. Portia and Dana hit it off immediately. Dana couldn't wait to show Portia what the Vegas lifestyle was like. Portia immediately felt at home and thought that living in a city like Las Vegas would be exciting. She and Dana kept in touch over the next year, so by the time Kenny and Portia made their move, she already had a friend.

Portia was a healthy girl. Some would say big-boned, if there were such a thing, and Dana was not exactly what you would call petite. She was a couple of inches shorter than Portia, but she was built solid. She and Dana were obsessed with the glitz and glamour of Las Vegas. They saw movies and pictures of the city and loved the brightness of the colorful lights at night. Portia was obsessed with pictures of the fancy showgirls. She always felt that she had a love and desire for the lifestyle of a showgirl, but she also knew that there was no such thing as a black showgirl on the Vegas Strip. And even if by some miracle they were taking black girls, she was way too big.

Portia graduated from high school and began working at Dillard's Department Store. As much as she hated retail, she loved the employee discount. Eventually, Dana got a job there, too and both of them worked and partied together for several years.

When Portia turned twenty-one she got a job as a cocktail waitress in a strip club in downtown Las Vegas. She figured that was as close as she was going to get to being able to fulfill her wild dream of being a showgirl. The club catered to men who liked big women. She hated being at the mercy of the clients, but the tips were really good. She was going to make the best of this life for as long as she could stand it and hope that someday she could figure out a way to become a star.

CHAPTER 19

Melissa

One summer, Junior Murdock auditioned for "Butter Pecan", a professional musical production that would be starting its 3-month tour in Dallas. He had gotten the audition through an agent who had connections in the theatre. When the director of the show came to Los Angeles looking to complete his casting, Junior was more than ready for the opportunity. Bud McKinley was a well-known musical theatre director with several hit shows under his belt.

Junior's audition was flawless. He had tried out for a small, significant part where he was able to show his charm. Bud saw how all the girls reacted to the young, fair-skinned stud and paired him with several young women, who were all smitten.

Karen Petersen, a pretty, petite white girl, was already locked in for the female lead. She was a local star in Dallas, known to be a good actress, singer and dancer. She was an example of the triple threat that many thought was required to have a great career in musical theatre.

Bud McKinley had several talented actors to pair with his star, but hadn't made a final decision yet. Then, Junior Murdock came onto the stage and had that special something that was missing in the young men who had tried out for the male lead; the young white men. Going against the grain, Bud was compelled to offer Junior the lead.

It was very bold of the director to pair an interracial couple in the lead roles, which were traditionally white, but Bud McKinley needed the best actor for the role and Junior fit the bill perfectly. "Hell," he thought. "With stage makeup, who can tell?"

Junior and the other LA cast members arrived in Dallas on a morning flight. By 2:00 pm, the entire cast gathered for their first table reading in the basement of the theatre. Junior, with his back to the door, was talking to Bud. There was a stir and Bud was momentarily distracted as Karen Petersen walked into the room, followed by several other actors. "Here comes your new lady love," said Bud, as he turned Junior towards the door. "Allow me to make the formal introductions."

At first glance, Karen was just another pretty white girl. Bud waved her over and as she headed in their direction, Junior's eyes followed her body. She was wearing a dance leotard with hot pants and tights. Everything was in perfect proportion and she had that funny way of walking with her feet slightly turned out that trained dancers seemed to have in common. Her long, golden hair was pulled into a tight bun, but little wisps of hair framed her face and made her look like an angel.

"I must be trippin'," thought Junior as he stared at her.

"Junior Murdock, Karen Petersen. Now get to know one another quickly," said Bud, looking at his watch. "You have to be in love in…oh, my…ten minutes." Bud rushed off yelling, "Where is Joanie with those scripts?"

"So, you're Junior Murdock?" asked Karen as she stuck out her hand.

The first thing Junior noticed was her brilliant green eyes. When she looked at him, he had a hard time turning away.

"Uh, yeah. That's me," he said as he took her hand, which was soft and small inside of his.

"I expected someone a little different," she said

"Probably expected some pale-faced dude with blond hair and blue eyes, huh?" he asked, releasing her hand.

"No, actually I thought you'd be taller."

Since Junior towered over her at 6'3", that comment caught him off guard with no response. Karen touched his arm, which sent a chill through his body. Then her lips broke into the most beautiful smile. He actually blushed as he realized that she was pulling his leg. They laughed as Bud came back and called for everyone to join him at the long table. There were ten cast members. Two of them were off to a wonderful start.

The dance chorus in the show was made up of thirty males and females, twenty-seven of them white. The three black dancers were female and beautiful. One of them was named Twanna. She was long and lean with a cute pixie haircut and sweet Southern drawl. She was constantly trying to get Junior's attention.

The singing chorus consisted of another twelve white males and females. A lot of them flirted with Junior: black, white and gay. What could he say? He was a very likable guy. He had dated many beautiful, black women. He knew the white girls were attracted to him, but he really didn't pay much attention to it. He was so yellow himself; he liked to see his skin up against some brown sugar.

For the first time in a long time, he had his pick of the litter, so to speak. But for some reason, it was only Karen who piqued his interest totally. He thought that he knew himself pretty well, but Karen Petersen had awakened something in him that he didn't know was there. He was feeling things that he never felt before.

By the third week of rehearsals, Junior was very confused about what he liked and didn't like. Of course, that was only when it came to women. Some of those guys were good looking, but Junior was definitely straight. For Junior, women were always plentiful, so he was not easily swayed by their charms, but he had met his match in Karen. She even changed the way he liked to move.

Junior loved to dance and he loved the sisters and their booty shakin' skills on the dance floor, but this white girl had something special. She was trained as a ballet dancer and on the first day of rehearsal with the choreographer, he knew that he was in trouble. Karen went through her warm-ups and his heart began pounding. She pointed her toes to the sky and all he could think about was grabbing them and sucking them.

As they began working on their dance numbers, he would get a little nervous. One move, in particular, sent his hormones into a wild frenzy. Karen had to put her leg up onto his shoulder and the way that she looked when she lifted that leg to the sky made him want to shove his face between her legs and find the whipped cream that he was sure would be there. This little white girl had turned Junior Murdock into a romantic idiot.

And then she had these beautiful green eyes with little flecks of gold in them. Whenever he sang the love song that was the climax of the show, she would look intensely into his eyes. Then she would smile a crooked smile with lips that were painted with rose petals. All that he could think about was how much he wanted to take her in his arms and kiss the lips off her face; however, Junior and Karen were specifically instructed to fake the kiss. Bud wasn't sure he was ready to be that bold. That only made their closeness more erotic: all that passion being withheld.

The entire cast got along great. They joked with each other and had a good time. Junior noticed that some of the dancers were competitive, but that seemed to be their nature, always trying to outdo one another. They would have miniature dance-offs during breaks, but it was all in good fun.

Even though Junior was the only black male, none of the white actors seemed to treat him any different than they treated each other. Being in the theatre was a great equalizer because Dallas wasn't the most liberal place in the world. The cast was really talented and most of the time they were one big happy family. And like every family, they had their moments of debate, and people took sides, but they got over things pretty quickly when it was time to pull it together for Bud. He didn't stand for any discord amongst his cast. Whatever was going on had better be resolved by curtain time.

The only person who didn't feel like family to Junior was Karen. That was probably because he wanted to ravage her. On stage, he was able to have his hands all over her, but as soon as the curtain went down, she became the untouchable white girl who barely gave him a second glance. Junior tried to talk to her alone after rehearsal sometimes, but she was simply polite and kept a professional distance.

One night during a late rehearsal, Junior was sitting about six rows from the front, rolling his neck around to loosen it up. Twanna walked up and sat behind him, rubbing his shoulders and whispering in his ear. "How does that feel, sugah?"

"That's good, Twanna. You have good hands."

"My hands are good for a lotta thangs, Junior."

She moved her hands around to the front of his shirt, and slipped her hands inside to caress his chest, which was lightly covered with soft, silky hair that continued down over his tight stomach. Her hands ventured there, too. "Oooh, that feels so good," she said, apparently in heaven.

"I thought I was the one who was supposed to say that," he said, stopping her hands by gently holding her wrists.

She kissed his neck. "I think you should take your shirt off and let me see what you're workin' with."

He removed her arms from around his neck. "Thanks, but no thanks. You can't handle me, girl. I might hurt you with my rock solid six-pack."

"I'll take my chances," said Twanna.

Bud, who was sitting in the front row, turned to look at Junior and Twanna.

"Oh, goodie! There you are, Junior. Now how about taking your dangerously tight body with all that pent up sexual energy and bringing it on up to the stage to do Act 2 Scene 4? Thank you very much. Where's Karen? Perhaps she would like to join you on stage. Twanna, I released the dancers twenty minutes ago. Go get a life."

"See y'all tomorrow," Twanna laughed.

"Make Joey walk you to your car," Bud called after her.

Twanna wasn't alone in her quest for Junior's attention. There were several girls in the chorus who would have been happy to have that black buck sweating all over them in a round of hot monkey sex, but those were the ones who would have been comparing notes. He didn't really want to get into that whole thing. He had been there and done that. Big mistake. After a while, the girls would all be fighting and then he'd have to deal with the aftermath. He didn't need that drama. There was plenty of sex to be had in Dallas with the black women he had met outside of the theatre, but for some reason unclear to him, his head was all twisted up with thoughts of Karen.

Of course, Karen had been enjoying Junior's discomfort. If only because it made it easier for her to hide how much she was attracted to him. Every time she looked him in his eyes, she saw something that made the blood rush to her head. She kept a straight face to keep from getting lost in his spell, but every time their faces got very close for the kiss, she wished that she could feel his full, sensuous lips all over her body. She had to snap out of it. She couldn't let things go too far, because her family was from the old school and didn't believe in mixing the races. Although, they would probably deny any prejudice at all "against the niggers".

It was sad, but true. Karen hadn't even mentioned that the man tossing her around on stage every night and holding her in his manly arms was a black man: a big, strong, handsome black man. No, that would be a bullet right through her father's heart. She might as well go pull the rifle from the dashboard of his pickup and go shoot him with it. And as far as her mother was concerned, Karen knew that she would simply pass out, right in the middle of blaming her for bringing on the apocalypse.

So, for weeks, Karen maintained her composure with Junior while avoiding questions from her family. They had gotten used to her doing several shows a year, so this was routine. She didn't make a big deal about it, so they didn't go out of their way to come see her perform.

"Just a bunch of faggots and sissies running around on stage," her father would say. "If that's what you want to do, fine. But it doesn't mean that I have to spend any of my good time looking at 'em."

Bud McKinley had made it a point to keep the identity of his stars under wraps. He sent out teasers rather than full-blown publicity pictures. Everything was going to be a big surprise, from the cast to the elaborate dance numbers. He had big ideas about shaking up this little city.

One week before opening night, during a rehearsal break where everyone left to get food, Junior and Karen stayed behind to perfect a move in their sensuous dance number. Without any warning, Karen began rubbing her butt against his crotch, which was not part of the choreography. Within seconds, Junior had a raging hard-on. He grabbed her, spun her around and kissed her hard, on the mouth, with tongue. She gave it back as good as she got it. They frantically worked their way backstage and onto a couch. She worked her hands down his pants and immediately got down on her knees and went to work like nobody's business. She sucked and licked and pulled and rubbed until Junior thought he was going to lose his mind. He eventually pulled her onto the couch, where he proceeded to introduce little white Karen to the big black snake.

Junior and Karen went at it hot and heavy and were on the second round when they heard the sounds of the cast arriving back from lunch.

They heard someone say, "Damn, it smells like funky sex up in here."

Others laughed as the sweaty couple quickly got themselves together and managed to slip out a side door without anyone seeing them. They arrived back separately minutes later. No one seemed to catch on. They were both better actors than they thought they were.

After that, no more cold-shoulder from Karen. She didn't go overboard, but she let it be known, in her subtle way, that Junior was off limits now. Their chemistry was palpable. Their preview week performances went from good to great. Opening night was a huge success. The word was out and they were an instant hit, complete with controversy. For four weeks, Dallas was buzzing about this hot, interracial couple burning up the stage every night at the Orpheum Theatre. Especially, the night that Junior Murdock grabbed Karen Petersen in the heat of the moment and planted a big, juicy kiss on her lips. Luckily, the show closed in Dallas that night.

For the next six months, the company of "Butter Pecan" toured all over Texas, Oklahoma, Louisiana, Mississippi and Florida. Junior and Karen became inseparable and had sex every chance they got. Everyone in the cast, like it or not, had to get used to the two of them being together. Anyone could see that they were very much in love. Now, the tour was coming to an end. Junior and Karen talked about a lot of things, but they never had a conversation about what was going to happen after the tour was over.

A week before the tour was going to close in Los Angeles, Karen, whose menstrual cycle was very regular, missed her period for the first time. She didn't really think too much about it at first. After all, she was on a very hectic schedule, performing with a hit show on the road. Her regularity was the last thing on her mind. Besides, she was on the pill. But after thinking about it, she realized that she couldn't remember the last time she got her period after finishing a monthly pack. The next day, Karen decided to get herself a check-up at the Women's Clinic of Los Angeles. Her pregnancy test came back positive. Now, that was a conversation.

The final performance was great. The cast received three standing ovations, and then people waited in the lobby for them to come out and sign autographs. The whole Murdock family came out to the closing night show. Junior was excited to introduce his family to the people who had been like family to him for a good part of the past year. He watched to see how they would react to Karen, without knowing who she was to him.

Gary Wilson showed up and couldn't help but put his two cents in. "Damn, Junior. I didn't think you could pull that shit off, man. That white babe is hot. I can't believe how real that kiss looked. If I didn't know you any better, I'd say you've been dreaming of a white Christmas…or a brown Hanukkah."

Junior had to laugh at his friend. "Boy, you a fool."

James Sr., Mama Susie, Ruth, Becka and Pete, all came dressed up and ready to party. They were drinking champagne and eating hors d'oeuvres. Bud, Junior, Karen and the cast had just finished taking pictures with some of the VIPs. Karen tried to wait until the last possible moment to talk to Junior privately. She didn't want to appear conspicuous. She knew that Junior wanted to keep their relationship quiet from his family for now. He was going to be spending a week with them in LA before coming down to Dallas to spend some time with her.

Karen finally excused herself and persuaded Junior to go for a walk with her. They walked upstairs to the empty stage, where workers had already begun to break down the set. "What's up, girl? You've been wearing that plastic smile for almost an hour." He took her in his arms. "I know you're gonna miss me. I'm gonna miss you, too." They kissed for a long time. Finally, Karen looked deep into Junior's clear gray eyes and said, "I'm pregnant, Junior."

He stepped back. "What? You've got to be kidding."

"Do I look like I'm kidding?"

Junior was in shock. "No, of course not, I'm sorry."

"I'm sorry, too," said Karen with tears in her eyes.

"Did you forget to take your pills?" he asked.

"You know how fanatic I am about that. I haven't missed a day in over a year. It's that damn unlucky percentage."

They were quiet for a few tense moments until Junior's shock began to wear off. Then a big grin came over his face and he unexpectedly pulled Karen into his arms and spun her around. "We're gonna have a baby, baby."

"Are you serious, Junior? You're not angry?"

Karen couldn't stop the tears from falling. Junior wiped her tears away and looked her straight in the eye. "I was there, too, remember? You're not in this by yourself. I love you, Karen."

"Oh, Junior, I love you, too. What are we going to do?" She was breathless.

"Hmmm," he moaned. "I guess that means you gotta marry me, little lady."

Junior knew that his family was not ready for this, but they would have to come around once they realized that he was serious about her. He just didn't have time to break them in slowly. If she were already his wife, then they would have to accept her.

However, as far as dealing with Karen's parents, they were a whole other story. They weren't going to accept them as a couple, no matter what. Junior and Karen would have to get married before her parents had a chance to stop them. The following afternoon, they went to a justice of the peace and decided to keep the marriage a secret until Karen began to show.

Karen's mother was the first person she told about the pregnancy and the quickie wedding, but didn't mention that Junior was black. She didn't want it to matter. She knew that they would be upset and disappointed, but they would get over it. At least, that's what she had hoped. She actually had no idea how they would react.

It's not like she had ever made any special effort to have black friends. She realized that she had never brought any around. Not that there weren't some black kids at her school, but she just didn't hang out with them. Perhaps she knew that it wouldn't have gone over well in her household. Her father didn't have any black friends and neither did her mother. Truth be told, the only black person who came to their house was the mailman, and her father put a wooden mailbox out by the gate so that he wouldn't come onto the property. It occurred to Karen how fucked up that was.

When Karen finally told her mother about her situation, Mrs. Peterson was really upset, but even more so because they had to tell her father. At first, they just told him that Karen had gotten secretly married to another actor and they were having a baby. That was bad enough, but when Mr. Peterson heard the news, he was more pissed off because it was someone whose family they didn't know.

"You couldn't get yourself knocked up by one of the Dalton boys?" he scoffed. "That woulda brought somethin' to the table."

"Sorry, Daddy. I didn't know you were looking for me to complete a merger."

"So, who's the lowlife son of a bitch without the decency to come see me first?"

"I told you, Daddy. You don't know him."

"He better not be no Jew boy," he roared. "Is he a fuckin' Jew?"

"It's not that bad, dear," Mrs. Peterson said. "He's just a colored boy."

"What?" he yelled.

"He's a very talented actor from Los Angeles, Daddy."

Mr. Peterson almost fell over. "Just kill me right now."

"He's a good man, Daddy."

"Then bring him over here so I can shoot his good balls off."

Mrs. Petersen was calm. "Alright, that's enough. Nobody's gonna be doin' any shootin'."

"The hell I won't," Mr. Peterson said, taking his shotgun out of the closet.

"You're not going to shoot my husband, Daddy."

"I'm not gonna have no little niglets runnin' around with my blood."

"That's ridiculous!" she screamed. "Why don't you just put a white sheet over your head, get your redneck cronies and go hang Junior Murdock. Then you can hang your daughter and your first grandchild."

Suddenly, Mr. Peterson held his chest and literally fell out in the middle of the floor. Karen thought that he was faking, but it turned out that he was actually having a heart attack. Mrs. Peterson called 911 and the ambulance came and took him to the hospital, where he spent the next six days. During that time, he refused to let Karen visit him and told his wife to keep her out of their home.

Karen's parents simply disowned her. She expected the confrontation to be dramatic, but she still wasn't prepared to deal with the reality that her family held such unprovoked hatred for other people simply because of the color of their skin. She realized that they were just as bad as any racist groups and went to let her feelings be known, as soon as her father was back from the hospital.

"Get out of my house," her father said, coldly. "You're dead to me."

Karen went to one of her favorite female cousins, who had a lot of money, and was able to get a loan. With that money, she and Junior were able to put a down payment on a little house and settle in for the baby.

Melissa Jane Murdock was born a few months later. She was a beautiful baby with pale, white skin and green eyes. Junior was shocked and surprised. He had to resist the urge to ask if she was his baby. After a while it was evident, but if it wasn't for Melissa's hair, which was thick and wavy like his, except hers was blond, there would be no trace of him at all in his daughter.

Things were good for Junior and Karen Murdock for a few years, but Junior could not take the pressure of being a husband and father in Dallas, married to a white woman who gave birth to a white baby. Things between the young couple deteriorated greatly as time went on. Divorce was inevitable.

For the first ten years that they lived as a family, Melissa rarely saw her white family. Only Karen's mother agreed to see her and Melissa periodically. While Junior's family was very accepting, Karen had a family who was the other side of the coin. Back in their lily-white world in Dallas, her family called Junior's family 'jiggaboos' and 'niggers'. Karen's father never failed to remind everyone that he would continue to disown her, "as long as she's living with that coon."

On the other hand, the Murdocks had welcomed Junior's wife and daughter into their family and never made either of them feel out of place, except maybe in the beginning, according to Karen. When Junior first brought her home to meet his parents and sisters, he and Karen had already been married and Melissa was three months old. The family was a little disappointed that he didn't have a wedding. He also hadn't warned them that Karen was white and that baby Melissa looked just as white. But, Mama Susie liked it. In some twisted way, it made her feel better about herself.

"My grandbaby got the prettiest hair, so golden and wavy."

Growing up, Melissa was surprised that her cousins didn't hold it against her, because sometimes it seemed that she was treated special. Her cousin Eleanor said that it was only because their grandparents didn't get to see Melissa that much. The rest of them all lived close by, so they were able to see them all the time. But Melissa knew better. She heard the way that her grandmother talked about Junior and couldn't help but to mention how beautiful his skin was. "So light and bright," Mama Susie would say.

Melissa visited the Murdocks with her parents every summer from the time she was three, and after her parents were divorced, Junior insisted that she spend the entire summer with her black family. As a result, she and her cousins were very close.

Typically, Melissa would spend the first two days fighting the neighborhood kids, trying to convince them that even with her wavy blond hair, hazel green eyes, and slim build, she was one of them. She was a beautiful girl who would have fit right in with the Beverly Hills, 90210 crowd, but this is where her people were...off Crenshaw, next to the hood. The kids in this black neighborhood just pegged her as another white girl trying to be black. Melissa was definitely white, but she was definitely black, too.

Now, here she was, fresh from Texas for her annual summer visit, still holding her own with four black girls who wanted to kick her ass, and wondering where her cousins were. She had tackled the biggest one and backed the second one off, but she could still use a little help. Eventually, her three cousins came to break up the fight. The big girl still tried to get at Melissa, so Eleanor, who liked a good rumble, grabbed her hard and pushed her.

"Back off, Patsy," she said. "If you fight her, you gotta fight us, too. She's family."

The girl named Patsy looked at Eleanor, and then looked at Johnny, who said, "I don't have a problem slapping the shit out of a big ass girl".

While the kids were outside, Mama Susie was at the stove putting the finishing touches on a huge meal to celebrate Melissa's arrival. Suddenly, Melissa, Eleanor and Leslie ran into the house from the backyard. Their clothes were dirty and they were scraped up, but they had big smiles on their sweaty faces.

"Hey, Blondie," Mama Susie said affectionately. "I know you haven't eaten this good since the last time you was here, so y'all go on upstairs and get cleaned up. Dinner's gonna be ready in twenty minutes."

They were followed moments later by Johnny, who never had any intention of getting into a brawl with a bunch of girls, despite what he had said. Therefore, he had chosen to referee and managed to come out of the whole incident without a smudge.

Johnny didn't really like to get involved with the girls and their issues, but he stayed close by just in case one of those prissy ass fools decided to play dirty. He was a good-looking kid with a slim build who liked to keep his clothes nice and clean. Even at fourteen, he was working on his image and had plans to be a movie producer someday.

Leslie, the peacemaker, was the youngest at thirteen, and would try to talk the girls out of fighting altogether. Eleanor, the oldest and the toughest, had just turned sixteen and was down for a fight whenever or wherever. The four grandchildren had a strong bond that renewed itself every summer at their grandparent's house.

Susie Murdock was a great cook, and she always had some tasty soul food prepared. The smells coming from the kitchen let Melissa know that she was about to have a religious experience. When else did she ever have a chance to eat real Southern fried chicken, ox tails, black-eyed peas, macaroni and cheese, collard greens, yams and cornbread? Don't even talk about the dessert: banana bread, red velvet cake, sweet potato pie and peach cobbler. Her mother surely never cooked like that. Her idea of a home-cooked meal was Hamburger Helper with a side salad.

The four cousins ran upstairs, trying to beat each other to the hall bathroom. Leslie managed to slip in and lock the door before everyone else. The other three spread out to get to one of the last two bathrooms. Eleanor slipped past Johnny, almost knocking him down, and tripped Melissa as she ran through her grandmother's bedroom to the master bathroom.

"Dirty little bitch," muttered Melissa.

Since Johnny still wasn't willing to get wrinkled, he let Melissa win the race to the last bathroom on the third floor.

Thirty minutes later, Melissa and her cousins were all bathed, changed and passing plates at the dining room table.

"So, how's Karen doing these days?" asked Becka.

"She's fine," replied Melissa, looking down at her plate.

"Girl, I ain't seen your momma git outta here so fast," Mama Susie chuckled as she chomped on a chicken wing. "Where she had to go in such a hurry this morning? She barely stopped the car long enough for you to git your behind out."

Melissa looked directly at her grandmother, began to respond, and then changed her mind. Instead, she asked, "May I have more macaroni and cheese, please?"

"You sound like a commercial, Missy," said Eleanor.

"I told you to call me Melissa."

"Oh, excuse me." Eleanor looked around the table. "She thinks Missy sounds too white all of a sudden."

"Call Blondie whatever she wants to be called," said Mama Susie, daring Melissa to challenge her. Melissa just flicked her blond hair and looked at her grandmother with a straight face and much attitude. "Can a sista just get some macaroni and cheese?"

Mama Susie looked at Melissa, with her serious hazel green eyes, and broke into hearty laughter, along with the rest of the family. Eleanor threw her head back and laughed, exposing chewed up food.

"Hey, Miss Ellie, we don't need to see your dinner moving past your tonsils, so close your mouth and pass that dish of macaroni on over here to Blondie."

Mama Susie's comment allowed Melissa to join in on the laughter.

Book Four

CHAPTER 20

Snookie

By the time Snookie McClain was sixteen, she was tall and lanky, with small breasts. It seems that she went through an awkward puberty stage and never came out of it. She didn't wear makeup and kept her hair braided with synthetic extensions.

What happened to her carefree youth? She had to wonder, because she cooked, cleaned, took care of nine children and still went to school most days. She wasn't able to enjoy extracurricular activities. Jessie Mae expected her to be home right after school to help her out with everything.

Snookie desperately wanted to get away, so when Billy McAllister, one of the football players from her high school, asked her out, she said yes. Billy wasn't very attractive, but neither was Snookie. He was big, almost fat, but that was good for the football team. He had a really big head and big ears, but he was very nice to Snookie and she liked the attention. They made quite a pair. He was quiet, shy and well mannered, and Snookie was...well, far from being all of those things.

Snookie and Billy hung out after school sometimes for a few minutes, before he had to go to football practice and before she needed to get home, but they managed to learn a lot about each other in the time they had. Billy was always waiting for Snookie by the locker room. Today she was late.

"Sorry, Billy," she said, running up to him as he was about to go inside.

"Hey, Snookie," he said. "What happened to you? I was worried."

"Fuckin' Mr. Lorenzo made me stay to lecture me about my history test."

"Damn. Well, I gotta go, Snookie. I'll call you later."

"Okay."

He went into the locker room and she walked down the hall.

"Hey, Snookie!"

She turned around to see Billy running towards her. He sure was light on his feet for a big guy, she thought. He looked nervous.

"Listen...um, there's a dance next Friday," Billy said.

"Yeah, I know," she said, hand on her hip.

"Well...um, I was wondering...um..."

"Oh, just spit it out, Billy!" she snapped. "You wanna go or what?"

"Yeah...I mean...if you wanna."

"Uh huh, Billy. Let's go to the dance together."

"Cool," he said. "Okay, so, we'll talk about it later."

"Okay."

"I really gotta go, Snookie."

"So go then," she said. "Ain't nobody stoppin' you."

"Bye." He awkwardly kissed her on her cheek and rushed into the locker room.

When Snookie got home, she immediately told Shawna about the dance.

"A few of my girlfriends are going," Shawna informed her.

"So, maybe you need to go, too." Snookie suggested.

"Momma's not gonna let us both go, Snookie," she said. "Plus, I don't have a date, and you do. So, go ahead and have fun."

Snookie was determined to make sure that they both had fun. "We never get to do anything special, Shawna. Momma can stay home wit her own children for a change. I'll work it out."

"Snookie..." Shawna recognized the look in her big sister's eyes and knew that she was already brewing a plan. "Don't you get yourself in no mess wit Momma."

One thing that Snookie had learned to do was manipulate Jessie Mae when it came to something that she really wanted. She knew just how far to push her mother before she'd be earning a slap in the face, but Snookie was very good. All she had to do was make a little suggestion about Jessie Mae's former afternoon delights. That was enough to keep her mother in line. It was a terrible thing to do, so she only used it when absolutely necessary. A big school dance for her and Shawna to attend seemed like a perfect chance to use her skills.

The next day, Snookie took Shawna with her to find a dress for the dance. Shawna already had a dress that she had never worn. It was supposed to be for church, but Vincent thought it was a little too short. It probably hadn't helped that Snookie had helped her to hem it an extra two inches.

The sisters went to several stores and nothing was good enough for Snookie. She couldn't afford a really nice dress and the ones that she could afford were too girly for her taste. Snookie didn't have good taste. She didn't really follow fashion trends. But she knew that she didn't want to look like the other silly girls. She wanted Billy to see her as more than a friend; she wanted to be sexy.

"What do you think about this one, Shawna?" Snookie asked as she came out of the dressing room in a bright red dress with a low-cut front.

"Oh, my goodness!" she exclaimed. "Where is your bra, Snookie?"

"I don't need a bra with this dress."

"You ain't gonna be able to wear that to a school dance."

"It's a perfect fit," Snookie said as she admired herself in the full-length mirror.

"I can see your titties clear as day," Shawna whispered.

"Stop lyin', Shawna."

"I ain't lyin."

"Does it look good or what?"

Shawna looked at her older sister and rolled her eyes.

"You look fantastic, Snookie, but Momma's gonna kill you."

"Momma's not gonna know."

Somehow, Snookie was able to sneak her dress into the back of her closet without Jessie Mae finding out. Then she had to convince one of the old neighbors, Mrs. Durham, to make her a dress for free: a nice proper dress, which meant that it was gonna be butt ugly. Mrs. Durham sat on her porch watching everything in the neighborhood. You couldn't get anything past her prying eyes.

The following Sunday, Snookie dragged Shawna and the other kids to church and made sure that Mrs. Durham saw them parading by on the way home. Snookie waved and Mrs. Durham smiled and waved back. An hour later, Snookie was in her work clothes standing in front of Mrs. Durham's house.

"Hi, Mrs. Durham," she said, smiling. "You look like you can use a little help cleaning up this front yard."

The night of the school dance was a lovely night. The weather was warm and not as humid as it had been lately. Billy walked the seven blocks to Snookie's house to pick her up. While he was knocking on the front door, Shawna was busy putting a large paper bag under a bush at the end of the driveway. The bag contained Snookie's sexy dress, extra shoes and a bra, which was her idea, but she figured that Snookie wouldn't wear it.

Vincent McClain opened the door and invited Billy into the house as Snookie walked in and introduced Billy to Vincent and Jessie Mae. Billy tried to hide his shock as he stared at Snookie in her dress.

"You look very nice, Snookie," Vincent said as Snookie stood awkwardly in a hideous powder blue dress with white and purple flowers. It had puffy sleeves and came down to her knees.

"What about you, Mama? You like it?"

Jessie Mae just stared at her daughter.

Vincent smiled. "You look nice, Snookie. Doesn't she look nice, Jessie Mae?"

"Do you like the dress, Mama?"

"It looks a hundred years old," Jessie Mae snickered.

"Mrs. Durham helped her make that dress," Shawna said, walking into the room.

"Well, that explains a lot!" younger brother Sam piped in, following Shawna into the room. Shawna turned and popped him.

"You look lovely, too, Shawna," Vincent added.

"Thank you," she smiled, as the doorbell rang. She ran to open the door for her three girlfriends, who couldn't stop giggling as they spotted Snookie in her hideous dress.

"Alright, that's enough," Snookie said, taking Billy by the hand. "We gotta go."

"Have fun, Snookie," Shawna said.

"Have fun, Snookie," Sam mocked.

"Shut up, Sam!" Jessie Mae yelled. "Go to bed!"

"I'll see you at the dance, Shawna," Snookie said with a knowing look. She turned to Vincent. "Thank you."

"Do you need some money?" Vincent asked.

"Sure. I'll never turn down any money."

Snookie and Billy had a good time at the dance. For a big boy, he moved pretty well. Billy was very attentive and made her feel special. Even when it was a good time to make a move, he was a perfect gentleman. It was Snookie who was trying to get her freak on. They slipped outside to get some air and after what seemed like an eternity, Snookie planted a big kiss on Billy's lips. Then she grabbed him around his neck and gave him his first hickey, and when he didn't seem to know what to do with his hands, she grabbed one of them and put it on her little breast. He didn't move it.

Snookie McClain lost her virginity to Billy McAllister right after high school graduation. She planned the whole thing out, all the way down to the sleazy motel and the triple pack of condoms. It wasn't exactly the romance of the year, but they had fun together. Their futures weren't particularly bright, either. Neither of them were good students, but at least they managed to get into a local community college in Mobile. Billy was an old-fashioned kind of guy and felt that they should get married.

"What makes you think that I want to marry you, Billy?"

"Don't you want to get married and have kids, Snookie?"

"Hell, no. I thought I made that clear a long time ago."

"Never?"

"I don't know, Billy," she snapped, frustrated. "I been taking care of kids my whole life. I sure don't wanna think about doing it for the *rest* of my life."

"Well, we had sex."

"So, now we have to get hitched and have a bunch of brats? I don't think so."

Snookie was adamant about not being trapped into the life her mother had. She liked the idea of being in a relationship, but only for the comfort it would provide. The whole idea of having to go out with a lot of guys didn't appeal to her. She didn't mind being with one boy, as long as she could have things her way. Most of the girls her age were planning their entire lives around getting married and starting a family. Snookie sometimes thought that there was something wrong with her, because she didn't care about those things. She really liked kids and was very good with them, but she wanted them to be someone else's responsibility. Not hers.

By the time Snookie graduated from the community college with a certificate in sociology, she had long since dumped Billy McAllister, but they remained friendly. She realized that they just didn't want the same things. He was set on being a father and having a big family. Snookie could have been much happier if she and Shawna were the only kids in her family. At least that's what she thought.

Snookie was about to turn twenty-one and still lived at home. She helped her mother out whenever she could, but the last thing that she ever wanted to be was a clone of Jessie Mae. She felt that her mother was the worst example of life's choices. She still remembers one of Jessie Mae's drunken ravings where she said that she had always dreamed of being an expensive whore and that if it weren't for the fact that she had gotten pregnant with Snookie, she could've been one of the best. What kind of shit was that? Who sets out in life wanting to be a whore?

Snookie knew that something was wrong with her mother's way of thinking. Then again, with ten kids from several men, Jessie Mae sure had done a lot of fucking. That could look good on a resume if you're looking for a job as a prostitute.

Snookie had to laugh as she thought, "I guess everyone has something that they are born to do well."

She was willing to work hard, but if she wanted a better life, she needed to get a good job. That way she could get out on her own, afford to look her best and then maybe even find a good man who didn't want children. That would be a life for her.

Her mind was set on getting a city job. She knew it was a steady income and that it was considered prestigious to be working for the city. Billy's mother worked for Social Services. Her job was difficult, but fulfilling. She helped kids who were in a bad situation find a safer and better home to live in. Snookie remembered hearing her many heartwarming stories when she was hanging out with Billy. Snookie decided that's what she wanted to do.

Billy's mother eventually set up an appointment for Snookie, who was a natural talker, very mature and confident. She certainly had enough experience under her belt after practically raising her nine siblings. The people at Social Services of Mobile, Alabama were impressed with Snookie McClain. She was given an entry level position from which she could advance in no time. She wanted to be someone with a noble profession. Certainly not a whore!

CHAPTER 21

Aurora

In the beginning, it seemed as though Baxter Duncan had made a change. He really did love his family and tried to be more attentive. He even took a job as a security guard to help ease Camille's fears about supporting them. She really wanted to stay home with their daughter, the way that her mother did for her. Baxter refused to let go of his music, though, and eventually began booking gigs out of town on the weekends.

Camille didn't like it, but she wanted to keep the peace. Most of the time they were able to put Aurora's needs first, but as the years went by, Baxter seemed to only grow more resentful of his life. His band worked steadily, but he had visions of being a star. That wasn't happening in any way, shape or form, and Camille let him know that.

Aurora was beautiful. She had Camille's complexion and amber eyes. Her hair was long; not wild and curly like her mother's, but straight and slightly wavy like her grandmother's. Over the years, Aurora watched her parents fight and make up constantly and it made her afraid. Although Camille tried to shield her daughter from the fighting that went on with Baxter, Aurora was sensitive. She surely felt the tension between her parents. Growing up in a volatile household was not good for building security in a small child. Nor was it good for her self-esteem.

The Kennedys were the one stable factor in Aurora's life. They insisted on keeping her for at least one weekend a month. Camille was fine with that. It gave her daughter a much-needed break from Baxter, and the Kennedys could keep building a strong relationship with their granddaughter without having to deal with Baxter. Aurora loved going to her grandparents for sleepovers. It also gave Camille an excuse to see her parents even when she wasn't sure they wanted to see her.

Aurora was too young to understand the dynamic between her parents. Baxter would get angry and sometimes hit her mother. Then he would rush out of the house. Aurora never knew if her father would ever come back. But, Camille knew. She would brush it off as though nothing was wrong. When Baxter did come back, he always had flowers or a little gift and was full of remorse. What a confusing thing for a child to witness. When Baxter and Camille fought, it seemed like they were in their own world. Aurora watched them, but they never saw her. She became good at being invisible.

But like most little girls, Aurora still loved her daddy. He was always affectionate with her and although he seemed to be absent a lot, he still managed to be a big influence on her. For as long as she could remember, she loved to hear him play his horn or sing. He often performed for her when her mother was not around.

As time went on, things got worse. When Aurora was ten, she was old enough to know that her father was changing. For the past year, he had seemed less and less content with his band, more and more impatient with everyone around him. Baxter was still waiting for a big break in his music. He began to think that the band was holding him back. He felt that he could be a star without them, and would benefit by dropping them, even though he had promised that they would stay together, no matter what. This self-serving solo career idea was fueled with a lot of outside influence.

There was an attorney who had promised to help. His name was Edward Kane and he had heard the band play at a private event. He invited Baxter to several meetings with him at the Harvard Club, a very prestigious private club in midtown Manhattan. He always required Baxter to come alone. They would have drinks and food in the outer dining area, but he never invited Baxter beyond the sacred walls of the actual club. Mr. Kane was very enthusiastic about Baxter and dangled promises of stardom in front of his face. It was the break that he and the band had been waiting for.

The problem was that Edward Kane was not interested in the Soul Bandits. He only wanted Baxter. In order to get Kane's considerable help, which would include financing, Baxter would have to leave the band behind. Baxter kept trying to convince him otherwise, but he wouldn't budge. This went on for about a year.

Baxter finally realized that his big shot was slipping away. It was time to make a decision to part ways with the band, but he had to know they would remember his promise. He went so far as to mention that he might be leaving, which caused major conflict, even though Edward Kane had made no solid moves to prove that he could back up any of his promises.

One evening, Baxter came home after a big argument with the band. Camille had dealt with his drama long enough. It was time for him to get serious about providing for them. The band was the only income, and even though it kept him away a lot, it was something. He couldn't maintain any other jobs. He just wasn't satisfied. Now he thought he had a ticket to fame and fortune, but he'd have to sell his soul to get it.

"You can't turn your back on the guys, Baxter," Camille reminded him when he finally told her about the lawyer's offer. "They've been very loyal to you."

"I know that, Camille.

"So, why do you keep talking to this guy?" she insisted. "He's been jerking you around for months and months."

"Nobody jerks me around!"

"You can't keep doing this, Baxter."

"What the hell do you want from me, woman?" he asked loudly. "I'm trying to make things better for you."

"Bullshit! You're doing it for you!"

"This is my shot. I didn't get into this game to worry about everybody else."

"Not everybody else, Baxter," Camille said, frustrated. "Just me and Aurora. Unless you forgot about your wife and your child!"

"When it works out for me, it'll work out for you, too."

"What does he want from you?"

"What does he want?" Baxter was yelling. "He thinks I'm talented."

"You are, Baxter." Camille was becoming irritated. "You don't need some rich lawyer to tell you that."

Baxter swept a bowl of potpourri, a potted plant and some books off the table and roughly grabbed Camille by her shoulders.

"You gonna tell me what I need now? Huh?" He stepped back and slapped her. "Is that it?" He slapped her again. "You gonna run things now?"

Aurora, who had been hiding, ran into the room to stop her parents from fighting.

"Daddy!"

Baxter barely looked at her as he pushed her to the floor.

"Aurora!" Camille screamed.

She ran over to comfort her stunned daughter, who had a look of terror on her face that Camille had never seen before. As far as she knew, that was the first time that Baxter had been violent in front of their daughter.

"Stay out of my fuckin' business, woman." Baxter stormed out of the apartment and this time Camille didn't care if he ever came back.

Two hours and several drinks later, Baxter stormed back into the house and demanded to see his daughter. It had taken a while for Camille to calm Aurora down and she wasn't about to let him upset her again. She was in the middle of vacuuming the mess that he had made knocking everything off the table earlier. He slapped her one more time.

"Go sleep it off, Baxter," she said.

"I'll beat the shit outta both of ya," he shouted, stumbling back in her direction.

Camille had grabbed a baseball bat from behind the couch and was holding it in swinging position. "I mean it. Put your hands on me or my daughter again and I'll crack your skull wide open."

She knew that this was the moment of truth. Putting his hands on her was one thing. Putting his hands on Aurora was the last straw. It was up to her to save them both. She refused to have her daughter suffer the same fate that she had at his hands.

After Baxter fell asleep on the couch, Camille got busy.

"Mommy, why do you and Daddy fight all the time?" Aurora sleepily asked a while later. "Doesn't Daddy love us anymore?"

"Of course he does, baby," Camille replied, as she stopped what she was doing to give her daughter a hug. "Now hurry up and get dressed."

She quickly continued packing Aurora's clothes and grabbing everything that was important to her before making a dreaded phone call. Shortly after midnight, Camille and Aurora were at the Kennedy's front door with suitcases in hand. Jonathan answered the door in his bathrobe and looked at his daughter, with her tear-stained face. He always assumed that this day would come and that he'd have a chance to give a good ol' "I told you so" speech. But then he looked down at little Aurora, smiling bravely and holding on tight to her favorite teddy bear.

"Hi Pop Pop!" Aurora said, as she gave her grandfather a hug. "We're gonna have a sleepover!"

His heart broke for them. No words were necessary. He reached out for the suitcases and stepped aside to let them in.

"I smell cookies!" Aurora ran off to find her grandmother.

As Camille stepped inside, she looked at her father and their eyes met in silent understanding. She was still his daughter, and no matter what happened, no matter how old she was, she could always come home. She knew that as long as her parents had a roof over their heads, she would always have a place to lay hers. That was the comfort and security that only a family could provide.

Maria came rushing to greet her daughter with a big hug.

"Mija! It's so good to see you. Jonathan, please take their bags upstairs. I already put fresh linens on the beds."

Jonathan headed upstairs.

"Thank you, . I'm sorry that it's so late."

"Not to worry. We were still awake."

"What were you two doing up?"

"Never mind all that," Maria said. "We are not too old to do whatever we want to at this hour."

"Okay, okay," Camille laughed. "I don't need to know."

"Mommy," said Aurora, who came out of the kitchen munching on a cookie. "Grandma said we could stay up all night!"

"She did?" Jonathan asked as he came downstairs. "That sounds like fun. Imagine how many games we can all play."

"Grandma was just kidding, honey," Camille said, smiling. "But you can stay up for another hour."

"Yay!" she said, jumping up and down. "Come on, Pop Pop. Let's get some more cookies."

"Okay," he said as Aurora took him by the hand and led him to the kitchen.

"Two more cookies, Aurora," Camille said.

"Okay, Mommy."

"We'll make sure that they're really big ones," Jonathan whispered to Aurora as the two of them disappeared into the kitchen.

"Come on, sweetheart," said Maria. "We can talk tomorrow. Tonight, let's have some fresh-baked cookies and warm milk."

"Just like old times, Mommy?" Camille asked as she put her arms around Maria.

"Just like old times, mija."

Two weeks after moving back into her parent's house, Camille found out that she was pregnant. Aurora was about to have a baby brother or sister. Life was going to become even more challenging, but Camille was ready to face it head on. She had made her bed, so she was damn sure going to lie in it.

Since Jonathan's businesses were running smoothly, he decided to take his best girls on a family vacation, so they all went to Jamaica and Puerto Rico to visit Jonathan's family and Maria's family, respectively. It was a happy and carefree time for Camille. She was able to relax and enjoy time with her daughter. Aurora was a smart and beautiful child who deserved to be happy.

When they returned to Chicago, Camille decided to get a job. Maria was willing to help out with Aurora, so there was no reason for her not to make her own money.

Baxter went on the road, playing over in Europe. He called about once a month to talk to Aurora, and sent a little money when he could. Camille didn't pressure him about it. She didn't even want to tell him about the pregnancy at first, but her parents convinced her that it was the right thing to do. The next time he called, she figured it was as good a time as any. She had several weeks to prepare herself.

"How the fuck did you get pregnant?" Baxter asked, upset.

"How the fuck do you think?" she shot back. "You were there, asshole."

"Was I?"

"Go to hell, Baxter!" she yelled, slamming down the phone.

Fifteen minutes later, Camille cried as she sipped a cup of tea. "Mommy, he had the nerve to be upset and even insinuated that the baby might not be his."

"Oh, mija," Maria said, consoling her. "He didn't mean it."

Camille didn't have time for Baxter's nonsense, so she didn't talk to him anymore when he called. Jonathan talked to him, though. He made it clear to Baxter that he expected him to step up and be a man. He told him to send more money for his family.

Camille began working in one of her father's salons as a receptionist. She wanted to be independent, so she stayed with her parents until after the baby was born and then tried to find a small apartment. However, the harsh Chicago winter was coming and Jonathan felt that there was no need to take on an apartment and a new baby when there was plenty of room for them to stay. Camille reluctantly agreed.

The baby came in the spring. Camille named her new daughter Sharon. She was perfect and looked just like her father, which made it difficult for Camille to forget about Baxter. She was having a hard time forgiving him for not being there for them. When he finally called, Maria insisted that Camille personally tell him about his new daughter.

"So, what did he say?" Maria asked.

"He tried to pretend that he was happy, but I know him. All he heard was that there's another mouth to feed. He wasn't so happy about that."

"Maybe, but deep inside, he must be happy, Camille. He loves Aurora. He'll want to see Sharon, too."

"It's not like he's going to come running back to the States, Mommy."

"What if he does?"

"It's over, Mommy," she said. "I'm not going back to him."

A few months later, Camille found a good job. With Maria's help, her children were being well cared for. Camille began working at an upscale clothing boutique. She was able to make her own hours and enjoyed being around nice clothes. She tried to give her parents some of the money she earned, but they refused to take it, insisting that she would need it to get herself together.

Baxter still hadn't come back from Europe. He couldn't even give Camille a time frame of how much longer he'd be gone. She was very frustrated over his lack of concern for his children. She expressed this to Maria one afternoon.

"Mommy, at this point, he can stay over there forever," Camille said. "He probably has some woman keeping him there."

"Aurora loves her Daddy. Sharon deserves to know him, too. He's not a bad person, mija."

"Oh, all of a sudden you're his biggest fan?"

"He's done some really stupid things with you, Camille. But you have to own your part. You taught him how to treat you, right?"

"What do you mean?"

"The first time he put his hands on you, you should have broken up with him and said something to us. Your father would have taught him a very different lesson."

"We were in high school. I was naive. I thought Daddy would've killed him."

"He might have lived to be a better man."

"Well, we'll never know. I stayed and tried to change him."

"You and he were too young. Not mature enough to be married and have a baby, and you didn't want the same things at the same time. But you love him still, I can tell."

"Well, you're right about *that* Mommy," Camille said.

One day Camille realized that she was wasting some of her talents, so she decided to apply to the University of Illinois. With the support of her parents, she went for her degree in Business. They all pulled together to give the girls a family routine.

During the week, Jonathan made breakfast for everyone while Camille got herself dressed and got the baby up. In the meantime, Maria helped Aurora get ready for school. They started their day as a family before everyone had to go their separate ways.

On her way to campus, Camille dropped Aurora off at school, a few blocks away. Jonathan went to the salon and Maria took care of the house and the baby. If the weather was nice, Maria took baby Sharon in her stroller to pick Aurora up from school and they would stop at a park down the street from the house.

By the time Camille and Jonathan got home, Maria had dinner ready and Aurora had her homework finished. After dinner, Jonathan helped his wife with the dishes while Camille spent time with her girls before putting them to bed. Then, while her parents had a little quiet time together, Camille spent the rest of the evening studying. She studied hard. She was determined to get her degree in record time.

Baxter kept in touch while he played all over Europe. He had quick conversations with Aurora, funny conversations with Sharon as she learned to talk, but rarely spoke with Camille, who was too busy getting her life together to be bothered with his bullshit. She was beginning to feel good about herself and needed to keep her eye on the prize.

Camille's dedication to her education rubbed off well on her daughter. Aurora was a good student like her mother and took her lessons very seriously: including the lessons that her father taught her. He taught her that you couldn't trust love. That even love could walk away from you without warning and without apparent reason. A hard lesson for a young girl to learn, but she was determined to learn it well. Aurora didn't know it at the time, but thanks to her father, a little piece of her heart was frozen. She became slightly introverted and didn't make friends easily.

Aurora loved her little sister, though. She had plenty of room in her heart for little Sharon, who adored her. She was a big help to her mother and the two sisters had a lot of fun together. The ten-year age difference didn't really matter as Sharon got older. She was very smart and wanted to do everything that Aurora did. For that reason, Aurora stayed out of trouble.

Aurora spent a lot of time singing and dancing in her room. She took a few lessons, but wasn't really passionate about it. However, it sparked an interest in Sharon, who was way more talented in those areas than Aurora was. Aurora helped her sister develop her natural gifts. Sharon loved to perform in front of people, so putting together little shows for Sharon and her friends kept Aurora busy. They had talent shows for the neighbors and got generous donations. Aurora used the money to buy costumes and props for the talented boys and girls. After a few successful holiday events, they began to have a show once a month at the dance school around the corner from the Kennedy's house. Camille was very proud of both her daughters.

Eventually, Camille got her degree and was able to start a new job at an international company where she was able to utilize her language skills. Soon after that, Jonathan helped her with a down payment and she bought a three-bedroom townhouse not too far from the Kennedys, where the girls were still close enough to their grandparents to get much needed attention and supervision.

In her freshman year of high school, Aurora needed someone her own age to be close to. She found a kindred spirit and became best friends with Deehna Masters. Deehna was a good student, too. They had a lot of the same classes together. Sometimes people mistook them for sisters. They were both tall and lean with long, pretty hair, but Deehna was a little darker. Her father was black, but her mother was East Indian.

Aurora had known Deehna since they were little, and Deehna always tried to be her friend, but there seemed to be a little jealousy going on. Deehna was very close to her father, who was always around to support his daughter and her activities. Of course, Aurora had Jonathan around, but it wasn't the same. Having her grandfather there to support her was nice, but Aurora really missed having a father to do things with.

One day, Aurora and Deehna tried out for cheerleading. Camille was surprised even though she knew that Aurora liked sports. Jonathan had taken her to a few Knicks games over the years and she understood the game pretty well. If anything, the family would have expected her to play basketball. But since Aurora and her best friend both made the cheerleading squad, she would be shaking pom poms for the next few months.

The family supported Aurora by attending the basketball games. Their team had a pretty good record and she enjoyed herself a lot. The cheerleaders had fun and she got along well with the other girls. At least, most of them. There was a little firecracker named Judy White. She was one of the tough girls who always liked to fight. Aurora stayed away from her and tried to mind her own business. There were girls who didn't like her just because she was light-skinned with long hair.

There was a Puerto Rican boy, a sophomore named Johnny Rodriguez, who liked Aurora. He always tried to carry her books. She thought he was cute, but wasn't trying to be his girlfriend or anything. She liked him as a friend. He was funny and nice to her. He caught up with her one afternoon after her cheerleading practice.

"Hey, Aurora. Wait up."

"Hi Johnny," she said. "What are you doing here?"

"Why you in such a hurry?"

"I have to meet my grandmother out by the front gate."

"Can I walk with you?"

"Sure, I guess. What's up?"

"Can't a friend just walk a friend?"

Aurora rolled her eyes, "If you say so."

She saw other girls falling for boys and getting their young hearts broken at an early age. She wasn't about to let that happen. She wasn't going to fall in love because love wasn't real. Not something that you could depend on. That's another lesson that she had learned from her father. He had taught her well. She wouldn't be letting love fool her, like it did her mother.

***

Baxter finally returned to Chicago after five years of moderate success in the music business. Although he was back in their lives, Camille immediately filed for divorce. It was clear to her that he was not going to be the man she loved ever again. However, he was a changed man and decided not to fight her.

Camille knew she was going to have to prepare Aurora for Baxter's reappearance, but she wasn't sure that her daughter was going to make things easy. Aurora was fifteen now, with all the drama of a teenager, and Sharon was five. Aurora made her displeasure about her father's return known to anyone who would listen. One day Camille decided to have a talk with her. Just because she wasn't going to have a husband anymore didn't mean that her girls should be deprived of their father. That's just what she believed.

"Why are you so angry all of a sudden?" Camille asked her daughter.

"We don't need him," Aurora stated with conviction.

"What are you saying, sweetie? You have a relationship with your father."

"What? Because we talk on the phone sometimes? I don't know him."

"He loves you."

"Yeah, right."

"Don't you want to get to know him better?"

"I don't know."

"That's all you talked about for years."

"Right. And now I'm over it."

"Aurora, he's back and you're going to have to continue a relationship with him."

"Why? You're not gonna take him back, right?"

"That's between us," Camille said. "He's still your father and he wants to spend time with you. Sharon's excited about meeting her Daddy. He wants to see both of you."

"I need time."

"Well, don't take too long. I can't keep him from seeing you. I won't do that."

"Oh, that's just great. Take his side. You don't give a damn about what I want."

Before Camille could respond, Aurora stormed out of the room. Camille took a deep breath and prayed that they would all get through this somehow. It was up to her to help her daughter to forgive. She had to laugh as she realized that she was going to have to do it herself first, and forgiving Baxter wasn't going to be easy.

Baxter wanted to be close to his daughters, so he rented an apartment a few blocks away from Camille's townhouse. He had saved quite a bit of his money from touring, but he took a job working as a security guard for a high-rise office building. That was the money that he gave to Camille for Aurora and Sharon. On the weekends, he played various gigs around town, trying to get his career going again in Chicago.

On a warm, sunny afternoon, one of those perfect Chicago days, Baxter came by to sign the divorce papers.

"Camille, I know that I turned out to be a disappointment as a husband and a father, but I hope that you'll give me a chance to be here for you now."

He looked her directly in her eyes and smiled. He still had the ability to melt her icy wall with those damn dimples.

"As what?" she asked.

"As a friend," he said sincerely. "And as the father of your children. That's all that I really deserve."

"You don't deserve my friendship, Baxter. I don't like you that much anymore."

He visibly flinched. It was as though she had shot a dagger into his heart.

"But because you are the father of my children," she continued. "I will always have love for you. And for that reason, and that reason only, I will agree to work with you. The girls need you in their lives. Especially now that Aurora is a teenager. I won't interfere with that."

"Thank you," Baxter said, relieved.

There was a moment of silence as they looked into each other's eyes. Each one had a flash of what could have been. How that old spark of first love had burned so brightly, but then somewhere along the way, it had exploded and almost consumed them. The fact that they survived and were standing here right now was a testament to how much they were once in love. It was heartbreaking and brought them both to tears.

Almost simultaneously, they reached for comfort in each other's warm embrace. So many emotions, so much wasted time. They both realized that this was their way of saying goodbye to that lost opportunity, to a life that was not going to be.

"What the hell's going on here, Mommy?"

Startled, they quickly separated. They turned to see their very pissed off daughter standing in the kitchen doorway.

"Aurora, watch how you speak to your mother," Baxter said gently.

He was amazed at how much his daughter had grown in five years. She wasn't a little girl anymore. She was a beautiful young lady. "I know I been gone for a while, but you ain't that grown yet."

"You've been back for two seconds," she snapped back.

"Hey, sweetie," Camille said, drying her eyes. "You're early. How was school?"

"What is he doing here?" Aurora pointed accusingly.

"Let's start over," Baxter said, smiling. "Hello, Aurora. It's great to see you. I know this meeting wasn't supposed to happen until you were ready, but hey, that's life. We're here now."

"So you see me. Now what?"

"You're beautiful. Much better than those pictures your Grandma Maria sent me. Looking at you here makes me regret being away so long. You grew up without me and I want you to know that I'm sorry. I missed you, baby girl."

"Is this the part where I'm supposed to forgive and forget?"

"Nobody's saying that, honey," Camille said.

"What do you wanna do?" Baxter asked.

"How should I know?" Aurora cried, frustrated. "You're pressuring me."

"I could really use a hug," he said.

Aurora noted that he looked genuinely remorseful, which was totally confusing to her, because she had spent so much time preparing to hate him when this moment finally came. Now that the time was here, it took all of her strength to resist running into his arms. She had been sure that she was going to be able to put on her icy cold attitude and her father would just be an annoyance that she could ignore. But this was her Daddy in the flesh. Aurora saw Baxter's smile and somehow she was ten years old again and those dimples seemed to have the same affect on her as they did on her mother. She couldn't help but realize how much she loved him.

Aurora remembered all of the fun times that they once had. Then, as quickly, she remembered the pain of her father leaving. She hadn't thought of those things as they casually communicated over the years. He almost didn't seem real then. But, this was real. This was as real as it got. She ran out of the room in tears.

"I guess we all needed to cry today, huh?" Baxter asked.

"She'll come around," Camille said. "Give her time."

"I will."

Although Aurora had a hard time warming up to Baxter, Sharon fell in love with her Daddy immediately. Camille continued to encourage the girls to spend time with him. She had forgiven him in her heart, so even though the divorce became final, they were able to have a friendly relationship and be loving parents. It was good because Baxter really wanted to get to know his daughters and try to make up for lost time.

Baxter started to take some of the responsibility for his daughters from the Kennedys. He would often take Sharon to school and pick her up to give Maria a break. He also showed up for the basketball games to watch Aurora cheer. Although she acted as though it was no big deal, she was secretly hoping that Baxter would show up. Some of her other friends had fathers living at home who didn't come.

Aurora's friend, Deehna, had been encouraging her to be more open to Baxter. Her own father had been suffering from lung cancer for the past two years and wasn't expected to survive past Christmas.

"You're really lucky to still have your father there for you, Rory," Deehna reminded her. "My daddy can't even make it to the games anymore."

"I know, Deehna. I'm really sorry."

"So, do something about it. I like your father. He's trying to get to know you."

So far, Baxter had only missed one basketball game, but that was the night that little Sharon had gotten the flu. He went over to help Camille take care of her. Aurora couldn't be mad at him for that. She began to see that he was really trying to do the right thing. She had spent enough time without him. Maybe it was okay to love him again.

As Aurora got a little busier being a teenager, Baxter took over dealing with Sharon and her performances. Sharon was becoming interested in all aspects of entertainment. Now she wanted to be an actress, too. Baxter was having a great time supporting his little girl's dreams. She really enjoyed having a daddy. However, getting his big girl to enjoy having him around was a much tougher job than he expected. He knew that his actions would speak much louder than his words, so he just wouldn't go away. He and Camille had something going on, although they refused to give it a label.

By Aurora's junior year in high school, she had resigned herself to the fact that her parents were still in love and making it work, living separately but in the same neighborhood. Sixteen-year-old Aurora was finally enjoying her teen years. Having Baxter in her life had brought her out of her shell. She was more popular at school and loved to be involved with the talent programs. She could still sing and dance a little, but mainly liked the whole concept of finding the talent in her fellow classmates and putting shows together for them. She had gotten very good with all that practice she had with Sharon and her friends. Those little divas were perfectionists!

Baxter began recording his original music in a studio. Aurora enjoyed stopping by the studio with her friends after cheerleading practice. It was usually Aurora, Deehna and Janice, the captain of the squad, who was a cute little Jewish brunette who had kinkier hair than either one of them. The girls were interested in the music, but really wanted to check out the musicians. Well, actually only one musician, the drummer, a young man in his early twenties named Dex Taylor. He was from Jamaica and had long, beautiful dreadlocks. Aurora's friends loved his accent and the way that he kept a beat.

One Friday was a typical day when the girls didn't have any special plans after school. While the band was on a break, Baxter ordered a couple of pizzas and they all enjoyed it in the lounge. Deehna went over to the vending machine and bought a couple of sodas. She walked over to Dex.

"I brought you a Mountain Dew," Deehna said, handing him the soda.

"Thanks, Deehna. Ya know it be my favorite."

"Yep."

Janice tried to demonstrate some new moves for the squad, which made Dex laugh. He seemed to be aware of his affect on the young girls, but managed to keep his reactions neutral. He really got a kick out of them, all taking turns to get his attention.

"Alright, let's get back to work," Baxter said. "I wanna lay that last track again. You girls get on outta here."

"Okay, Daddy," Aurora said. "See you tomorrow night?"

"I wouldn't miss it. Biggest game of the season, right?"

"Can me come, too?" Dex asked, smiling.

"Sure!" Deehna replied before anyone else could respond. "It starts at seven."

"Cool, mon. I'll be dere."

Why did that sound like a bit of trouble? Aurora wondered about it for half a second and then it was just as easily forgotten.

CHAPTER 22

Debbie

Debbie Marshall never lost her love of clothes, but New York City could be expensive and since none of her friends had much money to go shopping, which was something that she loved, shoplifting was one of their favorite things to do. They started out with cosmetics at the local drug stores and the next thing you know they were stealing clothes from their favorite boutiques.

It's amazing that they didn't get caught. Luckily, she grew out of that phase before any serious consequences occurred. However, for one of her friends, it wasn't just for fun anymore. It became a serious problem. Rosa, a Puerto Rican girl from her Harlem neighborhood, got addicted to shoplifting to the point where she would go on her own, secretly. She was arrested five times and ended up in a juvenile home until she was eighteen. It was enough to make Debbie take notice.

Bored, without any serious ambition, and looking for a father figure, Debbie was a vulnerable sixteen-year-old teenager when Harold Hamilton walked into her life. He was a twenty-six-year-old substitute teacher who frequented her high school.

The first time that Debbie laid eyes on Harold she had a strange reaction to him. She had walked into her art class late, expecting Mrs. Brown to be standing there absorbed in whatever project that she had prepared for the class. Instead, there was a tall, brown-skinned man with a handsome face and eyes that seemed to look right through her.

His voice was deep and seductive. "How nice of you to join us," he said, smiling. "What's your name and why are you late?"

Debbie hesitated, not used to being called out.

"I'm talking to you," he said, looking directly at her. "Are you deaf?"

The other students began to laugh as Debbie took a seat in the back of the class. What was this guy's problem? She tried to become invisible, but it apparently wasn't working, since this fine chocolate tormenter was making his way over to her desk.

Harold Hamilton had piercing hazel eyes and thick eyebrows. He had a strong face and wore a close-shaven mustache and beard. And apparently, he was not to be ignored. He stopped and stood directly over her. She looked up and got lost in his gaze. Debbie had heard about this substitute teacher whom a lot of girls had a crush on. She thought they were being ridiculous and immature. They had gone on and on about him. He was reported to be handsome, sophisticated and sexy as hell. They sure hadn't lied.

"Well, are you deaf?" he asked, with his intense stare.

"No, I'm not deaf," Debbie said, noticing how good he smelled.

"So, what's your name?" he asked, still smiling.

"Debbie Marshall," she said, staring at his full, sexy lips.

"And why are you late?"

"No reason." Was that a bulge in his crotch?

"See you after class. Perhaps by then you will have thought of something."

For the rest of the hour, all Debbie could think about was what he would look like naked. The idea that she was even thinking about a man in this way was disturbing. Those were not things that she wasted her time on. Girly fantasies were not a part of her life. She was serious and had real issues to deal with. She didn't play with dolls anymore and she sure as hell wasn't thinking about boys or sex. But here she was, thinking about sex. And he was no boy.

For a week, Harold gave Debbie a lot of attention. It made her feel uncomfortable at first, partly because he was her teacher, but mostly because she liked it. She knew that it was wrong, so she rejected his advances, pretending to be oblivious. But she did start to wear lipstick and even took her braids out and wore her hair in a simple ponytail.

When some of the other girls got jealous and began flirting with Harold, he politely ignored them and continued to pursue Debbie, who began to feel special. He had to be very careful, though. The school probably would not look favorably upon one of their teachers having a personal relationship with one of the students.

Harold began to bring Debbie little gifts and offer to take her places. The void in her life began to close a little bit and soon Debbie was able to believe that he genuinely cared only about her.

Next thing you know, Debbie began hanging out with Harold after school, even when Mrs. Brown came back and he was assigned to another school. Usually, he would pick her up a couple of blocks away from school and take her for a ride. He had a cute MG Midget convertible that he kept in mint condition. They would go down to Greenwich Village for a movie or to an arcade, where Harold encouraged her to let loose.

Eventually, Debbie was able to play a mean game of Ms. Pac Man. They had a lot of fun together and she never felt that he was too old to be her friend. He didn't seem to let the age difference bother him either. After a while, Harold would take Debbie to a secluded park where they would drink wine. He never let her drink too much, never tried to get her drunk. He didn't even try to kiss her. He let her do a lot of talking so that he could get to know her better. It made her trust him and confide in him. He realized that she needed someone to talk to and he was happy to be the one. She was a special girl.

With Michael Marshall fairly clueless and out of touch with his daughter, Debbie had free reign to do whatever she pleased. Harold didn't make any physical moves on Debbie, but he showered her with the attention that she needed. He constantly told her how beautiful she was and how much he wanted to put her on canvas. He claimed to be a talented artist. She was still shy, even with him, and ignored his compliments.

"My friend Madeline should be a model, not me."

"Anyone can be a perfect subject on canvas."

Eventually, he was able to talk her into coming to his private studio in Brooklyn. It was a pretty good-sized loft space with a small kitchen, bedroom and bathroom in the back. Once there, she was able to see what kind of work he did. There were mostly portraits of beautiful women in various stages of undress. Very few of the paintings were blatantly revealing any body parts however they all were extremely erotic. She was flattered that he wanted to paint her, but she still didn't think that she looked good enough to be a model. She was totally unaware of her sex appeal.

"A portrait of your back would be perfect. How about that?" he asked. "I think that you have a beautiful back."

Debbie laughed. "You've never seen my back."

"Then it's about time, don't you think?"

She didn't see anything wrong with that. It wasn't the same as being nude. It was all very innocent.

"Alright," she said shyly. "Just my back."

Harold warned Debbie that she was not going to be able to see his work in progress. As he painted her, she would have to wait until he was finished and satisfied with the results. That was the deal and she had to agree. The entire time, he still never made a physical move on her, but somehow he didn't have to.

"What do you want me to do?"

"Don't be shy," he said. "Models are not self-conscious about their bodies."

"I know."

"I'll set up my canvas and you can just go behind that screen over there, take off all your clothes and put on the robe that's hanging there. When you're comfortable, come on out."

After undressing, Debbie slowly walked out and sat on the edge of the table that Harold had set up for her, waiting for him to tell her what to do.

"Are you okay?" he asked.

"Yeah, I'm fine," she replied, her voice soft.

"Good. Now I want you to go around to the other side of the table and sit on the edge just like you're doing now," he said.

Debbie did as she was instructed.

"Now open the robe, lean back and put your hands on the table. Let your arms support you and allow the robe to drop naturally behind you."

Debbie followed his directions.

"Now turn your face to the left and tilt your chin like you're going to let it rest on your shoulder."

"Like this?" she asked, complying with his wishes.

"Just one more thing," he said, walking to her. "Hold still."

Without a word, he gently pulled her hair from the elastic band holding it in place. He used his fingers to spread her hair onto her shoulders and neck. He appeared to be oblivious to her nakedness, but was surreptitiously checking out every tender curve.

"Perfect," he whispered.

For the next thirty minutes, Harold worked furiously on his canvas. He barely spoke to her during this time and she didn't bother him. However, the fact that she was sitting in front of him with nothing on was very exciting to her. She was intrigued by how professional he was and by the fact that he wasn't trying to look at her body without her clothes on.

He didn't want her to get too tired sitting in one position, so he did the painting in three sittings. On the last day that Harold was going to finish the piece, he told Debbie that she didn't need to be present, but she insisted on coming to the studio anyway.

Debbie wore a little sundress that she could easily slip out of. She wanted to be naked again, but he said that he didn't need her to pose anymore and made her sit on the other side of the studio for three hours while he put the finishing touches on the painting. She was eager to see it, but he wouldn't budge.

Impatiently, she listened to music for a while, and then Harold eventually sent her off on an errand to pick up dinner for the two of them at a restaurant down the street. An hour later, after Thai food and a bottle of wine, Harold was ready for her to see his work.

"Are you ready to behold a masterpiece?"

She had been so anxious, and now that it was finally time, she cautiously walked over to stand beside him in front of the canvas. For the first time, Debbie saw herself through his eyes, the eyes of an artist. The portrait was beautiful. She looked like a real woman: a sensuous, mysterious, and desirable woman.

"Wow, do I really look like that?" Debbie wondered out loud over his shoulder.

"Absolutely," he assured her.

He turned his head to look at her while she admired her painted image. The front of her dress was hanging in a way that exposed her beautiful cleavage just inches away from his face. She caught the look of lust in his eyes and it almost frightened her. She jumped back and one of her shoulder straps fell. He stood up and for a moment they were frozen in time. Suddenly, he pulled her away from the canvas and she fell into his arms, where they shared an intense first kiss.

After that, the rest was easy. Harold ravaged her hot, young body for the next two hours and she finally felt like a woman. Once he was able to seduce her, she thought she was in love. She had no idea what she was getting herself into. It was a miracle that no one at her school found out about them. Since Harold worked at other schools, they weren't seen together very often. He was able to keep their secret and Debbie certainly wasn't going to tell anyone. She was smart enough to know that he could get into a lot of trouble if anyone found out that they were having sex. But it was true love after all, so there was no way that she was going to stop seeing him.

There was such a change in Debbie and her attitude. She couldn't think of anything except Harold. She stopped doing her schoolwork and some of her friends were beginning to question her lack of availability. If she was going to ditch school, she was supposed to be hanging out with them. Where was she going and who was she going with? That's what they wanted to know. For Debbie, it was just too many questions.

Desperate to avoid the scrutiny of her high school friends, Debbie decided that she wanted to drop out. She was a week away from her 17th birthday, so she felt that she could make that decision for herself. The way that she was performing in class, she was failing anyway. She knew that she had to tell her family.

While she was at her Grandma and Grandpa Marshall's house for her birthday dinner over the weekend, she decided to tell them first. The news obviously broke their hearts. They knew that she was being challenged, but they had no idea how bad things had gotten for her. They couldn't understand why she would give up her education and of course she couldn't tell them about Harold. She simply insisted that she was never going to graduate at this rate and wanted to become a model.

Her grandparents gave her a gentle lecture, hoping that she would be able to make up her schoolwork and get back on track. They even offered to pay for a tutor, but nothing that they said could persuade her to change her mind. By the time she went back home on Sunday night, they had all but given up on her. Michael was not so gentle.

"Girl, you better get your ass back in school unless you plan to get a job and help me pay these bills."

"I'm not…"

"Forget that," Michael interrupted. "You don't have a choice. You're going back to school tomorrow. You're gonna study hard and start improving your grades so you can graduate, or you can get the hell out of my house."

"Oh, all of a sudden you care about what I do?"

"Don't backtalk me, Debbie. This is still my house."

"Fine," Debbie cried as she ran into her room and slammed the door.

After falling out on her bed for several minutes, she jumped up and ran to her closet, rummaging through items on the floor until she made her way to the back of the closet and found what she was looking for.

Debbie pulled out a large suitcase and a couple of backpacks and proceeded to pack her clothes and personal items in them, slamming things around as she did. Michael heard all the commotion, but didn't pay her too much attention. He assumed that she would go running to her grandparents. She didn't.

When Debbie called Harold and told him that she was quitting school and moving out, she expected him to offer her sanctuary right away. He was shocked and surprised by her decision, but didn't discourage her. He also assumed that she was going to go to her grandparents. Debbie had other ideas. Big ideas that caught him off guard.

"Please, Harold," she begged. "It's not like we won't be spending all of our time together anyway."

"I know, but what about your family? Aren't they going to want to know where you are?"

"I'm going to tell them that I'm staying with Madeline at her sister's house."

"Oh, so you have it all figured out, huh?"

"Yes, I do. So just say yes. Please, please, please!"

Harold resisted for a short time, but he finally gave in and told her that she could move into his studio in Brooklyn, but she had to promise not to tell anyone.

"Well, I have to tell Madeline. She's going to cover for me."

"If you can trust her," he said. "But don't tell anyone else."

"I promise."

The next day, Debbie waited until Michael left the house, and then she grabbed as much stuff as she could carry and met Harold a couple of blocks away. She was on a wild adventure and imagined that she was eloping with the love of her life. She thought the entire thing was romantic. She might have given up playing with her dolls, but the little girl inside of her still believed in fairy tales.

Harold went to work every day, but he didn't stay with her every night. He was there about three nights a week. The rest of the time he was caring for his sick mother in Queens, but she was deliriously happy with whatever time that he spent with her. That fantasy lasted for several months. During this time, Debbie never called Michael. She spoke with her grandparents, so it wasn't like she was missing. She told her family that she was living with Madeline's sister in the Bronx and getting small modeling jobs. They didn't like it, but they saw how happy she was, so they were just thankful that she still came to visit them periodically. Debbie felt that her life was perfect.

Debbie played the happy little teenaged housewife, while Harold went to work every day. He bought her a sewing machine so that she would have something to keep her busy. He even gave her a little money, which she mostly spent on fabrics.

A lot of the nights that Harold was gone, Madeline spent the night with her. Madeline had the perfect model's figure and Debbie used her as a mannequin for the designs she played around with. She was getting really good at designing clothes.

One night Debbie was making a new pantsuit and had Madeline try it on.

"So, has Harold taken you to meet his mother?" she asked.

"Are you crazy? What can he say? Hi, Mom. Here's the girl of my dreams who can get me fired if I tell anyone about her."

"Yeah, I guess you got a point."

"Besides," added Debbie. "I told you that she's sick."

"What's wrong with her?"

"I don't really know."

The more she thought about it, Debbie realized that Harold had rarely talked about his own life. She really didn't know much about him at all. Madeline could sense her friend's discomfort and after a few minutes of silence, decided to change the subject.

"Maybe you should think about taking this fashion design thing seriously, Deb. You really have a gift, you know."

"You'd be my only client," Debbie responded, making one final adjustment. "Okay, it looks great. You can take it off now."

One evening, Debbie was walking home after spending the day with Madeline. They had gone window-shopping in midtown Manhattan, had lunch in the Village, and even caught a matinee. Debbie needed to vent her frustrations about Harold and there was no one who could put things into perspective like her best friend.

Debbie told Madeline about the big fight that she had started with Harold on the phone the night before. She was frustrated by the lack of time that she actually spent with him these days. Since she had left school and moved in, it seemed as though she hardly saw him at all. Weeks had rolled by and it seemed as though Harold had been spending less and less time with her at the studio and more time at his mother's house.

Debbie questioned him endlessly. He hated that, and his patience with her was getting short. One morning while she had him on the phone, she begged him to commit some time to her and he finally agreed to make an extra effort to be there that night, so she decided to prepare a special dinner for the two of them. Harold had a late appointment and wasn't going to get to the studio until after 9pm. It was just after 6:00, so Debbie had plenty of time. She had picked up a couple of Porterhouse steaks, a bag of onions, green beans and some baking potatoes. That was Harold's favorite meal.

When Debbie arrived back at the studio, she noticed that the door was unlocked. She was excited to think that Harold had gotten there early to surprise her. However, it seemed a little too quiet. There were a couple of lights on, but he hadn't turned on any music.

"Harold?" Debbie called out.

There was no response. As she walked through the studio, she felt that something wasn't right. Harold always turned on music or was busy in the front room painting, framing, or cleaning his brushes. She went into the kitchen to put the groceries down.

"Harold, are you here?"

Debbie went back into the workspace and turned on some more lights. Then she saw the last thing that she ever expected to see. There was a woman lying unconscious on the studio floor. She panicked, not knowing what to do. Who was this woman? What was she doing here? Did Harold know her?

Debbie paged him, but when he didn't call her right back, she called Madeline.

"Call 911 and don't touch anything," insisted Madeline, who watched a lot of cop shows on TV. Debbie did what she was told.

By the time the paramedics arrived, along with their many questions, Debbie was in a state of shock. She lied and said that she had arrived at the studio for a modeling job. She also told them that the door was open when she arrived and that she had never seen the unconscious woman before, which was true. Madeline arrived shortly after they rushed the woman to the hospital. In the bathroom, they had found sleeping pills and a note addressed to Harold. Apparently, the woman who attempted suicide in the middle of their apartment was Harold's wife.

"Well, I'll be damned," Madeline said. "That bastard!"

In what would be the longest night of her life, Debbie waited for Harold to call. He never did. Madeline stayed with her and then insisted that she move out that night.

"Forget that asshole, Debbie. He's not going to call you. Let's just pack your shit and get the hell out of here." Madeline was insistent. "And bring that painting of your naked ass with you."

Madeline vowed to Debbie that she would help her to learn the truth about Harold. Debbie didn't dare try to go back to Michael's. Instead she went to the Marshalls, who let her stay with them. They didn't ask too many questions. Her grandparents were simply happy to have her back.

In the meantime, Madeline discovered that most of what Debbie believed about Harold wasn't true. He had led her to believe that he was single, but in truth he was a married man with a two-year-old daughter. The sick mother that he took care of in the Bronx? She had died four years ago. Madeline was also able to find out that Harold had already been warned a few times about getting too involved with his young students, but he had never been disciplined.

"Madeline, you should really go after a job with the FBI," teased Debbie, who was able to find humor in her situation, despite the fact that she was hurting.

Madeline anonymously turned Harold in by calling the Board of Education and reporting his involvement with Debbie. This time, there was no getting out of the mess. The police arrested Harold Hamilton and charged him with statutory rape. An ugly scandal followed the trial, which continued for months, and dragged Debbie's whole family into it. Harold's wife, who had lapsed into a coma after the night at the studio, had remained hospitalized for several weeks before recovering. She eventually filed for divorce and sole custody of their child.

Michael Marshall wanted to beat the hell out of Harold, but he blamed Debbie equally. He demanded that she come back home, so out of guilt, Debbie went, but whatever was left of Michael's heart had been shattered. Michael couldn't deal with her. He tried to get her to go back to high school, but she was not his little girl anymore. She had a mind of her own.

Debbie didn't realize how her behavior had been affecting Michael. He was so depressed that he dove back into his vodka bottle and this time it killed him. He got drunk one night, got into his car and wrapped himself around a tree in Brooklyn. It was the eighteenth anniversary of Valerie's death, Debbie's eighteenth birthday. So now and for the rest of her life, her birthday will be remembered as the day that her mother and father left her in the world to carry on without them.

The Marshalls had to find the strength to bury their beloved son. Now they would have to focus all of their love and attention on their troubled granddaughter. Debbie appeared to deal with the whole situation very well, but the truth was that she was simply numb. So much had happened to her in her short life and she had always managed to bounce back even stronger. She always felt that she had to be strong for Michael's sake. He had carried enough grief for both of them. However, it was not meant to be this time. There was no bouncing back from this.

There weren't a whole lot of people at Michael's funeral. Most of the mourners were there for the Marshalls. Madeline was there for Debbie, of course. There were also a few of Michael's old co-workers. John Becker, Michael's best friend from college, unexpectedly arrived. Debbie liked him a lot. He had come around periodically over the years. He was a movie producer out in Hollywood now, so he was always very busy, but he showed up to say goodbye to his friend. He found Debbie after the funeral.

"Hey, little girl," he said, smiling.

"Hi, John," she smiled back.

"How you holding up, kid?" he asked sincerely.

"I guess I'm alright."

"Come here." He pulled her into a comforting hug. "You're going to be alright, Debbie." He let go of her and looked in her lovely, sad brown eyes. "Michael loved you very much. I know he had a funny way of showing it, but that man lived for you."

"I know," Debbie said, putting her head down.

John gently lifted her chin.

"Listen to me. I want you to know that if you ever need anything, anything at all, don't hesitate to call me. I mean it. Here, I'll give you my card." He took out a pen and wrote on the back of one of his business cards.

"This is my private number. Make sure that you use it. Check in from time to time and let me know how you're doing."

She took the card and absently put it in her purse. "Thanks."

He hugged her again and kissed her on the cheek. "I'm going to say goodbye to the Marshalls and then I have to catch a plane back to LA."

In the days after Michael's funeral, Debbie finally broke down. Not in front of her grandparents, but when she was alone or with Madeline. A week later she was still inconsolable. Madeline was worried about her friend. She gave Debbie a really big hug and let her cry on her shoulder as they sat in Debbie's bedroom at the

Marshall's. Debbie's grandfather had already made arrangements to move all of her things to their house and dispose of the items in Michael's apartment.

"I can't do this, Madeline," Debbie cried. "I'm suffocating."

"Here," Madeline said as she released Debbie and handed her a tissue. "You done soaked up my blouse, girl. It can't absorb no more water."

Debbie proceeded to blow her nose.

"I think you just need a little vacation," Madeline suggested. "Maybe we can go to Great Adventure or something."

Debbie looked at Madeline, who was very serious. The thought of all of her problems being solved by riding roller coasters and eating cotton candy made her smile. This time she was the one to give her friend a really big hug. She even began to chuckle.

"I love you, Madeline," she said. "Thank you for always being there for me. I'll never forget that."

"Stop being so dramatic," said Madeline. "I ain't goin' nowhere."

Debbie knew that, because she was the one who had to get away. Everything about her life was different and now she wanted to get as far away from New York as possible. She vowed never to celebrate her birthday again. Her mother died on the day she was born and now her father died on the same day. April 20th was a day to forget.

Because she didn't have the heart to say her final goodbyes in person, Debbie waited until everyone was asleep, and then took the letters that she wrote for her grandparents and for Madeline, left them on the kitchen counter, and headed to the Port Authority Bus Terminal. She had no idea where she was going to go or what she was going to do. She just knew that she needed a major change if she was going to survive.

As Debbie sat at the bus station trying to figure out what to do, a familiar face passed by and smiled at her. It was Lola Molina, a beautiful young Cuban girl who went to her high school and dropped out about the same time. They were never friends, but they recognized each other. A while later Lola came and sat next to her.

"Hi," she said. "Don't I know you from school?"

"Yeah, I recognize you."

"I'm Lola," she said. "And you're Debbie, right?"

"Yeah." Debbie was a little reluctant. She wasn't in the mood to talk.

"So, where are you off to?" Lola asked cheerfully.

"What?"

"I see you got a suitcase, so where you going?"

"Um…I don't know."

Lola looked at her for a minute and then began to laugh.

"What's so funny?" Debbie asked.

"I don't know."

"Whatever. Where are *you* going?"

***

Debbie and Lola arrived in Miami where Lola's three cousins lived in a large beach house. They were successful models who were often out of town working. This was one of the rare times that they were all home at the same time. They were more than happy to play host to their cousin and her friend.

Victor and Vito were gorgeous identical twins. They were twenty and very much in demand for runway and print. Their older sister, Meline, was a world-traveling runway model. They loved Lola, who had visited them every summer, even before they moved out on their own, and had spent two years trying to convince her mother to let her come and live with them, but Lola's mother was traditional and believed that modeling was not a respectable career choice, but apparently working at Burger King was.

Lola finally turned eighteen and made up her own mind. She was on the first bus rolling south. And after thirty minutes of swapping high school horror stories and fifteen minutes of glamour stories about her cousins' life in South Beach, she was able to talk a confused and reluctant Debbie into making the trip with her.

"You never know what's waiting," Lola said, excitedly. "It'll be an adventure."

As a matter of fact, after talking on the bus and looking at Debbie's design photos, Lola was sure that Debbie's talents as a seamstress would come in handy when she and the cousins were looking for something unique to wear out to the clubs. Debbie could be just the extra boost they needed to stand apart in that fashion forward city.

Debbie lasted only a few months in Miami. She liked the city, with all of its beaches and flashy nightlife, but she just couldn't get used to the cousin's lifestyle. Victor, Veto and Meline were cool, but they were fast, fun and rich, which was a dangerous combination. They liked to party a bit too much for her taste. They had money and spent it. They always had people hanging around drinking and taking drugs. Half the time, people didn't even bother to put on clothes. It was all too loose and easy.

Lola pushed Debbie to sew party clothes for her cousins. They were willing to pay and she made money of her own, but she didn't want to continue living off these people and she couldn't afford to pay for the luxury. She still had most of the money that the Marshalls kept in a bank account for her, but needed that to last as long as possible. Lola's cousins and their friends paid well for her sewing skills, but she could see herself easily getting caught up with these young, wild and beautiful people.

Since Debbie wanted to be on her own, she would have to learn to be disciplined. Even she knew that this lifestyle would be her demise if she continued. Somehow, between taking care of her father all those years and going through her ordeal with Harold, she had grown up. She understood herself a little better and came to the conclusion that she needed a little more structure than this Miami life was going to offer. She decided to save some money and head west. That's where she initially thought she would end up when she left New York. Meeting Lola was a detour. She was still being pulled by the idea of Los Angeles. She loved the ocean in Miami, and she would miss living on the beach with the beautiful people, but guess what? They had an ocean over there on the west coast, too. Her mind was made up.

Debbie decided to make one last collection of party dresses. She decorated them with fancy beads and feathers, anything to make them look like the expensive designer gowns. She sold them to Meline and her model friends for an outrageous amount that they were willing to pay. Within a week she was saying goodbye. Of course, they threw Debbie a wild party to wish her well and send her off in grand style. She couldn't even stay long enough to enjoy it. She called a cab, hopped on a Greyhound Bus and headed to the only place that she imagined being happy. Los Angeles, California.

CHAPTER 23

Candy

By the time Candy Martin was in high school, instead of being the outcast, she and her newfound confidence had worked her into a position where she was popular. The truth was that she had a beautiful face. She had actually grown into her big head and she had perfect skin and perfect teeth. As a matter of fact, if Candy didn't look in the mirror every now and then, she would have forgotten that she was black. African black.

"Are you still a virgin?" Katie inquired one day.

"Of course. I'm not thinking about anything like that."

"Girl, don't you go messin' around with none of those little, no good, nappy headed boys at school."

"Don't worry, Mama, I'm saving myself for a white man."

Candy was on a mission. She started by making friends with the white girls who were anxious to be friends with her. The black girls couldn't stand her. They thought her to be pretentious and arrogant. But the white girls seemed to be intrigued with the way that she carried herself. They treated her like she was some kind of freak, but a really cool freak that they wanted to hang around. She had one black girlfriend, who was also an outcast. She was a junior, her name was Anasi, and she was from Nigeria. A real African. The funny thing was that Candy was even darker than her.

The black guys at Candy's school thought that she was interesting, with her good manners and proper way of speaking, but they weren't attracted to her. She figured that they were intimidated. Some of the white guys thought that she was exotic, but most seemed afraid to cross the line. However, she did have three invitations to her senior prom. One was from Anasi's older brother, John, and the other two were from white boys. Talk about progress.

Candy damn near revolutionized her high school by going to the senior prom with Willard Branson, a freckle-faced redhead, who couldn't be much whiter. They made an odd pair. What no one knew is that they had been secretly dating for months, but decided to "come out" for prom.

Willard had a crush on Candy from the time they started high school. He had fantasized about her dark, chocolate skin against his pale, white body. He was the type of kid who didn't get off by looking at Playboy magazines. His erotic book of choice was National Geographic. Something about those naked African women with their dark, pointed nipples just made his teenaged blood boil with desire.

Willard and Candy began studying together after school and he had noticed that sometimes Candy didn't wear a bra. If he got lucky, she would bend over for some reason or another and he could see her naked breasts. Those dark, pointy nipples were what his wet dreams were made of. Willard was determined to make Candy his girl. Of course, he never told anyone about these fantasies, but since his parents were kind of liberal, he knew that dating black women wouldn't upset them too much. It's just that South Carolina wasn't the ideal place to be carrying on with a very dark girl. A black girl, no problem. But a *black*, black girl…Yikes!

The night of the prom, Willard thought that he had died and gone to heaven. He drove to Candy's house in his classic T-Bird. Katie was thrilled to see Candy going to the prom with this young, white boy. He looked nervous holding onto a plastic container that held a pink corsage. She couldn't believe that this pale, skinny thing standing in front of her was taking her baby to the prom.

Willard's family had a little money, and apparently had no problem with Willard dating a black girl. At least, that's what he said. Gwen was less impressed. She was constantly flip-flopping on her position. Now she thought Candy should have gone on to the prom with the African boy. Gwen said that they would have looked good together. This little pasty faced boy was going to be nothing but a whole lot of trouble.

"You gonna try and keep her out all night, boy?" Gwen growled, as she sipped on her glass of whiskey.

"Leave the boy alone, Momma," Katie admonished. "It's prom night."

"So?" Gwen persisted.

With perfect timing, Candy appeared in a beautiful, pale pink, silk gown that showed off her lovely cleavage. Willard almost had a hard-on right there in the middle of the living room. As he rushed to put the corsage on Candy's wrist, he accidentally brushed up against her breasts. Under the silk bodice was a bare nipple. The hard-on now raged in its full glory. Embarrassed, he got them out of there quickly.

Willard had a bottle of chilled champagne waiting in the car. By the time they got to the prom, they were nicely buzzed. Most everyone was shocked to see Willard and Candy walking into the school auditorium hand in hand. They knew how to make an entrance. Looking at the faces of her white girlfriends and their dates made Candy giggle as she and Willard moved toward them.

"I imagine they'd have the very same looks on their faces if I had walked in here with Abraham Lincoln," she whispered.

Eventually, their circle of friends got over the shocking news and managed to have a good time. At the end of the night, Willard and Candy gathered with a few select couples at a nearby motel. After more drinking and a little pot smoking, Willard and Candy retired to their room, where he had his fantasy fulfilled and she lost her virginity.

After that, the odd couple dated hot and heavy. She had her eye on Willard because he wanted to be a doctor. That would make him a desirable husband. Candy knew that Willard was crazy about her and would be devoted. In the fall, Willard was heading to California to begin his medical career. He had received a scholarship to USC, and she was on her way to a small college in nearby Columbia to study cosmetology.

High school graduation was a big deal for the Martin family. Candy was the only one to make it through without dropping out or getting pregnant. Katie was so proud. She attended the graduation in all of her finery, taking pictures and crying. Even Gwen managed to not be drunk.

"You'll make a fine doctor's wife," said Katie. "Willard will take care of you."

Gwen pulled Candy to the side.

"Listen, gal. It's gonna be twenty years before that boy pays off his school bills. Go get your beauty license, get a job and take care of your damn self."

A week after graduation, one of Candy's friends from Miss Kelsey's told her about a tryout for a local beauty pageant, which was taking place in Columbia. Candy knew that being a pageant contestant was something expected from Miss Kelsey's girls, but she hadn't seriously thought about it. Her mother had thought about it, though, and once Katie found out about the tryout, there was no way for Candy to get out of it.

Candy talked to Willard to get his opinion and he told her to go for it. Candy appreciated all of the support, but she didn't feel much like a beauty queen. She knew that she had some good qualities, but looking in the mirror, she didn't see a beautiful woman. She saw an improved woman and that was good enough for her. Katie wore her down, so after a little contemplation, Candy did make it to the tryout, and to her surprise, got into the competition.

After Willard left for USC, Candy went into full pageant mode. She and Katie went to work making dresses and trying out different makeup ideas suggested by the beauty magazines and the classes at school. Candy was excited about something for the first time in a long time. It gave her a purpose to compete on the basis of her looks. Who would have thought that the "little monkey" could compete as a beauty queen?

In her first competition, Candy came in fourth place, which only spurred her on to want to try out for other pageants. Much of the time, she was the only black girl, but that only made her try harder. She had no great talent, but the singing lessons from Miss Kelsey's were enough. She had a lot of everything else. Her body was perfect for strutting in a swimsuit. With her poise, charm and excellent communication skills, she became a good competitor.

Willard came home for Christmas. Candy barely recognized him. His pale skin was red and his red hair was blond. He had become a poster boy for Southern California. He was excited to see Candy and wanted to hear all about her beauty pageant career. They spent two weeks catching up, which led to talk about the future.

"I wanna marry you, Candy," he said one night in his car.

They had just come from the movies and he was dropping her off at home. She barely had a reaction.

"Really, Willard," she said, turning her head away from him. "Tell me something I don't already know."

Willard's red face turned even redder.

"What kind of acceptance to a proposal is that?" he asked.

"Well, what kind of low class proposal is that?" she shot back. "You didn't even get on your knees."

"We're sitting down," he replied.

"Then you should have waited until you were standing up so you could get down and do it like a normal person."

He couldn't believe that they were having this conversation.

"When has either one of us been normal?" he asked, with a grin. "I just figured I would let you know what I was thinking."

"Now you're being ignorant," she said, crossing her arms.

"That's it," Willard yelled. "We are not gonna have this conversation. You're gonna get out, I'm gonna pull off, you're gonna go inside and we'll talk tomorrow, okay?"

Without a word, Candy looked straight ahead and didn't move. After waiting several minutes, he finally got out of the car and went around to her door. He opened her door to help her out. She silently took his hand and walked towards her front door.

"Hey, Candy," he called after her.

She stopped, but didn't turn around. "Hay is for horses."

"I'm sorry, Candy," he said, sincerely. "Please come back."

After a slight hesitation, she turned around to see Willard on his knees, with his hands reaching out to her. She slowly walked back with a little smile on her face.

"Yes?"

"Will you marry me?" he asked, sincerely.

"Where's my ring?" she asked, with her hands on her hips.

"Well, I just thought of this whole thing a little while ago."

"What?" Candy couldn't believe her ears. "How long have we been together?

"I mean, of course I thought about it…I mean…I just wasn't prepared with a ring and everything."

"You're a fool, Willard Branson. A ring *is* everything."

Willard was left kneeling on the ground as Candy stomped off into her house and slammed the door behind her.

Realizing that Willard only had a few days before he had to leave, Candy decided to forgo the usual torture and forgive him quickly, especially when he showed up with flowers the next day. They were talking about their lives again. He shared with her how full his schedule was and the difficulties and pressures of being at a school like USC. She felt that her life was equally difficult as she navigated through the pageant world. He was patient and humored her as she entertained him with beauty pageant horror stories.

His last night in town, Willard took Candy to an expensive restaurant for steak, lobster and champagne. Oh, and for dessert…a beautiful, diamond engagement ring, which he presented while on one knee.

"Candy Martin, will you marry me?"

"Now, you're talking, college boy," she said, sticking out her left hand. "Wait until my mama sees this!"

Two hours later, Candy was standing in her mother's kitchen. Katie was ecstatic.

"Girl, that thing looks real!" she said, grabbing her hand.

"Of course it's real, Mama," Candy said, looking at Willard. "He knows better."

Willard was grinning from ear to ear. He knew that he was in for some good hot sex before the night was over.

After Willard went back to California, Candy had her eye on winning one of those pageants. Willard suggested that she get more involved in the local black pageant arena. She might have a better chance of beating some of the black girls without her qualities. The funny thing was that she had tried that, but didn't enjoy the black pageants. Every time she entered one of those, she couldn't even make the first cut. She felt that all the glory went to the lighter girls with the longer, straighter hair. Of course, that wasn't the reality. There were lovely black women of all shades, but it was mostly her attitude that prevented the judges and other girls from liking her. She appeared to be above the whole thing and couldn't be bothered.

Deep inside, Candy was intimidated by the black women around her. They reminded her of how she was never considered to be beautiful amongst her own kind. With the white folks, she was a rare beauty: a novelty. Her dark skin and beautiful complexion led her into the top ten each time, although never closer than second place. She was not to be deterred. She finally won a regional competition which led her to the Miss South Carolina pageant. She didn't get past the first round there, but it made the beauty queen feel like royalty. She could retire her crown.

After graduating from beauty school the following summer, Candy was ready for a change. She and Willard were still talking about getting married, but he was dragging his feet. He didn't come home for the last spring break and spent his vacation in San Diego with friends from school. Since Candy couldn't get away, they hadn't seen each other since Christmas. It was time for serious preparations, which required desperate measures. She decided to move out to Los Angeles to speed this marriage thing along.

Katie was happy to see her daughter taking her life into her own hands, although she was sad to see her go. She and Gwen cooked a special dinner for Candy and her friends the night before she left. As Candy walked her guests to the door, Katie turned to Gwen, who took a shot of whiskey, belched and looked back at her.

"Our tar baby's all grown up now," Gwen said. "Time for some little yellow babies to be runnin' around here."

"Don't let Candy hear you talkin' like that. You know she gets all sensitive."

"She the one always talkin' about how she don't want no black babies. I'm just sayin' it, too."

"What are you two hens cackling about?" said Candy as she returned.

Gwen took another swig. "Talkin' bout you, gal, and all your high falutin'…"

Katie interrupted. "Now, you make sure that y'all come back here to Camden when you get married."

"None of that runnin' off to Vegas shit," Gwen added.

"Of course not, Mama," Candy assured. "I wouldn't deprive you of the opportunity to plan a wedding."

That made Katie grin broadly. "It'll be an event fit for a queen. You know that."

“I know,” replied Candy, kissing her cheek. “I have to go start packing now.”

Candy ran off happily.

“Yeah, you do that,” laughed Gwen, who was well on her way to being drunk. “And don’t forget the suntan lotion.”

“Shut up, Mama!” Katie snapped.

Two weeks after arriving in Los Angeles, Candy celebrated her twenty-first birthday, landed a job doing makeup for a music video production company, and moved into an apartment near Willard’s campus. She shared the three-bedroom place with two female USC students. Willard was very busy with a full schedule of classes and chose to continue living on campus. Their time together was limited and he always seemed to be too busy. How was she ever going to plan a wedding when she could barely get a date?

Early one morning when she was scheduled to do make-up for a photo session, the job got cancelled. She decided to surprise Willard at his dorm room. She went in and realized immediately that his bed hadn’t been slept in. She was confused, because they had spoken on the phone around 11pm the night before and he was going to be up studying all night. She decided to wait. Maybe he went over to the library and fell asleep there. After a couple of hours, she decided to leave a note and go home.

As she wandered down the hall, disappointed, she thought she heard his drunken laughter coming from around the corner. She stood still and waited. What she saw made her want to run away. There was her red-faced surfer dude, arm in arm, and chuckling it up, with what could only be described as an ugly, black drag queen.

Needless to say, Candy lost her charm school manners and proceeded to beat the crap out of Willard. The drag queen was able to pull Candy off of Willard, and then quickly let her go as Willard ran as fast as he could down the hall and out of the building.

“That’s right,” Candy yelled after him. “Run like a little bitch. You better hope that you never see me again.”

She brushed herself off, surprised at her behavior and language in public. The drag queen smiled with his hands on his hips, and in a perfect baritone said, “You got yourself a freaky little white boy right there.”

Candy looked him up and down. "Not anymore," she said as she strutted off.

"Nice meeting you," the drag queen said.

Candy never looked back.

CHAPTER 24

Portia

Portia Taylor had given up the waitressing job at the Vegas strip club for large women because she was tired of the manager trying to get her up on stage. She had to agree with him that she would have made a damn good stripper, but she just didn't see herself in that role. Portia was almost naked already in the cocktail waitress costumes that she wore. She decided to save her money and put up with the job for a little while. She had put up with it for four years. That was long enough.

While working at the club, Portia began to have a warped idea about her body. The men came there to look at women like her. They loved her body and she loved the attention, but she couldn't date clients. Most of the men who she served at the club were married. Some even admitted that it was a secret desire to be with a big woman while they had a thin woman at home. Some even had a fetish for fat women. They considered some of the strippers too little, even though they were even bigger than her.

During that same time, Portia had claimed a few boyfriends, if you could call them that, men that she met outside of her work environment. These were decent men who seemed to like her voluptuous body, but ended up dumping her for skinnier girls. Just like the men at the club. She couldn't find a real man, just the ones in fantasy land. It happened enough times to make her insecure about a body that she always loved.

Portia had recently gotten dumped by someone who she had dated for a couple of months, but he never took her out in public. She finally confronted him and he admitted that he was embarrassed because he was used to dating women who were in shape.

"What the hell does that mean?" she asked when she related the story to her best friend. "I'm in shape! It's called large. That's the shape!"

"Shame on you," Dana replied. "One dumb ass man's opinion don't define you."

"Three times, Dana," she cried. "Three times in the past year is not a freakin' coincidence. They all think I'm too big."

"You don't know if that was the reason every time," Dana continued. "What about Harrison? You said that he encouraged you to eat because he liked your curves."

"Yeah, then I found out he was doing it so that other men would find me unattractive and I would keep my ass home."

"I forgot about that," Dana said. "What a jerk!"

"I'm done!"

"Portia, you will find a man who loves you for you. If you give up, we will never be able to double date again."

"Oh, okay," Portia laughed. "At least I have that to look forward to."

***

After quitting the club, Portia worked a variety of side jobs while taking some college classes, but she just couldn't figure out what to do with the rest of her life. At twenty-six, she felt like time was slipping away. She was ready for a serious relationship, but her only prospects were built for short term only.

"Where are all the single black men, Dana?" Portia asked impatiently.

"It's only been a half hour," Dana replied, smiling. "Just give it time. They'll be coming in droves."

Portia and her funky friend, Dana Turner, were working side by side as cashiers for the Auto Show at the Las Vegas Convention Center. Portia wasn't really into cars, but Dana had done it the year before and couldn't stop talking about all of the sexy men. Eventually, there were a lot of men, but not many of them were paying Portia much attention. There were so many skinny model types and flashy women with silicone boobs running around that the men barely noticed her and her hefty beauty. By lunchtime, she was starving and exhausted from flashing her pearly whites and pumping up her ample cleavage.

"Let's go get a burger," Portia suggested.

"I told you, girl. I'm on my week of veggies. I brought carrot sticks and celery sticks with cottage cheese dip."

"Sounds yummy. Now come on with me while I get a double cheeseburger, fries and a shake."

"Okay," Dana said with a sideways glance. "It's your ass."

"Whatever, Bugs Bunny. Let's just get something to eat."

As the pair walked through the lobby on their way to the food court, Portia couldn't help but notice that the Convention Center was filling up with quite a few fine men..

"Things are looking up," Dana observed.

"Humph," Portia grumbled.

An hour later, back at her post, Portia spotted a gorgeous young hunk standing in her line, smiling at her from six people back. He was looking at her with such lust that she found herself blushing. She couldn't maintain eye contact and continued to avoid him until she had no choice. He was finally standing right in front of her.

"Hi, beautiful," he smiled with his perfect teeth.

Portia finally looked up and stared directly into his sexy brown eyes. He was tall and had a buff body that didn't really match that baby face. Why did he have to look like he just got out of high school? It took her a second to find her voice.

"Good morning. How many tickets would you like?"

"Four please."

"For the wife and kids?" Portia queried innocently.

His response was an even bigger smile. "What's your name?" he asked.

"You don't need to know that in order to enter the show."

"No, you're right. But I need to know that if I'm going to ask you to marry me."

Portia looked at him like he was crazy, but crazy was looking pretty damn good.

"Please. You're holding up the line."

"Then you better hurry up and answer my question. I'm Chuck Adams and I think I just fell in love for the first time." He put out his hand, glanced at her cleavage and licked his lips.

Portia, who was flustered, shook his big, strong hand. "My name's Portia."

"Okay, Portia," he smiled. "Can I see you after the show?"

"That'll be twenty-four dollars."

"Wow. I would've paid a hell of a lot more for a voluptuous sister like you."

Portia had to laugh. "The tickets, stupid."

"Oh, right." He handed her the money and she handed him four tickets. He grabbed her hand. "So, what time do you get off?"

"Six o'clock!" Dana piped up from the next window.

Portia turned to give her a dirty look. Dana ignored her.

"I'm not going out with you," she said to Chuck, pulling her hand back. "Now go away and enjoy the show."

"Alright, but you don't know what you're missing." He leaned over to speak more quietly to her. "I know exactly what to do with a big boned woman. Um hmmm."

Chuck smiled and winked. As he walked away, Portia couldn't help but follow him with her eyes, even as she took the next customer. He had a nice walk and a nice butt.

"Damn," she said under her breath. "Why did he have to be so damn young?"

"You're a fool, Portia," Dana said.

The rest of the day went by quickly because they were very busy. The Auto Show was a popular attraction to Las Vegas natives as well as to the thousands of visitors. Portia and Dana worked for a company that hired workers for the various conventions and special events at the Convention Center. A lot of them were corporate events that were boring to them, but this one was fun. There were a lot of beautiful people. And one particularly beautiful man who Portia couldn't stop thinking about.

The girls had a couple of short breaks during the day, which they took together. As they sat in the lobby drinking water, Dana spotted a guy that she used to date.

"Oh, my God!" she whispered.

"What's the matter?" Portia inquired.

"Hey, Nick!" she called out.

Nick excused himself from the group of guys he was with and headed over to Dana with a big smile on his face. He was very handsome, but only about 5'6" tall, two inches shorter than her.

"Dana Miller! What's up, girl? You working here?" He gave her a big hug.

"Was it the lovely uniform that gave it away?"

He looked around at the other people wearing black pants and white shirts who are working the convention. "Either that or there's a major fashion crisis in town."

"You're right," she laughed.

"So, everything's going well with you?" he asked.

"I'm good. Haven't seen you in a while, though. Where you been?"

"Living in Phoenix for the past two years. I started a construction company there with my Uncle Jim and my cousin Edward. We've been doing extremely well."

"I'm so happy to hear that, Nick. You always were smart with that kinda stuff."

Nick looked at Portia. "How are you?"

"You remember my friend, Portia Taylor?"

"Of course. I see you're having the fashion challenge, too."

"Guilty as charged."

"Who did you come here with?" Dana asked. "That looked like Jason and Pete."

"Yeah, Pete's getting married and we came in town early for the bachelor party."

"Really?" Dana responded. "Tell them to come over and say hello. We're at the cashier's booth."

"As a matter of fact, we have to get back," Portia added. "Break time is over."

"You know my friend Jason had a serious crush on you, Portia," Nick added. "We're talking years."

Portia used to have a little crush on Jason, too. He wasn't that handsome to her, but he was always a gentleman. She also thought that he had a great body and she particularly liked his chest.

"Really?" she asked, truly surprised. "I thought he was dating Lori Pinto for the past hundred years."

"That didn't stop him from wanting to get with you. For the record, they finally broke up last year."

"Jason was always cool with me, but I'm hardly his type."

"You never know. He always complained that Lori was too skinny. She never wanted to eat."

Portia laughed. "Well, I'm definitely not that type."

"Jason was always comparing her to you. He wanted to know what it would feel like to hug up on a real woman.

"Is that so?" Portia asked.

"Maybe we can all go out for a drink tonight."

"See, Portia," said Dana. "You are just a popular gal today."

"Whatever. Let's go before we become unemployed."

"Alright," Nick said. "We'll check you all out later."

"We'll be here until six." Dana gave Nick a huge kiss. "Great to see you."

The girls rushed back to their posts. "Damn, I still can't believe you ever dated him," Portia said. "He's so short."

"Are you kidding?" Dana quipped. "He eats the best pussy in Las Vegas."

At five o'clock, Nick came to Dana's window. His friends were waiting close by.

"So, we're gonna do a little wedding commitment stuff and then we're heading back to Jason's for a barbecue. Just wanted to invite you ladies to come on by and join us anytime after seven. Very casual. Bring your swimsuits."

"Cool," said Dana. "You wanna come, Portia?"

"I'll think about it."

"Well, here's the address," Nick gave Dana a piece of paper.

"Yeah, I remember."

"Hey, Portia," Nick said. "Jason's a little shy, but he wants to hang with you."

Portia looked over at Nick's friends. Jason waved at her. She waved back.

"We'll be there," said Dana. "Should we bring anything?"

"Just your lovely selves," Nick answered.

"Cool."

"See you later, then."

Nick walked away and left with his friends. Dana turned to Portia, who put up her hand before Dana could speak.

"I said I'll think about it and I meant it, so don't bug me."

At 5:45, Portia looked up and saw Chuck Adams standing in the lobby watching her. If he wasn't so damn charming, it would have been a little creepy. He didn't seem to have any fear of rejection.

"That boy isn't giving up easily," said Portia.

"Oh, I forgot about your new admirer over there," Dana said. "He promised to put a hurtin' on your big ass."

"Shut up, Dana."

As Portia was closing up her window, Chuck approached her.

"Can we talk for a minute?" he asked.

"We have to go and reconcile our cash boxes."

"Will you come back and talk to me when you're done?"

"I'm sorry…" Portia began.

"Please," he clasped his hands together and flashed the smile again. High voltage. She couldn't resist. "Alright, for a few minutes."

Grinning, he said, "I'll be waiting right here."

Twenty minutes later, Portia and Dana headed back to the lobby. "So, I'm gonna go home and get cute," Dana said. "Then I'll pick you up around 8:00."

"Okay, I'll be ready," said Portia as she saw Chuck waiting. "See you later."

Chuck came to meet Portia half way. He was so confident and manly as he spoke. "Thanks for not ducking out the back door."

"Don't think it didn't cross my mind," Portia laughed.

"Now why would you want to avoid me? I'm a good guy."

"How old are you, Mr. Good Guy?"

"Aw, come on. You can't hold my youthful good looks against me."

"Not if you're old enough to drink," Portia said.

"I'm gonna be twenty-one next month."

"Oh, Lord! I knew it. You're just a baby."

"Really?" Chuck boldly grabbed Portia around her waist and pulled her to him, immediately planting a sexy, wet kiss on her lips. She was so stunned that she didn't even try to stop him when he slipped his hot tongue into her mouth. She liked it and was beginning to kiss him back. It was several seconds before she heard someone whistle and remembered that she was in the middle of the lobby of the Las Vegas Convention Center. She quickly backed off and pushed him away. She was lightheaded.

"Damn, you're a sexy woman," Chuck said.

"Oh, my goodness. We have to get out of here."

Portia rushed towards the front door with Chuck following close behind. She didn't turn around until she got to her car in the huge parking lot. When she stopped, Chuck was right there. He grabbed her again and this time she gave him as good as she got. They kissed for several minutes as he leaned her up against her Jeep Wrangler.

"Wow," Chuck said as he took her hand and put it on his crotch. "Look what you did to me woman."

"Shit!" Portia exclaimed.

"Will you go out with this baby?" he asked, kissing her ear.

"I have to get home," she said. "My friend's picking me up in an hour."

"You got another hot date, huh?"

"Just some old friends throwing a barbecue."

"Take me with you," he said, looking in her eyes.

"Damn, you're persistent," Portia said. "But, I'm invited as a guest, so I don't think it would be cool to bring someone else."

"Some dudes, huh?"

Portia was a little embarrassed. "Well, there's this one guy who supposedly likes me, but I don't think it's a big deal. I'm just going to hang out with my friend."

Chuck got close to her again. Close enough for her to feel his stiff erection.

"Tell her that something else came up," he smirked devilishly. "It won't be a lie."

"You're right about that," Portia responded breathlessly.

"I want you to come home with me. No games."

"What are we going to do at your place?" she asked coyly.

"First, I want to cook dinner for you." He backed up to look at her again. "You do like to eat, don't you?"

Her look said, "What do you think?"

"Alright, I like that," he said. "What's your favorite food?"

Portia thought about it and said, "I like anything. What's your specialty?"

"I can throw down on some soul food. I have a lot of Southern women in my family who love to burn in the kitchen."

"And they taught you everything you know, right?"

"Being the only boy in the family with six sisters, I learned how to make a lot of the stuff just from watching. But I really like to cook, so I just started experimenting with different kinds of food and now I can make just about anything."

"Hmmm. So that's all you want to do? Cook dinner?"

"No. I also want to play some sexy music and slow dance with you. You like to dance, don't you?"

"Yes, I like to dance."

"Then, maybe we'll make some ice cream sundaes or banana splits for dessert."

"Okay, so your intentions are purely innocent? All you want to do is feed me and dance with me?"

"Hell, no," he said seriously. "I told you, no games." He put her hand back on his crotch. "The truth is I want to have this all up inside you by midnight."

"Damn," Portia said as she felt tingling between her legs. The thought of having what she felt between Chuck's legs ramming up inside of her body almost made her come right then and there. She fumbled around in her purse for a pen and some paper. "Give me your address. I'll meet you there at 9:30."

Dana wasn't happy to hear that Portia was flaking out on her, but she couldn't be too upset. After all, she had every intention of getting naked with Nick that night.

"Go on, girl," Dana said when Portia called to tell her about her date with Chuck. "If it's as big as you said it is, you gotta check that out first hand. No pun intended."

"Well, have fun with Nick. You gonna give him some?"

"He can suck it, but I don't think I'm gonna let him fuck it."

"Dana, you're funny."

"That's the truth, girl. His tongue is longer than his dick, but like I said, he knows how to work that motherfucker."

By 11:00 pm, Portia and Chuck were like an old married couple, laid out on the couch listening to music. She had on a blue jean dress with a zipper up the front and a slit up the side. Her low-heeled sandals were left at the front door. She liked to wear her hair teased into a curly Afro. Her nails were perfect, her toes were perfect and she smelled good. Chuck was wearing black sweatpants and a wife beater.

Chuck wasn't lying about his culinary skills. He had fixed smothered pork chops, rice, macaroni and cheese, and green beans. Now he was feeding her chocolate covered strawberries and whipped cream, while they drank champagne and she laughed at his college stories. She found out that he was about to graduate from UNLV with a degree in liberal arts, and he also worked part-time for an air conditioning installation company.

Chuck kissed some whipped cream from Portia's lips. "So what did you do when you went home?"

"I took a shower, and then I got dressed and came straight over here."

"Oh, yeah?"

"And I called Dana to tell her that I wasn't coming to the barbecue."

"And what did she say?"

"She said to have a good time."

"You having a good time, Portia?"

"I'm having a great time, Chuck."

"So, when you got dressed, what did you put on?"

"Silly. You see what I have on."

"What do have on under this dress?"

"I thought you were going to try and find out."

"I want you to tell me," he said, running his hand up her leg.

"Oh, just a little black bra and little matching bikini panties."

"Let me see."

"Why?"

"Because I don't believe they're that little."

Portia giggled as Chuck began to unzip the front of her dress.

"Can I see?" he asked as he got up and pulled her to her feet.

He slow danced with her as Luther Vandross crooned on the stereo. While she languished in his strong arms, he continued to unzip her dress until it fell completely open, revealing her sexy, black lingerie. He wrapped his arms around her body inside of the dress and held her close as she felt his enormous erection pressing against her. Portia wriggled out of her dress and grabbed Chuck by his neck, planting a big kiss on him as he caressed her ample curves. He took her hand and led her to the bedroom.

"Make yourself comfy. I'm going to get some more wine."

Chuck had good taste. It was definitely a man's room, but not too masculine. When Portia walked over to the bed and ran her hands over the leopard skin blanket, she realized that it was a waterbed. She couldn't help but think that if she didn't get on that thing carefully, she might start a tsunami. She turned as he came back into the room."

"I've never been on a waterbed before," Portia stated, demurely.

"Go ahead. You'll like it."

As Portia floated on the king-sized waterbed, Chuck pulled off his wife beater, revealing a nice set of abs. His erection was making a tent of his sweatpants. When he pulled those off, Portia gasped. Chuck was endowed with a rock solid, foot long dick.

"Think you can handle this, Big Mama?" he asked.

"Bring it on over here, boy."

Two hours later, Portia was sore, drained and completely satisfied. Chuck was fast asleep.

After that night, Portia and Chuck saw each other almost every night, even though they both had busy schedules. Portia was completely in love and if she was to believe him, Chuck had fallen hard the moment he laid eyes on her at the Convention Center. She had never felt so wanted or appreciated, and Chuck was honest, told her everything, even things that she didn't want to hear. He said that he was going to break her in slowly. He had lived a full life in his nearly twenty-one years. He looked like a baby, but was all man.

A group of Chuck's friends threw him a 21st birthday party the following month. They rented a huge suite at the Fitzgerald Hotel and Casino downtown. The women were supposed to be in sexy costumes or wear sexy eye masks, which were provided at the door. Chuck invited Portia, but she didn't think she was going to be able to come. She had promised Dana that she would help her with her sister's bachelorette party.

Chuck's party was a fantasy come alive. The suite was full of horny young men and hot, sexy women of all shapes and sizes, including Celia, one of Chuck's ex-girlfriends, whom he was very close to. He had yet to mention that little fact to Portia. Chuck was slightly drunk and was getting a lap dance from one of the large women when Celia, who was dressed in a long slinky Elvira dress and wearing a silver eye mask, stepped over and cut in.

"Sorry, Gina. Gotta drag the birthday boy away."

"Celia!" he exclaimed, happy to see her. "I knew you wouldn't let me down. Where you been hiding your sexy self?"

"Hey, cutie pie," purred Celia. "Time for your present."

He turned to the girl who was giving him the lap dance and said, "Sorry…what was your name again?"

"Gina," she answered.

"Thank you, Gina," Chuck said as he grabbed her hand and kissed it. "That was hot." Gina quickly moved on to dance for another willing guy.

Celia pulled Chuck by the hand and asked, "Did you get my birthday card?"

"Yeah, baby, you sure looked great in your birthday suit."

"Come on and get your present," she said as she pulled him into a private room and locked the door.

Amethyst, Celia's busty best friend, was waiting by the bed in a French maid's uniform, complete with a silk feather duster. She held the current title for most beautiful female body in Las Vegas.

"Long time, no see," said Amethyst, her breasts spilling over the top of her costume.

"Oh, shit!" Chuck said, licking his lips.

"Happy birthday, Chuck," said Celia with a sexy smile.

Celia led him over to one of two king-sized beds, pushed him down and promptly pulled out a pair of furry handcuffs, which she clamped him to the bedpost with.

"Oh, Lord! I must've died and gone to heaven. Am I going to finally get to see Amethyst's famous 40DD's in the flesh?"

"Am I going to see that famous dick?"

"This is your lucky day, birthday boy," replied Celia as Amethyst straddled him and pushed her cleavage into his face.

"Oh, I think I'm gonna like this," he moaned as Amethyst bounced up and down on his chest and Celia pulled his pants down.

Out in the suite, the music was so loud that no one heard Portia knocking, so she had to wait until someone left the suite before she could get in. She left the bachelorette party early because Dana felt sorry for her and got someone else to help her out after the first couple of hours.

When Portia finally got in, she looked around and thought that she had landed in the middle of a strip club. The women, all wearing masks, were in various stages of undress and the men seemed to be having their way with them. Some people were eating, some were dancing and everyone was drinking. Before she could make her way to the bar, a bikini-clad woman presented her with a tray of freshly chilled Cosmopolitans.

"Thank you," Portia said, taking one. She had decided to be Mae West. She had a blond wig, tight gown, big hat, the works. She felt overdressed and immediately found a chair, sat down, drank her martini and observed. She didn't see Chuck anywhere or even recognize any of the guys she had met with him.

Portia eventually found out that Chuck had been there and had probably stepped out for some air, so she decided to wait patiently. By the time she finished her second drink she needed to walk around. All of the sexual tension in the room was making her horny. Besides, she needed to find a bathroom.

As Portia worked her way around the large suite, a young woman whose huge breasts were spilling out of a maid's uniform was coming out of one of the bedrooms. Portia glanced into the dimly lit room as she passed and could see a couple who appeared to be having sex. She quickly looked away.

"Don't be shy, honey," Amethyst said, shutting the door behind her. "If you win the raffle, you can get a piece of that, too."

"Can you tell me which one is the bathroom?" asked Portia.

"Sure, follow me." Amethyst led her to an empty bathroom at the end of the hall. "See you back at the party and don't forget to join the raffle."

Portia began to feel uncomfortable. "Do you know where Chuck is?"

Amethyst looked at her with interest. "The birthday boy? He's the prize, sweetie. Three top winners get to join the private party." She winked and walked away.

Portia quickly scurried into the bathroom and locked the door. She was stunned. Her man was in that room screwing some strange woman. She wasn't sure what to do. She didn't want to make a scene. It's not like they'd been together forever. It had only been nine days. Portia made a decision. Maybe she had lost her mind, but she got herself together and marched back into the party room to find two people; the girl with the martinis, and the person who was selling those raffle tickets.

Chuck Adams was truly in his version of heaven. Hot jazz was playing on the stereo. He was handcuffed and blindfolded, and had been rubbed, sucked and teased to the point of torture. These ladies were masters of the game and would not let him come. He had licked and sucked on Amethyst's nipples while fingering her to an orgasm with his free hand. At the same time, Celia was sucking on his dick and rubbing his balls with the feather duster. There was ice and hot oil involved. Then they switched positions. At times he felt as though his dick was going to explode, but it hurt so good.

Amethyst stepped out to the party to let them know that the raffle could begin. One of the martini waitresses pulled from the men's tickets. Only one man was allowed to win. The lucky guy was Chuck's friend, George Montana, who had come up from LA. He was a football star from USC who was on his way to play pro ball in San Diego. He would have been just as happy if he had won the California Lottery.

The next two tickets called were women who were probably servicing guests in another room. Portia was holding tight to her tickets. Amethyst spotted her looking anxious and decided that this was taking too long.

"That's it. Raffle over," she announced.

She grabbed Gina, the voluptuous woman with Chuck earlier, and then pointed to Portia. "You, with the blond wig. Wanna come? And I mean that literally."

"Yes," said Portia, excitedly.

George was waiting by the door, rubbing himself, when Amethyst brought Portia and Gina to the room. "Damn, George."

He grabbed Amethyst by the waist. "I can't wait to see this prize-winning body of yours."

"Calm down, tiger," she said. "It's the birthday boy who gets first dibs." She turned to Portia and Gina. "He likes you big girls, though," she said as she knocked with the prearranged signal.

Celia answered the door totally naked, except for her high heels. The room was dark, but a few scented candles were spread around the room.

"Holy shit!" exclaimed George as Celia pulled him into the room, shut the door and immediately blindfolded him.

"Shut up and do as I say."

"Yes, ma'am," he replied happily. Celia led him over to the other bed, where he was also laid down and handcuffed. Then she went back to let the ladies in. It took a minute for their eyes to adjust to the candlelight.

Chuck was blindfolded, his body completely oiled down. His long dick was standing straight up, throbbing in anticipation. Portia was speechless. Gina was not.

"Oh, my God!" she said. "It's not just an urban legend."

"You start over here, Gina," said Celia, who was setting up ice and hot oil by George's bed. "Take off his clothes. We need to get his dick standing at attention, too."

George couldn't contain himself. "Do whatever you got to do to me, baby."

Chuck recognized his friend's voice. "Is that you Big G?"

"Hell yeah, man. Cost me two hundred bucks in raffle tickets to win your special birthday prize."

"You better not try to kiss me, man."

They all laughed.

Amethyst walked over to the wet bar, where there were six bottles of expensive champagne on ice. She looked over at Portia, who couldn't help but stare at Chuck and his erection. He looked so damn hot lying there helpless. She couldn't believe that she was doing this. She should have been outraged and appalled. Instead, she was so excited and turned on that she began to sweat.

"What's your name, sweetie?" Amethyst asked, breaking Portia out of her fog. In full game mode, she changed her voice to a Southern accent, and said, "Lisa. Lisa Mae."

Amethyst looked at her and smiled. "Whatever you say, gal. Come over here and help me, Lisa Mae."

Chuck was intrigued. "How many people are in here?"

Celia answered, "Don't worry, sweetheart. In a minute, it's gonna be you and me. I've been waiting for months to get another piece of that rock."

"You never have to wait. Come on over here and get it right now, sexy."

Portia tried not to react as she realized that Chuck and this woman had some history together Amethyst poured champagne, and Portia carried a couple of glasses over to the bedside table where Gina was oiling George's body and he was grabbing her breasts. Amethyst brought glasses to Celia and Chuck, then she instructed Portia to sit down next to her while they watched for a while.

Celia was straddling Chuck and teasing him by balancing herself over him and allowing the tip of his penis to enter her. The ladies had a clear view of Celia's big, beautiful behind as Chuck tried to use his one hand to pull her down further onto him.

"Damn, baby," he moaned. "You're killing me."

"Be patient."

"Please let me have that sweet pussy."

"Shhh!"

"You promised," he said. "And where's Amethyst with that hot pussy of hers?"

"I'm right over here, Chuck," said Amethyst. "Ready and willing."

"I know you want more than my finger up in that hot shit."

"You know I do."

"Then bring that hot body over here."

"Celia?"

"Come on, hot mama." Celia climbed off of Chuck and unlocked his handcuffs. "But grab a rubber from the table over there. You know this boy can make a baby."

"What the hell did that mean?" thought Portia, who was feeling no pain as she watched Amethyst walk over to her man. Chuck sat up and took the blindfold off. He didn't see anything but Amethyst, who grabbed his penis with both of her hands. He helped her off with her clothes, kissing her deeply on the mouth and then all over her upper body, paying special attention to her perfect 40DD's. She was left wearing only her garter belt and stockings. He slipped his hand between her legs and made her come, and then licked the juices from his fingers. Finally, he threw her onto the bed, put on a condom and mounted her. She opened her legs wide and screamed out loud as he entered her with all of the pent up sexual energy of the past two hours.

"What the hell is going on over there?" George yelled as his own penis about to burst.

Gina had been sucking him well, and had been instructed not to let him come. Celia went over to take George's blindfold off, but left him cuffed as they all watched Chuck pumping his hard dick in and out of Amethyst's beautiful body. He flipped her and turned her in every direction until they were in perfect harmony and after several frantic minutes, climaxed together. It was a beautiful sight to behold. Except for Portia, who was out of her mind with jealousy and went for another glass of champagne. By the time Portia had calmed herself down, Celia was cooling Chuck off to get him ready for the next round. Portia went to George's bed and had Gina help her out of her dress, but kept the wig and the mask on. Amethyst came over to see what was going on.

"Don't you want some of that good birthday dick, Lisa Mae?" she asked Portia.

"I want some of this one over here," she answered in her fake voice. "Put the blindfold back on him."

"You girls are kinky," George smiled. "I like it."

Amethyst put the blindfold on George, "Okay, Gina. Go have some of that."

"Cool," Gina said.

They watched as Gina went over to Chuck's bed and while Celia was bent over on the bed with her ass in the air sucking his dick, Gina slipped up behind her, grabbed her ass and began eating her pussy.

"Unlock these cuffs," George said, getting their attention. "Let me feel you two."

"Is that alright with you, Lisa Mae?" Amethyst asked Portia.

"Sure," she said. "Let him feel us."

Once Amethyst released him, he was like a blind madman. He grabbed them both and laid them down. He found Amethyst's breasts and sucked on her nipples like he was a baby. Then he reached for Portia, rubbed all over her body until he found her wet and ready, and climbed on top of her. He did all of this without missing a beat.

"Wait!" said Amethyst, handing him a condom. He still had a suction hold on her right nipple. Once he penetrated Portia, it didn't take long for either of them to come, especially while they watched the ménage a trios taking place in the bed across the room.

The rest of the night went by in a drunken haze. Portia woke up and realized that she had taken part in her first orgy. She reached up to her head. Thank God she had pinned her wig on tight. She couldn't remember much after George mounted her, but she was pretty sure that one of those women ate her pussy and someone fucked her in the ass. Disgusted with herself, she grabbed her clothes and managed to get to the bathroom down the hall without being seen. She had to step over bodies because people had passed out in every area of the suite. After getting her clothes on, she quietly slipped out the door and hot tailed it to the hotel parking lot.

It was 5am, but as she got to the casino floor, it looked like midday. Hundreds of people were still gambling and drinking. Portia couldn't wait to get home. She had a splitting headache and hadn't even begun to process what she had just been through.

Chuck began leaving messages for her around noon. Portia wasn't ready to talk to him yet. He had no idea that she had been there the night before, not only to witness his sexual exploits, but to indulge in some debauchery of her own. The only person she didn't have sex with was Chuck. At least, she didn't remember.

As if that wasn't enough, she had a whole lot of questions about Celia and Amethyst. Several comments were made that created suspicions and doubts about who Chuck really was and if he had been honest with her about his life. She really liked him a lot and she deserved to hear the truth from his own lips. That meant she had to be willing to tell the truth herself. Could she do that? She sure hoped so.

Later that night, she called Chuck and asked him to come over. When she opened the door, he gave her a big hug and kiss. He didn't look any worse for the wear and tear on his body the night before. She felt like crap.

"So, I missed you at the party last night."

"Really?" she asked. "Did you have a good time?"

"Oh, baby," he said, gesturing with excitement. "It was off the hook! My friends treated me like a king."

"Oh, yeah?"

"One of my ex-girlfriends is a stripper. Her name's Celia. I'll tell you all about her later. She brought some of her stripper friends and some of her high class hooker friends over to serve drinks, dance for the fellas and do pretty much anything, you know what I mean?"

"Anything?" Portia asked.

"Anything and everything."

"Wow!"

"It was pretty fuckin' crazy, baby. I gotta admit they wore my ass out."

"You admit to having sex with these women?"

"It's just sex, baby," he said as he grabbed her and held her close. "I love you."

"You say that, but it's only words."

"Are you kidding me?" he said. "I have never told another woman that I love her."

"What about the mother of your child?" she regretted it as soon as the words came out of her mouth. He was being open with her and she wasn't giving him a chance to tell her in his own time. Too late to un-ring the bell.

"How do you know about my children? I was going to get my daughter and have you to meet her next week."

"Children?" she asked, shocked. "How many do you have?"

"Three."

"Holy shit!" Portia began to pace. "Celia has three kids?"

"Wait! Hold the fuck up," he shouted. "Have you been spying on me? How did you know that I had a baby with Celia?"

"You hold the fuck up!" she shouted back. "How many women did you get pregnant?"

"Three," he answered with no shame. "Yes, my kids all have different mothers, but you should know that if you've been spying."

Portia sat, exasperated. "We need to have a serious talk."

An hour later, he had told her all about his history with Celia and why he has three children. Then it was Portia's turn. She told him the birthday party story, including her having sex with George.

"Damn," he said, shaking his head.

"Like you said, it was just sex. I love *you*."

Chuck got up and headed out the front door.

"Where are you going?" she asked, following him.

"I'll be back."

She shut the door and leaned against it, regretting the day she was born. How could she have been so stupid? Men can't handle the truth when it comes to their woman having sex with another man. She should have never, ever told him the truth.

But Chuck was so open with her. He told her all about getting Celia pregnant when he was just seventeen. She's six years older than him and wanted to have a baby while she was still young. He supports his three-year-old daughter, Kayla and sees her whenever he wants. When Chuck was nineteen, he got two college girls pregnant at the same time. They both moved back to their hometowns and he doesn't see those children at all. However, he does send money when they ask, which isn't often. One of the girls has her parents raising the 18-month old boy in Minnesota, and the other one got married, so another man is raising his 15-month old daughter in Louisiana.

Two hours later, Chuck came back. Even though he seemed perfectly fine, Portia couldn't look him in the eye, so she almost didn't see him holding a beautiful velvet box in front of her.

"Portia Taylor aka Lisa Mae West, will you marry me?"

CHAPTER 25

Melissa

One particular summer proved to be a testing ground for the friendship between fifteen year-old Melissa Murdock and her cousin, Eleanor Foster, who were very close, only six months apart. Melissa developed more quickly and was a perfect size seven. Eleanor had a boyish build and outweighed her petite cousin by twenty pounds.

The weeks flew by every summer as the two girls alternated between being friends and rivals. They were getting older and starting to talk more about boys. Eleanor realized that Melissa was not only the favored one within her family, but within the neighborhood, too. Some of Eleanor's favorite people were the boys who got high and gave her free marijuana, especially when Melissa came to town. They went out of their way to give her extra bags of the good stuff, which she had no problem sharing with her favorite cousin.

Every guy on the block wanted to get close to the beautiful, white Murdock girl who blossomed more each year. Melissa ate up the attention and enjoyed flirting her shapely little ass off. She was a rare sight in the neighborhood and she knew how to work it. Eleanor took it all in stride and enjoyed the fruits of Melissa's labors.

"This is some good weed, girl," Melissa said as she took a nice long drag on the joint, passed it to Eleanor and blew the sweet smoke toward the starlit sky. It was a clear, beautiful night with a typical summer chill in the LA night air.

"Thank you very much," replied Eleanor.

"You got the hook-up, cuz."

"You know dat."

"Why you got to be ghet-to, Miss Ellie?"

"Oh, shut up. Blondie!"

The two girls giggled and continued to talk trash as they sat on a couple of makeshift swings in the park adjacent to the backyard. The park was an acre away from the house and separated by a grove of lemon trees. Suddenly, the girls heard a noise among the trees. It sounded like someone walking in their direction. As Melissa tried to put out the joint, Eleanor pulled a small bottle from her pocket and sprayed some air freshener around. A short, dark figure with a hood moved toward them. There were no other people around, so the girls got geared up for a fight. As the person got close enough, Eleanor yelled out.

"Hey! Who's that?"

"Boo!" The figure jumped closer, removing his hood.

"Dammit, Boomer," cried Eleanor. "You scared the crap outta me."

"Whatchu two doin' out here all late and shit?" he asked.

"Smokin' up that weed you gave me," replied Eleanor.

"So, what's up, vanilla homegirl?" he asked, looking at Melissa. "I see you came back to the hood."

"Yeah," she replied.

"Wait until I tell my brother that you're back in LA."

"Why?" Melissa tried not to seem too interested.

Boomer just gave her a sly grin and walked off, strutting cockily.

"What was that about?" wondered Eleanor.

Boomer was one of the Buckingham bad boys. He and his four brothers were from a good family and their parents worked hard, but the three older boys were into a few illegal activities: nothing to get them into trouble with the law, but only because they didn't get caught. They weren't bad like the gangbangers down the road, but they were bad compared to their neighborhood, where most of the kids went to camp and had activities to keep them busy. Kids like Melissa and her cousins basically just had a lot of fun.

At seventeen, Lester Buckingham was the oldest of the brothers. He was secretly in love with Melissa from the first summer that he noticed her, even though she was only eight years old at the time and he was ten. He didn't even know that he liked girls until he set eyes on her. Before that he had only been thinking about sports.

Melissa was shy and beautiful. He was a little shy, too. Kindred spirits, that's what they were. He could feel it, even though he didn't say it in words. Each year she got more beautiful. His infatuation grew as he silently watched her with the Murdock kids. He thought that she was white, but found out that she was actually related them.

The Buckingham boys were all brown-skinned and good-looking in different ways. Lester definitely got his fair share of the handsome genes. He was tall and slim and wore a little goatee, which made him look very sexy. His younger brothers, sixteen-year-old Matt, fifteen-year-old Ricky, and fourteen-year-old Boomer, each had their own appeal, but were shorter, stronger and more outgoing. Todd, the baby, was eight. The brothers protected him, so he was still innocent. Lester wasn't so innocent.

Melissa looked forward to her summers in Los Angeles. She felt more loved and at home around her black family. They took her to their Baptist church, where she was accepted as part of the Murdock family. No one ever questioned her right to be there. The preacher inspired her with his rousing sermons and she got a good taste of gospel music. They even had a band. That was exciting for her. Nothing at her family church in Dallas made her feel as good. She was filled with the spirit and sang her heart out.

Melissa had a great voice like her father, Junior. She loved to sing R&B music, but only in LA. At home, she had to listen to classic country or homogenized church music. She snuck some country like Alabama and Trisha Yearwood, but nothing could replace SWV, TLC, or Whitney Houston. She could sing them all. The Murdocks teased that she was the only soul singer they knew who had naturally blond hair.

That golden mane is what made the boys like Melissa. Especially, Lester Buckingham. When Boomer ran home to tell his big brother that the object of his desire was back in town, Lester knew that this was the year that he had to make his move. Only one thing could hinder his plan. Eleanor Foster, who had a serious crush on him and had been trying to get his attention ever since she started high school two years before. She was always athletic and a bit of a tomboy, but she started wearing makeup and dressing a little more feminine, hoping to catch his eye. Her pride and joy was a fake ponytail that she liked to attach to her shorter hair.

They all grew up together and Eleanor was close to Boomer, so she had spent a lot of time at their house. They played basketball together in the Buckingham's backyard and had barbecues at each other's homes over the years. The Buckingham boys were almost like brothers to her and that's how they treated her. That's how they treated Melissa, too, when she was around for the summer. But Eleanor loved herself some Lester Buckingham, and not in a brotherly way. She spent the entire sophomore year flirting with him. He could hardly take her seriously, having always looked at her like a sister. However, you could never underestimate the seriousness of a girl's first crush. Lester had no idea how serious Eleanor was about being his girl. No idea at all. Melissa knew, though. That's all Eleanor wanted to talk about.

"If you haven't gotten a response out of him, then maybe you should back off a little," Melissa suggested.

"Yeah, you're right. I don't wanna look desperate."

Melissa had been in town for three days when Lester finally stepped out on a limb. He strutted over to the Murdock's house one afternoon while Melissa and Eleanor were on the front porch reading trashy tabloids and trying to stay cool. They were giggling and sharing stories as Lester came up the front walk.

"What are you girls laughin' at?" he asked, flashing his perfect teeth.

Eleanor was happy that she had put on a cute pair of shorts, a sexy halter-top, and her favorite ponytail. Melissa was just intrigued by the fact that her cousin hadn't stopped talking about Lester. He was the quietest of the brothers and Melissa had never really paid that much attention to him. Until now. He was looking pretty good in his basketball shorts and a wife-beater.

"Hey, Lester," said Eleanor.

"What's up, Eleanor?" he said, and then turned to Melissa. "Welcome back, lady."

"How are you doing, Lester?" Melissa responded.

"I'm doing great, but I'll be better if you ladies come over."

"Why would we do that?" Melissa asked.

"Well, you two look hot out here," he said. "And since my parents went to take Todd to camp for the summer, my brothers and

I decided to throw some food on the grill. I thought you might like to come and join us for a swim and some grub."

Eleanor was about to jump out of her skin and couldn't find her voice.

"Y'all got any alcohol?" asked Melissa, calmly.

"Yeah," he grinned. "But you're too young to drink."

"So are you," she said, not flinching.

"Then, I'll have to share," he said. "So, come over in say…thirty minutes, okay?"

"We'll be there in twenty," Eleanor smiled as they watched Lester walk away.

Oh, that didn't sound desperate at all, Melissa thought as she looked at Eleanor, who believed that all of her flirting had paid off. Lester was finally taking notice and she wasn't going to blow it.

"I'll be back. I gotta go tighten up my hair." Eleanor said.

"You might wanna take it off. I don't think you can swim with a hairpiece."

"Shut up," Eleanor snapped, as she went inside. "Not everyone has perfect hair."

A half hour later, the girls were at the Buckingham's. The water felt good as Melissa dipped her hands in the pool. She was lying on an inflatable raft in the low end of the pool watching Boomer and Eleanor, who took turns diving into the deep end. Michael Jackson's Thriller was playing on a boom box and Melissa was singing along.

Eleanor, who was wearing a fire engine red bikini, kept calling Lester to watch her dive in. He was busy on the patio manning the barbecue grill.

"Lester!" yelled Eleanor, swinging her fake hair around. "Watch this one."

"I'm watchin'," he yelled back, humoring her.

Over and over, the ritual played itself out. It was a ridiculous spectacle that Eleanor was making of herself, but it kept Melissa amused. After a while, Melissa closed her eyes and took a little nap as she enjoyed the sun beaming down on her well-oiled body, unaware that Lester was enjoying the view. She was wearing a tiny, white bikini that left little to the imagination. She was well developed for her age and Lester had to keep reminding himself that she was only fifteen, but much more mature than her crazy cousin.

"Having a good time, sleepy head?"

Melissa opened her eyes and peeked over her sunglasses to see Lester standing over her with a glass of lemonade. Her raft had drifted over to the side of the pool.

"Of course," she said.

"Come on out and have a cold drink with me."

"Sure," she said. "Is the food ready?"

"Almost."

Lester extended his hand to help her as she climbed out of the pool. He watched her closely as she walked over to a deck chair to get a towel. Melissa had such a cute, tight behind. With her back turned, she bent over to dry her legs and feet and Lester's woody nearly popped out of his swim trunks. She turned around unexpectedly and caught his lustful stare. It made her feel funny inside, and she wasn't sure why, but she liked it. She liked it a lot. As she wrapped the towel around her waist, he walked over and handed her the cold lemonade.

"Here."

"Thanks."

She took a big gulp of the drink, which tasted a little funny, but was really good.

"There's vodka in there," he said. "So sip lightly."

"Okay."

"Let's go inside for a minute," he said. "You can help me get stuff together."

She followed him into the house.

"Where is everybody?" she asked.

"Matt went to get his girlfriend," he said. "Ricky should be here in an hour."

"What happened to Eleanor and Boomer?" Melissa inquired.

"I sent them off to the store to get some lettuce and tomatoes," he replied.

"They walked?" she asked.

"Yep."

"You're kidding?" Melissa said. "I'm surprised she didn't get you to go with her. Y'all could have taken your car."

"I'm the one running the grill," he said. "That's what the peons are here for."

Melissa laughed out loud.

"I guess that's the category I'm in, too," she said.

"No, little lady," he said. "You are my special helper."

"Yeah, right," said Melissa. "You're gonna get me in trouble with my cousin. You know she really likes you."

"That's why I had to get her outta here," he laughed. "She was getting on my nerves with all that damn pool diving."

"She just gets nervous around you, that's all."

"Lester, Lester, Lester," he said, imitating Eleanor, complete with the girly poses. "Watch me, look at me."

"Stop it," Melissa said, laughing. "That's not nice."

"She sure didn't want to leave you here with me," he said. "She wanted to wake you up and make you walk with them, but I assured her that I had every intention of putting you to work, too."

"So, put me to work, then."

"I'm going in my room to get a buzz first," he said. "Wanna come?"

"Okay."

After smoking a joint and drinking the rest of her lemonade, Melissa was feeling giddy. They were sitting on Lester's bed and he was sharing an old photo album with her. They were laughing and making fun of him and his brothers when he suddenly leaned over and tried to kiss her. She jumped up and shook her finger at him.

"Hey, none of that," she said. "You have a girlfriend."

"What are you talking about?"

"Eleanor Foster, the future Mrs. Lester Buckingham."

"How about I make *you* the future Mrs. Buckingham?"

"You have to catch me first," she said, running out.

Lester followed close behind as she squealed with delight and ran out the patio door, trying to shut it behind her. Lester got hold of the door, too, and since he was stronger, she abandoned that idea and jumped in the pool. He jumped in behind her and had her by the arm for a second, but she was able to slip away again.

"If I catch you," he said. "You're gonna get it."

"If you catch me," she teased. "You can have it."

"Oh, it's on now!" he said.

Several more times, she easily ducked and dodged him. He was so determined, it tickled her. She began laughing so hard that it slowed her down. Lester finally caught up. He grabbed her by the waist and held her tight against him. As she wriggled her body around and tried to get away again, he grabbed her from behind and accidentally pulled on her bikini top, exposing her left breast, which was now in his hand. She made no move to cover herself and allowed him to pull her to him. He rubbed and gently squeezed her long, hard nipple. She could feel his hardness against her.

Lester spun her back around, grabbed her under her butt, and lifted her up. She wrapped her legs around him and he put the exposed nipple into his mouth. They stayed in that position, kissing and fondling for several minutes until they felt water splash over them. Melissa ducked underwater and Lester jumped away.

"What the hell?" he said, wiping his face.

Ricky Buckingham was in the pool next to him.

"Get a room, bro," he laughed. "What you doin' out here in broad daylight with a white girl? You need to go check that grill."

Lester looked around for Melissa, who had made her way over to the deep end. She popped up to the surface with a splash, realized that her breast was still exposed, and adjusted her top.

"Damn!" Ricky said. "Who's that?"

Ricky swam to the other end of the pool to get a closer look as Lester climbed out of the pool and went over to check the grill.

"Melissa?" he asked.

"Hey, Ricky," she said. "You scared the shit outta me, jumpin' in like that."

Then Matt Buckingham entered the backyard with his girlfriend, followed by Eleanor and Boomer. "What's up, people?" Matt asked. "Where's the party?"

"In the pool, fool," said Boomer, jumping in.

"Oh, it's definitely in the pool," Ricky said, pointing to Melissa. "Over here."

"Don't say anything," whispered Melissa.

"Whatchu gonna do for me, girl?" he asked.

"Excuse me?" Melissa asked.

"I know your cousin has the hots for my brother," Ricky said. "Maybe she'd like to know that you two were fuckin' in the pool when I got here."

"That's not true!" cried Melissa.

"I'm just messin' with you, Goldie," he said. "I ain't gonna say nothin'."

"Thanks, Ricky."

"Nice titties, though," he said.

Melissa pushed him under the water and while he was down there, he pulled her bikini bottom down and swam off. Eleanor came over to that end of the pool.

"What's up, Missy?" she asked. "You messin' with Ricky?"

"Hell, no." Melissa said. "He's just being a jerk."

"So, did Lester say anything about me?" asked Eleanor.

"No, not really," she said. "He just appreciated you guys going to the store."

"I think I'm gonna go make a move," said Eleanor, taking off her cover-up.

Lester was taking overdone chicken breasts off the grill when Eleanor walked up.

"How did that happen?" she asked. "I thought your job was watchin' the grill."

"Two pans of perfectly grilled burgers, wings and hot links are in the kitchen."

"Oh, but it's okay to neglect the breasts?" Eleanor asked.

"I swear to you," Lester grinned. "I did not neglect the breasts. No, no, was all over the breasts. Trust me."

"What happened to the chicken?" asked Ricky, walking up.

Lester brushed barbecue sauce on the blackened breasts.

"I got distracted for a minute, man," he said. "Don't worry, it'll still taste good."

"No doubt," said Ricky.

Lester looked around, his eyes found Melissa and followed her as she walked into the house. Eleanor followed his eyes, too.

"Here," Lester said, handing her the brush. "Finish this up for me, okay?"

"Sure, Lester," Eleanor replied.

Lester went into the house. Eleanor was not too happy as she slapped sauce over the chicken. She wasn't sure what was going on, but something was going on. She was going to have a little talk with her favorite cousin.

"You guys can come on and eat now," Matt yelled from the patio door. "Everything's ready."

Eleanor brought the last pan of chicken into the kitchen.

Hours later, they were all in the pool. Some were standing in the low end talking and some were swimming or playing around. Eleanor was trying to get up the nerve to talk to Lester and tell him that she liked him. Melissa was even encouraging her. Eleanor was nervous, but eventually she swam underwater in Lester's direction, and when she emerged right next to him, she jumped up and kissed him on the lips, shocking him.

As she wiped the water from her face, Eleanor reached back and found that her ponytail was missing. Extremely embarrassed, she looked around and saw it floating in the deep end of the pool. Seconds later, Boomer was swimming towards it.

"Hey, Eleanor," he yelled, waving her ponytail around. "You missin' your tail?"

All the kids, except for Eleanor, laughed uncontrollably. Boomer laughed so hard he peed in the pool, which chased everyone else out. Then they laughed even harder, and were doubled over on the deck. Eleanor was mortified and left by herself.

Later at home, Melissa tried to make Eleanor feel better by saying what jerks the Buckingham boys were and that they should stay away from them. Eleanor agreed, and for the rest of the summer she refused to talk about Lester. Melissa wasn't even allowed to bring up his name. However, Melissa had no intention of staying away from Lester Buckingham. She snuck to see him and they had a good laugh at Eleanor's expense. Melissa got her thrills sneaking around with Lester and teasing him until he couldn't stand it. She had to keep coming up with creative ways to get away from Eleanor and her other cousins in order to be with him. She didn't realize how desperately he wanted to have sex with her. For him, it was just a matter of time before they actually went all the way, but she knew that she would be leaving soon and thought that she could continue teasing and flirting without any consequences.

Finally, one afternoon at the end of summer, Melissa, Johnny and Eleanor were swimming at the YMCA. Melissa sent them on a wild goose chase to the neighborhood record store, saying that one of their favorite singers was making an early appearance there. The artist actually wasn't scheduled to be at the store until the following week, but she knew that they would want to go and check it out. Since the record store was over a mile away, and they were going to have to walk or wait for the slow bus, Melissa figured that Eleanor would be gone for at least an hour.

Minutes later, Lester showed up in black swim trunks. Melissa had on a hot pink bikini, and after a short swim, he and Melissa wrapped themselves in towels and disappeared into one of the buildings where there was a piano room with a lockable door. Lester began playing some popular R&B tunes and Melissa sang along, watching herself as she performed in front of the large mirror on the wall.

"You know you sound like Whitney."

"Oh, I don't know about all that."

"Really. You should seriously consider a singing career. Isn't your father a good singer?"

"Yeah,"

"Well, you got the gift from him. You shouldn't waste it, girl. Go make you a hit record."

"And I like how you play. Are you going to be a musician?"

"Hell no, I'm going to MIT. Don't you know, I'm a genius?"

"Yeah, right."

"Okay. Don't sleep on this black man. I'm going to get a Nobel Prize someday."

"Okay, I believe you, Mr. MIT."

"Actually, I'm going to school in Atlanta," he said. "Too many white folks in Boston."

"What's wrong with white folks?

"Didn't mean to insult your tribe, but I forget sometimes."

"Ha! Half my tribe," she laughed. "At least you have big dreams. I hope they come true for you."

"I have one that you can make come true right now."

They tossed aside their wet towels and began kissing. Then, before she knew what was happening, he had picked her up and laid her across a wooden table, his hands all over her. He pulled off her bikini top and just stared at her pointy nipples. The tips were about ½ inch long when erect.

"Damn, you got some pretty titties."

"You like?"

"Hell, yeah. You got those Farrah Fawcett nipples. I just want to suck on 'em."

"Well, do it then."

He began sucking on her left nipple as he was pulling down her bikini bottom.

"Can we do this?" Lester asked, hard as a rock.

"Yes," answered Melissa, breathless.

He pulled her to the edge of the table and entered her with some difficulty. She cried out. "Wait. It hurts!"

"I'm sorry," he said, stopping. He saw that she was crying. "Are you a virgin?"

"Yes."

"Oh, shit," Lester said, standing up.

"It's alright," she assured him. "Just take it easy. This table is hard as hell."

"Wait a minute. Don't move."

Lester found a huge, quilted blanket on top of a piano. He spread it on the floor, picked Melissa up, gently laid her on it, and with the experience of a seventeen-year-old, properly deflowered the girl of his dreams on the music room floor of the local YMCA.

After they finished, Melissa realized that she was bleeding. Lester offered her the wet towels to cover herself with. They had to sneak out to the locker rooms.

"I'll see you later, Lester. I have to get home."

"Are you sure you're alright?" he asked, holding her.

"I'm great."

They kissed again until someone rattled the doorknob and banged on the door.

"Shhh," Lester put a finger to his lips. After what seemed like a long time, the banging stopped. They waited for another minute, and then he relaxed.

"Okay, let's go." He tentatively opened the door and looked around. "The coast is clear. Come on."

As they slipped out and headed for the locker rooms, neither of them saw Eleanor, who was hiding at the other end of the hallway. She and Johnny had gotten a ride to the record store and returned quickly. Lester and Melissa could not have known that one of Eleanor's classmates had told her she saw them enter the music room. They could not have known that Eleanor had been listening through a vent at the other end of the room.

Eleanor didn't believe it until she heard singing. Lester and Melissa were in that room. Their voices weren't clear, but she recognized the tone of her cousin's voice. Then there was quiet talking, but she still couldn't hear what was going on. Whatever it was, she decided to break it up. When she banged on the door and they didn't answer her knocks, she hid back down the hall and waited until they emerged.

When Melissa got home, she soaked in a hot bath. She was sore from having her cherry busted, but there was something about the throbbing between her legs that made her feel like a woman. She was really happy that she gave her virginity to Lester. He was mature, handsome and sexy. Yeah, she could've done much worse.

At dinner the whole family was present. While everyone was having lively conversation, Eleanor was unusually quiet and Melissa couldn't help but notice that she had cut her eyes at her twice. Then Eleanor refused dessert, which never happened.

"What's the matter with you, gal?" asked Mama Susie.

"Nothin's the matter," Eleanor said.

"Eat your cake," said Mama Susie.

"I don't want any stupid cake," Eleanor said.

"Eleanor, watch your mouth," Becka said.

"Yes, momma," Eleanor responded. "May I be excused?"

"You feelin' sick or somethin'?" Leslie asked.

"Mind your business," snapped Eleanor.

"Well, excuse me," Leslie responded.

Melissa watched Eleanor carefully, but kept her mouth shut.

"Go on, gal," said Mama Susie as she looked disapprovingly at Eleanor. "You can take your little behind and your bad attitude upstairs. And don't let me see you for the rest of the night."

Eleanor scraped her chair across the floor and stomped up to her room, lucky that she didn't get popped upside her head.

"I don't know what's got into that girl," snorted Mama Susie. "Hey, Blondie. Did you all have a fight or something?"

"No, ma'am," Melissa answered. "I barely saw her today."

"I thought you all went swimming together," added James.

At that moment, the doorbell rang.

"I'll get it," Melissa said, jumping up from the table, anxious to avoid any more interrogation about her day at the YMCA. When she opened the door, to her surprise, she was facing the last person she expected to see.

"Daddy!"

"Hey, baby girl," Junior Murdock said, as he scooped her into his arms and swirled her around. She giggled with delight.

"Put me down, you crazy man!"

"Damn, you're a sight for sore eyes," he said, as he got a good look at her. "You look like a little woman."

"Thanks, Daddy. What are you doing here?"

"Since when do I need a reason to come home? Where's everybody?"

Junior marched into the dining room, where everyone made a big fuss over him. Within minutes, there was a large plate of food and a glass of whiskey in front of him.

"I'm driving up the coast tomorrow morning and my baby girl's going with me."

"What about Mommy?" Melissa asked.

"I talked to her and I'll be sending you on a plane back to Dallas next week. As a matter of fact, you should call her and let her know that you're excited about spending time with your old man."

"Cool." Melissa ran off to call Karen.

"Where have you been all summer, Junior?" asked Susie.

"I've been around, Mom."

Becka howled. "Well, you must have been invisible, bro."

"Funny," Junior responded. "I told you that I was going to be traveling with that show I produced. Not that you ever care about the stuff that I do."

"Alright, that's enough," James, Sr. said. "The boy's here now. I'm glad to see you, son. Let's hear about this show of yours."

Junior Murdock spent the next thirty minutes entertaining his family with stories of his antics on the road. They were amused and impressed. Melissa came back excited about the prospect of going on a road trip with her father. The only thing that bothered her was the prospect of not seeing Lester Buckingham before she left. She might not be seeing him until the following summer. At first, she thought about not even calling Lester, but that would be awful, so she waited until everyone had gone in the living room to watch television, and then she snuck and called him on the kitchen phone. They agreed to meet later that night. She would have to sneak out one last time.

Lester picked her up and they went to a motel, where they smoked weed, drank vodka and orange juice, and made love over and over again. He was obviously a little more experienced than she ever thought. He really made her feel like she was grown.

Lester held her tightly. "I wish I could take you to Atlanta with me, Melissa."

"Really?" she asked. "What would you do with me there?"

"Protect you, keep you safe."

"You sound like an old man," she laughed. "Why are you talking like that?"

He laughed, too. "Maybe I love you."

"Love me?"

"Maybe."

"Well, when you are absolutely sure, let me know."

"Will you write to me?"

"Maybe."

"Let me help you to make up your mind."

They made love again before Lester took her back home. They agreed to write to each other while he was in college and she was back in Dallas. They also agreed to keep it just between the two of them. No Eleanor, no Boomer, nobody.

It was just after ten-thirty when Melissa slipped in the back door unnoticed. She stopped in the kitchen to get a piece of cake and sashayed into the dining room where she found her Aunt Becka and Aunt Ruth drinking and laughing at something Junior had said. She smiled and put her plate down, then continued over to the doorway where her Uncle Pete and her grandparents were in the living room watching television.

"What y'all watching?" she asked.

"Shhh!" Mama Susie hissed.

"Sorry," Melissa whispered, smiling. You can't bother Mama Susie when she's watching her favorite shows.

No one even noticed that had been gone, so she happily went back to the dining room to have her cake and laugh at her father's stories. When she was done, she went upstairs and found Johnny and Leslie in his room playing video games.

"I got winners," Melissa said, plopping onto Johnny's bed.

Ever since Eleanor stormed away from the dinner table, she had been in her bedroom licking her wounds. She felt betrayed by Melissa. While Melissa was telling her to forget about Lester, she was after him for herself. Eleanor knew that she wasn't as beautiful as Melissa and she had to deal with the family fawning over her all the time, but she thought that she had found a loyal ally in her favorite cousin. Now, she felt that she couldn't trust her anymore. Melissa had disregarded her feelings because of a boy: a boy that she had wanted for years. She would never forgive her. Ever.

When Melissa finally slipped into the room hours later, Eleanor pretended to be asleep. She was still stewing over Melissa's betrayal and couldn't wait for her to leave. She had even pulled all of Melissa's clothes out of her closet and tossed them on her bed. Melissa thought how nice it was that Eleanor was helping her out.

"Hey, Eleanor," Melissa whispered. "Are you awake?"

There was no answer, so Melissa finished packing her things before going to sleep. When Junior woke her at 6:00 in the morning, Eleanor was already up, so she didn't get a chance to have a conversation with her. It was hard for Melissa to tell, but if she didn't know any better, she would have sworn that Eleanor was avoiding her. Junior knocked again fifteen minutes later.

"Come on and eat so we can hit the road."

Mama Susie fixed a huge breakfast for the whole family, so that meant everybody had to get up early. After wolfing down bacon, sausage, eggs, waffles and grits, Melissa and Junior bid farewell to the family and headed north.

Book Five

CHAPTER 26

Snookie

After several years as a social worker for the city of Mobile, Alabama, Snookie McClain finally needed a change. She was a wild woman. She loved sports and loved jocks. But, between working and spending significant amounts of time and energy with her family, she just didn't do much for herself. Taking time away from Mobile was a rare occurrence. It was as though she spent enough of her life around other people and just wanted to be alone. But, she was never alone. She hung out with Jack Daniels, Jose Cuervo and Captain Morgan and they never turned her down.

When Snookie did go out, her idea of a good time was to hang at a local sports bar in her neighborhood. Dating wasn't her thing. She wasn't typically pretty, but she had long legs and a certain sexiness that some men liked. Not the one you bring home to meet your mother, but not necessarily one to hide. She always fit somewhere down the middle. Snookie never had a chance to build a real relationship because she rarely spent time with the men she met. She just had sex and kept it moving. Knowing that she didn't want to get pregnant, she even carried her own condoms.

Under peer pressure, Snookie decided to let herself get set up on a couple of dates. It was as though she had forgotten how to just have fun. Every encounter turned into a one-night stand. There was only momentary satisfaction, no real connection. After a string of dates with that type of result, she was back to being alone and miserable. Snookie certainly would never let it show that she was unhappy, but there appeared to be no true joy in her life. She gave to her job and her family because she was used to giving, but she didn't like it anymore. Maybe she never really did.

One day Snookie met a man named Fernando Watson. He was about to change life for her. He was a big guy who had played football in college, until a knee injury stopped him from playing, but didn't stop him from loving the game. When Fernando met Snookie at a sports bar one night, he was impressed by her knowledge of football and even liked the fact that she could cuss like a man, with no apologies. They hit it off immediately. After several drinks and a good game on TV, they began a conversation.

"So, Fernando. You married?"

"Nope."

"Got any kids?"

"Nope. Don't want any, either."

Snookie smiled, "I think I love you."

He laughed. "And, what about you?"

"Not married, no kids, don't want any," Snookie grinned.

"Perfect," he grinned back.

They clinked their glasses together.

Three months later, Snookie McClain and Fernando Watson got married by a justice of the peace. Shawna stood up for her and Fernando had his best friend Mickey. They drove to New Orleans, which was a couple of hours away, and enjoyed three wonderful days in the Big Easy, and then Snookie had to get back to work.

As Snookie soon found out, three months was not enough time to get to know her new husband. Since Fernando and Mickey had been roommates, Fernando immediately moved in with her when they returned from their honeymoon. All of his worldly possessions fit into two large boxes and a duffle bag.

While they were dating, Snookie had no idea what Fernando did during the day while she was at work. He told her that he and Mickey had a computer business. She thought that sounded pretty lucrative, since the computer people she knew of made very good money. Now that he was at her place all day, she realized that he was playing Super Mario Brothers, watching Jerry Springer and eating her out of house and home. Whatever money he had been spending on her during their short courtship had dried up and now she was taking care of him and his childish habits. How does a woman who doesn't want any children end up with a big ass baby?

“Do you actually make any money, Fernando?” she asked after a long day. “I can use a little help with the bills.”

“You know I got a bad knee.”

“What does that have to do with you getting a job?”

“You were doing just fine before I got here, so what’s the problem?”

“Are you serious?”

He reached into his pocket and pulled out a few bills. “Here, now stop bothering me, woman.”

Snookie counted out forty-three dollars.

“You’re lucky you rock my world in bed,” she snapped. “Cause the minute you slip up on *that* game, your ass is outta here.”

Snookie was willing to suck up her bad judgment, but she wasn’t a total fool. Having Fernando around kept her out of trouble. She had pretty much been through the pool of available black men in her area of Mobile without sleeping with completely undesirable guys or other people’s husbands. She really liked Fernando and was content for the moment. At least he finally got a job as a night club bouncer. Snookie appreciated the effort. He cared about her and didn’t want to lose her. A little help with the bills and great sex was all Snookie asked for.

They enjoyed another six months of ignorant bliss, until the unthinkable happened. Snookie found out that she was pregnant. In her mind, that was the worst possible thing to have happened to her in a long time. She had been taking birth control pills for years, so she was appalled and knew that she would have to immediately have an abortion. What she wasn’t prepared for was Fernando’s reaction. Even though Snookie was absolutely sure that she didn’t want to be a mother, somehow Fernando’s dumb ass decided that he would make a great father and was hoping that they had a son.

“What the hell are you talking about?” Snookie asked. “What happened to the guy who said that kids are just demanding little bloodsuckers and receptacles for germs?”

“What can I say?” Fernando innocently responded. “My sperm never made it to the finish line before.”

Weeks of begging and pleading did no good. Fernando insisted on her having the baby and Snookie was adamant about never going through the agonies of motherhood. Compromise came with a high price. Snookie would be willing to carry and give birth to the baby. That meant that she would stop drinking and try to take better care of herself. Fernando would agree to take full custody and Snookie would help out financially, but he would have to sign the divorce papers that she would file as soon as the baby was born. In a perfect world, they both would have had a change of heart, been thrilled to bring a child into the world, and experience all the joys of the blessed miracle. But Snookie knew better than that. The world was far from perfect. The former Snookie McClain, now Snookie Watson, filed her divorce papers and handed over her new baby boy to Fernando Watson on the same day, with no regrets.

For the next few months, Snookie kept herself busy. She wasn't one to hide how she felt, so her circumstances were no secret to the people around her. They didn't understand, some turned their backs on her, but they had to respect her willingness to follow her own heart and mind. She was a little more subdued than she was before, but still didn't indulge in real relationships. After her marriage fiasco, she just went back to her old, typical behavior. Her divorce became final and she was free again.

One night, Snookie was on a blind date with a retired pro football player she met through Jenna Casperian, her supervisor at work. His name was Oscar Beaumont and Jenna was his sister. He lived in Los Angeles and was a former player with the Rams before the team left the city. Oscar was in Mobile to visit his family and was looking forward to having fun on his vacation, so Jenna made a suggestion that he go out with Snookie. Most of the ladies Jenna knew were married or in other relationships. The ladies Oscar used to hang out with had either gotten married or left town. Snookie had vowed to give up the blind dates, but since it was her boss who was asking, what could she say? One more couldn't hurt, right?

"Wow, you got some skinny legs, gal," Oscar said as Snookie approached him in front of her building at work.

"Really?" Snookie snapped. "And you look fuckin' gay."

He was shocked for a second, and then broke into a hearty laugh. Even if it were true, he would be the last person that anyone would mistake for being gay by looking at him. He was big and rugged, just the way Snookie liked her men.

"Damn, with that mouth, you must be Snookie."

"And if you're Oscar, I'm gonna go back upstairs and slap a bitch right now."

"Don't call my sister a bitch. She's a really nice lady."

From that moment on, Snookie and Oscar had a fun, week-long relationship. The day that he went back to Los Angeles, she gave her job a 30-day notice and made plans to move to California. She wasn't even going there to be with him. She just got so caught up in all of the stories he told about his celebrity friends, that she had stars in her eyes and became obsessed with living in La La Land. Snookie finally found her motivation.

Fernando gave Snookie his blessing. She kissed him and her baby goodbye, but it was with the same fondness in which she treated her nieces and nephews. She was able to leave her baby in good hands. Fernando really did turn out to be a good father. Her sister, Shawna, agreed to help him with little Fernando, Jr. in any way she could. Snookie's family was supportive and all agreed to help out. They gave her a nice going away party. Shawna hugged her tight and said, "I'm gonna miss you, Snookie, but now I'm finally gonna have someplace cool to visit."

As soon as Snookie arrived in Los Angeles, she found out that her good friend Oscar Beaumont had gone to Las Vegas and gotten married to a stripper three days before, and wasn't coming back to Los Angeles for a few months. Luckily, Snookie wasn't depending on him to help her out. Jenna had connections that she used to get Snookie a couple of job interviews to compensate for her wayward brother, and Snookie was able to get a job right away.

***

For the next two years, Snookie worked in the Social Services Department for the City of Los Angeles. Even in Tinsel Town, it didn't take long for Snookie to burn out. Things were good for a while, but the hours were long and the booming social life that Snookie expected to find was hard to come by. All day, every day, she dealt with the less fortunate, and people in trouble. In a twisted way, it made her feel good. Most of Snookie's workday consisted of removing children from homes where their safety was in jeopardy. Observing these mothers reminded her of her own childhood. She never thought any mothers could be worse than Jessie Mae, but she saw things that made life in her dysfunctional family look like the Cosby Show.

As much as it could be satisfying to help these children, it could also be dangerous. She always worked with a partner and rarely was able to do her job without some sort of incident. A few of the areas she covered were in neighborhoods with a lot of gang activity. That was something she had to get used to dealing with.

After two years of this high stress routine, it took a toll on her. She was tough, but even she had her limitations. As always, she dealt with some of the strain by drinking herself into a state of numbness some nights. One thing about being a miserable person is that you take the misery wherever you go. Snookie kept searching outside of herself for the answers that would continue to elude her.

Once again, Snookie needed a break. In her leisure time, she tried to get to places where she could spot a movie star. On Saturday afternoons, she went window-shopping in the Beverly Center or strolled down Rodeo Drive. And she never missed an opportunity to catch a ceremony in Hollywood when a celebrity got a new star on the Walk of Fame or their footprints at the Chinese Theatre. That was her idea of stargazing.

The National Enquirer and People Magazine were Snookie's favorite sources of research material. Most of the stores and restaurants that the celebrities frequented were way out of her league. Even if she had the money, she would stick out like a sore thumb. She just didn't have the style or the personality to hang with the stars. Her socializing would look more like stalking. She would never admit it, though. But Snookie was dying to see someone famous in Hollywood. This was Tinsel Town, land of the beautiful people. She should be able to see some of them somewhere. Celebrities hung out all the time in Los Angeles, but they were surely hanging out somewhere else, because she never saw anybody that she wanted to see.

CHAPTER 27

Aurora

While Aurora and her friends were deciding where to attend college, Chicago had one of the worst winters on record. Snow, ice and that awful wind off the lake drove them to pursue greener and warmer pastures. Much to her mother's pleasure, Aurora decided to attend UCLA. That's where Camille was going to go before she gave up her college dreams for a man who stopped appreciating her.

The week of Christmas, for Aurora's seventeenth birthday, Baxter took Camille and his two daughters to see the musical, *Cats,* downtown in the Loop District. It was Chicago's version of Broadway. They had a late supper and an all-around fantastic time. It was Sharon's first time seeing a professional stage show. She was mesmerized and didn't say one word until the show was over, not even during intermission. However, once they were outside, she couldn't contain her excitement and declared to everyone within earshot that she wanted to be a Broadway star.

"I'll be in the front row every night," Aurora assured her.

"Me too, sweetie," Camille added.

"What about you, Daddy?" Sharon asked.

"I'll have to see if you can sing and dance first," he said.

"Daddy!" Sharon exclaimed with a disapproving look.

"Just kidding, baby," Baxter laughed. "I'll bring all of Chicago."

"Okay, that's better."

That night, Baxter spent the night in Camille's bed. Aurora wasn't sure how she felt about her parents sleeping together. They kept going back and forth. She would be happy if she thought it could last, but she knew that he would find a way to screw it up.

In the morning, the phone rang. Aurora heard it, but immediately fell back asleep. Thirty minutes later, the sound of her mother's voice screaming and cursing is what woke her again. She ran into Sharon's room and saw her sitting up, apparently frightened.

Aurora turned on the radio to drown out the voices, sat down and held her sister tight.

"It's alright, Sharon," she said. "Everything's fine."

Aurora could hear part of her mother's rant. Some woman had called looking for Baxter. Camille had answered the phone and spoken to the woman, whose name was Julie Carson. The same Julie Carson who had almost ruined prom for her mother so many years ago when she found out that Baxter was sleeping with her.

"What the hell was she calling here for?" Aurora wondered.

Next thing she heard was Baxter calling Camille crazy and slamming the door on his way out. So much for having peace. Things began to look like the old war zone that she remembered when she was ten. Baxter maintained his relationship with his daughters, but he and Camille were done. It was too painful, so Camille went back to treating him with an icy indifference.

Somewhere along the way, Aurora developed a crush on Dex Taylor, Baxter's drummer. He had come to a couple of basketball games and then taken them out for pizza afterwards. Deehna had been doing all of the flirting, but she was so eager that he practically ignored her and began to give most of his attention to Aurora.

Aurora seemed a little shy to him. Because she was so toughened by her attitude about boys, she wasn't that experienced, even though she had plenty of opportunities. He could see a little change in her and guessed that she was still a virgin. He wondered what it would be like to deflower a beauty like her, but wasn't sure that he wanted to deal with Baxter Duncan. Even a man like Baxter, who has ruined many daughters in his day, doesn't want his own daughter messing around with somebody just like him.

One night, Deehna convinced Dex to take them to his apartment where they could smoke weed and listen to music. Deehna fell asleep on the couch an hour later and Dex tool Aurora into his bedroom. She wasn't nervous, she felt that she knew him pretty well, but she had no idea what to expect. She wanted something to happen, though.

So, when Dex walked up to her and she could smell his pleasant musk, she merely closed her eyes. He quickly and efficiently removed her top and her bra. As she stood half naked in front of him, she made no move when he gently kissed her for the first time. He kissed her lips, slipping his tongue around the inside of her mouth. She shivered when his lips brushed her bare shoulders and moaned when his tongue flicked over her hardened nipples. He laid her on the bed, licked and kissed all over her for about twenty minutes, and then suddenly stopped.

"Get dressed. Time to go home."

He walked out of the room to wake Deehna, who was still a little woozy. Aurora came out a couple of minutes later, feeling woozy, too.

"You okay?" Deehna asked, gathering her things.

"I'm fine," Aurora responded. "C'mon, it's getting late."

"Be safe," Dex said as he closed the door behind them.

The next day, Dex quit Baxter's band and Aurora never saw him again. Apparently, an angry Baxter Duncan was not something that Dex was willing to chance.

***

Aurora Duncan managed to graduate from high school with honors, and with her virtue intact. After a hot summer working as a camp counselor, she was excited about being out of Chicago for the first time and going to UCLA to major in Business Administration. Her parents and grandparents went to Los Angeles with her to help her get settled. They bought her all kinds of things for her dorm room to make it homey. Most things she wouldn't need, but it made them feel good to spoil her.

As much as Aurora hated how Baxter treated her mother when she was growing up, she just couldn't stay away from musicians. One of her favorite places to hang out was a jazz spot in Westwood called The Indigo, not far from campus. She really enjoyed listening to the talented young singers and musicians and remembered how she liked to put together shows when she was in high school. She certainly didn't have time for any of that with her heavy course load, but she always made time to go to the Indigo.

During her UCLA years, Aurora made a lot of friends, mostly guys, and supported as many of their activities as she was able to without her grades suffering. So she was at football games, basketball games and music gigs in her spare time. She loved hanging around with the guys, and they loved hanging out with her, too. She was smart, beautiful, and mostly immune to them in any romantic way. She just didn't trust giving her heart to anyone. That somehow endeared her to them. They all felt protective of her and wanted to make sure that she didn't get hurt. If only they could.

One thing about a woman when it comes to men: she has to make her own mistakes and learn her own lessons. Aurora didn't trust a man to get close to her again, the way that Dex Taylor did, until she was twenty-two years old. Somehow, when her protectors weren't looking, she allowed a man inside of her walls, figuratively and literally. It was no surprise that he was a musician. His name was Walter Benson, an older black man in his forties, well established in the music industry as a keyboard player, producer and executive. He was also a regular at the Indigo and had many conversations with Aurora over several months.

While she received an education in how the music business worked, she found herself intrigued by him. In this case, he was the innocent. It never even occurred to him that he had a chance with a woman like Aurora, but as they became friends, she saw that there was something special about him. He was kind and gentle, and always took time to answer her many questions. He had lost his wife to cancer two years before.

One night after the show, she asked if they could go for coffee. She wanted to continue their conversation about licensing and royalties. He agreed and they found themselves at a local diner. He could see that Aurora had a special gift when it came to business. There was a determination in her that didn't allow for her to be intimidated by what she didn't know. She was willing to learn. That was her strength. By the time they got to dessert, he had offered her a job, upon graduation, as a junior executive at his company, Tazora Records. She was thrilled to accept.

Aurora also accepted a nightcap in his nearby home in Beverly Hills, where she lost her virginity and spent the night making love to her future boss.

CHAPTER 28

Debbie

The first thing Debbie Marshall had to do after arriving in Los Angeles was find a place to stay. The only person she knew was John Becker, so she called the number on the back of the card he gave her. He was happily surprised to hear from her so soon and immediately sent a car to pick her up at the bus station.

John had an office at Warner Bros. studios, where he was overseeing production of a feature film. He sent Paula, a production assistant, to pick Debbie up and bring her to the set. Debbie had two large suitcases with her. They walked onto the set just as the cast and crew were breaking for lunch. Actors were dressed in beautiful costumes. The movie was about dancers who lived, loved and prospered during the Harlem Renaissance.

Paula pointed to John, who was talking to the director. He waved Debbie over.

"Go ahead, I'll watch your bags," Paula said, smiling.

"Okay, thank you."

As they hugged, John said, "Debbie! I'm so glad you called. Are you okay?"

"Yeah," she replied. "At least I think I am."

"I want you to meet John Singleton," he said. "John, this is my niece, Debbie Marshall, fresh from present-day Harlem."

"Hi," said Debbie.

"Hi, Debbie," John Singleton said as he shook her hand. "It's nice to meet you. How do you like our Hollywood version of old Harlem?"

"Pretty impressive," she said, looking around in awe.

"Listen, I gotta run. Enjoy yourself, young lady. See you upstairs, JB."

Debbie watched him walk away. "Wow, that was really him? He was so nice."

"Yes. You'll get another chance to see him. Right now, you must be starving after that long bus ride. How about some lunch?"

"Yeah, I guess."

"Look, I have to go into a meeting, but I'm going to have Paula take care of you until I get back. Then we can talk, okay?"

"Okay," she said.

",Are those your bags over there by Paula?"

"Yes."

"Do you already have a place to stay?"

"No, but I have some money. I figured I'd get a room somewhere."

"That's ridiculous. I have plenty of room at my house. I'll call my fiancée, Rhonda, and have her get a room ready for you. End of discussion."

"I really appreciate it. Thank you."

"No worries." John kissed her on the cheek and managed to get Paula's attention. "See you a little later."

"Hey, John?"

"Yeah."

"You introduced me to John Singleton as your niece."

"Hey, kiddo, your father was like a brother to me. I think Michael would want someone looking out for you. Would you prefer that I didn't refer to you as family?"

"No, of course not. I just…no, not at all." Debbie said as Paula walked up.

"Cool," said John. "Paula, take good care of my niece. You can put her bags in the office for the time being. And make sure she eats lunch and gets some of that peach cobbler before it's all gone."

"Of course."

"Save me some, too."

"Thank you." Debbie said as she gave John a hug.

"See you later, kid."

Paula grabbed the handle to one of the suitcases. "Come on, Debbie," she said. "Damn lucky these things are on wheels."

Debbie laughed, and as she passed the beautiful set that looked like Harlem in the twenties, she felt something that she hadn't felt before. She wasn't sure what that feeling was and she didn't know why she felt that way, but she certainly knew that it was good.

There was a melancholy moment when she felt that her parents were watching over her and protecting her from up in heaven in a way that they never could here on Earth. She felt that she was exactly where she was supposed to be and that everything was going to be okay. It was a feeling of hope that was going to be enough to sustain her.

At the end of the day, which took seven more hours, Debbie was exhausted and stuffed. It seemed like she was eating something every fifteen minutes. There was so much food all over the place. She kept thinking that it was amazing that the set wasn't full of fat people. Then again, she couldn't help but notice that some of those cameramen were a little hefty.

John and Rhonda lived with their two German Shepherds in a beautiful, four-bedroom house in the Hollywood Hills. It was a Spanish style house with spacious rooms, a huge patio, and a view that overlooked the city and took your breath away, especially at night when the lights of the city sparkled as far as the eye could see. People who arrived in LA and saw a view like that, rarely wanted to leave, Debbie included.

For three weeks, Debbie had a blast meeting actors, producers and crewmembers. She loved the excitement and saw how much work and how many people it took to make one movie. She also learned a lot by paying attention to what everyone did on the set. John allowed her to work as an extra during the last week of shooting. She made money, but the long hours of sitting around bored her. She wanted to be doing something more.

Rhonda was very nice to Debbie. She was a voiceover performer. Her current job was as an animation voice on a huge Disney film. She worked a lot, but her jobs only lasted about two or three hours at a time. She didn't even have to get dressed or put on makeup to go to work. She took Debbie with her a couple of times and then they would spend the rest of the day shopping, walking the dogs, Savannah and Denver, and making wedding plans. John and Rhonda were getting married in October, five months away.

When Debbie went back to the movie set with John, she started to hang around the wardrobe trailer and got to know the wardrobe supervisor and other wardrobe people. That was mostly socializing. However, when Tracy Cook, the head costume designer, was around, Debbie asked a hundred questions. Now that was an interesting job.

John Becker was a blessing to Debbie. He helped her in many ways. Rhonda agreed that Debbie should continue to stay with them while she saved her money. John gave her a job in the wardrobe department on several movies and was able to buy her an inexpensive car. She really became part of the family. A family that was about to grow.

In July, Rhonda found out that she was pregnant. John was very excited. He had briefly been married after graduating from college, but that only lasted a couple of years and he and his wife never had any children. He had vowed to remain a bachelor forever until he met Rhonda two years before. Falling in love with her had changed his attitude and his life. Now he was actually looking forward to having a real family.

Debbie insisted on helping Rhonda prepare the nursery and Rhonda insisted on paying her. Debbie painted walls and baby furniture. She also made curtains, pillows and baby clothes. The two of them spent glorious afternoons preparing for the wedding and the birth. Rhonda recognized her talents.

"You are really handy with a sewing machine, Debbie."

"I've always loved to make clothes."

"I love the suggestions you made on designs for the bridesmaids' dresses. Would you consider helping to make them? I know that Tracy is going to have her hands full with my dress and I really want them to be fabulous."

"Of course I'll help," Debbie responded. "I think your ideas are beautiful. I could whip them up in no time."

"Well you'd better whip up one for yourself. I want you to be a bridesmaid, too."

Debbie squealed with delight and gave Rhonda a big hug. When they told John later that night, he was very pleased. He worked so many late hours, he was just grateful that Rhonda had some company at home when he wasn't around.

"I'm going to send you over to Desmond," he said. "He'll be a big help to you. He's doing the tuxes and he's very meticulous.

He'll want to make sure that things are coordinated. Tracy hasn't gotten to him yet."

"Lawrence Desmond, the famous designer?"

"The very same."

"Cool."

Life couldn't be better. Debbie was going to be a bridesmaid and help design gorgeous dresses. As for her love life, she was determined to forego relationships for a while. She didn't really have time for dating, with the long hours on the set, but it was hard to stay neutral in a place like Hollywood. She met handsome actors everywhere she went. They hit on her and she flirted back, but it was like having too much candy. It was good while you were eating it, but it made you sick after a while.

To her surprise, when she did develop a crush, it was on the wrong person. John took Debbie to meet Lawrence Desmond, a well-known fashion designer who was going to be one of John's groomsmen. Lawrence, in his late forties, was a very distinguished looking man who was well respected among his peers. He was also very married.

"So nice to meet you, Debbie," said Lawrence. "I hear that you are a very talented designer."

"They exaggerated a little," she said, embarrassed. "I'm very interested, though."

"Don't be modest, my dear," Lawrence said. "It doesn't go too far in this town."

"More is better," John laughed, "I told Debbie it's alright to leave folks with the impression that you're already doing what they think you can, as long as you back it up."

Debbie and Lawrence got together several times to coordinate the bridal party's attire. He was making the tuxedoes and she was working with Rhonda's designer on the bridesmaids' dresses. One meeting probably would have been sufficient, but Debbie found it difficult to stay away and kept coming up with reasons to visit the studio, which was big, but not very inspiring. Lawrence had a living space full of dark, wood furniture. Everything was conservative. His wife obviously had no hand in decorating this space. The décor was definitely manly. "Old manly," she giggled to herself.

Debbie enjoyed picking Lawrence's brain about the fashion industry. They had an easy chemistry and even though Lawrence was reserved and a little stuffy, he was able to loosen up and relax when he was around Debbie. She had found a friend, and although they were both aware of their physical attraction, neither of them dared to mention it nor had any intention of doing anything about it. She knew that he had a daughter around her age. It would be really crazy to think that they could be more than friends.

Finally, the big day arrived. The wedding and reception were held at the exquisite Malibu Beach Country Club. Debbie was excited. It was the first wedding she had ever attended and it was beautiful. Everyone and everything was new to her. She shouldn't have been so happy at the thought of walking down the aisle with Lawrence, but that was the truth. She had been paired up with him and it was everything that her little fantasy world had conjured up. Lawrence looked handsome in his tux. As a matter of fact, the entire wedding party looked amazing, thanks to the talented designers.

There was a nice selection of celebrities and celebrity photographers who came out to see John and Rhonda get married. John Becker was well known and well liked in Hollywood, so not too many people were going to turn down an invitation to the lavish event. Everything had been worked out to the last detail and went off without a hitch. Even the weather, which is often predictable, was especially beautiful for their day.

At the reception, Debbie was still glowing after taking pictures and enjoying her partnership with Lawrence. And as everyone else sat at the bridal table drinking expensive champagne and basking in the glow of happiness, she couldn't help but notice once again how elegant and sexy he was. It was something about the way that he looked at her when he answered her questions. Sometimes she found it easy to forget that he was married. Today, however, she met his beautiful wife, Anita, who was seated at one of the tables with some of her friends. If Anita had been paying closer attention, she might have spotted the first signs of trouble.

First of all, Debbie looked hot in a beautiful lavender gown with a low cut front. Rhonda had worked with a designer friend who helped her make the wedding gown, and also helped to design the bridesmaids' dresses. Debbie finished them off with her special touch. She did beautiful work and the dresses fit each of the women like a glove.

Lawrence noticed that Debbie had a hunger and a passion for fashion, and it intrigued him. He was a major player in the industry, but she treated him like he was special without sucking up to him like some of the people he had to deal with. With Debbie asking so many questions and being so excited about everything, he couldn't help but feel knowledgeable and powerful. That was very seductive.

At the bridal table, Lawrence felt the connection with Debbie and knew that he should limit his time with her. After dinner was over, he cut their conversation short, and decided to go over and pay more attention to his wife. Anita wasn't going to make it easy for him, though. She had developed an awful headache and wanted to leave early. Lawrence was more than happy to take his wife home, but she insisted that he stay. Not only was he part of the bridal party but because a lot of these people were in the industry, she understood that he could make a lot of new business contacts at an affair like this. His tuxedoes were as big a hit with the men as the gowns were with the women. Besides, Anita had already arranged to get a ride with a couple that lived around the corner from them. He walked her out to her car.

When Lawrence arrived back inside, the guests were dancing up a storm. The live band was very good. As he stood in the doorway, Debbie snuck up behind him.

"I thought I lost my partner there for a minute," she said.

"Only for a minute."

"Can you still manage a move or two?"

"Are you kidding me?" Lawrence grinned. "I was the Gregory Hines of my high school."

"That was a thousand years ago. What you got now?"

Lawrence laughed as Debbie took his hand and pulled him onto the dance floor. He tried to whisk her into some kind of fancy ballroom steps, but she wasn't having it.

"Come on, dude. No grandpa dancing. We're gonna do what you grown folks call boogie down." Lawrence had to laugh. Debbie was so full of life and very fun to be around. His wife, Anita, had become so serious lately. He really couldn't talk, though. He was serious most of the time. After working up a sweat, the music slowed down.

"Alright, I need to get some water," Lawrence insisted, as he led Debbie off the dance floor. "Not too bad for an old man, huh?"

"Not bad at all, Mr. Desmond."

One of guys that Debbie had worked with grabbed her back to the dance floor.

"Come on, sexy. Let me see some of those moves."

Lawrence watched as the man took Debbie into his arms, slowly moving to the rhythm. As she danced, she couldn't help but notice that Lawrence was watching her with a strange look on his face. She recognized that look. She had seen that look before. Lawrence wanted her, but heaven knows that she had been down that road already. Debbie really liked him, but she wasn't going to be messing with older men anymore. Oh, right. And, especially not if they were married.

John and Rhonda Becker honeymooned in Maui for a week while Debbie enjoyed their beautiful house in the Hills with the family dogs, Savannah and Denver. She didn't have to work that week, so she pretended that she was a wealthy lady of leisure. She finally had a chance to sit down and write a letter to her grandparents back in New York. She had been sending postcards to them and letting them know how she was doing. She had also sent a letter and some pictures to her friend Madeline Clayton. They all wrote back quickly to give their support. It was difficult for Debbie to reach back into the past. That's what it felt like to her now that her life had so drastically changed, but they were all genuinely happy for her and wished her well.

Debbie spent one beautiful afternoon sunbathing in a tiny bikini and sipping frozen margaritas on the patio by the pool. She fantasized about being a big time fashion designer one day. Suddenly, the dogs were barking at the sound of the front doorbell. Debbie wasn't expecting anyone, but she grabbed her cover-up and tied it on as she walked through the house to open the front door. Standing there was a UPS deliveryman, a very cute UPS deliveryman, in sexy brown shorts.

"Hi. I have a package for Debbie Marshall," he said.

"That's me," Debbie said as she took the pen that he offered.

"Sign right here, please."

Debbie smiled broadly as she signed with a flourish. He handed her the well-wrapped package. "And this is for you."

"Thank you."

"My pleasure," he said. "Have a good day, miss."

"You, too."

She looked at his tight butt as he strutted away. She had to laugh at herself. She shut the door and headed into the house with her package. She put it on the couch and while she went to look for a pair of scissors to cut the heavy tape that sealed the box, the bell rang again. This time she let the cover-up fall open. When she opened the door this time, she was looking into the handsome face of Lawrence Desmond, looking so proper in his preppy shirt and shorts.

"Oh, my!" he exclaimed.

"Lawrence!" she said as she covered herself.

"I…I'm sorry, Debbie. Am I interrupting you?"

"Yeah…I mean, no. Not really. I was just out by the pool."

"I was in the neighborhood and thought I'd stop by to see how you were doing up here all by yourself."

"Well, since you came all the way up the hill, you might as well come on in and join me for a margarita."

"Thanks." He followed her into the house.

"Go on out and make yourself comfortable," she said. "I'll get you a glass."

Minutes later she returned to the patio and they talked and laughed and finished a pitcher of margaritas. "I'm thirsty," Lawrence said.

"You've been drinking for an hour."

"I need some water, if you don't mind."

"Of course," she said, taking the pitcher. "I'll make a fresh batch."

While she was in the kitchen, she remembered her package, found the scissors and went to open it. Inside was a beautifully tailored black jacket, complete with a tan silk lining and the Lawrence Desmond label embroidered inside. Debbie was very touched. She put the jacket down and returned to the patio carrying a tray with a fresh pitcher of margaritas, salt, lime, two bottles of water, and a bowl of chips and salsa.

"Service with a smile," she said, placing the refreshments on the table with a flourish. "I'll be right back."

"Alright," he said, grabbing one of the water bottles.

Debbie went back to the living room, took off the cover-up and put the jacket on. It was a perfect fit.

"Look what I found," said Debbie, returning to the patio and spinning around to show off the jacket. "You are sneaky, Mr. Desmond."

"I was hoping that the UPS truck was here for you. You look fantastic," said Lawrence. "I ought to sell a million of those if they look that good on everyone."

"Why did you send this to me, Lawrence?"

"A thank-you gift for being so helpful to me during the wedding preparations."

"I probably shouldn't accept it, but it's so beautiful."

"You have to. It was made for you and it would be bad manners to turn it down."

"Alright, but I don't want to get it messed up. I'm going to hang it up properly."

"Alright, I'll pour us a couple of these refreshing drinks."

"You do that, Mr. Desmond," she said, bouncing into the house. "You still have a lot of catching up to do."

When she came back, she was in her bikini with no cover-up. Lawrence whistled. "Are you trying to test my heart?" he asked.

Debbie laughed as she took the glass that he handed her. "Well, thanks to you, I can't begin my nude sunbathing."

"Don't let me stop you," he smiled with a twinkle in his eyes.

"Oh, I'm sure."

After more margaritas, great conversation and a few laughs, Lawrence reluctantly got up to leave. Despite the strong physical attraction, they acted as though they were just two friends having a drink together. No pressure. They both were well aware that one step down that road and there would be no coming back.

"This has been lovely, but I've got to get home," he said. "Anita is having a cocktail party."

"Well, thanks for stopping by," Debbie said. "And thanks again for the jacket."

"My pleasure," he said, taking her hand and kissing it. "Enjoy your afternoon."

Debbie walked him to the door and waved as he made his way to his car. She breathed a sigh of relief. One wrong move by either of them and they would have made a huge mistake. She realized that her crush was strong. She wanted to have sex with Lawrence Desmond as much as he wanted to have sex with her. It could never happen.

CHAPTER 29

Candy

After Candy discovered Willard with the drag queen at USC, she got a bottle of vodka and took it back to her apartment. She looked into her bedroom mirror and hated her reflection. All she could see was the funny-looking black girl who grew up taunted by the other children. After years of etiquette classes and charm school, Candy still had emotional scars that she couldn't overcome, so instead she drank herself into a stupor. When Candy drank, she was in her own world: a world where she could look into the mirror and pretend that the image was white and pure. That was when she saw a product of Miss Kelsey's Charm School. That was when she saw a lady. But, no amount of charm school could make her love herself.

However, she knew how to give herself a temporary fix. After sleeping off the vodka, she got up around 4:00 pm and jumped into her shower. After a nice, hot scrubbing, she felt much better and decided to get herself dolled up. She threw on a skimpy dress, some strappy heels and headed to the nearest yuppie bar.

Candy spent the next few weeks barhopping and jumping into bed with whatever white man she could seduce that night. She felt no need to waste her time hanging around black people. And she sure as hell wasn't going to sleep with a black man. As Candy so boldly told Sam Atkins, a gay, white man who was one of her fellow make-up artists, "There's no way that I'm going to take a chance on getting pregnant by some nappy-headed Zulu."

Sam looked at Candy in shock. "Honey, have you looked in a mirror lately?"

"What are you trying to say?"

Sam saw that she was deadly serious.

"Well, I mean, come on, sweetie. That's a hell of a thing to say about your own people," he responded, carefully. "Isn't that like talking bad about your own father?"

"You're darn skippy. Although I never had the pleasure of meeting him personally, he probably *was* a nappy-headed Zulu."

They had a good laugh, but Sam realized how deeply wounded Candy was, and how self-hatred was eating her alive. Candy was a beautiful woman who didn't know how beautiful she was, inside and out. All she knew was that she never wanted children who looked like her. No black babies, no black men.

After a few years in LA, Candy discovered how cool black could be when you were the social curiosity. Most of the people she hung out with were white. Candy was ambitious and decided to get her real estate license while she was working steady as a make-up artist. She loved the film business, but she hated the long hours. She was ready to make some big money and she knew that with her ability to deal with white people, she would be very successful. They had money. She needed money. Simple.

She had always liked being the chocolate drop in a vanilla crowd and was actually intimidated by black women, which is why she didn't have many black friends in LA. The black guys she knew all wanted white girls, or at least light-skinned black girls. That was fine with her, because she didn't want them, either, and they knew it.

However, curious white boys, experimenting with forbidden fruit, wanted Candy. That was what made her feel special. It was superficial, but she had to take acceptance where it was offered. She could not stop craving the attention of white people. That was something that really annoyed the black women she encountered. Deep down she envied black women who loved their own dark skin, but just like back home in South Carolina, they thought she was trying to be better than them.

There was one thing that made Candy's life much better. She had replaced her good wigs with a good weave. Nothing gave her greater pleasure than sewing some Asian or Indian woman's hair into her scalp and swinging it around as if she had grown it for years. She put the discovery of the hair weave right up there with the invention of the brassiere: improved the quality of life for millions of women forever.

One summer, Sam Atkins invited Candy to come to New Orleans as part of his make-up team to work on the set of a movie called *Jazz Girl*. It was a three-month gig and he promised her top dollar, so she decided to go for it. She would be ready to concentrate on her new career in real estate once she returned to LA. She had a great time in New Orleans. There was great food, she could smoke pot out on the corner with some of the crew, even with the cops passing by, and she could take her Hurricanes to go.

One day while the cast and crew were breaking for lunch, Candy got to the catering area late and most of the seats were taken. There were about a hundred and fifty people working that day. It was hot and the tables and chairs were set up outside under a huge tent. The crew always got in line first so they could get back to the set. Candy could have cut the line, but even the extras had already gotten their food. After she made her way through the pasta bar, the salad bar, and the last of the dessert choices, she looked around and saw an empty chair next to Sam, who was chumming it up with Juan Figueroa, a guy he liked from the wardrobe department. She went over there.

"Hey, Sam," Candy asked, holding her tray of food. "Is anyone sitting here?"

Juan replied, "I was saving this one for Debbie, my wardrobe assistant, but we can squeeze you in."

Sam got up. "Hold on, sweetie. I'll get you a chair."

He got up and found a chair at the end of the tent.

"Thanks, Sam."

A few minutes later, Debbie Marshall came with her tray.

"Where have you been, girl?" asked Juan. "Lunch is over."

"Sorry, I had to make a phone call."

"Hope he's worth it," Juan laughed. "Do you know everybody?"

"I've seen you guys, but we haven't officially met."

Juan continued, "Debbie Marshall is my wonderful wardrobe assistant. Debbie, this is Sam Atkins, key make-up, and Candy, uh…what's your last name?"

"Martin," she said. "Nice to meet you."

"Candy is a very talented makeup artist," said Sam.

"Now that all the butts have been kissed, did anybody see that extra get thrown off the set for trying to get Eddie Murphy's autograph?"

They all laughed and ate until time to get back to set.

"You're not from here are you?" Candy asked Debbie as they walked back to the crew trailers.

"No, I came in from LA."

"Me, too," Candy said. "But you don't sound like you were born there. I noticed that you have a slight New York accent.

"You're right. Born and raised in Harlem. I can't tell where you're from. You sound like the lady on the six o'clock news."

Candy laughed, "I'm actually from South Carolina."

"Get outta here. I never would've guessed."

"I lost my accent a long time ago," Candy said. "So, you work in the business, you're from LA…I'm surprised we haven't met before."

"Is this your first John Becker production?" Debbie asked.

"Yes, it is."

"Well, I've only worked on his projects."

"Oh, good for you," Candy said. "His company has done some great work. Do you know him?"

"He's kind of my uncle," Debbie said, a little embarrassed.

"Kind of?"

"He was my father's best friend, but please don't say nothin' to anybody. People act different when they think you haven't paid your dues. Know what I mean?"

"Yes, but you know how Hollywood is. Everybody is using whatever advantages they can to get by. There's no shame in that."

"I guess you're right," Debbie said, thinking about it.

"You said he *was* your father's best friend. They aren't friends anymore?"

"My father died a few years ago."

"Oh, Debbie, I'm so sorry."

"It's alright. It was really hard at the time, but I'm good now. John came for the funeral and told me to look him up if I ever came to LA, so that's what I did and he took me under his wing. He and his wife accepted me as family and it's been great."

"What does your mother think about all this?"

Debbie put her head down. "My mother died when I was born."

"Good Lord!" Candy exclaimed. "I thought I had it rough. I don't even know who my father is."

They reached the area where they had to go separate ways.

"See you around, Debbie."

"See you."

Candy didn't make friends with black women very easily so she was surprised that she enjoyed talking to Debbie so much. Maybe it's because she was able to relate to her and some of the loneliness she must have experienced as a child without a mother. Candy had a different kind of loneliness, but she also realized that she wasn't alone. Poor Debbie never had a mother. At least she had Katie and Gwen to watch over her, a loving mother and a crazy grandmother. Debbie was an orphan.

They saw each other throughout the rest of the shoot and spoke at lunch several times. Candy even invited Debbie to hang out with her and her friends the night that the movie wrapped, which was a big step for Candy. She just didn't socialize with her own people, but something about Debbie caused her to make an exception, but the girl never showed up. Oh well, she tried.

The same week that Candy returned to LA, she got a call from Bruce Mullen. He was her first real estate client and was prepared to introduce her to the future. Candy had met Bruce while shopping one day at Trader Joe's. After a brief discussion about red wine, he had invited her over to his place around the corner to taste their selections. They had been having hot sex for about a month before she left for New Orleans to work on the movie. She didn't see any reason not to mix a little business with her pleasure. Bruce was white, wealthy, well connected and well hung: her favorite qualities in a man.

Bruce's grandfather, Popi Martini, was having a huge, star-studded birthday party that Saturday. Popi was the original owner of Popi's Place and had many celebrity friends. It was going to be the party of the year, or at least of the month. In Los Angeles, there was a "party of the year" every week. However, this was really going to be something special and Candy was not about to miss it.

“By the end of the night, you will have all the business that you can handle for a while,” Bruce said as she watched him prepare a welcome home dinner for her.

CHAPTER 30

Portia

Crazy as it seemed, Chuck Adams and Portia Taylor got married in a Las Vegas chapel five weeks after he proposed. He moved into her apartment and they began an unconventional union. After that infamous talk where they both came clean, they figured that they could talk about anything. They set a few ground rules for their marriage. He made her promise not to sleep with any other men and he promised to let her know if he slept with any other women. Crazy, but she agreed, as long as he never lied to her.

Chuck opened her up to every aspect of his life. She officially met Celia, who attended the ceremony with Chuck's daughter, Kayla, and George Montana came back up from LA for the wedding. After much pleading from Portia, Chuck promised to never reveal to anyone that his new bride was the "insatiable blond-haired big girl" that George said he had so much fun with at the birthday party. That would be their private joke.

Celia, who wasn't easily shocked by too many things, would have found it hard to believe that Portia was the masked blond, who had amazingly been able to make it through Chuck's birthday party without incident. Well, at least not any incident that was apparent at the time. Celia appeared to be truly happy for them. She took good care of Kayla, who was a sweet little angel, a perfect blend of both her parents.

A few months later, Chuck was working for the air conditioning installation company full-time and Portia had a long-term temp assignment as a receptionist in a plastic surgeon's office. Great sex was plentiful and Chuck knew how to make Portia feel good about herself. He really loved her curves and the way she took care of herself, always well groomed from head to toe. He shared the kitchen duties because he wanted her to have a break sometimes. She loved his cooking and he loved hers. Things were starting out just fine for the newlyweds.

Portia and Chuck hung out a couple of times a week. A lot of the time, she went with him to the Diamond Ball Gentlemen's Club to watch Amethyst, who was the star attraction. Celia danced there, too. Chuck and Portia were a great-looking couple having fun, and Portia trusted him completely. He left her no doubt that she was the one for him.

One morning, Chuck came running into the kitchen after being on the telephone for twenty minutes. Portia was making bacon, eggs and waffles for breakfast. He was grinning from ear to ear as he went to kiss her on the cheek and smack her on the behind.

"Hey, sexy. Smells good in here."

"Who was that on the phone, baby?"

"Remember I told you Uncle Richard wanted to talk to me?"

"Yeah, and you keep avoiding him."

"Well, I haven't been avoiding him. I've been trying to work some things out."

"What are you talking about?"

"My uncle wants me to come to LA to help him out," said Chuck as Portia put his plate on the table. "Thank you, baby. He's willing to pay me very well."

"Wow, sweetie," she said. "How long would you be gone?"

"It's a permanent job, baby," said Chuck.

"What are you saying?"

"Uncle Richard is very well off. He owns a bunch of properties and he needs someone to manage the places, do maintenance and stuff. We'd have to move to LA."

"Are you serious?" asked Portia, sitting down. "You want to leave Vegas?"

"Did you really want to stay here forever?"

"I don't know, but that's a big move. I don't even know if I like LA that much. People are too phony."

"Honey, that's not true for everybody in the whole city," he laughed. "You've only been there one time."

"I don't know, Chuck. I'd have to find a job."

"Come on, Portia. I'll be making good money. That's not a problem."

"Well, I like working for Dr. Mejak."

"You're only working as a temp right now. That job could end at any time. C'mon, baby. My uncle's gonna give us a three-bedroom apartment, rent-free, so you can take your time and get some kinda work that you really want."

"Oh," she said, running out of excuses. "How soon would we have to leave?"

"As soon as possible. Two weeks, maybe."

"Dammit, Chuck. You're not giving me a whole lot of time. Can I think about it for a minute first?"

"Of course, baby. Take your time. If you really don't want to go, we won't go, but this is a great opportunity for me. I think it would be a mistake to pass it up."

Chuck was very excited and she wanted him to be happy, but she also knew that being in LA would bring a whole new set of problems when it came to their social life. She had things under control here in Sin City, but La La Land was a whole new ballgame. So much for complete trust.

Three weeks later, Portia was having a good-bye dinner of Chinese take-out with Dana, who was helping her to pack up the last of her boxes. Chuck was hanging out all day with Celia and Kayla.

"Dana, can you believe how much has happened in the past few months?"

"Girl, if you ask me, y'all are moving faster than runaway slaves," Dana quipped. "Does Chuck owe somebody money or something?"

"No, of course not. And nobody asked your ass."

"You just did!" Dana laughed.

"Whatever."

"I'm just kidding, Portia. If I found a fine ass young man to sweep me off my feet, marry me and whisk me off to Hollywood, I'd be on the fastest train running, too."

"Don't say Hollywood. I hate that. Just say Southern California. Sounds better."

"Honey, when I come to visit you, I'm coming to Hollywood, and I expect you to make sure that I meet all of your famous new friends when I get there."

"You're not invited."

"See. You've gone Hollywood already!" Dana laughed as Portia threw a fortune cookie at her.

A short while later, with some classic Snoop Dogg bumping on the CD player, Dana was packing clothes in Portia's bedroom. She was grooving inside of the walk-in closet. Portia was on the telephone in the kitchen, talking to her Grandma Laurie.

Chuck arrived home after getting the U-Haul truck, blew Portia a kiss, and went straight into the bedroom, where he immediately took off all his clothes, preparing to take a shower. First, he decided to play some other music, so he picked out a Kirk Whalem CD and put the brakes on Snoop.

"Hey!" said Dana, rushing from the closet. There was Chuck standing there in all his naked glory. "Oh, shit!"

"Hey, Shorty," he said, surprised, but making no attempt to cover himself. "What the hell are you doing sneaking around in my closet?"

Dana tried to be nonchalant. "I'm here working. What are you doing, besides flashing the hired help?"

"Getting ready to take a shower and kick you out so I can make love to my wife."

"Well, if you two expect to be on the road at 3:00am, you don't have time for all that, so put your little stuff away and come help us out." She could barely keep a straight face as she said it, especially after getting a peek at what he was working with.

"You wanna stay and watch, that's on you, but I'm gettin' laid before I do anything else." Chuck grabbed his dick and Dana was momentarily mesmerized by how beautiful it was. She finally tore her eyes away.

"You wanna join us?" he teased.

"Can you please put my music back on?"

"You mean *my* music?"

Dana rolled her eyes and went back into the closet. Chuck laughed and put on the CD of his favorite horn player, then went into the bathroom. A few minutes later, Dana went into the kitchen looking for Portia, who had finished her phone call.

"What's up?" Portia asked.

"Girl, you got your hands full!"

They had a good laugh as Dana relayed the story of Chuck's antics. He even came out to the kitchen in a towel after his shower.

"Did you ladies save me some food?"

"No, you said you were going to eat while you were out."

"Damn, I can't get no food, can't get no sex and I think Dana packed all my clothes away. Looks like this is my traveling outfit."

"Boy, go get some clothes on and help us finish packing."

"As you wish, madam."

With his back to them, he opened his towel, shimmied it back and forth over his butt, and left. Portia and Dana looked at each other and began laughing again. Around 1:00am Chuck's buddies came over to help him load the truck and by 3:30am he and Portia were headed to LA and to their new life. He drove the truck and she followed him to LA in her car. There were scheduled stops that they made along the way. The first stop was in Barstow for breakfast and bathroom breaks. Then a quick stop in Victorville for snacks before they hit the 10 freeway heading west into Los Angeles.

CHAPTER 31

Melissa

Melissa and Junior had a grand time on the road together, driving up the coast, singing at the tops of their lungs. After a short stop in Santa Barbara, where they had lunch and enjoyed the beach, they had an overnight stop in Cambria, where they had dinner and walked along a quaint street filled with interesting gift shops.

Melissa found a pretty gold and ruby pin in a little store run by a woman who said she was ninety years old. She only had two teeth showing when she smiled and was very sweet to her. She told a couple of jokes and Melissa was having a good time until Junior burst into the store a few minutes later looking for her.

"What the hell are you doing?" he asked, agitated. "I've been looking for you for ten minutes. I thought you were right behind me."

The old woman's smile disappeared. "Is this boy bothering you, dear? I can call the sheriff."

"Mind your business, granny," Junior said, ignoring her scornful gaze. "This here's my daughter."

"Daughter?" The old woman looked at Melissa, her eyes narrowed. "You adopted or something?"

"No, she ain't adopted," he snapped, offended. "What had happened was...I had lots and lots of sex with a white woman and this beautiful girl was the result.'

The old woman backed away from the counter and made a sound that resembled a growl. Melissa had to suppress a giggle.

"Daddy, I saw this beautiful pin in the window. I want to get it for my mother."

He looked over at the old woman. "How much is this?"

"Thirty dollars."

"Hey," Melissa said, surprised. "You told me *twenty* dollars."

"I said thirty. That's what I said."

"Daddy, I swear..."

"Are you calling my daughter a liar?"

Junior and the old woman stared each other down for several seconds. Finally, Junior looked at his daughter.

"Come on, honey. We don't need this."

Melissa, who was hurt and frustrated, looked the old woman in her eyes.

"You told me twenty dollars when you thought I was white."

The old woman continued to be silent.

"You want it that bad?" Junior asked.

"Yes," Melissa responded.

"Here, lady," he said, throwing a twenty dollar bill on the counter. "Wrap it up or call the sheriff, but you're going to honor the price you gave my daughter."

The old woman thought about it for a few seconds, and then tossed the pin in a small bag that she laid on the counter.

"May I have a receipt, please?" Melissa asked, putting her hand out to the woman.

Silently, the old woman wrote a receipt and, ignoring the outstretched hand, put it on top of the bag.

"Thank you," Melissa said, taking her prize. She and Junior walked out of the store without another word.

"You okay?" he asked as they strolled past other shops.

"She was a bitch."

"Yes, she was."

"Why are people like that, Daddy?"

"I don't know, honey. Some people are ignorant. It's something you're gonna have to get used to, though. Especially if you're gonna be true to who you are."

Melissa was thoughtful for a moment. Then they passed a window that made her eyes almost pop out of her head.

"Daddy, let's go inside!"

They entered a museum filled with amazing blown glass pieces, each one more beautiful than the last. Melissa talked her father into buying her one that looked like a butterfly inside of a heart, which the clerk lovingly wrapped for her. She went back to the motel happy, almost able to forget about her unpleasant encounter with the old hag.

The next morning they headed to Yosemite, which was a wonderful treat. Melissa had never been to such a beautiful place. She saw the best waterfalls of her life. Pure white water rushing over the mountainside was a sight to behold. She even saw meadows. Who knew how amazing a meadow could be? Before that, it was just a nice word that appeared in books. But there she was, looking at a field of flowers and seeing all of the colors in her Crayola box. We're talking the box with the 64 colors.

Junior and Melissa also did a lot of walking through the woods. She had to go see the redwoods: the tallest and oldest trees that she had ever seen. It was like looking straight up into heaven gazing at those ancient branches. The Giant Sequoias are considered the largest living things on Earth. After that they went horseback riding. The horse she rode was named Harmony and looked to be as old as Methuselah, but was apparently very experienced. On the trail, those horses had to make their way up sections of the mountain that felt slippery and slightly dangerous. They had fun, though.

On the way back, they stopped at Bass Lake, a beautiful town several miles outside of Yosemite. Bud McKinley, the director from "Butter Pecan", owned a house there. Junior had kept in touch with him over the years and knew that he would be there for the summer. Junior had an open invitation. Bud's house on the lake was something out of a fantasy; a fairy tale princess could have resided there. It appeared that every house on the lake was built with a unique, artistic flair. It was very peaceful.

Bud was a great guy. He was very happy to meet Melissa and she was excited to hear stories about the show that her parents met on. She could see that Junior and Bud had an easy friendship and deep, mutual respect for one another.

About an hour after they arrived, Bud's friend, Gerard, came in with a bag full of groceries, excited to have company to cook for. Gerard was Bud's lover. Junior had explained to Melissa that Bud was gay and had prepared her so that she wouldn't be confused. Melissa immediately understood the situation. Gerard was very expressive and funny. She couldn't help but to think that he was, as Mama Susie would say...about "two ovaries short of being a woman". It was an all-around good time spent with her father and she knew that she would cherish this rare experience.

After a tasty vegetarian dinner that Gerard prepared, Melissa helped with the dishes and left the men alone to catch up. She went out to the backyard and sat alone, facing the lake. She took some time to think about her life. Melissa finally reflected on the past few weeks and everything that had happened with Lester Buckingham. She was still young and had time to make changes.

By the time Junior and Melissa got back to their motel in Cambria, they were both exhausted and ready for a good night's sleep. The next morning, they drove back to Los Angeles, talking and laughing like two old friends. Then Junior put her on a plane.

When Melissa returned to her mother in Dallas, she had a whole new outlook on life. She had a purpose. She decided that she wanted to sing. She was going to forget about boys and concentrate on singing. Maybe she would try out for the school musical at her high school this year. She always thought it was expected of her to be on stage because both of her parents did it. Of course, that's why she never did. And luckily her mother never pushed her, but Melissa was sure that Karen would nonetheless be ecstatic if she tried out. And so she did.

Melissa poured her energy into the arts. She got into as many singing and dancing groups as time would allow while keeping up her grades. Karen could clearly see that her daughter had tremendous talent and was willing to support her dreams, but she also wanted her to think about going to college. All Melissa could think about was performing. Once she received her diploma, she was going to be ready to dive right into a singing career.

By the time Melissa graduated from high school, she had received all sorts of awards, mostly for her performances on stage. She starred in *Cabaret* in her junior year and starred in *A Chorus Line* in her senior year. She had little trophies for Best Actress, Best Singer, Best Dancer, and Best Body. She left high school with high hopes of making a career out of her musical talents. But if she was going to do that, she needed to be in a bigger city, so she was going to have to formulate a plan.

Dallas, Texas was not going to be big enough to hold Melissa's dreams, so she convinced Karen to let her move to LA. It wasn't what Karen had wanted for her, but she agreed to let her go as long as she promised to take academic classes at LA City College while she pursued her musical career. She had already gotten the thumbs up from Mama Susie, who was more than happy to have her there. Her cousin, Eleanor Foster, was going off to attend Spelman College in Atlanta, where Lester Buckingham had gone to attend Morehouse two years before. Coincidence?

Melissa and Eleanor were never as close as they used to be after that summer of Lester Buckingham, but they wrote back and forth periodically and saw each other during the holidays. Lester became an unspoken subject between them. According to the gossip, Eleanor went to Atlanta and, within a few months, had managed to completely isolate herself from Lester, who had discovered all of the other fish in the ocean.

In Atlanta, Lester ended up treating Eleanor like a pariah. She was desperate and needy and couldn't make friends easily because her focus had been to get Lester into her bed. She apparently had one drunken night where she nearly passed out in a bar. Lester happened to be there, and since it appeared that everyone in Atlanta knew that Eleanor Foster had a thing for him, he was the one delegated to take her back to the dorm. Forty minutes later, after forcing Eleanor to drink two cups of coffee and endure a brisk walk to campus, Lester waited patiently while Eleanor fumbled for her key at the door. She finally found it.

"Bingo!"

"Alright," he said. "You're back safe."

"You're so sweet, Lester."

"Goodnight, girl. Get some sleep."

"Wait, Lester. Come to bed with me," she said, trying to pull him into the room.

"I gotta go, Eleanor."

"Pleeeeease...just til I fall asleep."

"Okay, okay. I'll stay for a few minutes."

Lester kept his word and waited for Eleanor to fall asleep. She might have been a pain in the ass, but Lester was loyal to the fact that they grew up together and he still looked out for her like she was a little sister. He really did have a good heart, but Eleanor somehow managed to take that act of kindness and turn it into something more.

She doubled her efforts to get Lester's attention. It was very embarrassing for him and any woman he tried to deal with. Eleanor became obsessed and openly blamed Melissa for Lester's lack of affection. She felt that Melissa stole Lester away from her. She told him that if it weren't for that bitch cousin of hers, Lester would love her. Deep down, Eleanor loved her cousin, but she insisted that Melissa had ruined everything. That's when Lester tried to separate from her. Eleanor didn't make it easy.

Months later, Melissa went to Atlanta, checked into the Purple Swan Motel near Spelman's campus and decided to surprise Eleanor, but when she found her at the dorm, her cousin made it very clear that she wanted nothing more to do with her. They were never going to be close again. In reality, Eleanor was actually pleased to see Melissa, but she just couldn't take a chance on her running into Lester. She had worked too hard to get him back and she wasn't going to let Melissa mess things up for her.

Of course, Eleanor was delusional. Lester was barely speaking to her after the drunken incident. But that didn't stop Eleanor from sending Melissa away. Hurt and rejected, Melissa headed back to the motel room and was going to go back to LA, but decided to see if she could locate Lester. He was handsome, talented and charming. All of the women knew who he was, though they seemed hesitant to lead this white girl to him without a lot of interrogation. Melissa was far from intimidated and managed to get the information that she needed. Now all she had to do was track him down.

Melissa met Justin Burke, one of Lester's teammates, who told her that Lester was tied up with classes and other obligations for the rest of the day, but he assured her that Lester would be hanging out at his favorite club later. Without much effort, she convinced Justin to escort her to the club that night, where she could surprise her friend.

Justin was tall and charming, but not very handsome, and although he managed to get his share of cute girls, taking Melissa out would be like hitting the jackpot, so he agreed to pick her up later, get something to eat and take her to see Lester.

Excited about surprising Lester, Melissa went shopping, got her nails and toes done, and then spent a couple of hours pampering herself. She put on a sexy, strapless red dress and high heels, then fluffed her hair into a gorgeous, wavy mess. She looked hot and she knew it. Now if she could just stir up a little action, she'd be happy.

Justin picked her up at the motel at exactly 7:00 pm.

"Right on time," she said, opening the door. "I like that."

"Oh, damn!" he exclaimed. "You look great, Melissa."

"Thank you."

"You sure you wanna see that knucklehead? Buckingham's got his hands full. Now me, I can show you a great time."

"I'm letting you take me to dinner, Justin. Don't press your luck. Let's go."

"Okay, but I warned you."

Justin Burke took Melissa to a very nicc, high profile restaurant where he could show her off. Even though he didn't normally date white girls, there was something special about Melissa. She had all the outer assets of a pretty woman, but she had a way about her that was very attractive. He was in heaven. During dinner, Melissa had to endure Justin's endless jabber about their basketball team, but it was worth it if he was going to help her find Lester. And find him she did, at The Oasis Nightclub, surrounded by what she imagined were several of the hottest black girls in town.

Even though Melissa looked white, she never saw herself as a white girl. She had soul. She could sing and dance as well as any of her black cousins and friends, and took for granted that everyone saw her blackness. It came from within. She realized that the club was going to be mostly black, but that didn't bother her one bit. She loved her black side, her black people, and was comfortable to be wherever they were. But until folks got to know her, she was just another pretty white girl trying to steal another good-looking, straight brother from the dwindling supply, especially in Atlanta.

Melissa didn't care. With her tight body, beautiful eyes, and wild blond hair, she knew how to make an entrance and even enjoyed it when people stopped and stared. The minute that Lester Buckingham spotted Melissa come through the door with Justin, he forgot all about the beautiful sisters who were catering to his every need. Everyone in the club saw him making a beeline to the hot, white chick, but all he saw was his vanilla chocolate fantasy. He was shocked and surprised as he made his way through the crowd and walked straight up to Melissa, towering over her, so close that she could smell the light scent of his perspiration, a pleasantly familiar musk that caused her heart to flutter.

"Go grab us a couple of brews, man," he ordered Justin, without taking his eyes off of Melissa. Justin hesitated for a moment, and then silently headed to the bar.

"You lost, little girl?" he asked, smiling that smile.

"Not anymore," she replied, licking her lips.

He put his hand under her hair and gently grabbed the back of her neck. His touch was like fire. The old flame was ignited. Without another word, he ran his hand across her shoulder and down her arm, then grabbed her by the hand and walked her out of the club, leaving a group of angry, black women in his wake.

Outside he never let go of her hand as he pulled her around the side of the building to the parking lot. She could barely keep up with him as her high heels clicked on the concrete. She was so excited that her heart was pounding. She was happy to see him again. They simply had great chemistry and nothing seemed to change that. Not time, not distance, nothing. She wondered if that was what love felt like.

When they reached his dark blue Tacoma, he gently pushed her against the side and looked into her amber, green eyes.

"Hey, beautiful."

"Hey."

Lester took his hand and pushed Melissa's hair away from her ear as he whispered, "I missed you, Blondie,"

"You know I hate that."

"What about this?" he said, as he kissed her neck.

"Love that." Melissa began to shiver.

As he slowly moved his lips over her cheeks, her forehead and her nose, she moaned. When he got to her lips, he suddenly stopped.

"What's the matter?" she asked hungry with desire for him.

"Let's go, Blondie," he said, unlocking the car. "Before I fuck you right here in the parking lot." As he helped her in, he grabbed her behind. "Shit, I missed you."

Lester and Melissa went back to her motel where they spent the entire night and half of the next day making love. When they came up for air this time, Lester sprawled out on the bed with a huge, satisfied grin on his face.

"Damn, Melissa," Lester said, getting up from the bed. "You still got it, girl."

She watched him as he walked into the bathroom. His body was even better than she remembered, and with all of his college experience, he was able to take her to new sexual heights. Equally satisfied, she looked in her bag and found a joint that she had brought with her. She found her lighter and began smoking.

"Oh, some things never change," Lester said as he returned, wiping his groin with a wet towel. Melissa offered him the joint.

"No more smoking or drinking for me," he said

"Oh, that's right. You jocks have to be good."

"Gotta keep the body clean."

"No doubt," she said, putting the joint out.

"You gonna try and reach Eleanor again?" he asked.

"No."

"You need to find her and take her ass back to California."

"Let's not talk about my cousin anymore," Melissa whispered as she leaned back on the bed seductively.

"Okay," he said, crawling across the bed to kiss her stomach and slowly work his way down. "Let's not talk anymore at all."

Melissa enjoyed the attention for several seconds before grabbing his head between her hands. "How about talking about some food? I've got some serious munchies."

Lester immediately abandoned his action and jumped up from the bed.

"You ain't said nothing, girl. Let's hit the Waffle House across the street."

Ten minutes later, they had showered, thrown on some clothes and headed out the door. Neither one of them noticed the hooded figure sitting at the bus stop in front of the Waffle House, but she saw them. As a matter of fact, she had been waiting all night to see who was going to come out of that motel room. She thought she knew, but she really wished that she had been wrong. That was the day that Eleanor Foster snapped.

A couple of days after Melissa was back in Los Angeles, James and Susie Murdock were in the den watching television when Becka and Pete called to tell them that they had to fly to Atlanta immediately. The police had called to inform them that their darling daughter, Eleanor, had been arrested for arson. She had allegedly started a fire at a motel not far from her campus. Eyewitnesses had identified her after seeing her hanging around the motel acting suspicious before the fire. A young couple, spending the night in the room where most of the damage was done, got treated for smoke inhalation and was kept at the hospital overnight for observation. They were expected to be fine.

The Murdocks were in the living room watching television when the call came in. Susie Murdock was in shock as she hung up the phone and relayed the information to her husband, James.

"I don't believe it," he said after hearing the news.

"Has somebody gone and lost their ever lovin' mind?" Susie asked. "How could they think she would do something like that?"

"That girl has been acting strange since she hit puberty."

"Don't say that, James," Susie admonished. "That's your granddaughter. Ain't nobody proved that she did anything."

"Bullshit! She's crazy like your Aunt Pauline. Didn't she go to the loony bin for trying to kill her third husband?"

"Oh, shut up!"

"Who tried to kill whom?" Melissa asked, standing in the doorway.

"Girl, your cousin Eleanor's goin' up the river," James stated as he got up and headed to the kitchen.

"Don't you come back in here tonight," Susie shouted after him.

"What happened?" Melissa asked, concerned.

"Something awful has happened to Eleanor," Susie began. "They're accusing her of trying to burn down some motel in Atlanta."

"What motel?"

"I don't know...something purple."

"Purple Swan?"

"Yeah, you know it?"

"Why would she do that?" Melissa asked, afraid to think about the answer.

"Maybe you should tell *me*," Susie asked. "Was she acting funny? What did you all do when you went to visit her?"

Melissa, who had failed to mention Eleanor's rejection of her, sat down and hung her head. "Damn."

"You said you had a *fantastic* time!" Susie said, mocking her. "Well, Blondie...did you or didn't you?"

"I'm sorry, Mama Susie. I didn't tell you the whole story."

Susie stood up straight, making an imposing figure. Melissa cowered under her gaze. "Guess you better spill it, gal. Spill it all."

Even though Melissa was intimidated by Mama Susie, there was no way that she was going to confess to being the reason why her cousin had gone insane. She told a half-truth, saying that Eleanor was under school pressure and didn't have a lot of time for her, so she looked up some other friends and had an enjoyable time. There were enough of Eleanor's college mates in Atlanta who could confirm that something strange was going on with her before Melissa ever landed. Lester Buckingham had to reveal to the police some of Eleanor's desperate behavior in the prior weeks, but managed to keep her name out of it. Apparently, Eleanor did, too.

Book Six

CHAPTER 32

Snookie

Snookie Watson's social life was lacking and so was her love life. Snookie hadn't dated much, not in the traditional way. Her idea of a good time was using her associates as a dating pool. She would go out drinking with people from work and there was often one man in the group who she hadn't met before. Once she got this guy in her sights, she would flirt and laugh until it was clear that she was willing to have sex. Not an ideal situation for a young woman to be in, but Snookie made it look normal. She would happily leave with these men, and later end up creeping out of a strange apartment in the middle of the night, wishing that she was someone else. Wishing that she gave a damn what other people would think about her if they knew. Her circle was getting too small. One day, it occurred to her that other people did know. They just didn't care. How many times had she found herself in a social situation where there were several men in the room who had screwed her, but not one of them had remembered her name?

One day, a guy at her job mentioned that Popi's Place in Hollywood on Saturday nights was the right place to spot the cool celebrities, so she started hanging out at the bar there and had been there for six straight Saturdays and even popped in for a couple of nights during the week. Finally, she saw her share of famous actors, musicians, sports figures and just regular people who were very cool. The food was great and the atmosphere made her feel right at home. But the main draw was the music. It was free to enjoy Sunday through Thursday and was still worth the ten dollar cover charge on Friday and Saturday nights. Popi's Place had the best jazz, blues and R&B in town, every night.

Snookie had spent hours chatting it up with Donny, one of the bartenders. He was a model and he was fine. Part black, part Irish, and part Japanese. All the ladies flirted with him, including her, but he wasn't really her type. He was almost too good-looking. She liked big, rugged athletes who looked like they could crush her with their bare hands.

However, Snookie loved Donny's conversation. He always made her laugh and had fun teasing her when she became star struck. One night, while Snookie was feeling particularly stressed out, Donny gave her a little extra attention.

"Here, Snookie," he said as he put a huge drink in front of her. "I made it special, just for you."

She took a big sip and almost choked. "Damn, Donny," she said. "You trying to kill me or something?"

"What's the matter, good lookin'?

"You can make two drinks outta this."

"You wanna give it back?"

"Hell no!"

"Sip light, sip right," Donnie said, walking away.

Twenty minutes later he delivered Snookie an order of barbecued chicken wings, mini crab cakes, and gourmet French fries.

"So, are you enjoying yourself tonight?" he asked.

"Always."

"Good," he said. "We love a happy customer."

"Well, I'm fuckin' happy. That's for sure."

Donnie walked away, laughing. A few minutes later, he brought a glass of water.

"How's your food, Snookie?"

"These are the bomb," she said, munching on a juicy wing. "I just love coming here on Saturday nights."

"You're gonna have to party somewhere else next week."

"What the hell are you talking about, Donnie?"

"Popi's having a huge, private birthday party next week. Invitation only."

"I guess my invitation got lost in the mail," Snookie said.

"Sorry, sweetie. Only the crème de la crème will be here next week," Donny said, torturing Snookie.

"Really?" she asked, totally hooked. "Oh, man. I would die to be here."

"You're a new kid on the block," he said. "The invites only go out to the big name celebrities and close friends who have known Popi for years."

"Damn!"

The wheels in Snookie's head were turning. Suddenly, her voice turned syrupy sweet and she leaned forward, squeezing her breasts together.

"So, you mean I can't come to my favorite bar next Saturday night to visit my favorite bartender?"

"Not without an invitation," Donny said, seductively, leaning over the bar to meet her halfway. "Or a really good hook-up."

"What did you have in mind?" Snookie asked, leaning in even closer. Donny whispered in her ear. She sat back and looked at him. "You've *got* to be kidding me."

CHAPTER 33

Aurora

Aurora was sitting in her office at Tazora Records in Hollywood when she first laid eyes on Krome Bumpa. She was familiar with him and his music, but didn't think much of him as a person. Actually, she didn't know much about him. In his music career he was known as a talented rapper and producer, but he had a bad reputation as a narcissistic womanizer, although she didn't believe half the things she heard. She knew how the business was. People gained reputations that they never earned. But she knew that he was very good looking with his chocolate skin, perfect teeth and shiny, bald head.

Over the past four years Aurora Duncan had risen to a powerful position at the successful record company. After she graduated from UCLA and went to work for Walter Benson, they ended the sexual part of their relationship. The fling didn't last because he realized that she was starved for a father figure even though he knew she had a father in Chicago. But for some reason, there was still a void inside of her that even Baxter Duncan couldn't fill. Maybe because he created it. Walter chose to take on that role, and they worked well together. He mentored her and helped her to excel at her job.

It was late on a Monday night. Aurora had been away on business for a couple of weeks and was catching up on some reports. She hadn't left her office since early afternoon and was trying to finish so she could get something to eat. She was starving.

"Hey, sexy," Krome said, as he passed her office, and then backed up. "Damn! Where they been hidin' *you*?"

Aurora, who was wearing a beautifully tailored, red silk suit, was busily typing on her computer. She looked up.

"Excuse me?" she asked, annoyed by the interruption, but trying not to show her pleasant surprise. Somehow Krome took that as an invitation to step further inside.

"What are you working on?" he gestured to her computer.

She couldn't have appeared less interested. "Who *are* you?"

"Oh, you wanna play me like that?" he laughed, covering his beautiful smile with his fist and flashing his diamond rings.

Aurora looked at him with no expression. He shook his head, amused at her indifference. "Alright, I'll play along. My name's Krome."

"Okay," she shrugged. "That didn't help."

He moved like a panther as he came closer to her desk and picked up one of her business cards. "If you were on top of your job, you would know exactly who I am…Miss Vice President."

"Miss Duncan."

"Aurora," he said with a sly grin.

Damn him and his chiseled face. She was thinking about how tight his body looked in the black t-shirt and cream-colored designer sweat suit. He was understated for a rap star. Not as flashy as some of his peers.

And he was right. Aurora knew exactly who he was. He had been signed within the past year and was immediately sent on tour. She had given her input about acquiring him and his music, but she hadn't actually met him yet. She enjoyed viewing a portfolio of Krome that her secretary had access to a few weeks before. She thought that he had class. He was a chameleon with his various looks. There was one picture where he was photographed looking very distinguished in a tuxedo designed by the talented Lawrence Desmond. He was sporty and casual in clothes by Sean John, with P. Diddy being one of his good friends. And on the final page of the layout, he was unforgettably naked and damn sexy, wearing nothing but a diamond Rolex with the logo covering his groin.

"What do you want?" Aurora asked, trying hard to get the image of his tattooed chest out of her mind. "I'm very busy."

"Alright, alright. I can dig it," he said, backing out. "Didn't mean to bother you."

After he walked out, she sat back in her chair with a sigh of relief and closed her eyes for a few seconds, conjuring up that shiny, dark chocolate image of his naked body. When she opened her eyes again, Krome was leaning back into her office from around the corner, smiling at her. Grinning like a Cheshire cat would be a more apt description.

"You eat dinner yet?" Krome asked, causing her to jump. Caught off guard, she didn't have time to make anything up.

"Uh…no. No, I haven't eaten since lunch, actually."

Why did his voice have to be so deep and sensual? He didn't sound that enticing when he was spitting rhymes. He practically growled then.

"So, what's your favorite food?" he asked.

"Sushi," she replied, regretting it the minute it came out of her mouth. "But..."

"I know the perfect place," he said quickly.

"But…"

"Get back to work, beautiful," he said. "I'll be back to pick you up in an hour."

Before she could protest again, he was down the hall. What the hell! She had a dinner date with the number one rapper on the label and she was starting to like it. She looked at the clock. It was 7:30. She tried to concentrate on her work for about ten minutes, but realized that she wasn't going to get any more work done now that she had Krome on the brain, so she grabbed her makeup bag and went to the ladies room. When he stopped by her office at exactly 8:30, Aurora was pretending to still be hard at work.

"Wow," he said, strutting in. "I didn't think you could look more beautiful than the last time I saw you, but here you are, making me feel all special and shit."

She looked up at him. Damn, he was fine. Why did he have to smile at her like that? "What are you talking about?" she asked, irritated.

"I know you like me, girl. You went and got yourself fresh and pretty for me."

"I did not." She was acting like a silly teenager.

"Whatever you say," he said, smiling that Colgate smile.

"Oh and why do you think you know so much about me?"

"Not you, baby. Women. I know women."

"Humph! I bet you do."

"You ready or what?"

"Yeah, I'm ready," Aurora said with a shy smile.

He walked over and reached out his hand. "Then let's go."

The first touch was electric. She whispered to herself, "You in trouble, girl."

An hour later, they were enjoying an excellent meal at Yamashiro, a fine Japanese restaurant in the Hollywood Hills. Despite her best efforts to be nonchalant, Aurora was enjoying herself immensely. Krome was a very charming guy. He might have started his career as a rapper, but he was no ignorant thug. He was an intelligent wordsmith and an astute businessman who was turning his name into a profitable brand. By this time next year, he expected to have his own clothing line.

"It's been a long time since I came up here for dinner," Aurora said, looking out the window at the lights of Hollywood. "I just love this view."

"I'm enjoying a hell of a view myself."

Aurora looked at him and their eyes met for several long seconds.

"I can't wait to get my lips on you," he said, as his tongue slid over his teeth.

On anyone else it would have looked sleazy; on him it was sexy as hell. She finally gave in. A smile lit up her face. She knew he was full of shit, but she decided right then and there that she would be having lots of hot sex with this fine male specimen, starting tonight. On that note, she helped herself to another cup of sake and plum wine.

Later, at Krome's townhouse in Inglewood, she had some of the best sex she could imagine. Walter had been gentle and adequate, but he wasn't very passionate. He had been her first, and she always felt like something was missing. With Krome, she let herself go and became a wild thing. He couldn't get enough. Unlike the trashy women that he was used to, with Aurora, he got the ideal woman, a smart, beautiful executive, holding her own in a man's world while still being a lady. And between the sheets, she gave him something more than her body. He felt her emotions, her passion, and her submission. That was sexy as hell to a man like him.

Aurora and Krome dated for several months in a whirlwind of publicity. Krome had always been known as a womanizer. Before Aurora, he had rarely been seen out with the same woman twice. He still had his groupies, and there were always women around the studio, but for all intents and purposes, Aurora Duncan became his woman.

CHAPTER 34

Debbie

The next few years for Debbie Marshall went by in a rush of activities. John and Rhonda Becker had a baby girl named Zora. They hired a live-in nanny who moved into Debbie's room, while they moved Debbie into the renovated guesthouse. It was a cute one-bedroom with its own kitchenette. Debbie thought it was perfect. She had offered to find her own place, but they loved her and wouldn't have considered having her move away unless she wanted to. Debbie traveled with John when his films were on location out of town. She learned various aspects of the business and did every job from production assistant to script supervisor, and from wardrobe assistant to craft services. John always made sure that she had a job on the set. Sometimes Rhonda would come with Zora and the nanny and stay for the duration of filming.

Lawrence Desmond was still a big part of Debbie's life. Debbie kept in touch with him by sending him postcards from the cities where they filmed and he called her at least once a week to see how things were going. She still constantly picked his brain for information and they became very close friends. She was pretty sure that after all this time, the crush was gone. She was in her early twenties now and it was time to grow up. There were a few short romances with guys she met in the Hollywood crowd, but she always seemed to pick the jerks. They were always too immature, too conceited or too ambitious to be considered serious partners, but she tried. She just couldn't help comparing them to her wonderful friend, Lawrence Desmond. So maybe it was her problem and not theirs. She'd have to think about that one.

More and more, Debbie was trying to make a satisfactory life for herself in Los Angeles. She needed to make some friends her own age. That was not going to be easy based on her past record. She really wasn't getting out enough. She made friends on the movie sets, but those friendships didn't always go outside of the set. During filming, the cast and crew became like family, spending so many long hours together, but afterwards, most people went their own separate ways. And if Debbie was honest with herself, it didn't help that most of her friends were men. If she stopped sleeping with the guys she worked with, she might have more female friends.

One day Debbie woke up and decided that she wanted a real boyfriend. That's it. That's all it took was the desire. So the next time one of John's projects wrapped in LA, she decided to take a few weeks off to have some fun. She began to visit some of the Hollywood hot spots, happy hours and weekends, hoping to meet people outside of her usual circle. That was always a challenge in Hollywood. You could throw a rock and hit an actor, or a writer, or a model. Most of those people didn't talk about anything but themselves and whatever project they were working on, or wanted to work on, or worked on a hundred years ago. Who the hell brags about getting a residual check for $2.35 for some movie they worked on that originally came out on VHS?

One thing that kept Debbie from getting too close to people was the fact that she was secretly ashamed that she had never gotten her high school diploma. It hadn't seemed to matter up to this point, but John Becker couldn't carry her forever. One day she would have to get her GED, especially if she was ever going to feel worthy of success. It was a desire she didn't know she had and refused to fully deal with. Nobody knew and she didn't tell anyone. Her secret was safe within the fear of her own heart.

The last movie that Debbie worked on was filmed on location in New Orleans. It was called *Jazz Girl*. She worked as a wardrobe assistant with Juan Figueroa, one of the best costumers in the business. He loved her work and invited her to come and work for his company after the movie wrapped. He was getting ready to go global with his own designs. John Becker gave her his blessing. He had hired Juan and knew him to be very dedicated to his craft. He liked him and his work ethic. He thought that by working with Juan, Debbie would learn a lot about the business that she loved so much.

There was a large cast and crew on *Jazz Girl*. Debbie was glad that her last movie was fun. One of the most interesting people she met was a make-up artist named Candy Martin. She was a beautiful woman. Very dark, perfect skin and a body to die for.

And Debbie was sure that if she wasn't looking right at her when she spoke, she would have sworn she was talking to a white woman.

Debbie and Candy hung with the diverse crew during lunch, but when they broke on the weekends, Debbie was more comfortable with the black people she befriended, or a mixed group. Candy only hung out with white people. It was the strangest thing. Debbie liked her though. She was funny and sometimes said things about black people that were so crazy, her being black and all, Debbie couldn't even be offended.

On the last day of shooting, Debbie and Candy walked back to the trailers together. They came to the spot where they would have to go in different directions.

"A group of us are going to go clubbing after the wrap party tonight," offered Candy. "You should join us."

"Thanks. Maybe I'll see you later."

"There won't be any of *your* people there, though."

"*My* people?" Debbie asked, bewildered.

"In case you haven't noticed, I don't hang out with the Zulu crowd," Candy replied with no shame.

"Oh."

What else could Debbie say? She stood in shock as Candy strutted off, waving.

"Ciao, bella!" she said, without turning back.

"Bye."

As Debbie headed to the wardrobe trailer, she thought what Candy had said was so outrageous that it made her laugh out loud. She couldn't wait to tell someone, and then thought better of it. They might not have a sense of humor and she wouldn't want to put Candy in a jam. Debbie never did show up for a drink with Candy and the anti-Zulus. Next morning she was on a plane back to LA.

Two days after arriving back in LA, Debbie received a bouquet of flowers from Lawrence Desmond with a note inviting her to the launch of his new line of men's shirts and ties. She smiled as she dialed on her cell phone.

"Hello, Lawrence," she said brightly. "Thank you for the beautiful flowers."

"Welcome back to LA," he said. "You haven't called in a couple of weeks. I trust that the remainder of your time away was pleasant."

"Travelling is good, but I worked my butt off, so I'm glad to be back."

"Will you be taking it easy for a while?"

"No. As a matter of fact, I have a job waiting for me."

"Really? Another film?"

"Actually, I'll be working for Juan Figueroa, the costume designer."

"That's wonderful, Debbie."

"I'll tell you all about it when we get together," she said.

"So, does that mean I'll see you on Saturday night for the launch?"

"I don't know, Lawrence. It sounds kind of formal."

"As a designer of formal wear, I do want everyone to get dressed up."

Debbie laughed. "Makes sense to me. Let me see if I can round up a date."

"Don't let that stop you. You can be my escort for the evening. Anita is in San Francisco for the rest of the week. I will absolutely need someone to talk to while everyone else is talking about *me*."

"I suppose I can whip up a dress in the next two days."

"Please do. I'd be honored to have you as my special guest."

The launch party on Saturday was a great success. Debbie wore a beautiful black gown that she designed herself. She felt like a princess standing next to Lawrence as he held court among the fashion elite. She could see how well his designs were received, although personally they looked pretty much the same as his other lines. But he was a classic, and so were his designs. The creative part of her just wanted to see something that made her say "WOW!" That certainly wasn't going to happen with Lawrence Desmond. She stifled a giggle.

"Are you having a good time, my dear?" he asked.

"Wonderful time."

“I’m planning to stop into a party later. Have you ever been to Popi’s Place?”

“No, but I’ve heard about it. Don’t you have to know somebody to get in there?”

“Not normally, but tonight is by invitation only because it’s Popi Martini’s birthday party.”

“Ooh, sounds special.”

“Good, then you’ll come with me.”

“I’d love to.”

“I’m exhausted, so I may not stay very long, but I’ll make sure that you meet some good people, so if you decide to stay, I’m sure that you’ll have a good time. Deal?”

“Deal. Just let me know when you’re ready to go and I’ll follow you in my car.”

CHAPTER 35

Portia

Portia and Chuck Adams enjoyed their new life in Los Angeles. Chuck's uncle owned really nice properties in LA and the building that the newlyweds moved into was a spacious two-story townhouse. Everything was like new. The kitchen and bathrooms had been remodeled and Portia loved it.

"This place is huge," Portia noted as she wandered through the space.

"Welcome home, baby." Chuck grabbed Portia and spun her around, and they immediately christened the freshly refinished hardwood floors.

Portia knew that she wasn't going to have any trouble finding a job. With a nice reference letter from Dr. Mejak, Portia had three interviews set up for the following week and had received offers from two of them. As a matter of fact, her first interview was the best. She lucked out and chose to work as a receptionist for Dr. Clayton, who happened to be Dr. Mejak's cousin and was one of the top plastic surgeons in the business.

Dr. Philip Clayton was a star. His Beverly Hills client list read like a who's who of Hollywood elite. He made beautiful people even better and was very discreet. He was, in fact, a gorgeous man in his own right, late forties, tall and tanned. Some women came just to look at his handsomely chiseled face. He could've been in the movie business himself if he wanted.

After six months, Portia could honestly say that she loved her job. She was able to hear all of the latest Hollywood gossip and get the best beauty products available. Right next door were the offices of a very expensive dermatologist and across the hall, an exclusive skin spa. Portia made sure that she got to know the other receptionists and assistants. She had people to go to lunch with and could find out about the LA happenings from people in the know.

He worked hard for his uncle and was often on call, but he was also able to fluctuate his hours sometimes when Portia came up with some exciting event for them to attend. Normally, Portia would be too tired to cook during the week after getting home from work, so Chuck would often have dinner ready for her. She loved that.

When it came to Friday nights, they liked to hang out together. They would usually go to dinner and the movies. Portia's number one spot for dinner, drinking and dancing was a great little restaurant and nightclub called Popi's Place. Two of Chuck's good friends had part ownership in the place, so Portia loved that they always received the royal treatment.

Once a month, Chuck would fly to Vegas to see his daughter, Kayla. Portia would go sometimes, but she liked to give him that private time. She had made her peace with the relationship between him and Kayla's mother. If he was going to have sex with Celia, there wasn't much she could do about it. She already had the visual of the two of them in bed together emblazoned in her brain from the wild night of this 21st birthday party. She couldn't imagine anything worse than that, so why bother thinking about it at all. She knew that her husband loved her and she believed Celia when she assured her that they were just friends. As a matter of fact, Celia had her hands full trying to make her own man secure about Chuck.

On Saturday nights, Chuck hung out with his buddies. Portia would go shopping and then come home and have a relaxing night to enjoy by herself until her husband came home to ravish her. Every now and then, they would hang out together at Popi's Place on Saturday nights if there was someone performing that she really wanted to see. Since it was the kind of place where a lot of people hung out regularly, she would sometimes go by herself to have a drink and chat with folks at the bar, and Chuck would meet her later.

What Portia needed was some girlfriends to hang out with. Sometimes she could talk one of her Beverly Hills associates into hanging out, but they were mostly white girls who were into rock music and raves. Popi's Place, was a little more on the mellow side compared to those types of clubs. If she wanted to make friends with women like her, she would have to make more of an effort the next time she hung out there by herself.

One evening, Portia was sitting at the dining room table going through the mail when Chuck arrived home late.

"Hey, baby," Chuck said as he walked over to kiss her.

"What took you so long? You said six o'clock."

"I stopped by the gym to play some ball and then I went to have a drink with George," he said, pulling off his shirt and heading into the laundry room. "He's having problems."

Portia yelled out, "George Montana is too damn fine and too damn rich to be having any problems."

A few seconds later, Chuck peeked around the corner.

"Portia, you know better than that. Since when do good looks and money stop people from having problems?"

"Yeah, you're right," she said. "He's not lucky enough to have a woman like me in his life."

"You got that right, baby," he agreed. "Hey, the blue hamper is full. Want me to put a load in the washer?"

"Yeah, honey. Thanks."

She could hear Chuck humming as he put the dirty clothes into the washing machine. She always appreciated the little things he did to help out.

"Hey, sweetie," she said. "We got an invitation in the mail for Popi's birthday party next Saturday."

"That's gonna be a great party, baby. You'll have to go shopping for a hot dress."

"It'll have to be hot and fancy," Portia said, smiling. "It's a black-tie affair."

"Really? That means I'll get to brush off my tux."

Chuck walked into the kitchen totally naked. "So, what's for dinner, sexy?"

"I don't know, hot stuff. Whatcha cookin'? I already ate."

"Oh, really?"

"You should've called. I would have saved you something."

"Uh huh, that's alright. Treatin' your man like that."

"My man should've picked up his cell phone and let me know what was up."

"I know you wouldn't punish me like that. Cause then there would be no dessert for you," Chuck said as he ran upstairs.

"Hah! Not until you take a shower," Portia laughed as she got up and removed a covered plate from the refrigerator.

CHAPTER 36

Melissa

The Murdock family hired a good lawyer and managed to get Eleanor Foster's sentence reduced, otherwise she would have been facing about twenty years. Eleanor had a speedy trial and was convicted of second degree arson. She was sent to prison in Georgia. Melissa knew that she would have to make some changes in her life after Eleanor's legal problems. Lester Buckingham distanced himself as far from the situation as possible. Melissa never tried to reach him. Soon after the trial he met a beautiful older woman from Barbados and married her.

While the family dealt with Eleanor's drama, Melissa went back to her plan. She decided that she wanted to be a singer, and that meant she had to put in some hard work. She spent the next few years getting into the music scene. She sang at several open mike venues and hung around anyplace where she could meet musicians and other singers. The biggest thing for her was that she loved to sing R&B, but she didn't get the warmest reception from the black female singers. They seemed to feel threatened by her talent and her looks. She didn't care. She would flirt with the musicians, get them in her corner, and that's what allowed her to get a lot of stage time. Survival of the fittest.

For a couple of years, Melissa sang backup with a cover band, always trying to get them to let her sing lead. No matter how good she sounded at rehearsal, they kept her as a background singer, saying that it made it easier for them to get gigs at the black clubs if the lead singer was black. If that wasn't bad enough, she started hanging out with local rappers and fell in love with the genre. She decided that hip-hop was a good way to go. She had a sexy style and was talented, but somehow her white girl look wasn't fitting in with the image. She and Eminem were out there alone.

One night, Melissa's group was singing at a release party for some of the up and coming rappers. The main attraction was a sexy hip-hop artist named Darren Cooper. He was extremely good-looking, smooth dark chocolate, the way she liked her men, but he had a reputation for using women like disposable diapers. Keep them handy, then piss and shit all over them, before discarding them.

Darren cornered her at the bar after the first set.

"Nice shoes," he said.

"Really?" she smiled. "That's your come-on line?"

"I'm not coming on to you. I like your shoes."

"Okay, thanks."

"Do you want me to come on to you?"

Melissa laughed nervously. Something about him made her shiver...in a good way. The way Lester used to make her feel.

"This conversation is ridiculous," she said.

"Okay, I'm sorry. Let's start over."

"Give it a shot," Melissa said, hands on hips.

You don't sing like a white girl."

"Oh, that's a better conversation!" she said, sarcastically.

"My name's Darren. I like your style, girl."

He smiled at her, and he sure didn't look like a guy who could be that bad. Luckily, she didn't get a chance to find out. At that moment, a beautiful black woman with short-cropped hair and a perfect bubble butt, walked up and draped her arm around his neck.

"C'mon, baby," she cooed. "Leave her skinny white ass alone." Then she turned to Melissa and said, "Go back to work, valley girl."

"Excuse me?" Melissa said, cutting her eyes at the woman. "Who the fuck do you think you're talking to?"

The woman was shocked, not expecting Melissa to respond.

"Ooh, the valley girl has some spunk," she said, releasing Darren.

Melissa got in her face. "You'll wish I was a valley girl when I start kicking your ass like a ghetto bitch."

"Whoa, whoa," Darren said, pulling bubble butt away. "Have a good set," he said over his shoulder to Melissa.

She shook her head. Was she actually going to get into a fight over some man she didn't even know?

"You better be careful," a deep voice behind her said. "My baby brother runs with a rough crowd."

"Really?" Melissa turned around and was face to face with another handsome hunk, this one with long, beautiful dreads. "You talking about me or her?"

"I'm not sure," he laughed. "My name's Dennis Cooper."

"Nice to meet you," she responded. "I'm Melissa Murdock."

"Can I buy you a drink?"

"Maybe later. I'm about to go back on stage."

Three weeks later, Melissa and Dennis were an item. She had tried to avoid him after the show, but he was persistent. A week later, she finally broke down and gave him her number after he found out where her band was playing and showed up.

"I really like you, Melissa," he had said, with his pen in hand. "You might as well give me what I want."

He called her the next day and they went out to dinner. Melissa thought he was charming, but she couldn't stop thinking about his bad boy brother, Darren. The one who made who heart go pitter-patter.

Both of the Cooper brothers were in the music business. Dennis turned out to be a jazz musician. He was a keyboard player with a modern jazz band and had traveled all over the world. He had been divorced for six years and was ready to settle down again. He made that clear as they were lounging in his apartment one night listening to music.

"I'm not out here messing around in the streets, Melissa. I'm looking for something real. How about you?"

"I want something real," she said. "But I want to take my time and make sure. I just don't believe it's going to happen in a couple of weeks."

"Okay, fair enough," he replied. "But I think that I need to warn you. You're the one that I want."

"What are you gonna do?" Melissa laughed. "Break into a song?"

"Am I too corny for you?"

"Just don't push it, Dennis. I don't move that fast." Melissa was surprised that she could say that with a straight face.

"Note taken. So, how about another glass of wine?"

"Sure."

Dennis refilled both of their glasses and then put his arm around Melissa. She knew that he was going to kiss her. She really enjoyed his kisses, but wasn't sure that she was feeling him sexually. She was going to need a little help.

"You got any weed?" she asked.

"As a matter of fact, I do," he said, as he walked over to get a box from the shelf and brought it over to the table. "I didn't know that you smoked."

"I don't do it all the time, but I like it."

"Cool, let's blaze."

While they were smoking, there was a knock at the door.

"Damn," said Dennis as he went to the door.

"I smell some good shit up in here," Darren said as he came barging into the apartment like he owned the place. "Oh, my bad. I ain't interruptin' nothin' I hope."

Dennis was unfazed. He was used to his brother's lack of decorum.

"Hey bro, you got time for a glass of wine and a smoke, and then get to steppin'."

"I hear you," Darren said, heading into the kitchen. "But I need a brewsky."

"Then you should've brought a six-pack with you, dude."

Melissa was sitting in plain sight, but Darren swept right past her without a word.

"I didn't have any cash on me," he said, checking out the refrigerator.

"You're full of shit," Dennis said. "You want anything from the store, Melissa?"

"Maybe some snacks. Thanks."

"Melissa, you remember my brother, Darren. Don't let him smoke all the weed. I'll be right back."

Dennis went out the front door and Darren came back into the living room. "Oh, shit. I didn't recognize you, girl. You're the singer from the club," he said, smiling.

"Yeah, the white girl with the nice shoes," Melissa responded sarcastically.

"Pass that joint," he grinned.

Then they smoked for a minute.

"You know, I've been dying to do something since I first saw you," he said.

"What's that?"

Darren came up behind the couch where she was sitting.

"Lean your head back," he said.

"What?" She tried to turn around.

"Just lean your head back," he demanded.

Melissa leaned her bead back while Darren gently grabbed her hair.

"What are you doing?" she asked, abruptly sitting up.

"Relax, woman," he said, pushing her head back down and wrapping her hair in his hands. Then he laid his large fingers against her temples and smoothed her hair away from her face, caressing her scalp with each tender stroke. She arched her neck back and he pulled her hair to one side, leaned over her and licked her neck, sending chills up and down her spine. He expertly unbuttoned the top of her shirt, reached his hand inside and released one of her breasts from its lacy confinement. He squeezed her nipple, which responded by standing to its full extension.

"Goddamn," he said, hopping over the couch and planting his hungry mouth onto her breast.

Darren roughly laid Melissa down and got on top of her. Melissa could feel his dick getting harder and harder as he began grinding against her. She was delirious. His hand was quickly unzipping her jeans, trying to get inside, and she was arching her pelvis forward to make access easier.

"Shit!" he said, getting up. "We can't do this."

"You're right." she said, flustered. "What the hell was I thinking?"

As she tried to fix her clothes, Darren pulled her up from the couch and kissed her hard, running his hands through her hair. Then he pushed her away.

"When I fuck you, I'm gonna fuck you in my own bed. Tell my brother I'll catch him later."

And without another word, he was gone. Thirty minutes later, Melissa was feeling mellow. Darren had made her horny as hell and she had to chill out. Dennis came back from the store, not surprised to find his unpredictable brother gone. He sat next to her.

"Now, where were we before we got interrupted?"

He reached over for a kiss and this time she gave him something to think about. Soon his hands were exploring her curves for the first time. She let him unbutton her shirt. The lacy pink bra she had on gave her breasts a nice presentation, nipples barely covered. She closed her eyes and remembered how Darren's mouth felt. Lucky Dennis. He was about to get what Melissa wanted to give to his brother. She got up to strip off her shirt and jeans, then gyrated in her bra and panties. She moved her body with soul.

"Damn, you are so sexy," he said, his voice husky.

"Oh, yeah?" She straddled him. "What's so sexy about me?"

"Everything."

Dennis pulled her close and kissed her deeply. She moaned in response, but it was the heat from Darren's departing kiss that fired up the passion in her.

***

Melissa was comfortable with Dennis. He was good to her and was the kind of man that a good woman dreamed of. If Melissa was honest with herself, she would admit that the passion between them was fired up by that one kiss from Darren, and hasn't been there since. Darren came around a couple of more times to visit his brother while she was there, and to her extreme aggravation, always managed to make her feel invisible. Dennis had told her about his brother's wild lifestyle and his affinity for blonds, so she wondered why he didn't find her irresistible every time he was near her. If she had any good sense, she would steer clear of him and be happy that he ignored her. But when did she ever have good sense?

"Baby, I'm so glad you're mine," Dennis said as they had dinner one night. "Otherwise, you might be in Darren's crosshairs."

"You make him sound dangerous," she laughed nervously.

"Only to the women who are foolish enough to love him."

A few days earlier, Darren came by to see Dennis and was bragging about some new woman who had captured his attention, and maybe his heart. Melissa was all ears, trying to appear disinterested, but it was making her sick to her stomach. Darren said that this woman was special, totally different from the women he normally played with.

"Man, I don't believe you," Dennis said.

"Believe it, bro," Darren said sincerely as he strutted around the room. "I'm going public, calling her my woman and everything. This one could get the ring."

"You still playing that game?" Dennis began laughing and got up to get a beer. Darren looked at Melissa, who looked back at him with simmering rage. He simply stared her down. Dennis came back with three beers.

"Well, since you found someone worthy of the ring, I guess this calls for a celebration," he said, handing Darren and Melissa each a bottle.

"Here's to small miracles," Dennis said, still laughing.

Melissa managed to put a smile on her face, but in her mind she knew that she was going to have to do something about this tension between her and Darren. There's no way that he could be falling for someone else when she felt this intensity between them. It was making her crazy. She also couldn't be in the same room with Darren and continue to hide her true feelings from Dennis, who loved her and trusted her. She couldn't take it anymore and had to get away. She jumped up from the couch.

"Baby, I have to get up early for a magazine interview with the band."

"I thought that was next week," Dennis asked, rising.

"We're popular these days," she said. "I booked two more."

"Well, give me a minute. I'll walk you out."

Dennis headed to the bathroom. Melissa walked towards the door, Darren on her heels. He grabbed her arm and turned her around. She was on the verge of tears.

"Why are you running away?" he asked, and gave her a kiss that made her weak in the knees, then whispered, "Call me."

"What about your future wife?" Melissa hissed back.

"I need to fuck you before I fall in love."

***

Two weeks later, Melissa was moaning and screaming as she and Darren rolled around on his wet sheets in the throes of passion. The sexy music playing on the stereo barely drowned out the sounds of her intense orgasm. He caught a glimpse of the two of them in the mirror that lined an entire wall. They made an interesting picture. She was sexy white chocolate with long, thick blond hair and a killer body. He was lean, dark chocolate with a muscular body, beautiful bald head and perfect teeth.

On the dresser, a cell phone was vibrating continuously, but neither one of them paid any mind. Melissa had the man she desired making love to her and nothing else mattered. After Darren was sure that she was finished, he began pumping faster and faster. Within seconds, he climaxed and rolled away from her, spent.

"Damn, Melinda," he said, exhausted. "That's some good pussy you got. You be wearin' a brother out."

She sat up immediately. "What did you just say?"

"I said you got some good snatch."

"You called me Melinda, asshole."

"What?" he laughed. "You're crazy, woman."

He reached for her but she jumped up, looking for something to hit him with.

"I know what I heard. If you forgot my damn name, you can go to hell."

Melissa found some pillows on the floor and began to beat him with them. He fended her off, still laughing.

"Okay, okay. Melissa, Melissa, Melissa. You happy now?"

Darren got up to check his vibrating cell phone.

"What's the problem, Darren? You got so many bitches you can't keep us all straight? Is that one of them calling you now?"

He put down his phone and looked her in the eye.

"I don't have to keep anything straight. You know there's only one woman that I really want, right? Only one woman for me."

He pulled her close to him, kissing her throat. She gave in to his animal passion.

"C'mon. Let me hear you say that you know it."

"I know it."

"You know what?"

"I know that there's only one woman that you really want."

"That's better," he said.

Darren tossed her onto the bed and climbed on top of her. He continued kissing her neck and then slowly moved down to her breasts and beyond as she moaned her pleasure. Then he stopped and climbed off.

"Now go make my brother happy."

Melissa was not pleased as she watched him walk away.

"What's the matter?" she asked. "Why did you stop?"

"Got to go."

"Don't leave, baby. I haven't had enough of you yet."

"Damn, girl. We been goin' at it for two hours."

"So?"

"How many times did you come? Don't be greedy. I'm late for a session."

As he turned again to walk away, Melissa leapt up off the bed and jumped onto his back. He flipped her over and landed on the bed with her on top of him. After a short struggle, he threw her over his knee and began to smack her on her behind.

"This is what you really want, right?"

She writhed in pleasure and he continued spanking her until she climaxed again. He tossed her off onto the bed, and then got up to get his phone again.

"Go on, now. Go get the shower hot for me. I'll be right in. You can wash my back for me."

"Okay." Melissa had to practically peel herself off the bed.

"Hey, wait a minute."

Darren grabbed her left hand and pulled a huge diamond ring from her finger.

"Fantasy over," he said.

Melissa gave him a dirty look before she went into the bathroom. Darren picked up a black, velvet ring box from the end table and put the ring inside. Then he opened the drawer and placed the ring inside. He checked his phone messages, and then hung up and made a call.

"Tanya, it's me," he said. "Meet me at the studio. Hell yeah, girl… can't wait to see your fine ass…later."

Darren had a satisfied look on his face as he hung up the phone and strutted into the bathroom, where Melissa had a nice hot shower waiting for him. In his mind, his little deception was working like a charm. He had everything he wanted and never thought for one minute that he was hurting anyone. Not Melissa, not his brother, and not the woman that he wanted to marry. He was feeling like king of the hill. Melissa was feeling like shit. She vowed that this would be the last time.

***

Months later, Melissa was in West Hollywood at Lonnie Gold's Salon getting her long, blond locks trimmed and tamed. Her friend Lonnie was the flamboyant owner.

She often said, "You ain't flaming, Lonnie. You're blazing."

Lonnie was tall and skinny and liked to dress like a cheap hooker, but he kept her laughing most of the time and had magical hands that kept her beautiful mane looking fabulous.

The salon was extra busy on this particular Saturday. A lot of women were going to be attending the big party at Popi's Place that night. Melissa was going to be there with Dennis, who was playing with the band. He was still treating her like a queen and she was doing her best to stay by his side.

Melissa was the only white-skinned person in the salon, but she was used to that. Her natural hair could get wild and unruly, so she liked to have it blown straight and then waved. Lonnie was the only one who Melissa let mess with her hair. And he took his time, too. Every strand was given loving attention. Melissa liked the fact that she was constantly entertained while spending the obligatory four hours at the salon. Lonnie had six other talented stylists working for him. There was Ozzie, who was also gay, but not as expressive as Lonnie. There was one straight guy named Travis, and three young female stylists named Olivia, Catherine and Jonelle. The stylists were all single, except for Travis, who was married to a soap opera actress, and all of them were full of stories.

After being shampooed, Melissa was escorted to Lonnie's station, where he began applying various styling products to her hair. A small television set on one of the high shelves was playing the top ten rap videos on VH1. Number one was being featured. Lonnie began straightening Melissa's hair with his new styling toys.

"Oh, lord!" Melissa said, looking at the TV. "Is that the only thing on? I can't stand his black ass."

"Whose black ass you talkin' about, Blondie?" Lonnie asked.

"Him," Melissa said, pointing to the TV.

"Krome Bumpa? Don't you know him?"

"Unfortunately."

"Well, I think he's fine," Lonnie said as he looked at Jonelle, who was finishing up a customer at the next station. "Jonelle thinks he's fine, too. Don't you, baby?"

Jonelle didn't say anything. Lonnie wondered why she was looking at him funny.

Melissa continued her tirade. "That's his problem. He's fine and knows it. He's the most arrogant son of a bitch I've ever met."

Jonelle cleared her throat, which Lonnie and Melissa both ignored.

"Yeah, that mothafucka always has some bimbo on his arm," Lonnie said, with lots of attitude.

"Exactly," said Melissa.

"Some white, blonde bimbo," added Lonnie, laughing.

Melissa shot him an evil look in the mirror.

"They be pure white, though," he said quickly. "Not white chocolate, like you."

"Like I said, I can't stand his black ass."

Jonelle had a small choking fit as she applied finishing spray to her client's hair.

"Girl, you need some water?" Lonnie asked, opening a bottle of Evian and handing it to her.

“Thanks,” Jonelle said, taking a long swallow.

Aurora Duncan swiveled around in her chair.

“Are we done?” she asked Jonelle.

“Yep,” said Jonelle, removing the protective cover from her.

Aurora stood up and looked at Melissa.

“I don’t mean to be rude,” Aurora continued, “but is that your natural color?”

“Yeah, it is.” she replied.

“Honey,” Lonnie interrupted. “Clairol ain’t got nothin’ on Mother Nature when it comes to this chile’s hair.”

“How nice for you,” Aurora said, not taking her eyes off her.

“Karen will take care of you at the front desk, Miss Duncan.”

“Thanks, Jonelle,” Aurora said, handing her a huge tip. “I like your work. I’ll come again.”

“Thank you.” Jonelle said, smiling.

Aurora turned and strolled off to the front desk to pay her bill. Jonelle followed to give the girl at the front desk her ticket.

“What was her problem?” Melissa asked.

“I don’t know that heifer,” said Lonnie. “That’s one of Jonelle’s new clients. Kinda snooty, if you ask me.”

They watched in silence as Jonelle walked back over to her station, looked at both of them and shook her head.

“You two should be ashamed of yourselves.”

“What?” Melissa asked.

“That was Aurora Duncan,” Jonelle said. “Krome’s lady.”

“At the moment, maybe,” added Lonnie, smirking.

“Oh, crap!” said Melissa, looking across the salon at Aurora.

“Why the hell didn’t you say something?” hissed Lonnie.

“I was trying to give you a signal,” Jonelle said. “But y’all was so busy crackin’ on Krome, you didn’t get it.”

“Hell, I thought you were having some kind of allergy attack with all that twitchin’ and coughin’ you was doin’.”

”Boy, you a mess!” said Jonelle.

“Shit!” Melissa said as she watched Aurora walk out the front door.

Book Seven

CHAPTER 37

Popi's Place - 2004

It was Saturday night and Popi's Place was jumping. Some of the best musicians in town came to play that night and to wish Popi Martini a Happy 75th Birthday. Excellent food and an open bar were provided for the attendees who were fortunate enough to have gotten an invitation to this private, black-tie event.

The club was glamorously decorated and guests went all out for the occasion. Things could get very casual in Hollywood and sometimes folks wanted an excuse to get really cute. People liked nothing more than to be on someone's exclusive guest list. An invitation to a private party at Popi's Place was worth fighting for. For two hours before the band started, smooth jazz was being piped throughout every room. As guests arrived there was an area for them to have their picture taken by a professional photographer.

Snookie Watson, dressed in a slinky black dress that she got on sale from Nordstrom's Rack, arrived at the club with her invitation in hand. The doors had only been open for fifteen minutes and the party didn't actually start for another forty-five, but that didn't matter to her. She wanted to make sure that she found a good parking space. She was grinning from ear to ear as she handed the invitation to Chantal, the hostess.

"I'm a special guest of Donny's," she stated proudly.

"Of course," Chantal said, amused. "Go on in, Snookie, and don't forget to stop over there to Jeremy and get your picture taken."

"Oh, really? That's so exciting. Thank you."

"Enjoy your evening."

Snookie pranced right over to the photographer, who had just finished setting up.

"Hi, I'm Snookie Watson."

"Nice to meet you," he said.

"You're Jeremy, right?"

"That would be me."

"Are you gonna take my picture?" she asked.

"Sure. Step on over here and give me your prettiest smile."

Snookie was feeling special. After the photo, she headed to the bar, where Donny had a stool waiting for her, as promised.

"Thank you, Donny."

"I'm a man of my word."

The restaurant was still almost empty at the time, but within thirty minutes, the bar was full and Snookie had already spotted two movie stars and a TV talk show host being seated inside the clubroom. Snookie was in her own personal heaven and told herself that it was well worth the blowjob that she gave Donny in the ladies room last Saturday night. Besides, as Snookie looked around the place, she was pretty sure that she wasn't the only bitch up in there who had earned her invitation on her knees. There was certainly no shame in her game.

"Donny," she said, as she looked around in awe. "Do you see all the famous people up in here?"

He winked at her as he delivered her a Long Island Iced Tea.

***

Aurora Duncan arrived at Popi's Place in a limo with Krome Bumpa. She looked great in a purple-sequined, designer gown. She had her long hair pulled up in a classic bun with pipe curls framing her face. Krome wore a black Lawrence Desmond tuxedo with a purple shirt and purple tennis shoes. He actually made the unorthodox ensemble look good. As they entered the club, Aurora stopped to look at the pictures on the wall.

"Wow," she said. "These are amazing."

"Come on, boo," said Krome. "I'm starving. You can look at all this shit later."

"Don't rush me, Krome."

"Girl, you better come on. You said you wanted to see Dennis, so let's catch him before he starts playing."

"Oh, right," Aurora said. "The older, more talented one."

"Yeah, you funny." he said, pulling her along. "Let's go!"

"Don't be so rough," she complained. "I can't move fast in this tight-ass dress."

They checked in with Chantal, who gestured for Jacques, the maitre'd.

"Bon soir," said Jacques, approaching them. "Welcome."

"These are guests of Dennis Cooper," said Chantal.

"Of course," said Jacques, with a flourish. "He has a wonderful table close to the stage. Allow me to show you in."

"See, Krome," Aurora whispered. "This is the kind of place that you should bring me to more often. It's classy."

"What you got to complain about?" he responded. "You're here now, right?"

"Yeah, well, it's about time."

After leading them over to get some photos, Jacques escorted them into the clubroom, where he pointed out Dennis, who was sitting in a booth by the stage, whispering into the ear of a beautiful woman with wavy, blond hair. Dennis, who was popular in the jazz world, was playing with an all-star band that night. Aurora had actually met Dennis briefly years before and they often acknowledged each other at various music events before she even knew Krome or knew that they were brothers.

"Enjoy your evening," said Jacques. "I'll send the waiter right over."

"Thanks," Krome said as he strutted over to interrupt his brother, leaving Aurora to follow closely behind. She hated when he did that. The paparazzi had photographed them a few times in the year since they had been dating and they always seemed to catch her walking several paces behind him like she was some kind of groupie.

Aurora knew that there were photographs being taken tonight and since she didn't want to see her face in the paper with a big scowl on it, she took a deep breath, smiled and went over to join Krome at Dennis' table.

"Whassup, bro?" Krome said.

Dennis got up and the brothers embraced.

Aurora noticed that Dennis looked extra good with his beautiful dreads. He was tall and dark, like Krome, with the same strong body and good looks. Krome told her that he also had a silky singing voice and played a hell of a keyboard.

"Hey, man, you made it!" Dennis said. "Damn, you two look like movie stars or something. Thanks for coming."

"Good to see you, bro."

Dennis looked admiringly at Aurora, who was trying not to look annoyed.

"So, finally! How long has it been since I've seen this amazing woman?" Dennis asked, hugging her. "Aurora, you're gorgeous."

"Thanks, Dennis," she said.

"Can I call you Rory?"

She smiled and tilted her head. "Some of my favorite people call me Rory."

"Not me," said Krome. "I hate it."

"So, how's everything going?" Dennis asked as he took Aurora's hand, looking for the ring that she wasn't wearing.

"Don't ask," said Aurora.

"What's the problem, bro?" Dennis asked Krome.

Krome ignored his brother to look at the beautiful blond in the booth. Aurora turned to look at her, too.

"Forgive my manners," Dennis said. "This is my girl, Melissa, who is absolutely the *most* stunning woman in the room. Sorry, Rory. Melissa, you remember my brother, Darren, and this is his…um…this is Aurora."

"My brother forgets that I only go by Krome these days."

"Sorry, man. You're always gonna be my little Darren."

"And I'm always gonna kick your ass."

Krome had not taken his eyes off of Melissa.

"Hey, girl," said Krome, with a lascivious grin. "Whassup?"

"What's up wit you?" asked Melissa, staring him down.

Melissa was sexy in a strapless, black gown. Her golden hair was full and wavy. She was able to hold her own amongst the beautiful people. Krome turned to Aurora.

"Hey, baby, I guess we ain't the only movie stars in the house," Krome grinned.

Aurora and Melissa looked at each other and smiled.

Dennis gestured to Melissa. "Slide over, baby. Go on and sit down, Rory," Dennis said. "Let me catch up with my little brother here while you ladies get to know each other better."

Aurora took a deep breath and sat down next to Melissa. Two waiters showed up. One had a bucket of champagne with four glasses and the other brought a tray of assorted appetizers.

After a few uncomfortable minutes of gathering food on their plates and getting their champagne poured, Melissa looked over at Aurora and held up her glass.

"I'm sorry," Melissa said. "I shouldn't have said those things in the salon today."

"That's alright, girl," Aurora said, clinking her glass to Melissa's. "Half the time, I can't stand his black ass, either."

They laughed and from that point on, they had a great time. Melissa knew that she had a lot more to be sorry for, but that was her secret to keep.

***

Portia Taylor-Adams and her husband, Chuck, stood near the bar sipping expensive champagne and looking elegant in their formalwear. Chuck had on a perfectly tailored black tuxedo and Portia looked voluptuous in her sapphire blue gown. If the top of her dress were two inches lower, she'd be indecent. Portia and Chuck had been to Popi's Place many times. Chuck knew some of the owners. One who was a pro basketball player, and another who was a fraternity brother. The fraternity had held a few of their events at the club over the past two years.

"Did I mention how beautiful you look tonight?" Chuck asked, putting his arm around his wife's ample waist.

"Yeah, baby, but you can never tell me too many times."

"You ready to sit down?"

"Honey, I'm not even sure I *can* sit down in this dress," Portia laughed. "Not without hiking it up like I did in the car. I'll just go stand at the end of the bar for a while and look fabulous."

"Well, I'm going to go and find Jeff, okay?" Chuck said, kissing her on the cheek. "He said he might be able to squeeze us into the clubroom. I'll be right back."

"Go ahead, baby," Portia said. "I'm going to mingle."

Portia strolled over to end of the bar and put her glass down. Snookie, who was sitting on the last stool, watched her carefully.

"Can you breathe in that thing?" Snookie asked.

"Girl, as long as I don't eat anything, I should be fine."

"That's a damn shame. These appetizers they been passin' around are the bomb."

Snookie had two small plates full of food in front of her.

"It looks like you already have my share, too," Portia said.

"I guess us skinny bitches can afford to eat a little extra."

Portia, with her hand on her hip, turned to look at Snookie full on. "Honey, some men like rump roast and some like ribs."

Snookie busted out laughing. "I like you, big girl. You funny."

Donny brought Snookie another Long Island Iced Tea. "Alright now, Snookie," he said. "It's gonna be a long night."

"I'll sip this one slow," she replied.

"How about you, Portia?" Donny said. "More champagne?"

"Hell, yeah. If I can't eat, then I damn sure need to drink."

"What happened to that husband of yours?" he asked.

"You know he had to go find his boys."

"Well, you can stay right here and make my night," Donny said.

"You better just go on and make some drinks, Donny," Portia laughed. "You can't handle all this."

Holding his heart, Donny pretended to be crushed as he rushed off to take care of a group of thirsty guests.

"I bet he'd like to try, though," said Snookie.

"Wouldn't they all?" Portia said, holding up her glass.

"Amen," Snookie said as she raised her glass. "Here's to a slammin' party."

Portia took a long sip and looked at her new friend. "And what the hell kinda name is Snookie, anyway?"

Candy Martin was feeling like a beauty queen again as she was helped out of the limousine by Bruce Mullen, one of her rich, white clients. He also happened to be one of Popi's grandsons. Candy was dripping in diamonds that sparkled against her flawless black skin. The sheer, silver halter dress that she wore with no undergarments left little to the imagination. The gown draped across her bare breasts, down below her navel in the front. The back of the dress was so low that it barely covered the crack of her behind. Bruce had bought her the dress and borrowed the diamonds.

Strutting into the restaurant, they were immediately treated like celebrities. The photographers couldn't get enough of Candy and she made sure to ham it up. Bruce finally dragged her away towards the back of the restaurant.

"Come on, star," he quipped. "I want you to meet Popi. I just hope he has a strong heart."

The men couldn't take their eyes off of Candy. Actually, she had the attention of the women, too. Some of them looked on in admiration for the way that her body looked in that dress. Others, of course, had their own opinions about what she looked like.

"Who the fuck is she?" asked Snookie, a little too loudly, as she looked at Candy with disgust. "She must be a porn star or somethin'."

"Stop hatin', Snookie," Portia said. "And keep your voice down. She's with Popi's favorite grandson."

"Oops!" said Snookie, covering her mouth.

"I think she looks hot," Portia said. "I sure as hell wish my big ass could get away with wearing no underwear. Maybe then, I could have a cracker and some cheese."

Snookie leaned over closer to Portia and lowered her voice. "You and I both know that she's too black to be wearin' that silver dress. Come on now."

At that moment, Portia saw Chuck almost break his neck to say hello to Bruce. She knew that her husband was just trying to get a closer look at the woman Bruce was with and her perky nipples, which were very visible under that sheer, silver material. The woman was barely giving him the time of day. Portia shook her head as Chuck finally made his way back to her. He grabbed her arm and tried to pull her away from the bar.

"Come dance with me, woman."

"Is this the hunky hubby?" asked Snookie.

"Yeah," Portia replied. "Chuck, this is my new best friend, Snookie Watson."

"Nice to meet you," he said, still pulling on Portia. "Come on, sexy."

"Alright, alright," Portia said. "See you later, girl."

"Later," said Snookie, sipping on her drink.

Chuck whisked Portia off into the clubroom and onto the dance floor.

As the band played, Krome joined the ladies at the table. He was trying to impress Melissa, who pretended to be intrigued, but every time he said something obnoxious, Aurora would tap Melissa under the table and the two of them would bust a gut, trying not to laugh out loud, and when they couldn't contain themselves, Krome thought he was the shit, entertaining two of the most beautiful women in the place.

***

Debbie Marshall felt like she was with the most distinguished man in the club as she looked around Popi's Place. She spotted several of them who were clients of Lawrence Desmond, all looking good in his tuxedo designs. For her, this was a business event. She was Lawrence's guest and she was definitely taking notes.

"Come with me, Mademoiselle," Lawrence said, taking her by the arm. "Let's get you a glass of wine and then I'd like to introduce you to some people."

"Okay," Debbie said. "Wine sounds perfect. Are you sure this dress is okay?"

Debbie looked great in a simple, black gown that she made for the occasion. She didn't own any fancy clothes and wasn't about to spend a whole lot of money. She whipped her dress up in one day and it fit her perfectly. Lawrence stepped back and totally absorbed her from head to toe.

"My dear, you should have all of your designs on a runway, with you in them."

Debbie had to laugh. Lawrence had a way of looking at her and reassuring her when she felt insecure. A waiter came by with glasses of red wine. Lawrence quickly grabbed one for Debbie.

'Here you go," he said as he handed her the glass. "Now you can handle anything that comes up."

"What about you?" she asked.

"Don't worry," he said. "I'll catch up later. I want to check on my clients first. Come, let's see who is going to give me a conniption."

Lawrence led Debbie into the clubroom, where he stopped to look around.

"Oh, of course it would be him," Lawrence said as he spotted Krome Bumpa.

"Who?" asked Debbie, amused.

"Yes, that's the one, right there in the front, talking to the keyboard player."

"The rapper?" she asked, intrigued. "Lawrence, he looks good. He could give you a whole new audience for your work," she said. "You should have made him a purple tuxedo."

"The day that I do that," he responded with a seriously straight face. "You can lay me out in a coffin immediately after I sew the last purple stitch."

Debbie laughed out loud. "Come on, Lawrence," she said. "Be open-minded."

"I have to go and say hello. Would you like to come?"

"Of course," she said. "I would love to meet him."

"Hold on," Lawrence said, grabbing a glass of wine from a passing waiter. "I guess I'll need this after all."

Lawrence actually had a good conversation with Krome, as Debbie chatted with Aurora and Melissa, who invited her to sit down. The three ladies got along well and so Debbie stayed in the booth for the band's next set while Lawrence went off to take care of his business. They all enjoyed the great music. During the next band break, Bruce brought Candy over to the stage to meet the musicians. Debbie recognized her as one of the make-up artists who worked on John Becker's movie. They actually had a fun time down in New Orleans, but Debbie remembered her being a little strange. The women at the table had a discussion about Candy's boldness.

"I like her confidence," said Aurora. "How many women can get away with that outfit without looking slutty?"

Melissa looked her up and down. "Oh, trust me, she looks slutty, but I think she's absolutely gorgeous for being so dark."

Debbie looked at both of them, wanted to comment, but decided to take the high road. "I met her on a movie set," said Debbie. "She's actually pretty cool."

Then Debbie giggled, wondering if Candy was getting better at hanging with the Zulu crowd these days. That's what Debbie remembered from the conversation they had the last time she her.

"What's so funny?" asked Mclissa.

"Nothing important." Then Debbie imagined that she'd like to duplicate Candy's dress in other colors.

By the time Bruce and Candy made their way over to the table for introductions, the women all wanted to talk to her. She immediately looked at Debbie with interest.

"I know you," Candy smiled. "Debbie Marshall, right?"

"Yeah, we worked on the set of *Jazz Girl* together."

"Good to see you again. We were in New Orleans forever on that film. Lots of fun, though."

Debbie gestured to her new friends. "Candy, this is Aurora and this is Melissa."

"My pleasure, ladies."

"You are workin' that dress, girl," Aurora said.

"Thank you," Candy responded.

"Not much to it, though," said Melissa. "You got guts."

"You gotta watch that backlight, Candy," said Debbie. "You look naked."

"I *feel* naked," said Candy. "And I like it." They laughed.

An hour later, Snookie was in the ladies room with Portia. They were both fixing their makeup when Candy strolled in. She headed straight for a stall. Snookie and Portia gave each other a look. When Candy emerged, she went to the sink to wash her hands.

"Hey, are you a porn star?" Snookie blurted out.

Without missing a beat, Candy smiled her beauty pageant smile and looked directly at Snookie.

"No, sweetie, but I do know some people. If you're looking for a job, though, you're gonna have to gain a few pounds and buy some breasts."

Portia couldn't resist laughing as Snookie turned red. Candy reached into her purse. "Now, if you're in the market for a luxury house or condo, here's my card."

She handed one to each of them. Portia read it, and then went into her own purse and pulled out a couple of cards.

"Candy, my friend here might need this before you do, but here's *my* card."

"You work for Dr. Clayton?" Candy asked, impressed. "He's one of the best in the business."

"That's right." Portia said.

"Very nice. Thank you. You ladies enjoy the rest of your evening."

"Thanks," replied Portia. "You, too."

As Candy strutted out the door, Portia was about to give Snookie the other card, but Snookie snatched it out of her hand first.

"Let me see that," she said. "What are you saying I need?"

Portia snickered as Snookie read the card. "Very funny," she said, rolling her eyes as she read that Dr. Philip Clayton was a Beverly Hills plastic surgeon.

As Candy returned to the bar, Chuck Adams approached her.

"Hey, you're Bruce's friend, right?" Chuck asked. "How you doin'?"

"Just fine," Candy replied. "You looking for your wife?"

"Uh, no, not really," he replied as he glanced at her breasts.

"Okay, then. Enjoy your evening." Candy walked away and immediately started a conversation with a good-looking white man at the bar. Chuck sneered as he watched her.

"What you got your face all twisted up for?" Portia asked as she slipped up beside her husband.

"I think he just got turned down for some white meat," laughed Snookie, following close behind.

"You don't know what the hell you're talking about," he snapped, turning to Snookie.

Portia gave him a chastising look. "I don't know what either one of you are talking about."

"Never mind," said Chuck. "Let's get a drink."

"Sounds good, babe," said Portia. "Later, Snookie."

"Later."

Chuck gave Snookie a dirty look as he took Portia's arm and led her to the bar.

At midnight, everyone sang "Happy Birthday" to Popi and watched him blow out the candles on his huge birthday cake. As the servers passed slices of the strawberry and banana-filled cake around to the guests, everyone was encouraged to dance. All of the guest musicians had played and the band wrapped up their last set by 1:00 am. Several guests had left, but there were a lot of people who wanted to linger, so guests who remained were invited to a private location nearby for an after-party.

An hour later, they were all partying in a tri-level townhouse owned by one of Popi's friends. It was designed like an adult playhouse. People were on every floor, in almost every room. They were playing cards, shooting pool, playing chess or backgammon. Some were eating and drinking, some were smoking weed and snorting coke. Whatever their indulgence, they were having fun.

Eventually, a new crop of people showed up from the cast and crew of a film that had just wrapped. One of Popi Martini's good friends was the executive producer and had brought him onto the project. Action star Bentley Dupree and his soap star girlfriend, Marcie McCray, caused a stir as they arrived, looking very Hollywood. There was dessert and plenty more champagne to be had by all. Old school R&B and funk played and the people danced until the wee hours. It was announced that this after party would take place randomly every few weeks, but you had to be at Popi's

Place on that night in order to be invited. Everyone present tonight was on the special guest list.

Dennis and Melissa were at the dining room table playing poker with other guests. Krome was standing behind his brother watching the game. He was cool as a cucumber, slyly watching Melissa, who was sweating bullets as she tried to concentrate on her game. Aurora was walking around socializing with a few of the other people she knew.

Snookie was the happiest one to hear the news about being on the special guest list. She was drunk and loud at the living room bar, flirting with some single men. She felt important to have slipped into this crowd. If she didn't open her mouth and say anything, no one would ever know that she earned this particular entry into the good life the hard way…on her knees. She was hoping to move from the bar at Popi's Place into the clubroom with this new crowd of friends.

Portia and Chuck were cuddled up in a huge closet, making out. They didn't hear the news about the special guest list, but they had no need to worry. They were on the permanent guest list and already had carte blanche.

Candy had let Bruce go home and decided to stay behind for the after-party. She had heard that this was also going to be a wrap party for a movie that Popi Martini had invested in. Some of the other investors were going to be there. That's what helped her along with her decision to hang out until the wee hours. Anywhere that there were white men with money, Candy could work that room

As Candy passed through the kitchen, she winked at Debbie, who was deep into a conversation with another up and coming designer who knew Lawrence Desmond. The designer invited her to a show that he was doing the following month. Both Debbie and Candy had gone to Popi's Place for the first time that night, but decided in their minds that this would certainly not be the last time.

By 4:00 am, the party was beginning to break up. The guests were all exchanging phone numbers and business cards. Snookie was too drunk to drive home, so Portia offered her a ride. She and Chuck lived near Olympic and Rimpau, which wasn't too far from

Snookie's apartment off Washington and Crenshaw. Chuck wasn't too thrilled.

"She better not throw up in my back seat," he grumbled.

***

Two weeks later, all of the ladies managed to be at Popi's Place again. Dennis' regular band was playing that night so Melissa was there. Krome couldn't make it to see his brother play that night because he had an all night recording session, so Aurora went on her own. She sat in the booth with Melissa, who saw her wander into the clubroom during the first set and invited her over. She figured that she should keep her rival close.

"What's up, lady?" Melissa asked as Aurora slid into the booth.

"Nothing much," she responded. "I just had to get out among some good energy. You know how it is."

"Sure do. Want a glass of wine?" Melissa asked as she reached for a bottle of merlot that was on the table.

Aurora thought about it for a second. "I need something stronger. It's been one of those days."

"I hear you."

The waitress walked up to the table and handed Aurora a menu. "Good evening."

"Good evening, how are you?" Aurora asked.

"I'm well," the waitress replied. "What can I get you?"

"I'll have a cosmopolitan."

"Okay. What about you, Melissa? Anything else?"

"Just have our food ready when the band goes on break."

"No problem. It should be about ten more minutes."

"And *please* make sure his steak isn't bleeding this time."

Teresa laughed, "Don't worry. I'm not planning to be on Dennis' bad side again. I'm still trying to get him to hook me up with the drummer."

"Girard?"

"He's fine, isn't he?"

"You *do* know that he's gay, right?" Melissa asked.

"You *do* know that I'm desperate, right?" Teresa shot back.

"Oh, Lord," Aurora said, as she rolled her eyes.

Teresa was unfazed by their reactions. "Hey, I have a plan, okay?"

"Good luck with that," said Melissa.

"I'll be back," Teresa said, smiling as she walked away.

"Is she serious?" Aurora asked.

"Seriously deluded," Melissa responded, as they laughed.

Portia and Snookie had become fast friends after the birthday bash and had spoken on the phone several times since then.

"I've been going to the bar to hang out every Saturday night for months," Snookie had told her on the phone one night. "I'm surprised we never met before."

"I like to hang out by myself sometimes, but my husband usually meets me there later in the evening, so Popi gets me a small table in the clubroom."

"Can you get us a table on Saturday night before Chuck gets there?"

***

Portia had no problem getting a reservation. One phone call and it was a done deal. There was going to be a large party in the clubroom, but Portia managed to get a small table, so the two of them agreed to meet for dinner at 8:00 pm. Fortunately for Snookie, Chuck had made plans to go to Las Vegas to visit Kayla. That was just fine with Snookie. She had gotten the distinct impression that he wasn't very fond of her, but she was happy that she had a chance to hang with Portia all night and feel important.

Snookie arrived at Popi's Place an hour early, as usual. She had to find a place to park on the street, still too cheap to valet park. Chantal, the hostess had her name at the door, so she went into the bar to wait until they were ready to seat her.

"Hey, Donnie," Snookie said as she plopped onto a stool. "Where you been?"

"I get to take a vacation every now and then," he replied. "How did you enjoy yourself at Popi's party?"

"Great! I made a few new friends."

"Good for you."

"Portia Taylor-Adams and I are having dinner tonight. You know her, right?"

"Of course, Snookie," Donnie said. "She and Chuck come in here all the time."

The restaurant was filling up quickly. There was a festive air and balloons everywhere. Donnie delivered Snookie a Long Island Iced Tea as Jacques walked up.

"Good evening, miss," Jacques said. "Chantal said that you will be joining Madame Portia this evening. I have a table ready."

"Yeah, thanks."

Snookie followed Jacques to a small table in the clubroom.

"Any celebrities coming tonight?" she asked.

Debbie and Candy had also decided to meet at Popi's Place for a drink. Debbie was wearing a simple black dress that she had made. Candy had on a tight green blouse and a black miniskirt. As they sat at the bar, they were able to find some common ground by remembering their days on the set of the movie in New Orleans. Candy confessed that she didn't have any black friends her age. They shared a few stories of their childhoods.

"I used to wish I knew who my father was," said Candy. "That never happened, so I had to deal with my ignorant mother and my drunken grandmother."

"That's a terrible thing to say," Debbie responded. "At least you had a mother. My mother died the day I was born."

"Debbie, this is not a contest to see whose childhood was more dysfunctional."

"I know. We all think we had it worse than everyone else. I do understand the drunken situation, though. My father became an alcoholic after my mother died."

"I'm sure he loved you just like my mother and Gwen loved me," Candy said.

"Yeah, the best they could." Debbie responded. "I didn't have a mother, but I had lots of love from my grandparents. I'm sure they miss me. I haven't been home in a while."

"Yeah, me either. I guess those crazy ladies miss me, too. I was always their little tar baby."

"That's not funny, Candy."

"Wasn't funny then, either."

"Absent parents, dead parents, alcoholics...damn, it's amazing that we ever survived," said Debbie.

Candy nodded her agreement. "Let's get another drink." After a few seconds, they had to laugh at each other.

"We better hope it's not in the genes, right?" Debbie said.

"Right."

As Debbie looked at Candy, she thought that Candy was exceptionally beautiful, but appeared a bit lost and lonely. She recognized that look. She had seen it in the mirror many times. With the things that they had in common, she wondered if they could really be close. She secretly felt that Candy was hanging out with her because she wanted to diversify her list of friends and come back over to the "dark side". The thought of it made her laugh out loud.

"What's so funny?" Candy asked.

"If I told you, you'd probably smack me," Debbie laughed again.

After the first set, Candy ran into Portia in the ladies room and promised to stop by her and Snookie's table, which she did. After a short chat, Candy spotted Melissa and Aurora in the front and decided to speak with them during one of the band's breaks. Eventually, all six women found each other and Melissa invited them to share her large booth by the bandstand. They were all so different from each other, but the one thing they had in common was that they loved Popi's Place. By the end of the night, they had gotten to know a lot about each other and had a lot of laughs.

Melissa and Aurora became natural friends by dating the brothers, Dennis and Krome. Dennis was one of Popi Martini's favorite musicians, so Melissa was an automatic hit with Popi. Beautiful Aurora, with her classy air, immediately captured Popi's heart. However, he believed that she deserved a better man than Krome to give her own heart to, even if he was Dennis' brother.

Candy and Portia had a mutual respect for each other after their encounter in the ladies room when they exchanged cards at Popi's birthday party. They discovered that they both had direct hook-ups with Popi Martini. Portia had hers through her husband,

Chuck, and now that Candy had the family thumbs up through her friend, Bruce, she could walk into Popi's Place anytime and get the special treatment. Portia and Candy both received Popi's blessing, so being friends with each other just made sense.

Debbie and Snookie were the insecure pair, compared to the other ladies, so they tended to ride the wave together and stay close to the others, which got them special treatment and allowed them to feel important.

Over the next year, the women socialized with each other sometimes outside of the club. Most of them really liked each other and had fun being friends, especially at Popi's Place. Debbie was beginning to open up a little. It had been a long time since she had a real girlfriend. Not since her high school friend Madeline Clayton. Even Melissa and Aurora couldn't help but like each other. Hell, they had the same taste in the wrong man. But Snookie was barely holding her own with her new girlfriends. She was caustically amusing before she began to drink, but her big mouth always got on somebody's nerves by the end of the night. Still, the six of them found some comfort in the chaos that moved in and out of all of their lives. They supported each other and grew to depend on the consistency of their weekends. They began to meet every Saturday night in the clubroom of Popi's Place, and that is where the true friendships began.

CHAPTER 38

Snookie

One Saturday while the ladies were partying at Popi's Place, Snookie walked into the bar and spotted George Montana drinking and laughing with a couple of his buddies. He was the former football player who was a good friend of Chuck Adams.

Snookie still had a thing for athletes, especially football players. She enjoyed screwing them, but she didn't think that they had much personality. She found that most of the ones she dated were too arrogant for her taste. They were used to having their fill of women and didn't take a lot of time for romance. As she once told her girlfriends, "From my years of experience, dumb jocks are mostly slam, bam, fuck you ma'am."

Snookie wandered over to make a move.

"Can I squeeze in here with you strong, handsome men to order a drink?" she asked, in what she thought was her sexy voice.

"Of course, slim," George said.

"Don't I know you?" asked Snookie, innocently.

"I don't know," he replied, looking at her more closely. "Have we met?"

"My name's Snookie. Portia Taylor-Adams is one of my best friends. You know…your boy Chuck's wife."

"Well, it's nice to meet you, Snookie. I'm George." He reached out to shake her hand and then gestured to his two friends. "This is David and that's Zachary." She nodded at them. "What are you drinking, Snookie?"

"I'll have a Long Island Iced Tea, please."

George gestured to the bartender, who came right over.

"Another round for you guys?" he asked.

"Yeah, and a Long Island for the lady. Put it on my tab."

"You got it."

"Thanks, man."

The bartender went to make the drinks and George turned back to Snookie. "So, I probably met you at Chuck's house, right? Are you one of the PP girls?"

"Is that what he calls us? The Popi's Place girls?"

"Well, that's a good one, too. But actually, we refer to you as the Pussy Posse."

"Get the fuck outta here."

"Of course, I ain't gonna fess up to saying a damn thing."

"Yeah, you ain't *too* stupid," said Snookie. "The Pussy Posse is in the clubroom."

"Then I better watch myself."

"Exactly."

"So, I feel a little bad about this," George said, looking at her intently. "I'm not sure that I remember you. When did we meet?"

"At Portia's Super Bowl party, but I got drunk and fell asleep upstairs."

"Oh, that was you. Well, I'm sorry to hear that. You missed a hell of a poker game afterwards."

"I heard all of the loud shit-talking that went on," Snookie said. "If I could've dragged my ass down there, I woulda taken everybody's money."

George was amused. "You consider yourself a pretty good poker player, then?"

"I can hold my own."

The bartender dropped off the drinks. "Should I keep the tab running?" he asked.

"Yeah, thanks, man," replied George. "Here you go, little lady."

"Thank you," said Snookie, as she took a sip. "Mmmm. That's really good."

"How many of those can you drink?" George asked.

"I usually knock down about three or four of these on a Saturday night."

"Really?"

"I'm from Alabama," Snookie stated proudly. "We can put down some liquor."

"Well, Miss Southern Lady, as long as you can *keep* it down."

"I might get drunk, but I'll still remember you in the morning."

George laughed out loud. "Is that so?"

"Shit yeah."

Three hours later, Snookie was sprawled out on the bed and was sweating so hard she left half of her face on George's nice blue and white striped sheets. When she finally managed to catch her breath, she got up to go to the bathroom.

"What's up, slim?" George asked, groggily.

"Gotta pee. I'll be right back."

"Can you get me some water on your way back?"

"Damn," Snookie said as she spotted two of her braids that had slipped off and were lying on the carpet next to the bed.

"You'll be right next the kitchen," George said. "It's the least you can do after draining me of all my bodily fluids."

"Yeah, sure," Snookie said, as she tried to pick up the braids and toss them into her purse without George seeing her.

"Hurry back."

After bringing back two bottles of water, Snookie began to collect her clothes. She was sore and moving a little slow, but she was determined to get out of there.

"Where you going, girl?" George reached out for her.

She began getting dressed.

"You don't even have time to take a shower?" he asked.

"I'll shower when I get home.

Snookie couldn't get out of there fast enough. As much as she talked a tough game, there were still things that embarrassed her, and losing some of her precious braids was one of them. She had worked hard over the years to keep her hair extensions looking fresh, but her own hair wasn't very strong and she was cheap, so she didn't spend the money to get good human hair. As a result, the synthetic hair was slowly pulling on her natural hair and causing damage to her roots, especially around her hairline. There were visible bald patches beginning to appear. She saw it, but was in denial.

Snookie was stubborn when it came to her personal style. All of her friends tried to help her at one time or another. Portia offered to make her an appointment with a dermatologist in the building where she worked, but Snookie refused to accept that she had a problem. Aurora tried to suggest that she take the damaging braids out and cut her hair short to give her scalp a chance to heal. Snookie's idea of healing her scalp was to smear Vaseline around the edges to plaster down the hair that was too short or too damaged to be braided in.

There was nothing that Candy or Melissa could say. With Candy's wigs and weaves, she had the same problem dealing with her natural hair, but she had the finances to make it look good. Snookie was extremely jealous of Melissa's beautiful mane, so even though she didn't say anything directly to her, Melissa knew to keep her opinion of Snookie's horsehair, as Portia called it, to herself.

As for Debbie, who barely paid attention to her own naturally curly hair, keeping it short and simple these days, she really didn't care what Snookie chose to do to hers. She found Snookie amusing, but steered clear of contributing to any conversations that would get her riled up. In the hair department, Snookie chose to wander alone.

CHAPTER 39

Aurora – 6

Aurora had been cooling her heels in Krome's apartment for over an hour. He had left a key for her under the mat. It was typical of him to keep her waiting. He was in a recording session, but promised to be done early tonight. After all, it was her birthday. It was also Saturday night. Aurora had fought with the ladies for a week because they wanted to celebrate her birthday at Popi's Place, but she insisted that Krome had made special plans for the two of them to celebrate alone, so her friends made plans to see her during the week. It's not that she cared so much about celebrating, but it was one of the few times that Krome had an opportunity to show how much he cared about her.

A week before, they had argued about this very thing.

"You don't give a damn about me, Krome."

"What are you talking about, woman?"

"You don't *act* like you give a damn," Aurora cried. "You don't do anything special for me. Most of the time you have three or four other things more important than me, but you talk a really good game whenever you want to get me into bed."

Unfortunately, it didn't take much for him to get her into bed. Aurora was pretty much hooked from the first time. These days, however, she felt that he strung her along like she was some kind of groupie. She saw how he treated them. One in particular. Her name was Tanya and she's the one who was always hanging around the studio. Whenever Aurora felt that he was ignoring her, Tanya was the one that she found with him. Sometimes she wondered why she didn't care more: probably because she wasn't threatened by some white woman who liked black dick.

As a matter of fact, Tanya was known as a video girl who got passed around. Granted, she was a beautiful woman, but she was common with flowing blond hair extensions and fake boobs. At least her butt and lips were real. For a white girl, she had it going on, but she gave herself to a lot of rappers. Why Krome felt the need to be on that long list was beyond her understanding. She needed for him to step up his game and put some real consideration into their relationship. It was time to leave the bimbos alone.

One afternoon, a couple of days before her birthday, Aurora met Portia for lunch and they went shopping in Beverly Hills.

"Come on, girl." Portia said, rushing her friend down Rodeo Drive. "My favorite skinny girl boutique is right around the corner."

Aurora laughed, "What the hell are you buying in a skinny girl boutique?"

"Sometimes I squeeze my curves into stuff," Portia said with a wink and a smile.

"Stuff like what?"

"Don't you worry about that," Portia said. "My husband likes it."

Aurora loved the store and they both tried on several items. Portia got a jacket for herself and bought Aurora a beautiful, form-fitting knit dress in a color that looked amazing on her. Magenta is what the saleswoman called it. It looked absolutely lovely against her skin. Aurora couldn't wait for her man to see how sexy she looked. She was all smiles as they left the store.

"I love it! Thank you, Portia."

"Krome is going to lose his mind," Portia assured her.

The next day, Candy and Melissa dragged Aurora from work and treated her to a day at the spa where they got all got scrubbed and polished. Then they got manicures and pedicures. They ended the afternoon at a happy hour, where Debbie and Snookie joined them. Debbie bought Aurora a beautiful African carving of a nude couple wrapped in each other's arms. Snookie gave Aurora a gift card to El Pollo Loco, which made her laugh.

It was finally Saturday and Aurora was waiting for Krome to come home so the fun could begin. She was excited to see what kind of plans he had made for her birthday. After two hours passed with no Krome and no phone call, Aurora was beyond furious. She was numb. She wandered into the kitchen and mindlessly opened the refrigerator. Krome didn't keep much food in it, mostly beer and leftover take-out. However, there were two bottles of very expensive champagne. Aurora decided to celebrate on her own.

"It's my birthday, so I'll do what I want to."

Aurora opened one of the bottles, poured herself a glass, and made a quick toast to herself. She practically gulped the champagne down. After drinking a second glass, she took the rest of the bottle and poured it all over Krome's brand new, silk sofa.

"Oops!" she giggled, as she watched the champagne spread into the beautiful, gold fabric. Minutes later she was on her way to Popi's Place.

By the time Aurora arrived at Popi's Place, it was packed all the way to the front door. While she was waiting in line for the valet, her cell phone rang.

"Hey, Candy," she said, sounding perky. The music in the background was already cheering her up. She was going to forget about Krome and have a good time with her best friends.

"What are you doing, birthday girl?" Candy asked.

"Waiting outside for these slow ass people to take my car."

"You're here?"

"Yes, and don't ask. I'll see you in a few minutes."

"Okay, Rory."

Minutes later Aurora walked past the line of people waiting to get into the bar. Jacques and Chantal greeted her at the entrance.

"Bon soir, Mademoiselle Duncan," said Jacques as he kissed both of her cheeks.

"You look fantastic!" Chantal exclaimed, as she opened the rope to let her in.

"Thank you, Chantal."

"Enjoy your evening, Aurora," Chantal said as she turned back to the line of anxious customers.

"Fantastique!" said Jacques with a flourish.

"Is that really a French word?" Aurora asked skeptically.

"But, of course, my dear," smiled Jacques. "And if it isn't, then it ought to be. How else can I describe your loveliness this evening?"

Aurora had to laugh. "Thank you, Jacques. It's my birthday, you know."

"Then you must let me buy your first drink."

"Too late. I've already had my first drink. And my second drink."

"Well, my dear, you weren't celebrating here with us, so that hardly counts."

"I'm sure."

"Allow me to escort you to your table."

"Absolutely."

They entered the clubroom and Aurora immediately noticed balloons and gifts at the table as her girlfriends jumped up to wish her a happy birthday. She was truly surprised, especially when Krome, with his pearly whites gleaming, got up and grabbed her in a huge bear hug.

"Hey, baby," he whispered. "I hope you can forgive me for the little deception."

Aurora was too shocked to respond. She was too busy trying to figure out how she was going to convince him to forgive her for ruining his beautiful couch.

"Come on and sit down," Debbie said.

"We have presents," Portia added.

Aurora was overwhelmed with the kindness of her friends. They had treated her during the week and still had more presents to surprise her with. However, Krome had prepared the biggest surprise of all. During one of the band's breaks, he got up to the microphone and called everyone to attention.

"I know that this wonderful establishment isn't used to being entertained by a rapper like me, but this is a special occasion. I want everyone to take a look at this beautiful woman. I feel so lucky to call you mine. Aurora, baby, this one's for you."

Krome spit out a special rap to Aurora. It was a little raunchy, but still appealing to the masses. Aurora was happy, but embarrassed, too. By the end of his two-minute tribute, he was on one knee, presenting her with a beautiful, 6-carat diamond ring.

"This man wanna know if you will be his wife."

"Oh, my God!" Portia exclaimed, while Aurora was shocked.

"Whatchu screamin' for?" asked Snookie, sucking down a Long Island Iced Tea.

After a few more seconds of silence, Krome became impatient and whispered, “Girl, you better speak ‘fore I take this motherfucker back to the jeweler.”

Melissa almost laughed out loud. The ring that Krome was so proud to give Aurora was the same ring that all of the women he slept with had to put on when he was in his strange mood. It was some kind of weird game that he played to make women feel special while he treated them like shit. He reminded Melissa of that many times. He was just addicted to her pussy but there was no love involved. Aurora was the only woman that he really wanted or had respect for, even though she never realized it.

“Are you giving up your woman-chasing ways?” Aurora asked.

He muttered, “Don’t be puttin’ my shit out there in front of these fuckin’ people.”

“Hey, it was your idea to do this with an audience. I would be happy to finish partying with my girlfriends and some of these fine ass men up in here.”

Snookie tried to get a little closer to the action. “What the hell is taking so long, Aurora?” Ain’t the ring big enough?”

Krome was furious, but he managed to suck it up.

“Yes, Aurora, I’m a changed man. I will be your man and only your man, okay?”

Aurora looked at the ring again, then looked in his eyes. “Do you love me?”

“Baby, you know I do.”

“Say it, Krome.”

“Dammit, woman!”

“Into the microphone…say it.”

“Aurora Duncan, I love you and I want you to marry me.”

“Then I accept.”

The crowd applauded, Krome put the ring on her finger and they embraced. He handed the microphone back and joined Aurora and her excited friends at the table. Even Melissa tried to be happy for her. She tried to stop seeing Krome and was totally focused on her own music career. Somehow, she had convinced herself that he loved Aurora in his own way. After all, she’s the one who got to wear the ring for real. Aurora was cool with her and she felt that she could find someone better. Krome was a dog and couldn't help himself. In any case, if he was full of shit, she knew that Aurora would figure it out.

CHAPTER 40

Debbie

Debbie Marshall wanted to be a designer. She knew that it would require dedication and persistence. Most of her spare time was spent perfecting her sewing skills. She had a great mentor in Lawrence Desmond and took full advantage of his vast knowledge and willingness to help her. She was determined to be the best and knew that it required her to overcome feelings of inferiority.

One afternoon she was at Lawrence's studio, drilling him with questions while he was working on paperwork, when he turned his full attention to her.

"Debbie, may I ask you a personal question?"

"Of course," she replied. "What's up?"

"With your deep desire to succeed, why haven't you pursued higher education?" Debbie appeared shocked by the question and didn't respond right away. He continued, "I mean, it seems only natural that you would have wanted to go to college or at least one of the prestigious fashion schools. As brilliant as I think I am, I can't be your sole source of information."

Debbie laughed nervously, but she was really embarrassed and intimidated by his inquiry. "Well…I, um…"

"Is it the money?" he asked. "Because I thought you said that your grandparents had some money saved for you."

"Wow," Debbie finally said. "I realize that we have talked about our lives a lot, and there are so many things that you don't know about me."

Lawrence moved closer to her. "I want to know everything about you."

"No, you don't. If I told you the whole story, you wouldn't want to know me."

"My dear, there isn't anything that you can tell me that would make me think less of you. But, something is holding you back and I would like for you to tell me what it is. You owe me that. With all the inside information that I've given you, you'll probably steal all of my clients one day."

Debbie laughed and put her head down. Lawrence took his hand and gently lifted her chin, forcing her to look him in the eye.

"Whatever it is, you have nothing to be ashamed of. I promise that I won't judge you. Tell me what it is."

Over the next hour, Debbie gave Lawrence a condensed version of her downward spiral in high school which led to her quitting before graduation. Although she trusted him, she still was not willing to reveal all of the drama about her affair with Harold Hamilton and how he ended up in jail because of her. True to his word, Lawrence was supportive and understanding.

"Sweetheart, it's not too late to go back to school. Get your GED and then apply to the school of your choice. I will personally write you a letter of recommendation. I'm sure you can get one from Juan Figueroa as well. You have no excuses."

"I don't want anyone else to know until it's official."

"Then we have a deal?" Lawrence asked, extending his hand.

"Deal!" Debbie shook his hand and they fell into an embrace.

For the first time in a long time, Debbie felt a ton a pressure lifted off of her shoulders. She almost broke into tears because of the wave of love she felt coming from Lawrence. He released her.

"I've got a lot of work to do, Debbie. You better go and get busy, too."

"Oh, okay." She felt like she was being dismissed.

"Don't worry," he said, "I'll see you soon."

Debbie immediately went about the task of finding out how she could get her high school diploma. This was a mission that she was determined to accomplish.

CHAPTER 41

Melissa

For Melissa and Dennis, the romance was over. They didn't get to spend a lot of time together over the next few months, mostly because of their schedules. He travelled a lot and she began to seriously work on her own music. It also didn't help that Krome kept coming around to taunt her. The attraction to Dennis' brother was strong, but she cared about Dennis and didn't want to hurt him in that way. After giving it a lot of thought and losing sleep, Melissa decided it was best for her and Dennis not to see each other anymore. Since he was performing with his band most evenings and his gigs took him out of town a lot, it was easy to use that as an excuse. Of course, he understood.

"The timing isn't right," she said. "You deserve a woman who can be there for you, and only you. With my desire to have a career, I don't think I'm that woman."

"I hope you know that I will always care for you, Melissa."

As they hugged each other goodbye, Melissa wished that she was a better woman. But she knew herself. The temptation to be with Krome, knowing how much he wanted her, was a dangerous game to play. Aurora wasn't a concern because she always broke up with Krome over some woman or another. It wasn't like Melissa was messing up some great love affair. Aurora and Krome were like oil and water.

Book Eight

CHAPTER 42

Popi's Place – April, 2005

It was Saturday night and the ladies were going to be celebrating Debbie Marshall's birthday. It would be the first time that she'd be allowing herself to celebrate. For years, she had a hard time celebrating because of the fact that her mother died on the day she was born and then she had to deal with the fact that her father died on her eighteenth birthday. No one could blame her for having a difficult time being cheerful. She confided those things to the other ladies as they had shared stories about their lives. They understood how difficult it was for Debbie, especially when she thought about her father. Michael was never too far from Debbie's mind. She thought about him often and really missed him. She remembered the rare times that were good. Sometimes it made her lonely for home. She also missed her grandparents and felt guilty because she didn't keep in touch with them the way that she should have.

Debbie was determined to free her mind as she was enjoying a manicure and pedicure after a day of pampering. Three hours before, she had been stretched out on a massage table, receiving an extremely soothing, extremely expensive body treatment, courtesy of Candy Martin. She and Candy were receiving the star treatment at the Golden Goddess Health & Beauty Spa and Salon. They had received facials, massages and hair services. Debbie had been there with Candy most of the afternoon and as Debbie looked at the clock on the wall, she saw that when they were done with their nails they would have about an hour and a half to get their makeup done, get dressed and arrive at Popi's Place by eight o'clock. She was really looking forward to the party.

Snookie was the first one to arrive at Popi's Place, as usual. Tonight she even got there earlier than her normal early. It was only

6:20 and the doors to Popi's Place hadn't even opened yet. She parked her car on a side street a couple of blocks from the club and grabbed a bouquet of flowers that was lying on the passenger seat. She had stopped at Ralphs supermarket on the way to Hollywood to buy a pack of condoms and realized that she didn't have a gift for Debbie, so she grabbed a bouquet of prepackaged flowers and a card. Snookie was not known for her extravagant gift giving.

Snookie was wearing a purple jumpsuit with a huge zipper up the front and low-heeled purple pumps. She had on a curly black wig and looked like a seventies throwback. Snookie was tapping her foot impatiently, waiting by the front door of Popi's Place, when Chantal came to open up.

"Good evening, Snookie," said Chantal, smiling. She was used to Snookie being one of the first customers on Saturday night. "Are you ladies doing a theme? You look very Pam Grier tonight."

"No, I just felt like being a little funky."

"I hear you. Pretty flowers."

"Thanks, Chantal," Snookie said. "Did y'all get the balloons we asked for?"

"Of course. Everything's set up in the clubroom."

"Good. Is Jacques here?" asked Snookie, as they walked up the long hallway.

"He's in the back having dinner with Popi."

"Get the hell outta here. I've never seen him eat dinner."

"He's usually finished by now, but there's been a little drama," Chantal said, lowering her voice.

"Really?" Snookie whispered. "What happened?"

"Well, you know who Blu Richards is, right?"

"Yeah, that old mother fucker who's always hitting on us."

"Well, apparently he's not that old. Jacques caught him having sex with some young woman in the men's room last night."

"Oh, shit!" Snookie said. "Are you kidding? That's gross."

"Well, that's what I said. One of the other customers actually heard them in the stall and went to complain to Jacques, who had to kick them both out. Blu is good friends with Popi, so it's a bit of a touchy situation."

"I guess so."

"Don't say anything. It's supposed to be hush-hush."

"Don't say anything? Now, Chantal, you know you done told the wrong person if this is supposed to be some kinda secret."

"Give me a break, Snookie," Chantal said with a grin. "At least pretend to be surprised when Jacques tells you about it later."

"You know he can't resist spillin' all the beans to me."

"Exactly."

"Alright, how's this?" Snookie made an exaggerated face of surprise, which made Chantal laugh.

"Oh, yeah, that's a good one. He'll never suspect a thing and I'll be fired on the spot." The restaurant phone began to ring. "Go on in and follow the balloons. I'll see you later. Enjoy your night."

"Thanks," Snookie said as she entered the empty clubroom.

Fifteen minutes later, as Snookie sipped on a Long Island Iced Tea, Jacques came over to her table.

"Bon jour, Mademoiselle Snookie," he said, sitting down. "How are you?"

"I'm cool, Frenchie," she replied. "What's the 411 up in this bitch?"

"You have a way with the words," quipped Jacques, amused.

Snookie leaned in, sipping on her drink. "Just get to the good stuff."

"Well, up in this bitch, as you say, Friday nights can be impossible."

"So I've heard, but I can't believe that it's any crazier than Saturday."

"Well, let me tell you. I had to throw somebody out of here again last night."

"No!" Snookie feigned shock.

"You can drop the act. Chantal confessed."

"Oh, good, cause I'm a terrible actress. Now tell me all the juicy details."

Twenty minutes later, Aurora showed up wearing a beautiful blue chiffon dress and bearing an armful of gifts.

"Hey, Snookie," she said. "I didn't recognize you. What's up with the wig?"

"You like?"

Aurora made a face that made it clear that she wasn't sure exactly what she thought about it.

"Whatever," said Snookie, ignoring the look. "I see you been shoppin'. Are those all for Debbie?"

"It took me a while to figure out how I was going to make this a really special birthday for her. I wanted to get a fabulous gift, but I couldn't make it happen with just one thing, so I got a few things to make it all work."

"Lucky for me, since I didn't have time to buy a gift I can give her one of yours."

"Damn, Snookie. You know that's trifling. How long have you been here? I see you had time to suck down a drink, though."

"I had to get a parking space."

"What the hell have you been doing all day?"

"I got somethin' for her yesterday. I just left it at my office."

"I thought you said you didn't have time to get anything."

"What the fuck, Rory? You got extra."

"I don't have extra, Snookie. All the gifts go together. There's a theme. I'm not breaking it up just so your lazy ass can look good."

"That's so goddamn selfish," Snookie whined.

"Deal with it."

"Bitch!"

"Damn, ladies," said Portia as she arrived with a huge gift. "I haven't even had my first drink and you two are fighting already."

"Oh, my God! Where the hell did you get that outfit?" Snookie asked Portia, who was stuffed into a hot pink pantsuit. "You look like you fell into a pool of Pepto Bismol."

"Thanks, Snookie," said Portia, sarcastically. "You always say the right thing."

Aurora shook her head. "I think that color looks good on you, Portia. Don't pay attention to what Snookie has to say."

Portia looked Snookie up and down. "Coming from discount Pam Grier over here, I took it as a compliment."

"I'm goin' to the bar," said Snookie, who got up from the table and walked away.

"She's crazy," said Aurora.

"Yeah, so what else is new?" Portia asked. "What time is Debbie coming?"

"Candy took her to Golden Goddess today. They should be here by 8:00."

"Okay. I have time for a drink. Where's Teresa?"

Fifteen minutes later, Melissa arrived. She had on a pair of sexy jeans and a low-cut, gold lame top.

"Hey, I thought I was gonna be late, but I see the birthday girl hasn't arrived yet."

"You actually got here on time," commented Portia. "How did that happen?"

Aurora added, "Must be a blue moon or something."

"Very funny. Where's Snookie? I know she must be here somewhere."

"Sulking at the bar, I imagine," replied Portia.

"Alright, so which one of you pissed her off?"

At 8:00 sharp, the band began to play. By then, the bar was crowded, the restaurant was busy, and the clubroom tables and booths were all filled. Snookie came back with a new attitude and the ladies enjoyed her retelling of the story about Blu and his antics. Snookie had her friends in stitches.

At 8:15, Candy and Debbie entered the clubroom. Candy was squeezed into a skin-tight, leopard mini-dress and her smooth skin was chocolate perfection. Debbie had been given a head to toe makeover and she looked fabulous in a black, sequined cocktail dress. She strutted up to the table glowing with an air of confidence. Her hair was done up in finger waves and her makeup was flawless.

"Oh, my God!" cried Portia. "You look fabulous, Debbie."

"Thank you," Debbie responded. "I *feel* fabulous, too."

"You clean up good," said Snookie. "You should wear makeup more often."

"I always wear makeup on Saturday night, Snookie."

"Oh."

Aurora stood up to give her a big hug. "And I think you always look pretty, but any chance we get to have someone beat our face for us, we should take, right?"

"Thanks, Rory. You're right. We can thank Candy for my fabulousness tonight."

Candy shrugged. "Look what they had to work with. They simply did a little enhancement."

"Well, Candy," said Snookie. "We all know that you get a lot of enhancement."

"Excuse me?" Candy looked at Snookie, ready for a fight.

"I'm just kidding," said Snookie. "Both of you look good so sit your asses down and let's bust this bubbly."

The ladies had a bottle of expensive champagne on ice and within minutes, Jacques came over to pour their first toast.

"Have a glass with us, Jacques," urged Debbie.

"Merci, mademoiselle," he said. "I'd be honored."

"Here's to the sweetest person I know," Aurora began, holding up her glass. "I wish you many days of joy."

"And may the wind always be at your back," added Portia.

"Oh, that's original!" Snookie said, snarling.

"Screw you, Snookie," Portia snapped back.

"Now, now ladies, behave yourselves," Jacques interrupted. "Miss Debbie, I wish you love."

"Here, here. I second all of that," Melissa said as they clinked glasses.

"I'm going to leave you ladies to your party," Jacques said. "Debbie, your dinner is on the house tonight. Order the most expensive things on the menu, please."

"Absolutely," Debbie replied.

Jacques walked away and Portia turned to Snookie. "Where's your toast, Miss Shakespeare?"

Melissa snickered. "You mean Miss Superfly?"

Debbie looked at Snookie. "No need to make a toast if you're not feeling it."

Snookie looked at Debbie, laughing. "I hope you find a man whose dick doesn't belong to another woman."

The ladies looked at each other, disgusted at Snookie, who apparently was on her way to being drunk already.

"It's okay. No need to say anything," Debbie insisted. "I'm sure that Snookie wasn't trying to be mean, right Snookie?"

Snookie continued to drink her champagne.

"We're about to cut you off," Portia said.

"I'm just about to cut her, period!" said Aurora.

"So, what's everyone eating tonight?" asked Melissa.

Debbie was eyeing the menu with interest. "I need to hear the chef's specials."

"Here comes Teresa now," said Aurora.

"Happy birthday, Debbie," said Teresa, walking up to the table. "You all look beautiful tonight,"

"Thank you, girl," said Debbie as the other ladies murmured their appreciation.

Teresa continued. "Ready to order, ladies?"

An hour later, after they finished their meals, the band played "Happy Birthday" and everyone sang to Debbie. She was embarrassed and delighted. Then it was time to open her presents.

"Start with Snookie," suggested Portia.

Snookie gave Portia a dirty look as she picked up the bouquet of flowers from under the table. She handed it to Debbie with the card. "Here, girl. I forgot your present."

"Oh, thank you, Snookie," Debbie said, taking the flowers and smelling them. "That was very thoughtful of you."

"Here, me next," cried Melissa, handing Debbie an envelope.

There was a card inside the envelope. Inside the card were three gift certificates to Debbie's favorite stores.

"Oh, this is great, Melissa. You know me like a book. I'm going shopping tomorrow."

"You're welcome, sweetie," Melissa said.

Portia handed Debbie the big present she brought. "Here, Debbie. I hope you like what I got."

"Are you kidding?" Debbie asked. "You all are so generous. You really didn't have to do this."

"You know we love an excuse to spend money," said Portia.

Debbie took the package. "Wow, it's kind of heavy." She opened it up. Inside was an array of expensive facial products from the Beverly Hills dermatologist next door to Portia's office.

"Wow, this is the top-of-the-line stuff, Portia," Debbie said. "Isn't this that $200 facial peel that you use to keep your skin flawless?"

"You're worth it, girl," Portia said. "Plus, I get a good deal from my friend, Isis. She orders all the products in her office and always hooks me up with the best ones."

"Thank you so much," Debbie said, sincerely. "I'm gonna be looking even better in a couple of weeks after all this."

"Last, but not least," said Aurora.

"Oooh, the big secret theme," said Snookie, snidely.

"Be quiet, Snookie," Aurora snapped. "I didn't interrupt your presentation."

"Ignore her, Rory," said Portia. "Snookie, one day, we're going to start going somewhere else on Saturday nights and we're not going to tell you where we are."

"Alright, here's the first one," Aurora said, handing her a medium sized package.

"How many are there?" asked Debbie.

"Don't worry about it. Just open the box."

"Okay, bossy."

The package contained a beautiful, silk kimono.

"Wow, this is beautiful," said Debbie, as the ladies agreed.

In the next box was a pair of designer sandals that Debbie wanted for weeks.

"You remembered!" exclaimed Debbie. "You even got the right size."

"Of course."

Next, Aurora handed her a very small box. Inside was a jewelry box that had a small, gold key hanging from a delicate gold chain.

"I like it." Debbie pulled the chain out of the box and held it up for everyone.

"What's the key for?" asked Snookie.

"Funny that you should ask," said Aurora.

"Oh, it's a real key?" asked Debbie.

"Yes, it's a real key. It goes to a beautiful piece of overnight luggage."

"Oh, I guess you've seen that raggedy bag I've been using for years. Thank you. I can finally throw that shit away."

"Now, you just need someplace to go," said Portia, as they all laughed.

"Here's the next one." Aurora handed Debbie a box with lots of tissue.

"It's like a treasure hunt," Debbie said as she tossed each piece of empty tissue aside. After rifling through the box for a few more seconds, she found an envelope. "Bingo!" she exclaimed. Inside was a $200 American Express gift card.

"Oh, damn. I am going to be so spoiled."

"Alright, can we get another round of drinks?" Snookie asked.

"Wait a minute," Aurora said. "There's one more."

"Jesus Christmas," Snookie complained. "I hope you all are this generous when it's *my* birthday."

Debbie opened the last box, which was also full of tissue. Finally, she found the last envelope. When she opened it up, she squealed with delight.

"Is this for real?" She jumped out of her seat to give Aurora a big hug. "I don't believe this."

Candy got up and snatched the envelope from Debbie's hand.

"Hey!" Debbie said, snatching it back.

"Share, woman," Candy laughed. "What is it?"

Debbie could barely contain her delight. "It's a plane ticket."

"Damn, Rory," said Portia.

"Yeah, that's a hell of a gift," said Melissa. "Where are you going, Debbie?"

Aurora smiled. "I'm taking Debbie to Hawaii with me next month to shoot Krome's new video."

"Get the fuck outta here," said Snookie.

"Love it," said Candy. "I might make that trip with you guys. I need a vacation."

"Come on, then," Aurora responded. "I have a huge suite reserved."

"Thank you all so much," Debbie said, her voice trembling. "This is the best birthday I've ever had."

"Oh, so the three of you are just going to leave me, Portia and Melissa here?" Snookie asked.

"Actually," Melissa said. "I'm going to be featured in the video."

"How fucking selfish," Snookie hissed. "You know I can't afford to buy a ticket. How come you didn't invite me, Rory?"

"Snookie! Be reasonable," Aurora said. "First of all, you said that you would never go to Hawaii because you have no desire to fly all the way across the ocean in the middle of nowhere to be on an expensive piece of sand with a bunch of little pig-eating men. They couldn't pay you to go there. Now, did I quote you accurately?"

At midnight, Melissa had to leave because she had a photo shoot in the morning. Minutes later, Chuck Adams showed up with three of his buddies: George Montana, who had married and divorced in the past two years. David Hooper, who was happily married with three children, and owned a chain of soul food restaurants. Zachary Jackson, who owned a real estate company, had two children by two different women, but had never been married. All of them were professionally successful, and Chuck liked to hang around with successful brothers. "No point in being a broke ass player" was Chuck's motto.

All four men arrived bearing gifts for Debbie.

"Well, hallelujah, look what the wind is blowin' in," exclaimed Snookie, as she spotted the attractive group of men closing in on their table. Jacques was right on their trail with a busboy to add another table and additional chairs to their group.

"Hey, baby," said Chuck, kissing Portia. "Ladies."

They smiled and greeted him. He handed Debbie a gift.

"Happy birthday, Debbie." Chuck kissed her on the cheek. "You remember these ugly dudes."

"Out of my way, Adams," said Zachary, who handed Debbie a huge bouquet of red roses. "Happy birthday, beautiful."

"Wow," said Debbie. "You guys really went all out, I see."

"Damn, I can't wait until my birthday rolls around," said Melissa. "You all are definitely invited."

"Yeah, I'm having a party, too," added Portia.

"Alright, stop hating," said Candy. "We've been getting our fair share of presents over the years. This is a special birthday for Debbie. We never celebrated hers before."

"Yeah, whatever," said Snookie, as she looked directly at George. "I need another drink. Which one of you generous guys is going to buy me one?"

"Here, Debbie," said George, ignoring Snookie and handing Debbie a wrapped package. "Happy birthday and I'll buy the next round of drinks for you ladies."

"Thanks, George," said Debbie. "That's very sweet."

David handed Debbie a card. "Hey, girl. Hope you have many more."

"Thank you so much." Debbie was overwhelmed and brought to tears by the thoughtfulness of her friends.

Snookie jumped up from the table. "Who wants to dance?"

"I'll dance with you," said David.

"No, I want to dance with this one," said Snookie, grabbing George's hand. "Come on, big guy."

"You get the next one, Snookie. I promised this one to the birthday girl." He reached for Debbie's hand as she rose from the table and led her to the dance floor.

Snookie was irritated. "This ain't the fuckin' prom."

Portia tapped Snookie on the behind. "Chill out. It ain't about you."

"It ain't about you, either, Portia."

"Why can't we have one night where you don't get drunk and make a scene?" Portia asked. "Just one night?"

David grabbed Snookie gently by the arm. "May I have this dance?"

"Fuck you, married man." Snookie snapped angrily as she marched off to the bar.

"Whoa, Portia, your friend's a little uptight," said David as he shrugged it off.

"My friend's a bitch. Plain and simple."

"She's playing that tough Cleopatra Jones with her Afro wig and her seventies outfit," said Chuck, who was cracking up. "She needs some dick."

"Stop it, baby," Portia admonished with a smile of her own. "She can't help it. She's having flashbacks."

"How about you, Mrs. Adams?" David asked. "Will you bite my head off if I ask you to dance?"

"Not at all," replied Portia.

He looked at Chuck. "Do you mind if I take your wife to the dance floor?"

"Don't worry about him," Portia said, taking his hand. "Let's do the damn thing."

Zachary offered his hand to Aurora. "May I have this dance?"

She rolled her eyes. "Sure, whatever. Why should they have all the fun?"

"Well, I guess that means you're stuck with me," Chuck said as he plopped down into a chair next to Candy.

"Oh, so you're not gonna ask me to dance?"

"I've been working all day. I need to chill the hell out."

Candy shook her head. "What is the point of being a young man if you can't hang like a young man?"

"Oh, don't you worry about how I'm hanging, little lady. I'm hanging just fine, thank you."

"Get your mind out of your pants for a change."

"Ha! You a funny girl, Candy."

"You can sit your lazy ass down by yourself," Candy said. "I'll be back."

Candy headed to the ladies room and spotted Blu Richards as she passed through the bar. She wandered over to him, kissed him on the cheek, and snuggled up close.

"Hi, Blu."

"Hey, good lookin'," he said, smiling. "Damn! To what do I owe the honor of having your warm body against mine?"

"Just stopping by to say hello."

"Is that all?"

"Maybe," she said as she allowed her breast to rub against his arm. He could feel her hard nipple.

"Damn, girl."

"What are you drinking, Blu?"

"My usual. Stoli and cranberry."

"Let me buy you another one."

"Sure, baby."

Candy raised Blu's glass and gestured to the bartender.

"Thank you," he said, grinning. "Now, what can I do for you, sexy lady?"

She lowered her voice and leaned in closer. "Got any candy for Candy?"

"You know I do, sweet chocolate. If you reach into my right pocket, you might find something sweet." She reached into his pocket, felt his erection, gave it a little rub and extracted a small packet that she held tightly in her hand.

"Thank you," she smiled.

"No. Thank *you*," he replied.

"I'll be right back."

Candy didn't like spending her own money on her favorite vice. It was plentiful and readily available to her through any number of colleagues in her real estate business or various musicians and patrons at Popi's Place. Blu Richards was her favorite source because she rarely had to ask. He was always ready to provide the boost she needed.

Candy managed to keep her cocaine indulgence undercover for the most part, but she suspected that some of the other women knew about it. They didn't indulge and she didn't partake in front of them, so they didn't say anything. Minutes later, Candy returned to the crowded bar and squeezed through until she was by Blu's side.

"Hey, baby," he said. "You better now?"

"I'm better now. Thank you."

She kissed Blu on the cheek and slipped the packet back into his pocket. This time her hand lingered there so long, she almost made him come.

"Go on and get outta here, woman. I'm about ten seconds from fucking you right here in this bar."

Candy removed her hand and smiled.

"Later, handsome."

As she approached the table in the clubroom, a handsome white man intercepted her by gently grabbing her arm. Startled, she turned around and summed him up in three seconds. His perfect tan, his expensive suit, and his diamond Rolex. She flashed a smile.

"I'm sorry, beautiful," he said, taking both of her hands. She didn't mind. "I've been trying to get your attention all night, but you seem to have a lot of admirers."

"Well, you haven't been trying that hard."

"I am now. I don't even want to let you go. Would you join me for a drink?"

She looked at the crowded table where her friends were having a great time, then looked back at the handsome man.

"Sure," she said, as he led her to a small table near the bandstand.

"My name's Ken Cortland. I'm the band's manager."

"They're very good."

"They work very hard."

"I'm Candy Martin."

"And what do you do, Miss Martin?"

"I broker some of the best real estate in the city."

"Really? I just happen to be in the market for a prime piece."

"I'm sure that I can be of service."

"I'm sure that you can," he smiled. "What would you like to drink?"

About an hour later, Candy slipped out with Ken as the rest of her friends partied and enjoyed the rest of the night drinking and dancing.

CHAPTER 43

Portia

Portia Taylor-Adams made up her mind that she wanted a baby. She felt she wasn't getting any younger and it would be a good time to plan a family. She and Chuck were making good money and were secure in their marriage. Chuck was open to the idea, as long as she knew what she was in for. Being a parent was a lot of work. With their schedules, it was going to be a challenge. Celia and her new husband had brought Kayla to Los Angeles to visit them recently and Portia really liked that Chuck was a good father. Kayla adored him. He still had no relationship with his other two children, but he made up for it by putting in an extra effort with Kayla. It brought joy to Portia's heart to see him with her, but she knew that he missed not being able to see his son.

As hard as they tried, Portia could not conceive. They had not been using birth control, but Portia figured that once she had made up her mind to get pregnant, it would happen. She had been experiencing heavy menstrual bleeding and even some pain, but was determined to make it happen. A year went by with no results. She knew how powerful Chuck's sperm was, judging by the kids he already had, so she began to question her own health. Her symptoms were getting worse.

Portia finally got her answer when she visited her gynecologist, who discovered that she had large uterine fibroids. Because of her size, she hadn't noticed the swelling of her stomach. She didn't even realize how the condition had affected her overall health. Her doctor recommended a hysterectomy, which she refused to accept.

"I'm trying to have a baby," she cried. "You have to save my uterus."

Although there were less invasive methods to deal with fibroids, they weren't going to work for her. The position and aggressiveness of her fibroids made radical surgery a necessary lifesaving procedure. With the support of her husband and her friends, she accepted her fate and had the hysterectomy.

She was devastated for a while, but she knew that she had to go on. The hole in her heart was not going to be filled with a baby, so she just went back to being a loving wife to her husband, who appeared to be just fine. Chuck, to his credit, made sure that she had the extra attention she needed and did his best to make her feel loved and wanted. Whatever insecurities Portia had about her age, size, or inability to bear children, didn't come from her husband. Long before her body healed, Chuck had done his best to help Portia heal her spirit. She would love him forever based on that alone.

Portia wished that she could talk to her friend, Dana, back in Las Vegas, who always gave her the best perspective on things in her life. They had tried to keep up with each other over the years, and she had recently received a letter from Dana saying that she was in Singapore. Apparently, the guy that Dana had been dating for almost a year took a job overseas, so when Dana decided that she wanted to be with him, they got married in a quick and simple ceremony and left town as soon as possible. Portia was happy for her and only regretted that she could not be Dana's maid of honor.

Portia was still thankful for her LA friends. The ladies visited Portia often at home during her recuperation. They even brought a couple of their Saturday nights to her so that she wouldn't feel left out. They played her favorite oldies on the cassette player, made her laugh with the gossip at Popi's Place, and proved to be true friends. Even Snookie managed to behave herself as she and Melissa cooked, and Debbie made her famous margaritas. Of course, Portia had to take it easy on the alcohol, and after weeks of recovery, it was time for her to get back to the business of living. It was time to return to work, her friends and Popi's Place.

CHAPTER 44

Candy

Roger Nichols was a handsome white man. He had lots of money and had no problem throwing it around. That's what got Candy Martin's attention as she sipped a glass of champagne at the Sofitel Hotel bar. She had just attended a real estate seminar where Roger was a speaker, and several attendees decided to continue mingling and networking. Candy was dressed a little conservatively for her taste, but she still had plenty to show. She had on a beautifully tailored navy suit with a skirt that was two inches too short to be professional, and a silk white blouse that had one too many buttons undone, but that was Candy. She had a way of making it all work and it didn't stop her from getting clients. As a matter of fact, she wore her clothes with such confidence that she could have been wearing a burlap sack and would have been able to make it look sexy.

It appeared that Candy wasn't the only one interested in Roger. Many other women had their eyes on him, too. Apparently, they had found out the same bit of information that Candy managed to find out. Roger Nichols was an extremely eligible bachelor, handsome, rich, and charismatic. And he obviously loved all of the attention from the ladies, a few of which were putting their best moves on him right now.

However, Candy had a talent for making herself stand out amongst any crowd, not that she had to do anything special. Her striking features and flawless dark skin were an automatic head-turner. Combine that with her brick-house body and charm school manners and you had quite an interesting woman. Most white men couldn't resist. The brothers seemed to think that she was full of herself and "acting white". Go figure.

While Roger had his hands full with four women fawning over him, Candy quietly admired him from the opposite end of the bar. Periodically, she would look down there and catch his eye. Without words, she knew she was getting her message across. Soon he extricated himself from the group and made his way down to her. She quickly dismissed the old geezer that couldn't keep his eyes off of her cleavage. Roger smiled and walked up to her. The bartender replaced her glass of champagne with a fresh one.

"So, you come here often?" smiled Roger, as he raised his glass in a toast.

Candy clinked her glass against his. "I didn't think people actually used that line anymore."

"They don't. I retired it twenty years ago, but take it out for special occasions."

"Real estate seminars?" Candy asked.

"Meeting magnificently beautiful women."

"Ahhh."

"I'm Roger Nichols," he said, reaching out to shake her hand.

"Candy Martin," she said. "And I enjoyed your presentation very much."

"Thank you. Hope it helps you to make tons of money."

"Me, too."

"So, Candy, would you like to join me for dinner? Those little appetizers were good, but I could use a big, fat piece of meat right now. How about you?"

Candy looked at him, sizing him up. He was probably in his mid-forties, tall, physically fit with a head full of dyed black hair. She had already spotted the Rolex watch and the diamond cufflinks. He was very well put together.

"That sounds delicious."

"Very well, then."

Roger turned and made a big show of inviting everyone at the bar to join him at Lawry's Steakhouse, a restaurant down the street. Candy was shocked, but didn't flinch. She was intrigued by his unpredictability. Fifteen other people accepted his offer, including the four women who were pretty pissed off that he had abandoned them "to go talk to that black woman".

"Wait for me," he whispered in Candy's ear.

Within twenty minutes, Roger had made arrangements to pay everyone's tabs at the bar and instructed them to wait for him in the lobby of the restaurant. Candy lingered as Roger made a call to secure tables for him and his guests. She went to the ladies room and took her time. When she returned to the bar, he was signing his credit card receipt.

"Hey, Mr. Nichols, you want a ride or something?"

"Well, Ms. Martin, I should be offering *you* a ride."

"You already offered me dinner. Oh, wait! Everyone got that invitation."

Roger laughed. "I suppose that didn't make you feel very special, did it? I need to make that up to you."

"You don't know me," she replied. "It's not your job to make me feel special."

He grabbed her and kissed her, taking her by surprise. He was an excellent kisser.

"C'mon Ms. Martin, let's see what kind of wheels you have."

Minutes later, they were zipping down La Cienega Blvd. in Candy's Mercedes with the top down. Roger couldn't keep his eyes off of her smooth, brown thighs. He put his hand on her leg.

"So, how hungry are you, Candy?"

CHAPTER 45

Aurora

For the entire time before their engagement, Aurora Duncan and Krome Bumpa had been in a power struggle. He hadn't been able to mend his cheating ways and kept getting caught. It seemed like every other month she had to break up with him. She didn't care about the women he screwed, he was just using them, but she couldn't let him walk all over her, so she made a point of ending the relationship. Then he would pursue her relentlessly and she would take him back. But he hated those breakups, so to keep her from walking away, he had finally given her the diamond engagement ring that he had bought a couple of years before, waiting for the perfect woman to come along.

Before Aurora became the lucky one, Krome played a sick game of putting the diamond ring on the women he slept with, to experience what it would feel like to be committed to a woman. By the time the sex was over, he took the ring back. The women played along, but somewhere in their minds, they hoped that he would let them keep it.

Once Aurora got the ring, she made him promise to be faithful and he agreed. None of her friends believed it, especially Melissa, but they tried to give him the benefit of the doubt because they wanted Aurora to be happy. If Aurora herself had any doubts, she buried them deep inside of the love that she hoped was real. As Portia liked to say, "They might be the perfect pair because Aurora is afraid of commitment and Krome can't keep his commitment."

Although Aurora had no proof, she began to feel that something was wrong, although he constantly assured her that he wouldn't jeopardize their relationship anymore. She had always been ready to forgive and forget, but the past couple of weeks had been a little different. Aurora realized that *she* was feeling used, like one of his bimbos. A strange sadness came over her which forced her to examine her feelings. She knew in her heart that she couldn't take it much longer, but Krome was in her blood. She said she was leaving for good, and she meant it, as much as she could. He swore that he could change, so she decided to give him one more chance.

A few weeks later, as the two of them were in Krome's bed making love, he was being very attentive and Aurora was feeling special. She had been away on one of her business trips for the past week and had just gotten back the night before, but Krome told her that he was going to be busy in the studio all night, so she had to wait until he had gotten some rest the next day. Sounded like one of his old lines, but she decided to trust him. He wouldn't dare take a chance on losing her this time.

Krome said he couldn't wait to see her, so she had surprised him earlier in the evening by bringing groceries and offering to make dinner. Aurora left the office early, went home to get cute, and then appeared at his door looking hot and ready in a slinky, lime green sundress. She had even taken extra time to put a little bit of curl in her hair.

"Wow, baby! You look great!" he exclaimed, giving her a juicy kiss.

"Feel like Italian?" she asked, handing him the bags

"Let's skip dinner," he said, following her into the kitchen. "That's not what I'm hungry for."

Krome put the bags on the counter, grabbed Aurora in a passionate embrace and kissed her deeply. As his hands caressed her back and moved down over her lovely curves, he worked his way under her dress and slipped his fingers inside of her green lace panties to the sweet honey pot that he knew would be awaiting him.

"Oh, good," he moaned. "Nice and wet the way I like it."

Aurora almost came right then and there, but she wanted them to have a date night. She knew that in another minute they'd be rolling around on the kitchen floor and that would be all she wrote. She decided to make him wait a little bit longer. She reluctantly pulled away and picked up a corkscrew, which she handed to him.

"I don't know about you, but I need a glass of wine and something to nibble on."

"I'm trying to give you something to nibble on if you bring your sweet ass back over here."

"Patience, lover," she purred seductively. "Woo me."

"Woo you?"

Krome wasn't too happy about this little game she was playing, but she had his juices flowing, so he was going to have to go along with it. It was times like this that made him happy that he always had a white girl on the back burner. He could just "hit it and quit it" with the blond sexpots that he kept in his stable. They were so happy to get some black dick, they were willing to let him treat them any way he pleased. But Aurora was a lady. *His* lady. And for that he had to wait.

After a bottle of chardonnay and assorted cheese and crackers, Krome decided that he had waited long enough.

"Alright, woman. I'm all wooed out."

He picked Aurora up and practically threw her over his shoulder. She squealed, but didn't protest too much. He carried her into the bedroom and they began to make up for their time apart. He started by stripping her naked and spreading her legs wide. He took a moment to savor the view of her perfect vagina, and then he dove face-first into her treasure. He licked and sucked her into two intense orgasms, and by the time he entered her, Aurora had disappeared into a world of pleasure. They were really into each other and Aurora felt very happy and satisfied.

An hour later, Aurora was luxuriating in the glass shower, when she suddenly saw something that made her want to get a wooden bat and break something. Particularly, Krome's skull...because between her slender fingers she held several long, blond hairs which she pulled off the shower wall.

"Hurry up, babe," Krome said, yelling into the bathroom. "I gotta get to Hollywood in a half hour."

"Be right out," she yelled back.

Minutes later, she rushed out of the bathroom, mumbling about a forgotten appointment.

He kissed her and said, "I'll call you later," and went in to take his shower.

Aurora quickly got dressed and left. She was long gone by the time Krome rushed out of the bathroom, calling her name and holding the diamond ring that she had left in the bottom of the toilet.

***

Aurora wasn't taking any of Krome's calls. It had been two weeks since the night she found the blond hair in his bathroom. He had been calling and sending flowers, trying to get her to explain what the hell had happened to make her so mad.

"I'm being real, hoping it's not a game," Aurora told the other ladies. "Krome's been playing games, hoping it's not real."

She had no one to blame but herself. She didn't demand anything from him, not really. Every time she took him back, she was telling him that it was okay to treat her like crap. He didn't appreciate what a good woman he had.

"Men are stupid," she thought.

Krome didn't appear to have a clue. He had gotten away with his shit for so long he couldn't even smell it anymore. Aurora just wasn't willing to hear him talk his way out of it this time. She knew that he had been screwing other women, and it never really mattered in the past. It was the fact that he promised over and over again: now that they were engaged, he wasn't going to do it anymore. Obviously, his word was of no value.

Aurora was through with Krome, but she wasn't over him by any means. Portia took Aurora to lunch at The Cheesecake Factory in Beverly Hills.

"Girl, I told my boss I might be late getting back," Portia said. "What the hell is going on with Krome?"

"I just can't do it anymore," Aurora replied. "Pretending that I don't care."

"Honey, you know that Krome sleeps around. Everybody knows that. What's so different this time? Cause you got a ring?"

"Yes, because I got a ring. It was part of the deal."

"Oh, shit! You made a deal with the devil and expected not to get burned."

"I guess," Aurora sighed. "It feels different. It feels like I don't have his love anymore. I just refuse to believe that he fell for one of these bimbos he's screwing."

"Rory, you can't control anything. Much less where his dick is going to end up. Apparently, that trumps where his heart is."

"I feel so stupid, Portia. You can't understand. You and Chuck have something good. You don't have to imagine him with other women."

Portia laughed out loud. "You are right about that, girl. I don't have to imagine shit! I know exactly what he looks like with other women."

Shocked, Aurora lowered her voice. "You caught Chuck cheating on you?"

"Oh, hell no! But I can tell you a little story I've never told before, about how we ended up married."

As Portia told the story of Chuck's 21st birthday party and the hotel orgy, Aurora listened intently. She alternated between shock, disbelief and gut-busting laughter. By the time Portia finished, Aurora was in tears from laughing so hard.

"George Montana? Oh, my God! You know that Snookie fucked him, right?"

Portia stated with a very serious face, "If you ever repeat a word of this, *to anyone*, I will kill you with these claws."

Portia waved her long fingernails towards Aurora's throat, which caused Aurora to burst into another fit of laughter.

Book Nine

CHAPTER 46

Popi's Place

Snookie was glad it was Saturday. Jacques gave her a booth in the clubroom with a perfect view. She sipped on her first Long Island Iced Tea. She decided not to get too dressed up tonight, but instead managed to look mysterious. She wore a nice pair of black pants and a black top that stretched across her breasts like it was a size too small. She had on a black hat that partially covered her face and wore dark sunglasses.

In about an hour or so, she'd be enjoying a great meal and all the dirty gossip that her friends would bring as they joined her throughout the night. Snookie amused herself by checking out a group of guys milling around the entrance of the clubroom. They were the same old regulars. Same old shit. Not one person that she felt like talking to and nobody fun to talk about. These days she got bored very easily.

"Why can't those bitches ever get here on time?" Snookie muttered.

For several minutes, Snookie sipped her drink and gazed into her glass until the sound of heavy breathing penetrated her funk.

"Wake up, Snookie!"

Portia sat down with a thud, bumping the table as she slid into the booth, spilling some of Snookie's drink. Snookie grabbed her glass, momentarily startled.

"Damn, Portia," she snapped. "You scared the shit outta me. I thought we were havin' a fuckin' earthquake."

Portia was squeezed into a bright orange pantsuit with silver studs along the low-cut neckline. She had on a wide silver belt and orange shoes. Even her long nails were painted orange. Her hair was perfectly coiffed.

"Wow!" Snookie was amused. "Where did you get that outfit? Did you jack one of the inmates on freeway duty?"

"Very funny," said Portia, noting Snookie's all-black ensemble. "Who died?"

Jacques walked up. "Bon soir, Madame Portia," he said gallantly. "I didn't see you come in."

"Bon soir, Jacques," Portia said. They exchanged double-cheeked smooches while Snookie rolled her eyes.

"You look lovely," Jacques said. "Very colorful."

"Merci, Jacques," replied Portia, as she adjusted herself in the booth.

"Allow me to buy you a drink," he offered. "What are you having tonight?"

Portia smiled and said, "Champagne, sil vous plait."

"Coming right up."

Jacques hurried off while Snookie still had a sour look on her face.

"I gotta kiss up to somebody to get a free drink around here," she said. "You just waltz your big, black ass in here and pretend to be French."

"And it works every time," Portia smiled.

"Those are the only damn French words you know."

"Well, I know how to say 'kiss my big, black ass' in plain English. You understand that?"

"Whatever," replied Snookie.

"And what's with the dark shades?" asked Portia. "You hiding from somebody?"

Snookie pulled her shades down slightly. She had a black eye. Portia stared at her for a moment, and then waved her off.

"You are way too Hollywood for me right now, Snookie," she said. "Guess who I saw up in my office today?"

Unimpressed, Snookie snarled at her. "Let me think. Whose fake ass woulda been up in your snooty facelift factory today? A thousand names come to mind."

"Go ahead. Guess."

"Viveca?" Snookie asked.

"I wish she would come up in there. On her business alone, my boss could retire early and pay me a tidy little pension."

Snookie laughed, "So, who was it?"

"That model you can't stand from the Victoria's Secret catalog."

"Which one?" Snookie asked. "I hate 'em all."

At that moment, a small woman with huge breasts passed by. Snookie scrunched up her face and poked out her lips.

"Daaaaamn! That's exactly the kinda shit I'm talkin' about. I mean, really. How big do they have to be?"

Teresa arrived with Portia's champagne. "Hallelujah! Thanks, Teresa."

"You're welcome," she said.

Portia turned to Snookie. "I wasn't going to drink tonight, but after five minutes with your negative ass, you can see why I need a damn drink."

"Oh, shut up!" Snookie snapped.

"You want another Long Island, Snookie?" asked Teresa.

"Yeah, but I'm hungry now and I'm tired of waiting on those heifers," Snookie said. "Let's just go ahead and order some food."

"Cool," said Portia. "I know I want some escargot."

"I'll be right back." Teresa walked away to get some menus.

Snookie looked around the club for a minute and sucked down the last of her drink while Portia began sipping her champagne. The horn player hit a few preparatory notes as the band set up to play.

"It's about damn time," growled Snookie impatiently. "Every time these dudes play they're always late getting started. Where's the waitress?"

"Give her a break, Snookie. She's busy."

Snookie looked around and saw another waitress deliver several plates of food to a nearby table where a large woman was sitting alone. Snookie turned back to Portia and shook her head.

"That's a damn shame. She don't need to be eatin' nothin' else for about a year."

"Who are you talking about now?" Portia asked.

"See that big, fat girl over there?" Snookie laughed.

Portia looked, but didn't find anything funny. "Why do you have to call her fat?"

"She has four plates over there."

"She's not fat, you're just skinny. Let's change the subject."

Snookie continued, "Look at her, she's huge!"

Teresa returned and handed them each a menu. Portia sipped on her drink and looked around, ignoring Snookie. Until the girls showed up, she would have to put up with Snookie's derisive comments. Portia was usually guilty of contributing to Snookie's gossip and bullshit, but for some reason, Snookie's comments about the fat woman were hitting a nerve. Suddenly, she was aware of her own insecurities about her weight.

Snookie was still talking. "She put the pig in Piggly Wiggly."

"Can we talk about something else, Snookie?"

"Now, you a big girl yourself, Portia, but this chick is even bigger than you."

"Excuse me?" Portia was livid.

"I mean it," Snookie continued. "She's a whale!"

"See, bitch, that's why you got punched in the eye."

Snookie didn't flinch. "For your information, I walked into a door."

"Whatever, Snookie," Portia snapped loudly. "I don't really give a shit. Just cut the fat jokes, alright?"

"Sorry," she said insincerely.

Snookie stayed silent long enough to drink the rest of her Long Island Iced Tea. She signaled for Teresa to bring her another one, and then she squinted her eyes and looked at Portia, who quietly took another sip of her drink.

"What's got you all in a snit?" Snookie asked. "You're the queen of gossip and all of a sudden, you got scruples."

Portia didn't respond, so Snookie decided to have a little more fun.

"Anyway, I know you think you a big-boned, sexy mama and all that, and I guess ol' Chucky boy gets off on it, but your ass is fat, too, if you wanna know the truth about it," Snookie laughed. "Now imagine how fat you'd be if you got pregnant."

"Dammit, Snookie!" cried Portia.

The look on Portia's face stopped Snookie dead in her tracks. It was like she had taken a knife and stuck it into Portia's heart.

"Oh, shit," said Snookie. "I'm sorry, Portia. I forgot."

This time she truly felt bad about what she said. Portia simply took a deep breath, shook her head and sipped on her drink as Teresa appeared with Snookie's drink.

"Wow, that was fast," said Snookie with exaggerated enthusiasm.

"Danny had one ready for someone who went outside, so he gave it to me."

"That's my boy!"

"Can I bring you another glass of champagne, Portia?"

"Sure, why not?"

"Your escargot should be ready, too," Teresa said. "You ladies decide what you want to order for dinner?"

"We need some more time, please," Portia responded.

"No problem," said Teresa.

"Wait!" said Snookie. "I need food now. Just bring me some hot wings quick."

"Sure." Teresa left and Portia looked over the menu.

Snookie began feeling the effects of her strong drink. "Hot wings, my asssh," she said, slurring. "I really wish I had a Fatburger right now."

Portia was irritated. "And I really wish the other girls were here so you'd have somebody else to talk to. You're giving me a headache."

One of Snookie's problems was that she never knew when to leave well enough alone. So in her inimitable way, she decided to press on.

"I can see right now that workin' in Beverly Hills is turnin' you into one of them 'I'm better than you' bitches wit your snow white teef and no goddamn sense of humor."

"For once, I wish you would keep your fucked up opinions to yourself," Portia hissed. "Don't even get me started talkin' about your buck teeth or your bald head."

"What?" Snookie said as she calmly sipped her drink.

"Have you taken a good look at yourself lately?" Portia was fuming. "Your braids are too damn tight. That fake horsehair's been pulling at your scalp for so long that your hairline starts on the top of your fuckin' head."

Snookie choked on her drink.

"I'm tired of your bitchin' and moanin, Snookie," Portia continued. "Go home, get laid, something. Just get your own life and leave everybody else's the fuck alone."

The band began playing, not giving Snookie time to respond. They sat in silence as Snookie studied Portia over the rim of her glass. Portia knew that this was probably the reason why the others were always late. Nobody wanted to listen to their negative ranting about everybody else in the club, because that's what she and Snookie always did while they waited for the band to play. Now, they had finally turned on each other.

Snookie eventually broke the silence. "Fuck's wrong with you?"

Fifteen minutes later, Portia and Snookie were still pissed off as they ate. Debbie arrived looking casual in a light blue halter-top with designer jeans and jacket.

"Hey! Why you guys looking so serious? I'm on cloud nine."

"Hi, Debbie," said Portia. "I'm so glad to see a happy face."

"What's with the sunglasses, Snookie?"

"Don't ask," said Portia.

"I have a black eye," Snookie replied.

"What?" Debbie turned to Portia and asked, "Do I really wanna know?"

"Save yourself the trouble, sister," replied Portia.

"I have some news, but I'll wait until everybody gets here."

"You don't wanna tell us? Who cares?" said Snookie.

"Who's our waitress?" Debbie asked. "I need a drink."

"I'll be back." Snookie got up and headed to the bathroom.

"What's her problem?" asked Debbie.

"I just had it up to here with her negative shit."

Debbie chuckled, "So you gave her a black eye?"

"I wish. Somebody beat me to it. No pun intended."

"Stop it, Portia," Debbie said, laughing hard. "I can't do this hungry." She snatched one of Snookie's hot wings. "Think she'll miss it?"

"You know she counted them before she left," said Portia. "Anyway, Snookie just got on my *last* nerve. She kept talking shit and pissed me the fuck off."

"Well, that's really funny, Portia, because you usually give as good as you get."

"Yeah, well… she pushed the wrong buttons tonight. So, what's up with you?

"Hi, Debbie," Teresa said, walking up to the table.

"Oh, good, Teresa," said Debbie. "I was hoping we didn't get stuck with that German chick. She's just awful."

"Don't worry," said Teresa. "Her days are numbered. How's it going?"

"I'm great," Debbie said, getting another wing. "How about you?"

"I'm bloated, but who cares?" said Teresa. "Hey, thanks again for hooking me up with that suit. It fit perfectly."

"Of course, girl. That's what I do."

"What are you drinking tonight?" asked Teresa. "Your first one's on me."

"In that case, Miss Teresa, your best merlot. None of that house shit."

"You been drinking house shit all *this* time," laughed Teresa.

"Well, tonight is special. I'm celebrating."

"What's the occasion?" asked Teresa.

"She isn't telling us yet," added Portia. "It's a big secret."

"No secret. I just don't want to have to repeat myself over and over."

"Yeah, yeah, yeah," said Portia.

"Did you guys order dinner already?" asked Debbie.

"No, just something to munch on."

"Teresa, you better bring another order of these wings, too."

"Alright, I'll be right back."

Minutes later, Candy and a stumbling Snookie walked into the clubroom and up to the table together.

"Look what I found in the bathroom," said Snookie.

"What's happening, colored girls?" said Candy.

"Look at you, sexy mama," said Debbie as she let Candy slide into the booth.

Candy had on a lemon yellow spandex mini-dress that hugged every curve on her body and didn't allow for any undergarments. Her nipples were prominently on display and practically every eye in the club was on her. She didn't care a bit.

"Girl, you sure know how to make an entrance," said Portia. "Any normal person would be arrested wearing that dress. How the hell do you get away with not being hauled off for indecent exposure?"

A drunken Snookie said, "She probally fucked half the police force."

"Ouch," said Candy. "That was a little brutal, even for you. What happened? Somebody take away your Milk Bones?"

"Hey, who been eatin' my food?" asked Snookie, counting her wings.

"Snookie's looking for a swollen lip to match that black eye," offered Portia.

"Oh, is that what's up, Snookie?" asked Candy. "You've been getting whipped on by your new man and taking it out on everybody else?"

"Alright, let's make nice," said Debbie. "I have good news."

"I thought you were gonna wait for everybody," Snookie snarled. "You're a liar."

"For your information, Snookie, I *am* gonna wait," said Debbie. "I was just telling Candy that I have some news. Mind your own business, why don't you?"

"Yeah, Snookie," said Candy. "I think you need to keep your big mouth shut."

Portia said, "She couldn't keep her mouth shut if somebody held her down and put a cement brick over her lips."

They all got a big laugh out of that, except Snookie, who just sipped on her drink.

Within the next ten minutes, Aurora and Melissa arrived. Aurora was elegant in a silk, cream coatdress with brown shoes and accessories. Melissa was dressed like a video vixen, in a hot little black dress, lots of cleavage, and clear, five-inch "fuck-me" pumps.

"The gang's all here," said Debbie.

"Alright, divas," Melissa said, smiling. "Guess what happened to me today?"

"Hol' up," interrupted Snookie. "Just hol' da fuck up. Debbie has some news that I been waitin' for. Yo ass just got here, so get a drink and chill."

Melissa was taken aback. "Who the hell are you?"

"Melissa, just go with the flow, girl," suggested Portia.

"Whatever! Can we get drinks first?" asked Melissa.

"She's drunk, I don't care," said Debbie. "Just tell us."

"Now I don't feel like talkin' about it," said Melissa. "Let's hear what you got."

Teresa interrupted to take drink and food orders and Debbie said, "Let's just listen to some music and when the band goes on break we can both talk about our news."

After settling in with drinks and food, Debbie decided that the time was right to reveal her secret. She didn't understand why she was so nervous. These five ladies were the most important women in her life. She had nothing to fear. She waited for a break in the conversation as the band stepped off the stage for a break.

"So, I'd like to celebrate a little something," Debbie said, raising her glass.

The ladies turned to her and raised their glasses. Debbie cleared her throat nervously. "There's something that I never told you. Pride, fear, I don't know the reason. But you are my favorite people in the world… except for you, Snookie…"

"Hurry up," Snookie said. "My arm's about to fall off."

"Alright, I want to share this with you all now," Debbie sighed. "I'm a high school dropout and just got my GED last week."

"Holy shit," Snookie blurted out as they clinked their glasses.

"I would've never guessed that, sweetie," Aurora said. "Why didn't you tell us?"

"I never told anyone, except Lawrence. He encouraged me to get my certificate."

"I'm sure," said Snookie. "If he's gonna be gettin' some on the side, he sure don't wanna be fuckin' no dummy."

"Snookie!" Aurora shouted.

"What?" Snookie asked, trying to look innocent.

"Sometimes I think you're addicted to gettin' your ass kicked," Aurora said.

"Really?" asked Snookie. "Is that what you said to your mama?"

Aurora responded by calmly looking at the other ladies and saying, "Should I take her out of her misery now?"

"Girl, don't wrinkle your dress," said Portia, who turned to give Debbie a hug. "Congratulations, Debbie. That takes a lot of guts to go back to school."

"Yeah, good for you, sweetie," Aurora said, hugging her from the other side.

"Does that mean you can get a real job now?" Snookie asked.

The ladies all turned to look at Snookie.

"Sometimes I wish I didn't know you," Candy said as she slid out of the booth.

As Candy passed the bar on her way to the bathroom, she happened to see Chuck at the end of the bar talking to some blond who had her huge, fake titties all up in his face. He looked like he was drunk, but he certainly was not looking didn't look like he was married. She looked back into the clubroom. Portia was having a good time, so she went into stealth mode. She knew that if Portia spied this little scene, she'd scratch the scrawny bitch's eyes out with her claws. Then she would slice and dice ol' Chucky boy. "Can't have that," Candy whispered to herself. "Time to go rescue his stupid ass."

With quiet determination, Candy squeezed her way through the crowd and startled Chuck and the blond woman by planting herself tightly between them, boldly rubbing her body up on him and forcing the blond to back off. Candy put her hand on Chuck's shoulder and reached out to give him her cell phone.

"Hi, honey," she said as she kissed his cheek. "The kids want to say goodnight."

The blond moved away as quickly as possible, which caused the crowd at the bar to push in further. Now Candy was squeezed up against Chuck involuntarily.

"Funny," Chuck said as he tried to push Candy off. He was able to back her off just enough to check out her body in that tight yellow dress. He stared at her nipples and licked his lips. Yeah, he was drunk.

"Damn, girl," he said. "You trying to get fucked tonight?"

"Well, it sure as hell won't be by you," Candy smiled. "I just came over here to keep your wife from starting a riot in here."

"Don't worry about *me*," he laughed. "You're the one about to be charged with attempted manslaughter."

"What the hell are you talking about?"

"You trying to give one of these white boys a heart attack."

Candy had to laugh. "You're stupid."

Chuck leaned over to whisper in her ear. "Do you have on any underwear?"

"What do *you* think?" she whispered back.

"I could just slip my hand right under there and be home?"

He slid his hand down under the bar.

"No, you can't. Hey!" Candy protested as Chuck's hand slipped under her dress. He caressed her inner thigh and quickly moved his hand higher.

"Damn, you're smooth as a baby."

"Stop it, Chuck," she whispered, trying to wriggle her body away from him. "I'm not playing...ooh!"

Candy squealed as Chuck's finger found her wet center. She struggled a little, but could barely move, so she just leaned on him as he moved his finger around, making her squirm. She was on the verge of an orgasm when the crowd shifted and she quickly backed up into a man behind her, forcing Chuck to stop.

"Sorry," she said, turning to the man, who responded with a grin, "No problem."

Candy turned back to punch Chuck in his chest.

"What the hell's wrong with you?" she asked.

"Stop fuckin' with me, woman. I ain't one of your boy toys."

"Don't nobody want your black ass, Chuck. You need to go and find your wife."

Candy turned around in a huff and squeezed back through the crowd of thirsty customers trying to get to the bar, leaving Chuck smirking to himself as he wiped his fingers on a napkin. He gestured to the bartender for another Jack Daniels and Coke.

CHAPTER 47

Snookie

Snookie had been seeing a football player named Domingo Johnson. He was very big and liked skinny women. They had been having a lot of fun for a few months, but he had a bit of a temper. One night, they went out to dinner and Domingo ruined the entire date by getting angry because they were seated fifteen minutes late for their reservation. He was a real pain in the ass, but he was great in bed, so Snookie put up with him. Unfortunately, he had taken her right out of the mood with his arrogance. They hadn't spoken a word since he grumbled over the expensive check.

"I think I'll get to bed early tonight," Snookie said as the valet pulled up with Domingo's Range Rover.

"What?" he asked. "You not comin' home with me?"

"Look, Dom..."

"Shut up and get in the car."

Snookie got into the car and without tipping the valet, Domingo sped off and drove a couple of blocks before looking over at Snookie.

"What the fuck is your problem, Snookie?" He was really pissed off. Snookie knew that she had been through enough for tonight.

"I'm really tired, Dom. I just want to go home and read a book or something."

Domingo burst into a belly laugh. "You stupid bitch! You don't own no damn books. Those fuckin' trash magazines you read don't qualify as books."

"You're the one who's stupid," she snapped.

Before she knew what hit her, blood was dripping from her mouth and she was screaming at the top of her lungs.

"Mother fucker!" Domingo shouted. He had backhanded her so hard he broke her tooth and hurt his hand. He pulled over, bringing the Range Rover to a screeching halt.

"Get the fuck out!" he yelled as he jumped out of the truck and ran around to her side of the car. Domingo opened the door and pulled Snookie out of the car. "Get out, bitch, before you bleed all over my goddamm car."

Snookie fell to the ground crying as Domingo drove away and left her there. She was there for what seemed like a long time before a couple of teenage girls saw her and stopped to help. At first, Snookie couldn't find her purse, and then realized that Domingo had tossed it out of the car a few feet away. One of the young girls gave her a towel to wipe the blood. They wanted to take her to the hospital, but she just wanted to get to her cell phone. She wasn't too far from Tazora Records.

Twenty minutes later, Aurora picked Snookie up in the parking lot of a CVS Pharmacy close by, where the girls had taken her and stayed with her until Aurora arrived. After she got Snookie settled in her car, she went over to the teenagers.

"Thank you, girls," Aurora said. "That was a real nice thing you did tonight." She handed the driver a fifty-dollar bill. "Here's something for your trouble."

"We can't take your money, lady," the girl said. "Our momma got raped and beaten five years ago. I just wish somebody would have helped her. She spent the whole night on the street with people passing right by."

"I'm really sorry about that," Aurora said. "Just take it. Buy yourselves a little something. Your mother should be very proud."

"Thank you," the girl said, taking the money. "Hope your friend will be okay."

"She will," Aurora said, getting into her car. "Drive safely."

Aurora took Snookie to a doctor friend who ran a late night clinic. He stitched up Snookie's lip and gave her a prescription for painkillers. Aurora insisted that Snookie come home with her so she could take care of her. Snookie, not usually one to go in for the sentimentality, was in too much pain to protest, so Aurora took her to Redondo Beach and settled her into her comfortable guest room.

"I know you got your own problems, but I appreciate you coming to my rescue."

"It's alright, Snookie," Aurora said. "You don't deserve to be hurt like this."

"You probably wanna whack me sometimes."

"Sometimes?" Aurora smiled. "Listen, Snookie. I'm the last person to be judging anybody. We all get ourselves into situations that require some reevaluation."

"You never let Krome put his hands on you."

"Girl, there are all kinds of abuse. Just because you don't see my scars, doesn't mean I'm not damaged."

Aurora talked with Snookie for another half hour until Snookie fell asleep.

Snookie had to go to a dentist the next day and begin the procedure for replacing her tooth. She was pissed. Aurora told Snookie to lay low for a few days until they could get Domingo arrested, but instead of taking her advice, Snookie talked to some of her friends at work, who dealt with a lot of gang members. Somebody made a couple of phone calls and a few days later, Domingo Johnson got jumped by three guys after leaving an afterhours club in Compton and got his ass kicked good.

A week later Domingo went after Snookie as she was getting out of her car near the DMV. When he snuck up behind her and grabbed her by the throat, she jammed her car key into his hand, hard enough to make him release his grip on her. But he immediately pushed her into the street, directly into the path of a truck driven by a teenage boy who had recently gotten his driver's license. The boy swerved to avoid hitting her and ended up running into Domingo, pinning him against a light pole, breaking both of his legs and his right hip. Snookie and the teen were both held for questioning, but since there were several witnesses to Domingo's attack, they were both released. Domingo Johnson was lucky to be alive, and would be going to jail after his release from the hospital.

Of course, Snookie got a grand lecture from her friends. Things could have gone so much worse. Even Snookie had to realize that there was a lesson to learn here.

CHAPTER 48

Candy

Candy Martin spent three nights in Roger Nichols' hotel room having hot, nasty sex. Roger was a wild man in bed and he took Candy to the edge of sanity with his insatiable sex drive, assisted by his love for cocaine. He didn't have much of a dick, in her opinion, but he more than made up for it with his sex toys and perseverance. Roger screwed her royally and didn't let her up for air until he had made her come several times each night.

During the day, Roger whisked Candy off to nearby Beverly Hills for expensive dining and upscale shopping sprees. She was in her element. Although she could afford these extravagances on her own, there was nothing better than a rich, white man who was willing to do it for her. Roger was the kind of man she needed. One who didn't mind having a beautiful, educated, black queen on his arm and was willing to treat her like one.

Candy might have been a freak in the bedroom, and she might have dressed like an expensive whore, but when it came to her public persona she wanted to be treated like the lady who came out of Miss Kelsey's Charm School. She expected her doors to be opened and to have all of her needs catered to. You see, Candy Martin was still in the market for a white husband. She wasn't getting any younger and it was time for her to get serious about starting a family. She was ready to have some little café au lait babies. Roger was looking like an excellent candidate for the job.

Roger had a house in Malibu, but his sister was visiting from Florida and was there with her husband and children for a couple of weeks. That's why Roger continued to stay at the Sofitel. Hard to have kinky sex with a bunch of kids running around. Candy had no problem hanging out with Roger, but she was dying to be invited out to the Malibu house. After Roger's family left, she was finally able to see how Roger was really living. He had a great house on the beach. Almost 10,000 square feet of prime real estate that Candy would love to become more familiar with. He also had a private plane, four beautiful cars, including a Rolls Royce, and a speedboat in Marina del Rey.

Up to now, Candy thought that she was living pretty well. She owned a beautiful six-bedroom home in Thousand Oaks, a condo in Westwood, had two luxury cars, expensive jewelry, and a designer wardrobe fit for a movie star. But here was this man, truly living large. It's just the kind of life that she always dreamed of.

For the next few weeks, Roger flew back and forth in his private plane from his home in Monterrey to his beach home in Malibu. He also owned a vineyard in the Napa Valley and a villa in the south of France. One weekend, Candy went upstate with him. All of his homes were grand. She was having a fabulous time. She was in the middle of a dream come true and wanted to play her cards right. She wanted the end result to be a fairytale wedding.

It was time to let him come to Popi's Place to meet the girlfriends. She had flaked on them for several Saturday nights and they were adamant about meeting this guy. Only serious prospects were allowed to take the ladies away from their Saturday nights. Casual dates were reserved for any other day of the week. Candy had assured her friends that this guy was a serious keeper. Now it was time for the test.

Candy had prepared Roger for the worst, but nothing could have matched up to the reality of the situation. The night that Candy had planned was designed to make it special for Roger. He had been so generous with her over these past weeks, so now it was her turn to return the gesture. She picked Roger up in a limousine at 6:00 pm from his Malibu house and had his favorite champagne and caviar in the car waiting for him. She also had an eight ball of the best cocaine in town. Candy had pampered herself all day. When Roger entered the limo, she was wearing a trench coat with sexy black lingerie underneath, so the driver was told to take the scenic route to her condo.

Once Candy and Roger reached her place, they went in to shower and change. By the time they pulled up to Popi's Place at 9:00 pm, they were feeling pretty damn good.

The ladies were all at Popi's Place waiting patiently.

"So, who's this guy we're meeting tonight?" asked Snookie.

"You know who he is," said Portia. "Why are you acting dumb all of a sudden?"

"I know who she said he is, but that doesn't mean I know who he is."

"Why don't we all just give the guy a chance?" offered Aurora. "Candy obviously likes him."

"Whatever," said Snookie.

"At least he's not married, is he?" Debbie asked, rolling her eyes. This caused a burst of laughter from her friends.

Candy and Roger appeared ten minutes later, all smiles.

"Hey ladies!" Candy was flying high. "Here we are."

"Well, it's about time," said Debbie.

"This is Roger, everyone." Candy made the introductions all around while Portia directed everyone to make room for the couple.

Before they slid into the booth, Roger said, "I'm a little shocked. I didn't expect to be meeting the entire NAACP."

"What the hell did you just say?" Snookie asked.

"Roger!" Candy laughed nervously, as she looked at her friends, who weren't amused. "He's just kidding."

"No, seriously," Roger continued. "I had no idea that so many of you were black."

"What color did you think we were?" Snookie asked. "Purple?"

"Candy just doesn't seem like the kind of person to hang around with blacks." He looked directly at Melissa. "I see that you're the token in this group. You must be the one who works in Beverly Hills."

"No," Portia offered. "That would be me…one of the black ones."

Melissa found that funny and started laughing.

"What the hell are you laughing at, Melissa?" Portia asked.

"You, Portia," Melissa replied. "You're taking this clown seriously."

"I assure you, I'm no clown," Roger said.

"You better be if you want these women to take a joke," Melissa giggled.

"Is that the white half of you talkin' right now?" Snookie asked her.

"Come on," said Candy, apologetically. "Lighten up."

"Can you speak for yourself, Roger?" Aurora asked.

"Have I offended anyone?" he asked, oblivious to the uproar he was causing. Then he mumbled under his breath, "You people are so sensitive."

Snookie heard him loud and clear. "What the fuck?"

The other ladies were looking at each other in disbelief. Snookie wasn't finished with him yet. "You got a huge pair of balls, white boy."

"Darn it, Roger," Candy snapped. "Just chill out."

"Chill out?" Roger looked at her incredulously. "Since when did you start speaking slang? What happened to your charm school manners?"

"Please," Candy pleaded, trying to salvage the night. "Let's just sit down and have a drink."

"I'm sorry, but there's no room at the inn," Portia said, scooting her ample body over to make sure. "Y'all got to take your party somewhere else…shit!"

"It's alright, we already ate," Candy smiled, grabbing Roger by the arm. "We'll be at the bar." She led him out of the clubroom.

"Am I the only one who was ready to knock that sucker down?" Portia asked.

"She's whipped," Aurora offered, matter-of-factly.

"You think?" Debbie asked.

In the meantime, Candy and Roger made their way to the crowded bar and ordered drinks. It took them a few minutes to make space for themselves.

"Your friends weren't very friendly, were they?" Roger asked. "What the hell was their problem?"

"You're the one who was acting like some crazy man."

"What? Because I acknowledged that I was surprised?"

"Surprised about what? I told you all about them."

"No, Candy, you didn't tell me everything," Roger stated emphatically.

"What you said was very rude. You don't make comments like that around *your* friends or other people. Why would you act like that with *my* friends?"

"What are you trying to say?"

"I'm saying that you treated them differently because they're black."

"*You're* black."

"You know what I mean."

"No, actually, I don't," said Roger, downing a shot of tequila.

"You sounded like a bigot."

"If I was a bigot, I wouldn't be fucking your black ass."

"Excuse me…."

"Shut up, Candy," he snapped.

Her first reaction was to throw a drink in his face, but when she looked into his eyes, she saw something that she hadn't seen before, something that scared her, silenced her. Something evil.

"We're outta here," he growled, tossing money onto the bar.

He began to walk away, and then turned around. Candy was rooted to her spot. She couldn't find her legs.

"You coming?" he asked.

Candy couldn't find her voice either. After a few more painful seconds of silence, she finally responded. "No." It was almost a whisper. Roger roughly grabbed her arm and began pulling her away from the bar.

In seconds, a strong forearm covered Roger's throat, forcing him to let Candy go. As a shocked Candy turned around, she saw a familiar face that looked like a black superhero to her right then.

"I believe the lady said no," the deep masculine voice rang in Roger's ears as he struggled to get out of the viselike grip.

"Fuck you."

"Do you want to go with this asshole, Candy?"

"No, I don't," she replied clearly.

"You bitch!" Roger was furious.

Without too much fanfare, Chuck Adams casually dragged Roger by his neck down the long hallway. George Montana was right behind him. The crowd at the bar erupted into applause as the people nearby had witnessed the altercation.

“What the hell’s goin’ on?” Portia asked as she rushed up to Candy, who was still shaken.

“You just full of trouble tonight, ain’t ya?” Snookie piped in, hot on Portia’s trail.

Snookie, who had been on her way to the ladies room, had run back to tell Portia that Chuck and Roger were at the bar fighting over Candy. Portia couldn’t get her big-boned behind over to the bar fast enough.

Since their food had just arrived, Debbie and Aurora decided to stay at the table. They were more hungry than nosy.

“Was that my husband brawling in here?” Portia asked Candy.

“He wasn’t brawling. I don’t think Roger even knew what hit him.”

“How did Portia’s husband manage to get caught up in *your* shit?” Snookie asked. “You shoulda never brought that asshole up in here in the first place.”

“Maybe you’re right, but I swear he never acted like that before. And when I called him on it, he started yelling at me. He wanted me to leave with him and I didn’t want to go, so he grabbed me, and then Chuck just came out of nowhere. He and George escorted him out to the front.”

“Come on,” said Portia, exasperated. “My food’s getting cold.”

In the meantime, Chuck tossed Roger out the front door so hard that Roger fell down.

“Don’t let me see you in here again, asshole.” Chuck said. “Next time you’ll be taken out in a bloody heap. Understand?”

Roger, who was furious, got to his feet, looked at the two big men and decided to cut his losses for the night. “You’re going to regret this. I guarantee it.” He walked away and didn’t look back.

Chuck slapped George on his shoulder as they headed back into Popi’s Place.

“What the hell were *you* supposed to be doing, George?”

“Making sure you didn’t need any help.”

“That guy was a pussy.”

"The very ones you gotta watch out for," George said with a wink. "Punks like that carry weapons because they can't fight."

"Oh, okay Superman. So you can stop bullets now?"

The girls were on their next round of drinks by the time Chuck arrived at their table and scooted beside Portia. He had left George at the bar.

"Hey, sweet thing," Chuck said, giving his wife a kiss. It did little to placate her.

"Is that supposed to make me forget what happened?" Portia asked.

"No, baby. It's supposed to remind you how much I love you."

"Uh huh. Here, I ordered you a Jack and Coke."

"Thanks."

"So, where's your partner in crime?" asked Snookie.

"At the bar."

"Then, I'll be back." Snookie got up.

For the rest of the night, the ladies enjoyed the music and the food. Candy's cell phone kept ringing, so she finally turned it off and did her best to forget about Roger Nichols. She even managed to have a good time. Snookie did her best to get George Montana to take her home with him, but he effectively avoided her advances. Debbie and Aurora left a little early, each one claiming a Sunday morning commitment.

Melissa had flirted with the guitar player in the band, so after they stopped playing, she continued to get to know him. Portia and Chuck danced until the very end and took their energy home, where they made love until the wee hours of the morning.

CHAPTER 49

Aurora

Aurora was exhausted. She had a rough week in Chicago where she had been visiting her parents and Sharon, who was in high school and would be turning eighteen soon. Aurora was going to fly back for a big party that her parents would be throwing for her. Baxter and Camille had been divorced for years, but they were still fighting and sleeping together, which boggled Aurora's mind, but they were still in love, so who was she to judge? Fighting was a part of their love dance. They couldn't live without each other. She should have been able to relate to that.

As a matter of fact, witnessing their dynamics made Aurora afraid that she was repeating the same messed up pattern, even though Krome's abuse was mental and emotional, where Baxter's abuse had been physical, too. Aurora was proud of her father because Baxter had changed. He had gotten that degree of his anger under control a long time ago. He would never even think of physically hurting Camille these days. Of course, a lot of that had to do with the fact that Camille was no longer afraid of him and would be happy to clean his clock if he even thought about threatening her in any way. They still had their verbal battles, but she didn't have the strength to walk away.

While Aurora was trying to relax after unpacking and returning phone calls, Krome was breaking his neck to get her to call him back. She had to deal with some of his business professionally during her time away, so she had corresponded with him by email and sent her assistants to deal with him personally. However, she wasn't trying to give him the time of day outside of the studio.

After a few days of begging on her voicemail, Krome finally got Aurora to call him. She was feeling rested and had talked to her girlfriends, so she called him back.

"I just wanna see you," he said. "Just let me see you."

An hour later, Krome was at her door with a sad look and a bouquet of flowers. She let him in and they talked, but it was the same old thing.

"I never intended to hurt you, Aurora," Krome said.

"That is so typical," Aurora responded as she held back tears of anger and frustration. "You never intended to get *caught*."

"Please forgive me, baby." Krome said.

"Forgive you for what? You never admit to doing anything wrong. Ever!"

"I slept with another woman," he said.

"Good," she responded casually. "Cause there's a fine ass brother who lives in my building and I always said if you ever hurt me again, he's the one who I want to comfort me."

"Damn baby, that's fucked up," Krome said, walking away from her. He looked like he wanted to hit something.

"Really, Krome?" she asked, following him. "What do you expect me to do, just let you continue to roll over me?"

He turned to face her, furious.

"I expect you to forgive me and don't bring up some other motherfucker while I'm trying to deal with me and you."

"So, you want me to forgive and forget what you did to me, and stay in this relationship?"

He changed his tone, gently trying a sweet approach. "More than anything."

"Really?" she asked, surprised at the balls he had.

"You know how much…"

"Do not talk right now," she said calmly, and then thought about it for a long minute, making him sweat. Finally she said, "Okay."

"Yeah?" Krome was optimistic. "So we're cool?"

"Absolutely."

"Great!" he said as he tried to grab her for a kiss.

"Whoa! Not so fast," she said, pushing him away. "There *are* conditions."

"Oh, shit!"

"Hey, you're the one who wants to keep this together. I'd just as soon be rid of your cheating ass."

"Oh, come on, baby. You don't mean that."

"Fine." She looked him straight in the eye. "Goodbye."

"Okay, okay. I'm sure we can come to some kind of compromise."

"You're not exactly in a position to negotiate, are you?"

"Yeah, whatever. Go ahead. But you know I don't like no fucking ultimatums."

"No ultimatums, sweetie. Choices."

"Humph," he groaned. "Alright, shoot."

"Since it's obvious that we're no longer in an *exclusive* relationship, you have two choices. Either we are now in an *open* relationship, in which case nothing will change for *you*, but I will begin to pursue men who I'm attracted to, while still kickin' it with you…"

"Or?" he asked as he tried to hide how pissed off he was.

"Or…you are now single and free to do whatever the fuck you want to...without me. *You* choose. I'm cool either way."

"Oh, it's like *that*?"

"Yeah, it's like that."

He began pacing. "That's not even fair."

"What you've been doing is fair? Sleeping with any tramp that opens her legs?"

"But I love *you*," he said, pleading with his eyes. "You know those bitches don't mean nothin' to me. It was all about the pussy."

"Oh, and you don't think I have men waving dick at me on a daily basis?"

"I'm sure you do."

"That's right, I do. But I know how to say no, even if I'm on the other side of the country, even if the man is fine and sexy as hell. I do that to be loyal to *you*."

"And that's what I expect from the woman I love."

"You say you *love* me? But you break my heart every chance you get? What kind of love is that?"

"This kind," he said as he reached into his pocket and pulled out a black velvet box. "I love you. Aurora. You know that. I want you to be mine forever."

He flashed his biggest, sexiest smile and opened the box to show her a brilliant diamond ring, twice the size of the last one.

"You bastard."

"Marry me, girl."

"I can't deal with this right now," she said tearfully. "Get the hell out."

"Come on, baby."

"I mean it. Get out now." She turned her back on him.

"Alright, alright. I'll leave you alone for now. Give you a little space." He headed for the door. "I'll call you later."

"Wait," she said, turning back around.

He stopped. "Yeah?"

"Leave the ring."

Book Ten

CHAPTER 50

Debbie

Over the past year, Lawrence Desmond had invited Debbie over to his studio often. She still liked to pick his brain about the fashion industry and he really enjoyed her company. She made him feel important, but also didn't mind letting him know when she thought he was being overly conservative, or as she put it…stuffy. Her biggest criticism was of his studio decor. She found it to be very dark. The furniture, the lines and angles, everything was square and overly masculine.

"Doesn't your wife ever try to do a makeover in here," she asked one day.

"Never. She doesn't come here very often. She's busy with her own life."

"Oh. So, she doesn't give you support, but she reaps the benefits."

"That's not fair, Debbie," Lawrence said. "Anita and I have been married for a long time. I suppose she's just not impressed anymore."

"Well, she's a fool."

Lawrence was rarely offended by Debbie's comments. He found her refreshing. Most people kissed his ass to gain favor. His friends were used to him, and his wife took him for granted. He liked having a different energy in his life. Debbie had great energy. Whenever she visited, he had a hard time letting her go.

One afternoon, Debbie invited Lawrence to come over for lunch to look at her sketches. She was enjoying her position with Juan Figueroa. He was very talented and gave her a lot of creative freedom. She was working on a line of her own, though it was going to be a while before she could get it off the ground. In the meantime, she needed professional advice and encouragement, something she could get from Lawrence.

"Hello, my dear," he said, entering the guest house. "You look wonderful."

Debbie had a sarong around her waist and wore a little tank top that showed off her lovely stomach.

"Thanks, Lawrence," she said. "I appreciate you taking the time to stop by."

"What's on the menu?"

"Shrimp fajitas and margaritas."

"Sounds tasty. Any excuse to come by for one of your famous margaritas."

Debbie laughed. "Really? Only one?"

"Let's see how it goes."

"I guess I'd better whip some up right away."

"Please, if it's no trouble."

"Not at all. I'll have to go up to the house and get some more tequila."

"Are John and Rhonda here? I haven't seen them since the premiere."

"They took Zora to see John's parents in San Diego. They'll be gone all week."

"So, you have your solitude up here on the hill."

"Yep," she said. "Once again, I'm here all by my lonesome."

Debbie returned with tequila and Lawrence watched her as she made the drinks. She poured them into fancy, colorful glasses.

"Are you hungry?" she asked.

"I'm ready to eat whenever you are."

"Let's have a couple of drinks first."

As always, Debbie felt comfortable with Lawrence. They never ran out of things to talk about. He wanted to hear about her job and she wanted to know about his exciting life as a successful designer. Eventually, Debbie prepared the fajitas and they ate.

"I'm full. How about you, Lawrence? Want some more?"

"Not another bite, but I'll have another drink and then I'd like to see these brilliant sketches."

Thirty minutes later, he pored over her portfolio.

"I'm impressed with your natural ability, Debbie. You will be doing wonderful things in this business."

"That's not the margaritas talking?"

"Absolutely not. I wouldn't say it if I didn't mean it."

"Well, thank you. Your opinion is very important to me."

"Of course, my dear. Anytime."

"Well, now that's out of way. I'm going to change into my bikini and go out to the pool for some sun. Wanna join me?"

Fifteen minutes later, Lawrence had his shirt off and was rubbing sunscreen on Debbie's back as she laid face-down on a chaise.

"I don't want a tan line. I have to wear a backless dress in two days. I'm modeling in a fashion show for a friend of mine."

"No problem."

He released the hook on her bikini top and massaged the lotion into her soft skin. It felt so good that she almost went to sleep. She was slightly drunk and barely acknowledged what an awkward position she was in. Here she was, a young single woman, half naked, attracted to a half naked married man, and both of them full of margaritas: a recipe for disaster.

Lawrence was relaxing on a chair when Debbie awakened from her short nap. "Lawrence? Can you give me a little more sunscreen?"

"Sure," he replied. He got up and sat next to her on the chaise. He poured the lotion into his hands.

Suddenly, Debbie had to pee. "Get up!" she said.

Lawrence stood up so she could get past him. "Where are you going?" he asked.

"Don't move." She jumped up and ran topless into the guesthouse. Lawrence had his hands covered in sunscreen. He was rubbing it on his chest as she returned to him, young perky breasts on display, naked except for her tiny bikini bottom.

"What about me?"

Lawrence couldn't look away and was nervous as he reached out to caress her. She turned around and leaned her back against him, moaning as she felt his rock hard penis in the small of her back. Lawrence closed his eyes, wrapped his arms around her and continued to caress her breasts. She felt so good under his hands. He must be out of his mind, he thought. He had never cheated on Anita before, but here he was with this beautiful young girl and the only thing that he wanted was to be inside of her.

Lawrence softly moved his hands across Debbie's flat stomach and down between her legs, which she spread to allow him better access to her wetness. Before either of them could stop, he scooped her up into his arms and carried her inside the guesthouse. Between hot, passionate kisses, she directed him to her bedroom, where they fell onto the bed and he ripped off her bikini bottom. They wildly and passionately made love.

Even though Lawrence and Anita had a healthy sex life, she never made him feel like this. Anita wouldn't perform oral sex and this nubile young thing was sucking him into a coma, bringing him to the brink and then pulling him back. He rode her on top, on the bottom and from the back. When he finally came inside of her, he exploded with a force that he hadn't experienced since he was in his twenties. The alcohol didn't diminish his performance one bit. He guessed that he had made her come three times. They were totally satisfied wrapped in each other's arms.

"This can never happen again," he whispered, barely audible.

"Absolutely not," she agreed.

Lawrence went home, completely satisfied, two hours later.

CHAPTER 51

Candy

Candy hadn't talked to Roger Nichols in over a week. She still had feelings for him, but after the way he had acted at Popi's Place that night, she knew that he was bad news. Even though he had sent her flowers and cards, she ignored them. He had several pieces of jewelry delivered to her, but she returned them all. For once, she just wasn't impressed and no longer saw a wedding in their future, but he had really captured her heart like no one else and she had it in the back of her mind to eventually forgive him.

The other ladies tried to convince Candy what a bad idea it was. She would have her work cut out for her if he was going to be a part of their collective lives. If they refused to accept Roger, then Candy would be missing on Saturday nights. She already knew that if she took him back, he couldn't be left out.

One Saturday she received a special delivery from Roger at her Westwood condo that got her attention. It was a brand new Porsche in Candy Cane Red, topped with a giant bow. She was intrigued enough to call and find out what he expected from her. Candy cancelled her plans with the girls to meet Roger for an even bigger surprise that he said he had been preparing for her. She was instructed to get all dressed up and call him on his cell phone at 6pm. She started phoning him at exactly six and had been trying to call him for two hours but he wasn't answering his phone. She was ready to give up and head over to Popi's Place when she got a phone call from Roger's personal assistant, Joanna, informing her that Roger had been arrested.

"What?" Candy couldn't believe it. "What on earth would he be arrested for?"

"I'm not at liberty to say," Joanna responded. "However, it seems to be serious."

"Is anyone hurt?"

"I'm sorry, Candy. You really have to hear it from him."

"Is that all? You can't tell me anything?"

“Well,” Joanna said reluctantly. “You can wait for the eleven o’clock news.”

Candy sat at home in shock long after the news came out. She didn’t know what to do first, call her friends or take a drink. She finally decided to confide in Jose Cuervo. That conversation lasted for the rest of the night until she passed out. Meanwhile, the other ladies were having fun at Popi’s Place without her.

CHAPTER 52

Melissa

Krome was in rare form. He knew how badly Melissa wanted a record deal and he had no scruples about making her a pawn in his game. He invited her to meet Palmer Whitmore, a producer friend who was looking for new talent. Palmer was a misogynist, with a lot of money and major influence in the music business. Melissa was excited about meeting him. He was one of the most powerful men in the record business, particularly when it came to discovering and developing new female hip hop talent. Krome promised that he would make it happen. She had no reason not to believe him.

Even though he was married, Palmer Whitmore had a reputation for hanging out with beautiful women and Melissa knew that she was definitely his type. She decided to sex it up a little to make sure that he was interested. Her green mini dress with the low-cut front was just the thing to set off her hazel green eyes and looked great with her wavy blond hair. It was one of Krome's favorite colors on her. He hadn't seen this one, yet.

When Melissa arrived at the beautiful Malibu estate, she had to leave her car with a valet in the spacious driveway. She couldn't help but think that she could have a place like this someday. Palmer's home was like a playground for rappers. When she got out of the car, she could hear music pumping from inside the house. There was a speaker somewhere outside, too. It sounded like Krome's new record.

As she approached the door, a handsome, young Asian man in formalwear, complete with white gloves, opened the door. The first thing she did was walk into the foyer and turn to admire all of the gold and platinum records collected on the walls.

"Just follow the hallway to the end, miss," the young man offered.

As she continued down the hall, Palmer was headed in her direction to greet her.

"You look absolutely scrumptious," Palmer said. "Are you Melissa Murdock?"

"That would be me," she responded, grinning widely.

"Well, Krome certainly didn't do you justice when he said that you were every man's fantasy. I'm hard as a rock just looking at you."

"You're making me blush, Mr. Whitmore."

"You must call me Palmer," he said, taking her gently by the arm. "Come and have the best apple martinis in town. I made them just for you."

Melissa loved apple martinis. Palmer had done his homework and she was immediately impressed. The house was very modern and well maintained. Palmer himself was well maintained. He had dubbed himself some sort of black Hugh Hefner. As they entered the main room, she could see that the party was in full swing. There were about fifty people enjoying food and drinks. His bevy of beauties consisted of video vixens, rapper groupies and wannabe actresses with plenty of visible assets, but no talent. She recognized several rappers and athletes, who were mingling.

"Krome tells me that I need to hear your voice."

"He's right. You do."

"I could have listened to the demo, but I like to be 'hands on' with my artists."

"I heard that about you, too, but I thought we were having a private meeting."

"I do my best business in this type of atmosphere," he said. "Just have a drink, relax and enjoy. We have plenty of time for business later."

"Okay," Melissa said.

Palmer gestured to a waiter, who walked over and handed her a martini, complete with a fresh apple slice. She took a sip.

"Umm, that's so good. Thank you."

"Enjoy yourself, my dear. Mingle. I'll be back in a few minutes."

Palmer walked away and two black girls immediately swarmed her.

"Hi, I'm Amber," said the taller one.

"I'm Jackie. You gonna be in the video?"

"Uh...no, I don't plan on it," replied Melissa. "Why?"

"Just wondering," Jackie replied. "Krome always has at least one blond bitch in his videos. He has a soft spot for white meat."

"Really? Well, I'm not white."

Melissa said it with such a straight face, that they barely had time to react before a familiar, sexy voice roared over the music. Krome had just walked into the room, rapping over his own track. He was dancing and strutting, being pawed by the lovely women in his path. Krome looked like a prince. He was dressed in white and gold. His perfect dark skin and bald head were glistening under the ambient lighting in the room.

Krome spotted Melissa, stopped several feet away and looked at her with such passion that she could feel her panties getting soaked with her own juices. He spent a lot of time flirting with other women and even disappeared a few times, causing Melissa unexpected anxiety. She was never at a loss for attention, though. She was easily one of the sexiest women there, and there were a lot of sexy women. Melissa wondered how Palmer's wife felt about all of this. There was a rumor that he was happily married. Apparently, his wife preferred to live half of the year in Palm Springs and rarely attended her husband's wild parties, but certainly was not blind to his activities.

About two hours after Melissa arrived, Palmer asked her to come into his private recording studio with him. She was finally about to get her chance to sing. She only hoped that she hadn't had too much to drink. Earlier, Krome had provided Palmer with a track, so he let Melissa get into the vocal booth to do her thing. She need not have worried. Her voice was golden, just like her beautiful hair.

Melissa sang with the rhythm and passion of a soul singer. Palmer was very impressed. If he closed his eyes, he wouldn't know that she was white. After she finished, Palmer played another track that belonged to one of his young stars. She broke into a rap that was raw and current and which rivaled any of his current stars.

CHAPTER 53

Candy

Candy was depressed and physically ill after finding out that Roger Nichols, her perfect, white millionaire boyfriend, was arrested for distributing child pornography. She couldn't really wrap her brain around it. From her understanding, he had been under investigation and was caught red-handed. All of his computers were confiscated, along with actual photos. His team of lawyers was working overtime to get him out on bail.

Aurora went to see Candy after she refused to return any of their calls. She wouldn't leave until Candy let her in.

"They must have made a mistake," Candy cried. "That's not the man I know."

"I don't think you know him at all, Candy."

"He may be a jerk…but, a pervert?"

"Even if there's only part of it that's true, you don't need to be involved. He's not your husband, and he's not even your man anymore. Let him go."

"You're right."

"And get rid of that damn car," Aurora added. "It's like a bright red flag and you don't need to be reminded of him every time you move around town."

Aurora kept her company until she felt that Candy was thinking clearly.

"I have to go back East on business for a few days," Aurora said. "I'm going to be calling you and your ass better answer the phone."

Candy agreed, but after Aurora left, Roger was all she could think about. She realized he needed to face him and hear the story from his own mouth. A few days later, Candy went to visit Roger in jail. He was in denial and pleaded for her to stand by him.

"You know that I've been set up, right?" he asked. "There's a conspiracy to bring me down by a competitor or even someone in my company who wants to take over."

"Are you serious?" she asked, incredulous. "They have tapes and pictures."

"Those tapes were doctored, not like the ones of us."

"What the hell are you talking about?"

"They have tapes of us fucking."

"Are you trying to tell me that you taped us having sex?"

"Don't worry. I edited them so that your face doesn't show."

"Then what's the point of taping it?"

"I didn't think that you'd mind the taping, but I thought you might not want everyone to know who you are."

"Everyone? Like whom? Did you show other people the tapes?"

"I have this little website...white men who have sex with black women."

"Oh, my God!"

"I love you, Candy," he said. "I really didn't think that you'd mind. You're a freak. I wanted to have something special of us."

"You sick bastard!" she hissed. "You better pray that I don't sue you for everything you've got."

"Sure," he grinned. "If you want the whole world to know that your black ass is the one all over the internet. Ooh, some of the things you did to me should be patented."

For the first time, Candy could clearly see the sleazy man that she had actually considered for a husband. She felt sick to her stomach.

"I don't ever want to see you again," she said before walking away. Somehow it didn't seem like enough.

Candy hadn't left the house in two days. If she needed to be shaken up and pulled out of her fantasy funk about Roger Nichols, it was done. As if the child porn scandal wasn't bad enough, now she was being pulled into his sick world. She should have listened to Aurora and never gone to see him. She certainly could have lived without ever knowing that her body was plastered all over the internet. The only one Candy confided in about the tapes was Aurora, who was still in New York and suggested that she retain a lawyer immediately just in case any of this came to light or he involved her in any way.

"I'll be away a little longer, but call if you need me, and let the girls know what's going on. They can be there for you, too. You don't have to tell them about the tapes."

"They've been calling, but I'm just not ready for the whole crew. Roger's shit is all over the news, so they can figure out why I'm not coming around."

"Just take care, Candy," Aurora said. "Don't be stuck in that condo. Get out and do something constructive. Keep your head up."

"I will."

Candy tried to be brave. After two long days, she was finally purging Roger out of her life the best way she knew how. By sitting in her favorite short, white silk bathrobe, drinking shots of tequila and stuffing pictures of Roger Nichols down the garbage disposal. When she turned it on, a loud clanging noise came from the sink, and then silence, as the disposal broke down. Candy was frustrated.

"I can't even do that right."

In a fit of anger, she pushed everything off the kitchen counter, except the bottle of tequila, which she turned up to her lips.

"What I need is a doggone handyman."

She stumbled over to one of the cabinets and pulled out the yellow pages. She took another sip and suddenly a huge grin appeared on her face.

"Wait a minute. I know a handyman."

She laughed like a drunken hyena as she dialed the phone, changed her mind and hung up. She poured herself another drink.

"Darn, it's too late. I know Portia has to get her freaking beauty sleep."

After a few minutes, she picked up the phone again.

"What the heck. It's an emergency."

***

Chuck Adams was sitting alone on his couch, drinking beer and playing a video game. His wife had thrown a blanket down to him before storming upstairs and slamming the bedroom door. He hated fighting with Portia. Before he got married, he rarely had to fight with women. Back in those days, he could send the bitches packing when they pissed him off. If one didn't play nice, there was always another one waiting to be sweet to him. When the phone rang, he grabbed it immediately.

"Hello?"

"Chuck. I'm glad you're home," purred the seductive voice.

He perked up. "Who's this?"

"It's Candy. I have an emergency and I need your help."

He looked at his watch. "Girl, do you know what time it is?"

"It'll be even later when you get here," she said.

"I'm tired, woman."

"I thought you were a twenty-four seven kind of guy," Candy taunted. "What you got going on that can't wait?"

"Where's your man?" Chuck said, his voice dripping with sarcasm. "I thought Roger took care of your needs these days?"

"Roger?" Candy screeched. "Who the fuck is Roger? He's not a fucking man. I need a fucking man."

"Hey, hey, hey," Chuck said, surprised. "What's with the potty mouth, Miss Beauty Queen?"

"Sorry, but I need a real man right now."

"That's your emergency?" he asked, amused. "Goodbye, Candy."

"Come on, Chuckie," Candy said, pleading. "I really have a problem over here. I need professional help."

"Well, I sure as hell can vouch for that," he said, laughing.

"What are you doin' right now?" she asked, her voice seductive again.

"I'm busy," responded Chuck.

"I know that you're not that busy," Candy began to slur. "Iss not like you were having sess when I called."

Chuck laughed, "How do you know I wasn't having sex?"

"Because you answered on the first ring, dummy," she snapped. "Now are you coming to help a sissa out or what?"

"A sista?" Chuck was tickled now. "I thought it was *you* who needed help."

"Very funny, asshole."

"That mouth of yours! You're totally shattering the charm school image for me."

"Chuuuuuuckkk….." she whined.

"What's the problem, Candy?"

"I'll see you in fitteen mince," she slurred.

Candy hung up with a satisfied look on her face as she poured herself another drink. She looked at the mess all over her kitchen and decided to try and clean it up before Chuck got there. She knew that he would show up. He couldn't resist playing the hero. He was a man. It was in his nature.

Candy began to move papers around on the counter. She saw a picture that was taken of her and Roger last Valentine's Day. He almost looked like a pervert now. How could she have missed this one? How could she have been so stupid?

Twenty minutes later, the doorbell rang. Candy grabbed the bottle of tequila and shuffled over to answer the door. As she passed herself in the mirror, she realized that she looked a mess, but she just didn't feel like doing anything. She wasn't going to get dressed, she wasn't doing her hair, and she was not going to leave her house ever again. She opened the door and was shocked to see how fine he looked. Chuck was wearing a tight, green workmen's jumpsuit that zipped down the front. He had it slightly opened at the chest, which showed off his amazing upper body and made him look extremely sexy. He was equally shocked by her unusually disheveled appearance, but couldn't help noticing her hard nipples poking through the little, silk bathrobe.

"Damn, girl," he said, looking her up and down. "You look like hell."

"Thanks, Chuck," she said. "I told you I needed help. Here, have a drink."

"I don't know why you called *me*," he said, taking the bottle. "You better call a shrink. You look kinda crazy."

As he took a swig, she picked up a pillow from the couch and threw it at him. It hit him in the back of his head.

"Hey!"

As Candy bent over to pick up another pillow, Chuck got a quick glimpse between her legs. The little robe barely covered her ass. She turned around, but decided not to throw the pillow.

"I'm not crazy, you moron," she moaned. "I'm drunk and depressed. There's a difference."

"What do you have to be depressed about?" he asked, taking another swallow of tequila from the bottle. "You got out just in time. You should consider yourself lucky."

"I don't want to talk about it." Candy pointed toward the kitchen. "Let's go in there. Thass where the problem is."

Chuck moved past her to the kitchen where he stopped to observe the mess.

"Well, this is pretty fucking depressing," he said. "Did you fire the maid? What happened in here?"

"I lost it a little bit."

After Chuck got his tools from the car and unclogged the disposal, he was about to say something else sarcastic, but as he turned to look at Candy, he saw something that he had never seen before, her vulnerability. She was standing in the kitchen doorway, looking like a broken doll. He wanted to be like a big brother and say all the right things to make her feel better, but she looked so fucking sexy with that white, silk robe clinging to her chocolate skin. If he had any good sense, he would have turned away, but there was sadness in her eyes that begged to be recognized. He wanted to reach out and take her into his arms and tell her that everything would be all right, but he knew what would happen. What he wanted to happen.

He started to turn away, but before he could make a move, she was in his arms, crying like a baby. Candy could feel his body, which was warm, yet she was shivering under his touch. She couldn't help but notice how strong his arms were and how gently he held her. He even smelled like comfort. He continued to hold her like that, and after a minute, Candy felt him getting hard. It snapped her out of her tears because she couldn't believe how big he was. She pulled away.

"I'm sorry, Chuck," she murmured.

He looked around and found a box of tissues on the kitchen table. He smiled and handed her the box.

"No problem," he said. "What's a strong shoulder for, anyway?"

Candy blew her nose.

"Thank you," she mumbled.

Chuck was a little uncomfortable and began picking up the mess from the floor. He looked around and found a broom in the corner.

"I guess I better help clean up this kitchen before you *totally* lose it."

Candy stopped blowing her nose for a moment, then burst out laughing. Chuck joined in and before they knew it, they were holding onto each other again. After she calmed down, Candy moved slightly away from him and looked into his eyes.

"I went to see Roger," she said.

Chuck replied, "Why would you waste your time? What did he say?"

"Oh, God. He's such a freakin' pervert. He's a nasty ass white man who needs to have his penis cut off."

Chuck backed away from her and grabbed his crotch.

"Hey, hey. None of that kinda talk, little lady."

Candy began laughing again. "Oh, your penis is your pride and joy, isn't it?"

"My what?"

"You know what I said."

"No, call it what you want to call it."

"Your dick," she said softly.

"Why are you whispering?" Chuck asked loudly. "Hell, yeah, my dick is my pride and joy. But you wouldn't know anything about that. Not after hanging around all those white boys."

Chuck grabbed the bottle of tequila and took another drink. Candy thought about it for a minute. She took the bottle from him and said, "Lemme see it."

"See what?"

Chuck began to rub his crotch, getting harder with every stroke.

"*It*," Candy said, looking at him as he rubbed himself.

"You mean, what you been missing all these years?"

Candy looked at him with a sexy grin.

"There are lots of men with big ones. What's so special about yours?"

Before she had a chance to catch her breath, Chuck unzipped his jumpsuit all the way down and Candy was looking at his long, hard penis.

He said, "You ain't the only one who walks around with no underwear on."

BAM!!! Candy and Chuck had sex for three straight hours as they ravaged each other's hot bodies. He had often fantasized about having sex with Candy. She was so damn sexy and always put it right out there, but she would never give him or any other black man the time of day. And knowing that he was the first black man to have sex with Candy turned him on so much that he couldn't get enough of her. He made sure that he represented well and kept coming back until she just couldn't take anymore.

"Alright, alright, that's enough!" Candy said as she rolled off Chuck's hard body.

"Shit, girl. That's all I got left," he replied with exhaustion.

"You act like you haven't had sex in weeks, she said, breathing hard.

"Me? You tried to break my dick off. It feels like you ain't had none in months."

"Oh, yeah?" she grinned. "Well, you were like a starved dog. What's up? The big girl been holdin' out on you?"

Chuck forced himself to get up.

"On that note…" he smiled with exhaustion.

"Right. Time for you to skedaddle your tired ass on home."

CHAPTER 54

Aurora

Every time Aurora came to Krome's house, she had a suspicious feeling in her gut. She knew he was screwing around, even after he promised to be faithful, but it didn't stop her from being hurt when there was evidence. He wasn't man enough to admit that he couldn't do it. Instead, he lied. Lied through his perfect, white teeth. It drove Aurora crazy.

One night, Aurora returned home early from a trip. She decided to surprise him; partly because she missed him, and partly because she was hoping to catch his ass in a lie. Before she boarded the plane, she called him and he said he was going home after the studio because he was coming down with the flu. He swore that he had been faithful while she was away and had only been at the studio, working, or at home alone.

Aurora, who was now a Vice President at Tazora Records, had recently hired Mark Sullivan, a handsome, young limo driver, to pick her up from the airport after her long trips. He was 5'10", very strong, with light brown skin and had a head full of curly dark hair. Mark was the younger brother of one of her UCLA friends who now played professional football, and he had a crush on her. He constantly smiled, happy to be around her. He owned the company with his brother, but insisted on being her driver.

Since Krome lived in Inglewood, his place was a ten-minute ride from the airport. He lived in a gated townhouse complex and when she arrived at the gate, the guard, who was new, mistook her for someone who had been there the night before. The look on Aurora's face let him know that he had made a huge mistake. His face turned completely red as he called Krome on the phone to announce her arrival. Aurora could hear Krome's muffled curses through the phone. The guard tried to keep a straight face.

"Do you know where the building is, Miss?" the guard asked.

"Yes."

By the time she directed Mark to Krome's building, which took several minutes, she saw a woman running out of the doorway and down the street. It was a huge complex of buildings, and since there were several units in each building, there was no way to prove it, but she knew the half-dressed blond was running from Unit 3G.

"Please get my small overnight bag and take the rest of my luggage to the house," Aurora said as she handed him her spare key.

"No problem," he said. "You gonna be okay?"

"I don't know," she replied. "I'll call you tomorrow."

When she got to Krome's door, it was open. Aurora called out for him and then proceeded up the stairs to his bedroom, where he pretended to be fast asleep already.

"I know you didn't get to sleep that fast, Krome."

"Nyquil," he mumbled.

"Really? Is it helping you to feel better?"

She tried to wake him up, realized that he was drunk, and began to take inventory of the bedroom. The first thing that she noticed was a pile of dirty sheets on the floor. The sheets he was lying on had been thrown onto the bed haphazardly.

"What's with the sheets?" she asked.

"Nothin', baby," he mumbled. "I know you like clean sheets."

"Is that so?" Aurora asked as she walked around to the other side of the bed. "You changed them just now? Just for me?"

"Of course," he said as he trailed off into a drunken sleep.

"Uh huh."

Aurora was relentless. Krome had removed the sheets, but obviously forgot to change the pillowcases. Dumb ass. She wanted to scream at him, but instead she immediately went into action. As far as she was concerned, the house was now a crime scene and she was the CSI bitch in charge. She immediately picked up the pillow on her side of the bed and found the first piece of evidence: smudges of tan makeup and red lipstick. This prompted her to investigate further, so she got down on her knees and looked under the bed, where she found a pair of panties that didn't belong to her. She could feel blood rushing to her head as she got up and stood over

Krome's sleeping body. It took all her strength not to pick up something hard and crack him upside his bald head.

Getting her emotions under control, she went downstairs into the living room. More evidence. A pair of unfamiliar earrings lay on the coffee table. There were two cocktail glasses, one of which had red lipstick on the rim, and an almost empty bottle of Grey Goose vodka. That was enough for her. What kind of a fool did he think she was anyway? Obviously, the kind of fool who would believe that his lying ass could ever change. She decided to give him one chance to come clean. She went back upstairs.

"Krome, wake your drunk ass up and talk to me right now," Aurora yelled, shaking the bed. "Get up!"

"What the hell's wrong with you, woman? I'm trying to sleep."

"You've been fucking around again, right?"

"What? You're crazy. Come to bed."

"I'm not playing with you, Krome." Aurora could barely contain her rage, but she didn't want to wake up the entire neighborhood, so she kept her voice as calm as possible. "Tell me right now. Have you been fucking around?"

"Dammit, we'll talk in the morning."

"I won't be here in the morning."

"Yes, you will," he said, as he rolled over to go back to sleep.

And with that simple statement, he told her everything that she needed to know. She had allowed herself to be mistreated by him for so long, she didn't even recognize herself as she caught her reflection in the mirror. She saw a woman who was well put together on the outside, but was an empty shell inside. That woman in the mirror was expected to take the crumbs that Krome rationed out. That woman was expected to climb into a bed that he had just defiled with another woman's scent. That woman was expected to have a peaceful night's sleep.

In the morning, he would expect to climb on top of that woman and make her forget that she was ever mad at him. He would fix that woman a big breakfast, because he knew how to throw down in the kitchen, and then he would make love to her again. After a hot shower, he would whisk that woman off to

Beverly Hills and spend a shitload of money trying to keep the peace. That was the routine. That's what he expected.

Aurora grabbed her purse and, without another word, walked out the front door, for what she hoped was the last time. *That* woman's ghost could be there when Krome got up in the morning, but *this* woman, Aurora Duncan, was going to get the hell out of there while she still had the nerve.

Aurora had no idea how she was going to get home as she made her way to the front of the building, but Mark Sullivan was a very smart and sensitive man. He was sitting outside in the limo, looking like the answer to a prayer, because when Aurora walked out that door, she was broken. Mark immediately jumped out and watched carefully as Aurora approached him. He opened the door and, without a word, Aurora climbed into the back of the limo.

As Mark drove her home, warm tears rolled down her face: tears for all of the mistakes that she had made, and all of the ways that she had allowed herself to be used. How could she be such a powerful woman in her business life and such a failure in love? With everything that she knew, how could she pick a man just like her father? Baxter Duncan was her role model for men. How fucked up was that?

Life had to change. Aurora had to make it change if she was ever going to find true happiness. She was going to have to learn that not every man was going to treat her this way and that she deserved better. What the hell was she afraid of? This was no way to live. This was no way to love.

Twenty minutes later, Mark had driven Aurora back to her townhouse in Redondo Beach. She still had not said a word. He opened the door for her and held out his hand. She didn't try to fight his offer of assistance. She actually wasn't sure that her legs were going to carry her. After walking only a few feet, her knees buckled and Mark had to catch her. He scooped her up easily and carried her up to the front door.

"Can you get to your keys?" he asked.

Aurora reached into her purse and found them. She leaned forward and unlocked the door. Mark carried her into the house and silently walked her up to her bedroom and laid her gently on the bed.

"Thank you," she said quietly.

Mark looked at her. She was not the fiery, bossy lady that he had come to know and love. This woman was a shell, as though the essence of her being had been sucked away. He could barely stand to look at her this way. He preferred it when she lit into him or one of her business associates with her razor tongue until they submitted to her. That was sexy. Apparently, her love life, if you could call it that, didn't allow her that freedom. Darren Cooper, Krome Bumpa, whatever he wanted to call himself, was a piece of shit. Mark always had an extreme dislike for the man who could break Aurora down on a regular basis. But, even then, she still had fire. This was something new.

"I'll be right back," he said. "Don't move."

A few minutes later Mark returned, carrying her luggage.

"Can I get you anything?" he asked.

"A new life would be great," she said softly.

"The life you have is just fine. Just needs a little fixin', that's all."

"This can't be fixed."

"Just take it easy," Mark said, confidently.

Mark went downstairs and returned with a bottle of wine and two glasses.

"I found this in the fridge," he said. "How about it?"

"A glass of wine would be nice."

"Okay."

He poured the wine silently, waiting to see how she was going to manage. She looked sad as he handed her the glass.

"I've got a cure for you," he said, happily.

Aurora shook her head as Mark got up and went into her spacious bathroom where he proceeded to fill the tub with hot water and poured a lavender and vanilla bubble bath. When he emerged, she looked curious.

"What are you doing?" she asked.

"I want you to relax in a nice hot bath and go to bed."

"Have some wine with me," she said. "You don't have to drive anymore tonight."

"Sure, Miss Duncan."

"You can call me Aurora," she smiled. "You're off duty."

"Okay, let me turn on some music for you."

Mark walked over to her CD player and turned it on. Then he poured himself a glass of wine, took off his jacket and shoes, and sat in a chair near the bed.

"Do you feel like talking?" he asked.

"No, I don't," she replied.

They sat in silence enjoying the music for a few minutes until Mark got up and went to check on the bath. He came back with a smile.

"It's all ready for you," he said. "You need help?"

"Yes, please."

Aurora was like a limp doll as Mark slowly helped her off with her clothes. He needed to be strong for her, so he handled her very gently and very carefully. She needed him and he didn't want to make her uncomfortable. He did his best not to touch her in any way other than as a caretaker. He found her bathrobe hanging on the door and covered her with it as he helped her to the bathroom.

"Can you manage from here?" he asked.

"Yes, but don't go far," she said, sadder than ever. "You can sleep in the guest room. I don't want to be alone tonight."

"I'll be right here."

Mark sat on the edge of the bed and got comfortable. He knew that Aurora was vulnerable, and he had no intention of taking advantage of her. He really cared about her and knew that she needed a friend, not a lover. He decided then and there to be that friend…for now. After all, he was a healthy man. And she was a hell of a woman.

Forty minutes later, Mark heard Aurora calling his name.

"You okay?" he asked, getting up from the bed.

"Please come help me."

He walked into the bathroom. She was standing in the tub, wrapped in a towel.

"Feeling better, beautiful?" he asked.

"Yes, much better, thanks."

Mark helped her out of the tub and into the bedroom. He had prepared the bed for her to be comfortable and had found some lotions and oils. Aurora sat on the bed and he poured another glass of wine and watched her carefully as she sipped it. Mark got up to change the music. She finally noticed the lotions and oils on the nightstand.

"What's all this?"

"Let me give you a massage," he said. Aurora looked at him skeptically for a moment. "No hanky panky," he laughed. "I just want to put you to sleep."

"Really?" she asked.

"Really," he replied, smiling. "Come here."

He helped her to lie down and covered her discretely with the towel. For the next thirty minutes she allowed her body to be pampered and caressed until she felt fully relaxed and completely aroused. She was almost too limp to move, but felt more alive than she had in a long time. Mark thought that she was asleep, so he covered her up and rose from the bed to go into the guest room.

"Will you just lie here with me for a little while?" she asked, barely audible.

Uh oh, he thought.

"If that's what you want," he managed to say.

Mark sat back down on the bed. Aurora laid her head on his chest and enjoyed the smell of him for a few minutes. He put his arm around her bare shoulders and held her. Just when he thought he might have to reconsider waiting for another time to make his move, she began to cry. It brought him back to the reality that he was there to take care of her, and that's what he was going to do. He let her cry it all out. It took over an hour. By that time she had a snotty, runny nose that she had to blow for fifteen minutes. That certainly killed the sexy factor for the night. He laughed to himself.

"I'm so sorry, Mark," Aurora whispered softly.

"Don't sweat it, Miss Duncan," he smiled.

"I told you…"

"Just kidding, Aurora. Relax."

He held her tight, without anything on his mind or in his heart except love. That night, she got the best night's sleep she had gotten in a long while. And with the beautiful Aurora Duncan in his arms, so did he.

CHAPTER 55

Candy

Ever since Chuck Adams pulled his dick out of his pants, it was all Candy Martin could think about. She kept replaying that moment in her mind. How she heard that hard, black penis calling her name.

"That's the most beautiful thing I've ever seen," she had said to him as she dropped to her knees and began licking all over it. Chuck had scooped her up, carried her to her bed and fucked the shit out of her.

Candy had to tell somebody because she was about to bust, so she broke down and called Aurora. Candy knew that Aurora had a good head on her shoulders. Maybe she could help her to figure this out. They met at a little coffee shop in Hollywood where they could talk. Aurora was still dealing with her feelings about leaving Krome, so she wasn't in the mood for any new "Candy drama" but she was a good friend so she met her in the late morning when there weren't a lot of people there.

Candy and Aurora were sipping on cappuccinos. There wasn't anyone in the coffee shop who knew them, but they still sat in the very back. Aurora was fuming.

"Please, Candy…explain it to me like I'm a six-year-old, and I don't give a fuck about Roger. Start with ol' Chuckie boy."

"Well, I called Chuck because my pipes were all messed up. He had fixed one for me before and I just thought that it was easier to call him again."

"Uh-huh." Aurora looked at Candy with no expression.

"It was an emergency, so he came right over."

"I see," Aurora said. "And how, exactly, did your pipes manage to pull his dick out of his pants?"

"We started talking. I didn't have anyone to talk to...you know... about Roger," Candy whined. "It was late. None of the other girls would have talked to me about him."

"That's because nobody could stand his white ass," Aurora snapped. "Did you ever consider that there was a reason for that, Candy?"

"I've been depressed lately, not that any of you have noticed..."

"Bullshit! I told you to call me, Candy."

"You weren't here. I needed a hug."

"Oh, my God...," Aurora sighed.

"Chuck was there. He was very sweet and he genuinely seemed to care."

Aurora rolled her eyes. "Yeah, he's a real prince," she said.

Candy continued, "I know that I've flirted with Chuck in the past, but it's always been very innocent because, of course, there was no way I could have sex with him."

"Right. Because..." Aurora waited for an answer.

"Because he's black," she blurted out as though it was the obvious answer.

"Uh, yeah, right...that's a good reason," said Aurora, sarcastically. "And?"

"And what?" Candy asked innocently.

"Don't mess with me, bitch. Right now I want to snatch you by your neck and spin you around until your head comes off, okay?"

"Dang, Rory!"

"Just tell the damn story."

"Well, I had been drinking before he got there and after telling him about Roger, I got all emotional and started crying. He put his arms around me and then, next thing I know, I was hugging him really tight and I could feel him getting bigger and harder and...he didn't have any drawers on."

Aurora accidentally spit out her drink.

"Lord have mercy! What's with you people airing your private parts out in the wind?" Aurora quickly dabbed herself with a napkin. "Go on."

"Well, we started kissing and then he unzipped his jumpsuit and....BAM!! He pulled it out in all its glory. It was beautiful. Big...and long...and looking like a giant chocolate Popsicle. I was mesmerized. I couldn't see anything else. And haven't been able to see anything else in my head since."

"Great!" Aurora said. "Now I've got the same problem. Thanks for the visual."

"Chuck is a damn handyman," Candy said with disgust. "What was I thinking? I know I must have been drunk."

"Unbelievable!" Aurora said, shocked. "That's what you feel bad about? That you fucked a handyman?"

"I don't know why I never got with a black man before," Candy said, as she appeared to have a revelation.

"Yes, you do," Aurora said. "You have a serious problem, but we're not even going to go there."

"Good." Candy was not up for that subject.

"How did this happen?" Aurora asked, irritated by Candy's nonchalant attitude about sleeping with her friend's husband.

"I told you," Candy said. "I clogged up my garbage disposal, then…"

Aurora took a deep breath and spoke slowly. "I want to know…how his dick…ended up inside of you. Are you that stupid?"

Candy was unfazed by Aurora's insult and said, "He turned me on. What can I say?"

"You could have said no. That dick didn't belong to you. As a matter of fact, that should have been the last dick on your list."

Candy looked at Aurora with all sincerity.

"You haven't seen this one, have you?" she asked.

Aurora looked at her like she was crazy. "Shall I slap you?"

"I'm serious," said Candy, as she fanned herself with a napkin. "It's a freaking twelve-inch wonder of the world."

"I doubt that," said Aurora.

"Well, it's damn close then."

"Girl, you act like you've never seen a big dick before. I know some of those white boys you dated must have been hung, or you would've been long gone."

"Rory, I haven't seen anything this good."

"You're losing your mind over something that you should have been used to a long time ago," Aurora said. "Put Chuck's ass in a lineup with some other brothers and I'm sure that his dick would fit right in. No pun intended."

"Really?"

"You should've asked somebody. Damn."

CHAPTER 56

Melissa

Two weeks after Aurora walked out on Krome, it was his birthday. He wanted to do something freaky and knew exactly who he was going to do it with. He made three phone calls. The first one was to Aurora's cell phone.

"Aurora Duncan," she answered, voice all business.

"Hey, baby," he said. "How ya doin'?"

"Fine, thanks." Her voice was less than cordial. "How can I help you?"

"Why so formal?" he asked.

"I'm very busy, Krome. What do you want?"

"I want you to join me for dinner this Saturday."

"Why?"

"I didn't think that I'd have to remind you, but I have a birthday coming up. Thought you might like to celebrate with me."

"And why would I do that?"

"C'mon, girl. Don't be so hard."

"Krome..."

"Just think about it, okay?"

"Nothing to think about. Happy birthday. Have a good time. Gotta go."

The connection was abruptly ended. Krome looked at the phone, slightly surprised, and then proceeded to his next two calls.

Later that evening, Melissa was at Krome's front door with a bouquet of flowers and a bottle of expensive champagne.

"Happy birthday, old man," she said, prancing through the door in a tight black miniskirt, red tank top and red thigh-high boots.

"Who are you supposed to be? The Happy Hooker?" he asked, laughing.

"You said that you wanted to get your freak on...this is my freaky outfit."

"You forgot the whip and chains," he said.

"Oops, left those at home. Just got these," she said, holding the bottle and the flowers up in the air.

"I ordered Chinese," he said, taking the champagne. "Let's eat. There's a vase in the kitchen for those."

Melissa admired the flowers as she arranged them. "Beautiful, right?"

"You or the flowers?"

"I don't need to fish for a compliment," she grinned. "I know I look hot."

"Come here," Krome said.

Melissa slowly walked around the table to give Krome a kiss. Instead, he smacked her on the ass and walked over to the cartons of take-out sitting on the counter.

"Grab some glasses from the cabinet," he ordered. "I'm hungry."

"Asshole."

An hour later, they were slow dancing. Krome had turned on some exotic music and turned the lights down. Melissa was feeling sexy. He kissed her neck softly.

"You said that I could have *anything* for my birthday, right?"

"Yes," she whispered.

"Do you trust me?"

"Yes."

After about fifteen minutes of dancing and kissing, Krome took out a blindfold and gently put it on her. She was ready for anything. She knew that he wasn't going to hurt her. Krome leaned up against the wall and turned her around, her back to him. Unknown to Melissa, a man was sitting on the couch, smoking a joint and watching the two of them. Krome ran his hands slowly up and down Melissa's slim hips. Her dress was already short, and with each stroke, he slowly lifted it higher and higher.

"Just relax, don't say anything," he growled into her ear. "We have company. He's on the couch right in front of us."

Melissa let herself go, feeling Krome's hands all over her and being intoxicated by the fact that someone was watching. Finally, the hem of her dress was above her crotch. As Krome pushed her panties aside with one hand, she spread her legs, knowing that whoever was there had a clear view. Krome's fingers found her wet spot and he dipped his fingers inside. Melissa moaned as she came all over his hand. The man on the couch had a raging hard-on as he continued watching Krome's big, black fingers sliding all over Melissa's smooth, white skin and in and out of her hot, pink center.

The man continued to be mesmerized as Krome slowly walked Melissa over to the couch. He laid her across the man's lap, facedown. The man began to rub his hands over her smooth skin, caressing her legs and her butt. He gently spread her legs wider and wider, and then slid a finger into her hot pussy as she lifted her ass slightly into the air. Krome sat himself on the couch next to his mysterious friend and positioned himself in a way that when he pulled out his dick, Melissa was able to take him into her mouth while the other man slipped a wet finger into her waiting ass.

For three hours, the two men took turns fucking and sucking Melissa, who was happy to return the favor. At one point, Krome carried Melissa, still blindfolded, into the bedroom, where he tied her to the bed and the two men continued to take pleasure in her. Eventually Krome walked his friend out to his car.

"So, we have a deal?" Krome asked.

"Hell, yeah."

The two men shook hands and Krome happily returned to the bedroom to untie Melissa, who had fallen asleep. Palmer Whitmore drove away, savoring the past few hours in which he enjoyed Melissa's talents. It would be a wonderful memory, but it was her singing, and how her voice could blend so well into the mainstream, that caused him to be excited about the future of his business. She was his perfect crossover artist.

CHAPTER 57

Portia

Portia and her husband, Chuck had not had sex in weeks. Actually, he had not touched his wife at all lately, not since his night of hot sex with Candy Martin. That was a night when his wife had been pissed off about something insignificant, and for the third time in a month, had sent him downstairs to sleep on the couch.

Chuck and Portia had always enjoyed a good sex life. She was always hot and kept him satisfied, but ever since the hysterectomy, she had been irritable and unloving. No hugging, no kissing, no sex. He sympathized with the things she was going through. She was forced into early menopause and there wasn't a whole lot of medicine that she could take to make it better. She found that she was allergic to a lot of the medications that might have helped. Chuck understood that it was hard on her, but it was challenging for him, too. Portia was only six years older than him, but it was like she turned into an old woman overnight. It was wrong, he knew it was wrong. But that didn't stop the thought from crossing his mind.

It had been a week since Chuck had cheated on Portia. He had come in drunk, managed to throw his clothes in the wash and slip back onto the couch without a word from Portia, who was fast asleep upstairs. The next morning and for every moment since, he had been feeling guilty. They had always been able to tell each other anything. That was one of the reasons that he married her. Their relationship began with both of them expressing their strong sexuality and sharing it with each other. They both liked it that way, but if Chuck had ever done anything without her, she surely never knew anything about it. As far as she knew, he had honored his commitment to tell her if he slept with another woman. And he had been faithful until now. She knew that he was no saint. He flirted, he had his fun, but he saved the good stuff for his wife. She always assumed that if he did anything, it was with Celia, his daughter's mother. Truth was he hadn't had sex with her either. Not since the party years before.

It was Friday night and Chuck decided to cook Portia a special meal, the same meal that he had fixed for her many times when he was trying to make her feel extra special. The tasty meal that he cooked for her the very first time she came over to his house. Smothered pork chops, rice, macaroni and cheese, and green beans. And for dessert, chocolate covered strawberries, whipped cream, and her favorite champagne.

When Portia arrived home from work, the first thing that hit her was the pleasant aroma coming from the kitchen.

"Wow, it sure smells good in here," she said as she put her purse down on a chair.

"Hey, baby," Chuck said from the kitchen. "Come bring your fine ass in here."

As Portia headed into the kitchen, she was surprised to see all the trouble that Chuck had gone through to make her favorite meal.

"Go freshen up and meet me in the dining room," he said.

"Oh, baby!" she said, noticing the new candles burning on the dining room table. "What you got up your sleeve? This is the seduction meal."

"Just wanted to do something nice."

"I'm hungry. Let me get out of these clothes and I'll be right back."

"Sounds sexy!"

"Hmmph, don't even think about it," Portia said as she headed upstairs. "I am not in the mood for your foolishness."

Chuck just shook his head. "Hurry back," he said. "I have your favorite bubbly." He opened the bottle of champagne.

An hour later, Portia was more relaxed and completely full. She and Chuck were on the couch, listening to music.

"How are you feeling?" Chuck asked, putting his arm around her.

"Listen, sweetie," Portia began. "I know I've been a little crazy lately. I ain't stupid. You've had something on your mind and I guess it's time to talk."

"Yes, baby," Chuck said. "I've never been so nervous to talk to you. You're usually so open and loving."

"I haven't made it a safe place for you, and I'm sorry. That wasn't a part of our agreement."

"I understand, Portia. You know how much I love you. I want my wife back."

"Alright, Chuck," she said, taking a deep breath. "What do you want to tell me?"

"I had sex with another woman."

"Well, I know that," she laughed. "I just haven't wanted to hear it, I guess."

"Damn, baby," he said. "I didn't think I'd actually be saying those words."

"Boy, you're a sex machine. I used to be one, too."

Chuck had to laugh at that.

Portia continued, "I haven't been able to take care of your needs, so I figured you were gonna have to be getting it from somewhere. That's what we agreed on when we got married. I just thought that I would be keeping you so busy in the bedroom that you wouldn't have to. I knew that you would tell me, because you promised that you would."

"Okay, so what do you need to know?" Chuck asked

"Did you use protection?"

"Yes."

"Do you love me?"

"More than ever."

"Then I don't need to know anything else."

"Portia, I…" Chuck began to speak, but Portia put a finger over his lips and gave him a kiss.

"I'm so sorry, Chuck."

For the rest of the night, all Portia heard was the sound of her own moans as she made love to her husband. She tried very hard to be the passionate wife he was used to.

Portia was rejuvenated after her night with Chuck. She didn't know if she had her mojo back, but she sure was going to take advantage of the feeling she had. It was time to get back to being herself. First thing in the morning she made another appointment with her doctor so that she could attempt to get her hormones under control.

CHAPTER 58

Candy

A few weeks after her encounter with Aurora, Candy Martin wasn't feeling like herself. She was depressed, in need of a boost. Aurora had been away on business, Melissa was working in the studio on some music project, and Candy couldn't face Portia, so Popi's Place had been off limits. She sure as hell didn't want to be sitting up in there alone with Snookie. Debbie was okay to hang out with, but Candy needed more than a friend. She needed some help. She needed cocaine. Candy decided to take a chance and get ready for a night at Popi's Place.

A couple of hours before it was time to get dressed, she felt terrible. She decided to lie down for a few minutes, but ended up sleeping into the early morning. Before she had a chance to wake up and shower, she felt an overwhelming wave of nausea. After a couple of miserable hours, she managed to get to the drugstore to find something to settle her stomach. Going through the aisles, she passed a shelf with home pregnancy tests and impulsively grabbed one. By the time she got home, she had convinced herself that somehow she was going to be punished for her indiscretion with Chuck.

She took the test and it came back positive. She was pregnant. The only problem was that she didn't know who the father was. It could be Roger Nichols, who was on his way to prison, or it could be Chuck Adams, the husband of one of her best friends.

"Hmmm, what do I prefer?" she wondered. "Fucked up or more fucked up?"

Candy rarely cursed, but the way her life had been going lately, some of Snookie's colorful language had started to be peppered into her vocabulary. As much as things had been crazy for her, she finally realized that one of her dreams might come true, although not quite as she had imagined. If Roger was the father, then she would have something that she always wanted: a baby that was half white. Unfortunately, the father wasn't supposed to be an imprisoned felon, and she wasn't supposed to be raising a child alone. But what if Chuck was the father? What kind of choice was that? Since there was no way that she was going to raise a child alone, and she didn't believe in abortion, Candy had a real problem.

The first thing she wanted to do was tell Chuck. As wild as it seemed, she felt better about that than anything else, that he might be the father of her child. She abandoned her dream of wanting a white man. She just wanted responsible man. Candy called him, and he reluctantly met her at the coffee shop where she met with Aurora.

"What are you talking about?" Chuck asked, shocked. "We used protection."

"Obviously, it wasn't 100% reliable."

"Damn, Candy!" Chuck exclaimed. "How do you even know it's mine? Shit, it hasn't been that long since your white boy had you all wrapped up."

Candy put her head in her hands. "I know, I know. I'm afraid to find out."

"What the hell are you planning to do?" he asked.

"That depends. Will you come with me?"

Two days later, Chuck and Candy were sitting up in her gynecologist's office, nervously awaiting the official results of her pregnancy test.

"How long is this shit gonna take?" he asked.

"Shut up, Chuck. You're making me nervous."

The doctor finally called her in. It was the more fucked up news. She was pregnant by her friend's husband, a friend who couldn't have any babies. What a nightmare! They stepped out into the hallway.

"So, now what?" Chuck asked.

"I'm just so glad that Roger the pervert isn't the father."

"Yeah, good for him, wreck *my* life."

"Nobody's trying to do anything to you, Chuck. You're married."

"What are you trying to say?"

"I'm saying that I don't want anything from you. I can't get rid of the baby, so I guess I'll have to lie to everyone."

"You're kidding, right?"

"You got any bright ideas?"

"I don't lie to my wife."

"Oh, so she knows about our little tumble?"

"Yes, as a matter of fact she does."

"You're a liar. She's not an actress. Trust me, if Miss Portia knew that I had sex with you, the whole world would have known."

"Well, I didn't tell her it was you," he said. "I tried. She didn't want to know."

"But now you want to fill her in on the details?"

"Look, Candy. Portia and I have something special. I have to tell her, no matter what. She'll understand. I already have two kids that I can't have relationships with. I'm not going to let that happen again."

"Yeah, yeah, yeah, Portia's a saint," Candy said. "Do I need to come with you?"

"I can handle it."

CHAPTER 59

Portia

Chuck went home to tell his wife the hardest thing that he ever had to tell her. Portia and Chuck had been through a lot of things together, some things that the average couple would not have handled. Chuck was hoping that she could handle this and allow him to do what he needed to do.

As he sat Portia down, handed her a stiff drink and explained the circumstances which led up to him sleeping with Candy, he could see the understanding draining completely out of her. She had been able to deal with many things in her marriage that she didn't think she could, but the idea of Chuck and Candy having sex was something she had a hard time wrapping her brain around. The fact that one of her best friends was pregnant with her husband's child was more than she could take. She was speechless. She just kept shaking her head and sipping on the drink.

"Say something, baby," Chuck said as he grabbed her hand and held it tight. "Tell me what you're thinking right now."

"It's like someone has ripped my heart out."

"Is it because I slept with Candy?"

"I don't know," she replied. "I don't think so. She's a beautiful, sexy woman. I get that. But, she doesn't even like black men. Are you some irresistible exception?"

"Well, baby…" he began as he grabbed his crotch.

"Don't even play with me right now."

"I'm sorry."

"I need some time to sort this all out," she said. "I need you to leave."

"Portia, you know we can work this out. I'll just sleep down here like always."

She downed the rest of her drink and got up. "I need you to leave this house."

Chuck, although he didn't want to leave, knew that he needed to give his wife time to process the information that was forced on her. He went to stay with George Montana, but he called Portia several times a day. Sometimes she would answer the phone and they would have a short conversation, and sometimes he would simply leave a message of love and support for her and the very difficult position that he had put her in.

After thinking about her situation for a few days, Portia realized that she had many choices. Thank God for that. Without choices, people are simply puppets who are slaves to their circumstances. She had never felt like a slave. She always made choices based on whether or not she could live with them. She remembered the stories of her beginnings and how her parents had made difficult choices. Choices that were made to ensure her survival. It was time for Portia to make some difficult choices for her and her marriage right now.

First, she had to deal with her feelings concerning her husband. She loved Chuck and she knew that she would take him back. When she took her vows, she meant every word: for better or for worse. If this was part of the worse, then she could survive it.

Second, Portia felt an overwhelming need to talk to Candy, who had practically disappeared after the debacle with Roger Nichols. Even though Portia had reached out, she had never really tried that hard to talk to Candy. She thought of her as being strong and self-sufficient. Not the broken doll that Chuck had described. In any case, she wanted to deal with Candy woman to woman, but who knows how that would end? The baby was the innocent in this equation. As much as Portia was upset with Candy, that baby was part of her family now and that meant that Candy was, too. Portia headed upstairs to shower and change.

Before Portia could get dressed, her doorbell rang. She expected to see her husband there, but to her surprise, it was Candy Martin standing on her doorstep.

"Hi, Portia," she said, holding a bottle of chilled Dom Perignon. "Can we talk?"

"Come on in," Portia replied, practically snatching the bottle from her hands. "There's sparkling cider in the fridge for you."

For almost an hour, Candy endured Portia's probing questions, basically telling her the same story Chuck had told, except for her added devastation over the way Roger Nichols had deceived her. At the end of her story, Candy took Portia by the hand.

"Please, please forgive me, Portia."

Candy was so sad and so remorseful that Portia found herself reaching over to comfort her with a soothing hug. Hell, Portia thought, no wonder Chuck's ass couldn't resist. Candy had needed a knight in shining armor and Chuck certainly had played the part to the hilt, no pun intended. Portia smiled to herself and took a deep breath. Candy Martin rarely showed her weaknesses and always put up a good front. It almost hurt Portia to see her this way. A flood of compassion filled Portia. She released Candy and looked her straight in the eye.

"So, what are you going to do about the baby?" Portia asked. "I know that you won't get rid of it."

"No, I won't. Chuck wants to have a relationship with the child."

"Of course he does," Portia said. "We'll talk about it, the three of us."

"I don't want to cause any further problems, Portia."

"It's going to be alright, Candy," Portia said sincerely. "I promise you. Everything will be just fine."

CHAPTER 60

Snookie

A lot had been going on lately and Snookie had taken all that she could take. Her wonderful world was falling apart and none of her friends seemed to care. She wasn't sure what everyone was going through, but she sure as hell didn't like it. Obviously, she wasn't the first one they came to in a crisis, but at least she was able to be in the loop at some point. Lately, she couldn't keep a good table in the clubroom at Popi's Place because she and Debbie were the only ones who agreed to show up. They ended up in the dining room or at the bar. Snookie also missed the special treatment at the door because Chantal had moved to Atlanta, and they had some ditzy white chick at the door named Roxanne, who couldn't remember her from week to week. Thank God for Jacques, who still knew how to make her feel special.

Snookie made it her mission to bring her girlfriends back together, thereby putting her life back in order. So for the past week, she was relentless in calling each of them, securing promises to show up the following Saturday night, July 15th, like old times. Most of them said they would at least try. Snookie hoped it was good enough.

First there was Aurora who was spending more time in New York than in Los Angeles these days. Probably because she broke up with that asshole boyfriend of hers and needed to be far away. But who could blame her? Krome was a man whore. Snookie had seen him around town with some blond named Tanya, who was all over him like a bad rash. Unfortunately, Aurora wasn't planning to come back until the following week, but Snookie wouldn't give up begging. Aurora had admitted to her that the extra week was more pleasure than business.

Then Snookie reached out to Portia, who was still cranky about all of her health problems and wanted to lick her wounds at home. When Snookie asked about Chuck, Portia was very vague and changed the subject quickly. As a matter of fact, the last time she saw George Montana and Chuck in Popi's Place, she could have sworn she heard something about Chuck crashing at his place.

There was definitely something wrong in paradise, but Portia promised to work things out so that she could be there. She even said that she would get Candy to come. Since when did Portia have any influence over Candy? Snookie thought Candy was supposed to be hiding from the press or something because of that white jerk she had the nerve to try and pass off as a boyfriend.

Snookie never thought that she would ever be able to feel sorry for Candy Martin, with her perfect body, perfect job, perfect home and perfect car, but even Snookie wasn't insensitive enough to think that she deserved to be humiliated that way by a man who should be strung up by his balls. Portia was right, though. Candy called Snookie herself and said that she was looking forward to Saturday night.

And who the hell knows what Melissa was up to? She was busy in the studio trying to be a rap star or something. She came around a couple of times, only to spend most of her time meeting with music industry types. She said that she would definitely be there, and even said that she'd be there early for a change. That would be a first.

Debbie was the reliable one. She said she had to stop by Lawrence Desmond's studio first. She hadn't seen him in weeks and it was important. She promised to come straight to Popi's Place after she was done. Things were looking up, but there was a whole lot of mess going on. For Snookie, this was more intriguing than those trashy tabloids she liked to read. She couldn't wait to find out what it was all about.

Book Eleven

CHAPTER 61

Aurora – July 14, 2006

It was Friday afternoon and Aurora was drinking a delicious Godiva Chocolate martini at a private listening party in New York City. There were a lot of influential people there to celebrate the launch of a new CD by R&B sensation, Kyria. Aurora discovered the young woman waiting tables at a restaurant in London three years before. Kyria was only eighteen at the time and knew who Aurora Duncan was. She had followed the music business religiously and read an article in a London paper about Aurora's success at Tazora Records and her visit to the city.

Kyria was originally from Martinique, but was raised in London. She had beautiful dark skin, spoke French with a Cockney accent, and could sing like a young Minnie Ripperton. Aurora listened to her demo and was hooked. She got back to Los Angeles and passed the demo to a friend of hers at Sony Records. She had to fight hard, but the industry finally took notice. The rest was history. Kyria's debut album went platinum and Aurora expanded her reputation for having a keen ear for talent.

It had been the best week Aurora had enjoyed in a long time. She was really enjoying New York, but LA was calling. Or more specifically, Snookie Watson was calling. Snookie had some kind of idea that the girls all needed to get together to rekindle their relationships and all of the drama needed to be squashed. She agreed with Snookie, but they were going to have to wait another week, because she wasn't ready to leave yet.

Aurora was feeling pretty amazing in her new silk emerald green coatdress when she spotted a familiar face. She walked up behind the handsome gentleman in the expensive Lawrence Desmond suit and whispered in his ear.

"Thought your wife wasn't letting you out of your cage these days."

Palmer Whitmore turned around with a smile.

"Wow," he said, looking her up and down. "I certainly could be considered a dangerous animal that should be caged."

Aurora always hated how easily Palmer made her feel like a piece of meat, but he was a powerful man in the music business and she had always been able to handle him. He had tried unsuccessfully to get her into his bed for years, but she knew that keeping him on a string had garnered her many favors. These days, Aurora was able to maintain a good relationship with him by putting up with the stories of his conquests. He had some warped idea that by him telling her about his sexual exploits, she would get weak at the knees and want to be ravished by him. It was a joke.

"It's been a long time, Aurora. You look fantastic."

"Thank you, Palmer."

"How's your love life these days, beautiful?"

"Better than yours, I'll bet."

"Then you'd better come to my hotel room later. Help a poor man out, right?"

"Sexual harassment is so beneath you," Aurora said, smiling.

"But, you don't work for me, dear."

"Oh, that's right. Now I remember why."

"So, what's on your mind, Aurora? You still hanging out with your thug?"

"No, I finally got over him."

"Is that so?"

"I'm certainly trying."

"Well, would it help if I told you that he's moving on to blonder pastures?"

"Whatever pastures Krome has moved on to, well…they no longer concern me. I don't care anymore."

"That's good to hear. You're better off without him, doll. He's pimping a fantastic singer now."

"He's always had his bimbos, Palmer, but to think that they have any talent is giving them way too much credit."

"I don't know...there's one *particular* one," he confided. "This chick is the real deal. She's got gifts."

Aurora squinted her eyes and took a sip of her drink, trying not to show any further interest. "Don't tell me…she can sing *and* suck a mean dick."

He broke into hearty laughter. "You're right, Aurora," he said. "All that and some shit you really don't want to know about."

"You're right, I don't."

Palmer got very close as he whispered, "You sure? It might be a hell of a turn-on to hear what Krome and I did to that hot...."

"Stop it, Palmer!" Aurora snapped, backing away. "Damn! Do you think I really care about some stupid bitch you two fucked?"

"Gotta give the girl credit, she's something else, more than just a great piece of ass. Hot white chocolate, like Teena Marie, only blond and gorgeous."

Aurora's head began to spin and she had a funny feeling in the pit of her stomach. She downed the rest of her drink.

"I know you never allow your dick to make business decisions for you, so forget Krome and his new discovery. Who cares? What's going on in *your* world these days, Palmer? What's making your career look brighter?"

"That's what I'm trying to tell you, sweetheart. I just signed this chick. Krome is co-producing on this and she's gonna make us millions. You watch."

Obviously, Aurora wasn't going to get out of this conversation alive. She took a deep breath. "So, Palmer, tell me. Who is this phenom?"

Three hours after Palmer Whitmore dropped a bomb on her, Aurora Duncan was rushing to JFK, where she spent the night trying to get on an unscheduled flight. Now, she was so anxious to get back to LA, she was willing to accept a series of flights that would force her to change planes twice. Krome was not her man anymore, but she still had serious feelings for him. She knew that she deserved someone better. She knew that Krome couldn't keep his dick in his pants and she had simply gotten tired of dealing with him and his random white women, who had never been her concern. She knew that they didn't mean anything to him, but now the entire game had changed.

"How could I have been so stupid?" she thought.

CHAPTER 62

Debbie 6:55 pm

Debbie Marshall managed to successfully avoid Lawrence Desmond after the one steamy afternoon, with too many margaritas, which led them into a fateful encounter that could not be taken back. For Debbie there was shame. She had wanted to make love to Lawrence for a long time, but his being married created the emotional aftermath. Debbie forced herself to keep her distance. Six weeks went by. Then Lawrence called her out of the blue and she dropped everything to come to the studio once more, even though she had promised to be at Popi's Place for an important night with her girls. That should have taken precedence, but here she was, giving her honest opinion about his new creations and trying to be the friend she used to be.

"So you teamed up with Krome Bumpa, our resident bad boy," Debbie said. "Well, I have to say, I like it."

"We call the collection Krome B by Lawrence D".

"Well, at least you didn't say Larry D. Don't think I could deal with that one."

Thcy laughed as Debbie carefully inspected the surprisingly colorful line of men's suits and discussed how he had changed his personal look into a more casual, sexy one. He was looking very comfortable. A little too comfortable, she thought, as he began moving into her personal space, which was a little more than Debbie could take. Lawrence was way too sexy for her to be alone with him like this. She had promised herself she wouldn't come around him anymore, but here she was again. She had always kept her cool around him, but the memory of their lovemaking came rushing back and she knew that she would be sucked back into a place that she just couldn't go again.

Debbie stepped back. "I think I'd better go."

"You waited all this time and now you're just going to run off?"

"I have to be at Popi's Place, and you obviously need a cold shower."

"You don't bite your tongue, do you?" he laughed.

"That would hurt."

Debbie turned to leave and Lawrence gently turned her toward him.

"Debbie, I won't hurt you," he said sincerely.

He pulled her into his arms and kissed her passionately. After a long moment, he pulled away, stunned and embarrassed by his actions. He released her and stepped back.

"I apologize, Debbie. I shouldn't have been that adventurous."

"No, you shouldn't have, Lawrence. What would your wife say?"

He was devastated.

"I love Anita," he replied. "And she doesn't deserve to be hurt, but Debbie, my sweet, sweet Debbie. What am I going to do about you?"

He reached for her again and she slipped away.

"Lawrence, we agreed."

"I know. I'm sorry. What should I do? You tell me, I'll gladly oblige."

"Coming here was a big mistake," Debbie said, as she quickly headed around the corner towards the door. Lawrence immediately ran after her.

"Please don't go!"

The look in his eyes was so pleading that Debbie just wanted to fold herself into his arms and never leave. Why did he have to look so damn good when he was begging? A man should be very unattractive in this sad, pathetic state. She took a deep breath and hoped that she would be strong enough for both of them.

"Look, you know that I'm attracted to you and we do have a strong connection, but if we're gonna see each other at all, then we're gonna need to stay in the 'friendly place'. You know what I mean?"

"Alright, Debbie, I surrender to whatever you say. You've been a good friend. I respect you and I respect your opinions. I really appreciate someone like you in my life."

"Someone like me?" she smirked.

"Okay. You. I appreciate *you*."

"And I need someone I can trust," she said seriously. "I trust *you*, Lawrence."

"That means a lot, so you've got me."

"Good," she said. "Then, we're cool."

"I guess I want you in my life more than in my bed."

"That's because it's your only option," she reminded him.

"Exactly." They both laughed and the tension was broken.

Debbie began to relax. "It was really, really good, though," she said, sighing.

"Best I ever had," he smiled.

"Wow." She was otherwise speechless.

"I love you, Debbie," he said, meaning it with all his heart.

She allowed Lawrence to take her into his embrace and they enjoyed a wonderful moment of real love. Neither one of them saw Anita Desmond, whose heartbroken eyes were watching in disbelief from the unclosed door. Anita immediately ran off, more furious than she had ever been in her life.

"I really have to go," Debbie said. "The girls are expecting me at Popi's Place. We've had a really rough few weeks. We haven't seen each other, so tonight we're supposed to be mending fences. Everybody promised to show up."

"I'm sure that whatever it is, you beautiful ladies will work it out."

"I hope so," Debbie responded. "Otherwise, I'm gonna need some new friends."

"You always have me," he said as he took her hand. As Lawrence Desmond walked Debbie out to her car, there was no evidence of the emotional devastation that had just taken place minutes before.

CHAPTER 63

Aurora 7:15 pm

Aurora returned from the East Coast on a mission. Her mind had not been able to settle down since she talked to Palmer Whitmore and found out what her good friend Melissa Murdock had been up to. She no longer wanted Krome, but what hurt so much was the fact that she had been betrayed by someone who was like a sister to her. She wondered how many times Melissa and Krome had been in bed together, laughing about their deception and her ignorance and stupidity.

After Mark Sullivan dropped her off at home she didn't stop long enough to shower and change. She was so determined to confront Krome and Melissa that she literally couldn't see straight. Drinking the champagne that Mark provided in the limo had not helped. After several unsuccessful attempts to reach both of them, she was so angry that she did something foolish. She rummaged through her closet, found a gun that she kept hidden, jumped in her car, and went hunting for her tormentors.

Aurora called Riptide Recording and yelled at Stevie.

"I'm on my way over there right now and there's one blond bitch that better not let me catch her with him."

"I'll tell Krome that you called," Stevie had said, nonchalantly.

"You do that!" she screamed. "Unless you want to witness a motherfuckin' murder tonight."

It had been twenty minutes since Stevie had hung up the phone and casually passed a blunt to one of the guys watching Krome in the vocal booth having sex with one of his favorite bimbos. Krome was kissing on Tanya, who was all sex, no substance. They were both naked now.

"I forgot what I've been missing," said Tanya.

"Don't talk, Tanya," Krome said. "It ain't your best talent."

The buzzer rang and Stevie looked up at the security monitor and saw Aurora, who appeared to be furious. He pushed a button to the vocal booth.

"Yo, K. Your girl A.D. is here with the devil ridin' shotgun on her broomstick. Better wrap it up."

"Send her away like you did before," Tanya said.

"Go on, Stevie, let her in," Krome said.

"It's your funeral, man," Stevie responded. "You lucky if you got sixty seconds."

Stevie buzzed Aurora into the building.

"You naughty boy," cooed Tanya. "You're going to get us in trouble."

Tanya kissed Krome again while Aurora banged on the studio door. Stevie opened the locked door and let her in. She watched for several seconds as Krome made out with Tanya in the dark vocal booth. Aurora walked right up to the window to get a closer look. Krome stopped when he saw her, wiped his mouth and grinned. Aurora recognized Tanya, who appeared smug as she looked back.

"Stevie, turn on the mic so he can hear me."

Stevie complied, not wanting to suffer the consequences. Aurora looked a little psycho to him at the moment. He had seen her mad, but this was something else. There was a murderous look in her eyes.

"Go ahead, Rory," Stevie said.

"You threw it all away for her?" asked Aurora, incredulous. "You stupid son of a bitch. You must have lost your damn mind."

"He likes me," Tanya squealed. "What can I say?"

"Nobody's talking about you, whore!" Aurora shouted. "Krome knows the blond bitch I'm talkin' about. The one who's gonna pay."

"What the hell are you talking about?" Krome asked, noticing an unfamiliar tone in her voice.

Aurora stormed out and that was just the reaction that Krome wanted, except that he was confused by what she said and the way she said it. Tanya was the only woman that he ever allowed himself to be caught with, because he knew that Aurora didn't give two shits about him fucking Tanya. But she wasn't talking about Tanya. She had something deeper on her mind and he was afraid to think about what she might do. He hadn't given it that much thought before, because he never intended to get caught, not really caught. He always had Tanya around the studio whenever he was fucking around with Melissa. That way if there were ever any questions, the musicians and engineers always talked about Tanya.

Melissa was his dirty little secret. Krome had no intention of anyone finding out about his obsession with his brother's ex, who was now one of his woman's best friends. Shit, if things had worked out differently, Melissa would've been his woman and maybe he would have been fucking Aurora on the side. That's something he had to live with.

Inside the vocal booth, Krome stopped humping on Tanya, caught his breath and pushed her away. He grabbed his shirt as Tanya laughed and tried to kiss him again.

"Sorry, no more for you, boo," he said. "Get dressed."

"You called *me*, asshole," she said.

"Doesn't matter," Krome replied, "Show's over. You gotta go. That's it."

Tanya grabbed her clothes off the floor and began to get dressed. Stevie and the boys found the scene funny. Tanya looked at Krome, her voice dripping with sarcasm.

"I like the way you break up with me. It makes me feel so special."

"You got jokes now, huh?" Krome asked. "There's only one woman I really want. You know dat. Just hurry up."

Tanya got up in his face.

"What I know is that you'll sweet talk your way back to Aurora…again. And you'll fuck up…again. Then she'll dump you…again, and you'll be back…again."

Krome, who was not amused, pushed her toward the door. She struggled against him and he grabbed her roughly.

"Do I need to repeat myself…again?"

"Get your hands off me, Krome," she snapped. "I'm tired of your shit."

"Order shit, you get shit," Krome replied. "Now, get the fuck out!"

Tanya mumbled curses under her breath as she tried to dress herself. She decided to grab the rest of her stuff and get out of there quickly. Krome yelled after her.

"Wait a minute!"

He grabbed her wrist and pulled a diamond ring off her finger.

"Fantasy over."

The sexy blond rushed passed Stevie and the musicians, ignoring them. As she hurried out, they started laughing. Krome came out of the booth with a scowl on his face.

"What the hell y'all laughin' at?"

They stopped immediately and Krome went back into the booth and placed the diamond ring in a small, black velvet box.

Aurora was equipped with the truth. There were facts that she could no longer ignore. First, there was the fact that one of her best friends not only had sex with her fiancé, but had fucked him and Palmer just to get a record deal. And the second was the fact that Krome was a lying dog who used sexy blonds like Tanya to cover up his deviousness. Well, Aurora had been blind for the last time. She was done with Krome, but now she had to deal with someone who broke the remaining pieces of her heart.

Over the years with Krome, Aurora had found blond hair everywhere, and although it made her fume and threaten to leave him, she was never going to give up a good man simply because he wasn't the marrying type. So, he would romance her and they would stay together. He was willing to let her compromise her soul, giving him the opportunity to have his women on the side, because he had her convinced that she was the only one he really loved. She chose to live with that and it was good enough for her.

However, once they became engaged, everything changed. She made demands and he made promises. There were expectations that she didn't know she had. For a brief moment, Aurora saw a future. She had hoped with all her heart and soul that Krome saw it, too, but her reality was so different. She knew that he couldn't keep his promises, so she began finding easy ways out. She wasn't exactly the marrying kind, either. Her fear of rejection was in direct proportion to her fear of commitment. When it came to love, Krome only reinforced the beliefs that Baxter had instilled in her: love wasn't real, wasn't something you could depend on. That's the lesson she learned from her father.

And what about the lessons she had taught? Obviously, Krome thought that he could do to her whatever he damn well pleased. Well, that's where she had to admit that she taught him how to treat her and he learned his lessons well. It was her own fault for making it so easy for him to get back into her good graces after he had messed up.

Aurora had convinced herself that her man could have his fun as long as he took good care of her. And certainly he should never let her find out about it. Any half-assed player can get caught. She wanted a man who was good enough to really play the game.

But that wasn't even the real issue any more. It was no longer a game. It was now about a friendship that Aurora could no longer believe in. She knew Melissa, and she knew Krome. How many times had the two of them made a fool of her? She should have known that there was something between them the first time she saw the passion with which Melissa despised him. She would have figured it out sooner if she hadn't been so sure that he was only out for pussy. By going after Melissa, he took his betrayal to a whole new level. All of the other women he screwed were easy to forgive and forget. They meant nothing. Didn't affect her life that much. But how does that work with someone who has been an integral part of your life? The pain Aurora felt showed that she loved Melissa like a sister, and as difficult as it was for her to love and be loved, that's what hurt the most.

So now, as Aurora sat in her car in front of Melissa's building, she could see her moving around the apartment and stopping near the window periodically to stand in front of a big fan. Aurora thought about how angry she was and how much she needed to hurt someone. She thought about all of the times that she had put her trust in someone she loved and had been disappointed, used and betrayed. As she reached into her purse, she put her hand on the gun and took a deep breath.

CHAPTER 64

Melissa – 7:30 pm

It was the biggest night of Melissa's life. All of the drama of the past few weeks was dying down and she was finally getting a chance to prove that she had what it took to be a star. And when that moment came, she wanted to look fabulous, so she had a multitude of dresses and assorted accessories laid across her bed.

"Should I be sexy, sophisticated or shocking?" she asked herself out loud.

There was a sound at the door. That must be the landlord, she thought. Thank God he had finally shown up to fix the air conditioner. She was in her bedroom, but had left the front door open for him when he said he was on his way. The temperature was in triple digits and she couldn't even put her makeup on without stopping to stick her face in front of a fan. She had three large fans whipping warm air around.

"Well, Alex, it's about damn time," Melissa said as she entered the living room, carrying several dresses.

But, it wasn't her landlord. She was facing someone she loved. Someone she hadn't seen in a while, but who was like a sister to her. Someone holding a gun that was aimed right at her. Melissa was shocked, but put a smile on her face.

"Wow," she said calmly. "I wasn't expecting to see you. I didn't even know you were back. What are you doing here?"

"Don't fuck wit me, trick. I think you know exactly why I'm here."

"You missed me, right?" Melissa asked, attempting a little humor.

No response. This woman was not in a lighthearted mood, so Melissa decided to address the issue at hand. "What are you doing with a gun?"

"I think you know that, too."

"Sweetie, a lot has happened since the last time I saw you. I know you must be upset. Can we talk about it?"

"There's nothing to talk about. I came to settle a score."

"C'mon now," Melissa said, trying to reason with her. "You sound like a fucking movie character. Give me a hug or somethin'."

Melissa tried to make a move toward her, which only made her tighten her grip on the gun. This was a woman who meant business. "Don't come any closer," she warned. "Or I swear I'll splatter your white ass all over this nice, shiny floor."

CHAPTER 65

Popi's Place 7:30 pm

As Snookie took large gulps of her Long Island Iced Tea, she was still wondering if her five friends were going to show up. Somehow, she had become the peacemaker over the past few weeks. The ladies had all agreed to get back together at Popi's Place. They had rarely been in town and not shown up for weeks. Their world had gone crazy.

Snookie left messages for Aurora, whose plane should have landed a while ago. Debbie was on her way, but still went to see that fine married man of hers. Candy was at the white man's happy hour bar trying to see if she could turn back the hands of time, or at least see if the saying was true…once you go black, etcetera, etcetera, but Snookie only knew that she was on her way to Popi's Place shortly. Portia should be hauling her behind in there any minute. And Melissa was keeping some kind of secret and would only say that we would see her like never before. But that was days ago. Snookie couldn't reach her tonight. What the hell did that mean?

Snookie took a deep breath. It was still too early to tell, but there was no guarantee that any of them would show up tonight. It had been that kind of a week. This was perhaps the last night of their friendship.

Sucking down the last of her drink, Snookie looked up and saw Portia.

"Thank you, Lord!" she said as Portia sat down.

"Hey, lady in red," said Portia, happily. "You look nice. I see you went and got your hair did! Looks like a new dress, too."

"Feels like a special occasion, but I didn't know the whole club was celebrating."

"Yeah, what's up with that?"

"That shows you how out of the loop we are," Snookie said. "It's the 20th anniversary of Popi's charity and Palmer Whitmore is providing the entertainment from his record label."

"Who knew?

"We shoulda known. Remember how much fun it was last year?"

"Yeah, that's right," Portia replied.

"At least we got our table back," Snookie said. "We finally became the ones that somebody else gets bumped for, right?"

"How about that?" Portia replied.

"I'm glad to see you, Portia."

"Just like old times, huh? You and I are still the first ones here."

"It's only been a few weeks," Snookie said.

"Yeah, well it feels like a lot longer. You talk to anybody else?"

"Just Debbie and Candy," Snookie replied. "Still can't reach Aurora or Melissa. Guess they'll show up in their own time, eventually."

"Well, if I'm willing to be here, those other bitches…oh, sorry…those other women should be able to drag themselves up in here, too."

"I hear you, Portia. What are you drinking? The waitress should be right back."

"Girl, I couldn't wait," Portia said. "You see this crowd up in here. I stopped Jacques on my way through the bar. Something strong should be here any minute."

They laughed and Snookie looked at her watch. "It's 7:45."

Candy arrived thirty minutes later. "Hi, I made it."

They all hugged. "Back together again," Snookie said.

"Wow, this is going to be fun, huh?" Candy said, looking Portia in the eye.

"Yes, Candy," Portia said. "I'm really glad to see you."

"I'm hungry," Snookie said. She was unaware of the drama going on between Candy and Portia. "We don't have to wait, right?"

Portia laughed, "No, just like old times."

The band began to play and it was announced that some special guests would be performing. The three ladies enjoyed food and drinks. Several minutes later Debbie walked in smiling and happy to see everyone. Things were beginning to feel normal between them as they laughed and joked about unimportant things.

Snookie broke up the lighthearted fun by saying, "Alright, enough of the small talk. I just checked my messages and Aurora is on her way. Says she had something important to take care of, but she'll be here shortly."

"Good," said Portia. "We've all had some important things to deal with."

"I wanna know what the hell you bitches have been doing that was so important that you practically left me alone for weeks?"

"Giving you time to stop using that word to describe us," said Candy, sincerely.

"Damn, what happened to you?" asked Snookie. "Just cause you don't use the word, all of a sudden I can't use it, either?"

"It's a new day, Snookie," Candy responded.

"I agree," said Portia.

"Okay, Benedict Arnold!" said Snookie as they laughed.

The conversation remained light as they waited for Aurora and Melissa to show up. They were all silently praying that this reunion wouldn't turn out to be a disaster.

"I can't believe that damn Melissa," Snookie said. "She said she would be early, so I'm going to curse her out when she comes."

What Snookie didn't know was that she might never get the chance to face Melissa at all. What she couldn't possibly know, what none of them knew, was that Melissa was sprawled out alone on her lovely hardwood floor, bleeding to death from a bullet wound to her head. Melissa was barely alive, cold and afraid, unable to move or to hear, and wondering if she was already dead.

CHAPTER 66

Melissa

"What the hell is happening to me?" Melissa thought.

Suddenly, she felt herself being lifted into the air. She couldn't actually feel anyone touching her. It was more of a sensation of floating that she felt. The more she floated up, the freer she felt. Melissa looked below and could see herself lying on the floor in a pool of blood. It like she was watching a movie.

"Is that blood coming from my head? Why is there so much blood?"

The sight of her own unmoving body mesmerized her until she heard a noise at the door. Someone was trying to get in. Good, because she definitely needed help. It was the LAPD, followed by Alex and a team of paramedics with all of their equipment.

"Now, the stupid landlord shows up," Melissa said. "If he had come when he was supposed to, maybe I wouldn't be bleeding to death on my living room floor."

"Are you ready, Melissa?"

The voice was almost whispering. Melissa looked around at the scene below her to see who was speaking. None of the people below were speaking in that tone.

"Are you ready?" asked the voice again.

Melissa looked around again. Was the voice only inside of her head?

"Who is that?" she asked, confused, but unafraid.

"Are you ready?" the voice asked again.

"Ready for what?"

"Are you ready?"

"Yes," she responded, hoping to get an answer.

Immediately, Melissa found herself in another place. Not a floating sensation this time. It was as though she was standing on a cloud, and she was aware of weightlessness. It didn't feel real. The space around her was brighter than it was a moment ago and she felt as though she was breathing misty air.

Melissa looked around. There was nothing and no one within her vision. She saw colors in the distance, but no forms. It was a strange feeling being in this place. Even though it was unfamiliar to her, she also felt like she had been there before. Melissa walked in the direction of the colors. She loved how natural it felt to not be touching anything. Her feet could not feel the floor. Actually, she realized that there was no floor. She wasn't even walking. Her mind told her to walk, but she just seemed to be moved in the direction of her intention.

As Melissa approached the area of the colors, it became brighter and then began to take the shape of more familiar things. Some of her favorite things in life.

"Are you ready?"

There was that mysterious voice again, beckoning her. Melissa spun around several times, almost uncontrollably. She really had to get this "out of body" thing down. From the colors, a shape began to form. Not a person, but the idea of a person. The energy emanating from the form was not threatening. She actually felt intense love.

"Am I dead?" Melissa asked.

"That's a tricky question."

"Really? It sounds like a yes or no question to me."

"Since the snippy attitude of your personality is still present, I would say that you surely remain attached to the earthly realm."

"So, I'm not dead?" she asked. "Cause I was just about to get the biggest break of my life. How messed up would that be if I died on a day like that?"

"Your human body is at rest," replied the entity. "However, your spirit is here to receive instruction. There are some things that you need to take back with you."

"Take back?" Melissa was relieved. "Thank God!"

"You're welcome."

Her eyes suddenly got really big and she was humbled.

"Oh… my… God!"

"Yes."

Melissa just stood there, speechless. Her brain would not allow her to comprehend the concept of standing before her maker.

After another moment of shock and awe, she slowly squinted her eyes and put her hands on her hips.

"Stop playing with me," she said, attitude intact.

"Okay," said the entity, laughing. "I do have a sense of humor."

"Who are you?" Melissa asked. "Really?"

CHAPTER 67

Aurora

Aurora thought about what she had done since returning from New York. She certainly wasn't proud of herself. Sitting in her car stalking Melissa was the last straw. She had gone too far. While she listened to Kyria's new CD, she wished that things had turned out differently. A beautiful song came on called *I Should Have Gone Home* that allowed Aurora to think about her present circumstances. She had been so happy in New York these past weeks, knowing that she had helped to build a talented young singer's career and change her life. She had done that many times over the past few years. She tended to forget how good she was at her job. Then she thought about how her sister Sharon looked up to her, and how difficult it would be for Sharon to lose her over something like this. Making a huge mistake could cost Aurora everything. She didn't think that she could live a life behind bars.

"I almost killed someone tonight!" Aurora shouted out loud as she was driving back home to Redondo Beach to clean herself up and join her friends at Popi's Place. Before leaving Melissa's she called Mark Sullivan and asked him to come back to her house and pick her up. He agreed, without hesitation. He had the rest of the night off and didn't have to respond, but that's the kind of guy he was. He always made her a priority. Slightly dazed, she avoided a couple of accidents. She was right not to trust herself to drive for the rest of the night. It was time for Aurora to get a grip on reality and let it all go. She even smiled at the thought that Krome and Melissa might be in love, but immediately dismissed the thought when she remembered what Palmer Whitmore told her. Krome had practically pimped Melissa out.

When Aurora returned home, she locked up the gun in a safer place than she had it before. She had wasted a lot of time, not just tonight, but for a large portion of her life. It was time to put herself first and manage her personal life with the same precision that she ruled her business. She could weed out bullshit like nobody else.

That's what she needed to do, weed out the bullshit and go after the life she deserved.

She wanted to look extra good after feeling so shitty for the past 24 hours. When she tried to call Snookie and Portia, the calls went to voicemail, so she left a message that she was on her way. She jumped in the shower and while letting the hot water wash over her, she prayed really hard that she could face Melissa tonight.

Mark Sullivan was ringing the bell at Aurora's front door. There was no answer. He could see that her car was there and the lights were on. Because of the abrupt way that she asked him to come back here to get her, and the strange way that she sounded when she called, he was worried about her. He still had the spare key she gave him the night she walked out on Krome, so he decided to risk her anger by using it.

"Miss Duncan," he called out, with no response. "It's me, Mark."

He looked around for any signs of distress, but other than being very quiet, everything seemed okay. He listened at the bottom of the stairs and heard the sound of the shower running, so he slowly walked up the steps towards her bedroom. Her room was a little messier than he would have expected, but he didn't see anything to worry about. The bathroom door was ajar. He walked over to the CD player and turned it on, dimmed the lights and lit some candles.

A couple of minutes later, he heard the water turn off and Aurora appeared in the doorway wrapped in a towel. He turned to look at her. She was momentarily surprised, but happy to see him. As a matter of fact, her entire demeanor had changed from when he saw her earlier. He took off his jacket as she walked towards him, maintaining eye contact. She stopped directly in front of him.

"You used my spare key?"

"I was worried about you," he said. "You didn't answer the door."

"I was busy."

"I see."

"How come you don't have a date tonight?" she asked softly.

"I did have a date," he responded, enjoying the smell of her close to him.

"So, where is she?" Aurora asked with a sly smile.

"I dropped her off after you called."

"Are you upset with me for calling you back to work?"

"It doesn't feel like work."

"It doesn't feel like anything at all."

Before she had a chance to say anything else, Mark pulled her to him and began kissing her passionately. She responded immediately and after a long embrace, Mark stepped back and pulled the towel away from her body. The candlelight made her look soft and vulnerable. He couldn't get naked fast enough.

"Are you feeling something now?" he whispered as he spread her legs and buried his manhood into her wet vagina. For the first time, Aurora Duncan let herself be free to enjoy making love to a man who always put her first. It was a hell of an aphrodisiac and at this rate, she figured she wouldn't make it to Popi's Place until after 10pm.

CHAPTER 68

Melissa

As an ambulance rushed Melissa to the hospital, the police were notifying Mama Susie, who contacted Junior, who was doing a show in Phoenix, and the rest of the family. They immediately rushed to be by her side. Her condition was critical and although her body was traumatized, her mental, emotional, and spiritual experience was enhanced by the presence of the entity who was keeping her company.

Chuck and his friends were at a sports bar in Studio City watching an Angels game when the news report came in:

"Melissa Murdock, an R&B singer, was shot in her Hollywood apartment this evening and left for dead. Ms. Murdock was scheduled to make her musical debut tonight at a star-studded event being held at Popi's Place on Melrose Avenue. Her condition is considered to be critical and she remains in a coma at this hour at Cedars Sinai Medical Center. The search for the shooter is underway at this time. Tune in for the full story along with other headline news, weather and sports at ten."

"Oh, shit!" Chuck said, immediately jumping up. "I gotta get to Popi's Place."

"Go," said George. "We'll take care of the tab and meet you over there."

"Thanks, man."

Chuck raced through the traffic into Hollywood wondering what could have possibly happened. Portia wasn't picking up her phone.

Melissa wasn't clear what was happening to her, but she felt peace being with this entity. Then suddenly she remembered what happened on the greatest night of her life. How she was so afraid, shocked and disturbed that she couldn't believe her eyes and ears. A woman who had once been her best friend had threatened to kill her. Now, she was able to remember clearly, without the pain.

After she was threatened with the gun, Melissa had a good reason to be afraid, so she had put her hands in the air and slowly backed away.

"Okay, but you really need to put that gun down. This ain't right. You love me. You're not really gonna shoot me."

The look in the woman's eyes held no love. No compassion. Just hatred and vengeance. "You don't know what the hell I'll do."

"He isn't worth it," Melissa said.

CHAPTER 69

Popi's Place

Candy was wondering where Aurora and Melissa were. She took out her cell phone and saw that she had several missed calls and messages.

"My goodness, somebody's trying to reach me badly."

Portia pulled out her phone and said, "Maybe it's the other girls. Damn, Chuck's been calling me."

While they began checking voicemail messages, trying to hear over the music, Portia stood up, shocked.

"What's wrong?" Debbie asked.

At that moment, Chuck came running into the clubroom. Portia ran into his arms.

"I'm so glad to see you," she said.

"Are you okay, baby?" he asked.

"Yes, but we need to get to the hospital."

The ladies were gathering their belongings and Jacques came rushing over.

"Ladies, I am packing up your food to take with you. Everything's on the house. Please give Mademoiselle Melissa my very best."

"I just picked up a message from Aurora," said Snookie. "She got in late from the airport, but I guess she's home now getting dressed to come here. I tried to call her back, but now she's not answering her phone."

Portia asked, "Did you leave her a message?"

"I told her to meet us at the hospital."

"Let's go," Portia said.

The ladies hugged Jacques, thanked him and rushed out with Chuck. There was chaos at the front door as people were still trying to get into Popi's Place.

CHAPTER 70

Melissa

"Oh, no!" Melissa exclaimed. "Did that really happen? She shot me?"

"Yes, she did."

"And you're sure I'm not dead?"

"I'm sure."

"And who are you? You never answered me."

"I am one of your spiritual guides," responded the entity. "I am here to let you know where you stand in your evolution."

"What does that mean?" she asked.

"The purpose of your earthly life; the reason why you exist as the person you are. You made this incarnation with five others and were born to help each other evolve."

"You talking about my girls?"

"Yes," he responded. "You each had fears to overcome in this lifetime."

Something awakened in Melissa's spirit. She saw her entire life clearly. She saw the lives of her five best friends, viewing them in her spirit as though she was watching individual movies of their lives. She understood things about them that they had never shared. In that moment, she became their true soul sister, their survivor, their savior.

Snookie Watson, a loud, obnoxious Alabama girl with low self-esteem. Not knowing who her father was and being raised by a woman who didn't want her or know how to love her, was painful knowledge for a little girl. If your own mother doesn't love you, then maybe you aren't lovable. That was the message received. Unfortunately, Snookie continued the vicious cycle by abandoning her own child. She learned to cover her pain by being funny. And she really did keep her family and friends laughing, because she could be so outrageous at times.

Unfortunately, Snookie's idea of being funny usually meant sacrificing someone else's feelings. Her perceived value was in the way that she took care of her siblings. She knows that she did a good job, the best job she could, being a child herself, and if she could see herself through their eyes, she would be able to feel the success of her sacrifice. She had been forced to work so hard as a child, that she never had time to *become* a child. Snookie wasn't able to develop into a woman who could look back and appreciate her life. She always found momentary validation in the arms of men who could never love her, therefore proving that she wasn't worthy of love in the first place. A viscous cycle that will continue to cause great emotional pain until she finds her value and lives up to it.

Aurora Duncan is afraid to be loved, feeling that she would lose herself, and therefore has a fear of commitment. If she would stop accepting less than she deserves from the men in her life, she would get the love that she so desperately wants and needs. After spending much of her childhood being disappointed by the main man in her life, her father, she learned that love hurt you. Love disappointed you. Love walked away from you. Therefore, the best way to avoid getting your heart broken was to make sure that you were in no danger of falling in love, which would require submitting your heart and soul, having that love returned, and being vulnerable to losing it all. It was a chance that Aurora wasn't willing to take.

She wasn't sure that what her parents had was love. It seemed some warped version of it. Would she have even known what it looked like if it knocked her in the head? She was too afraid to let her guard down long enough to find out. It was safer to have a man who would give her exactly what she wanted and expected: a love-free relationship. He would never commit to her, which gave her an excuse to run, and run back, which in turn made him her only weakness. By being afraid, she has created a life just as lonely as the one she is trying to avoid.

Debbie Marshall has to learn forgiveness. She never forgave her father for not being present for her, and at the same time, blames herself for a lot of the things that happened. She uses that excuse to run through life without considering consequences. She threw away her education and isn't feeling worthy. Sharing the day her mother died with the day she was born was tragic for her. She took it upon her young shoulders to be responsible for her mother's death and her father's decline into alcoholism. When her father basically killed himself while driving drunk on her 18th birthday, she felt responsible: she should have been a better daughter, and not dropped out of school and caused a scandal. She never consciously told herself these things, but it was in her heart.

Being a high school dropout represented her failure to herself and her family, but somewhere inside she found the strength to go on. She forged a career while harboring her secret. A secret that made her cover feelings of inferiority, but not something so terrible that it would make the people she cared about look down upon her, although that was her greatest fear. Getting her GED represented something very important to her: reparation to her dead father for the disappointments and humiliation that she felt Michael endured at her hand.

Candy Martin, the dark-skinned, former beauty queen, who is stunning, yet filled with self-hatred. The extreme damage done to her as a child by her well-meaning mother and drunken grandmother created a perception of herself that has never been erased. Like Snookie, she had an unknown father, referred to as "the African." A girl like her needed to feel watertight security in her world. Instead, she was treated like something dirty, something to be ashamed of and something undesirable. Her wounds are so deep that she has a constant need to avoid any relationship which might create a person that looks like her. In other words, if there is even a small chance that she might conceive a child, it better be with a white man.

Candy can't see her inner beauty because of her preoccupation with her skin color. Whatever confidence that she gained from being accepted by white people did nothing to heal the deep wounds of rejection by her own people. The sad result is that she's artificial and escapes reality with drugs and alcohol. Candy craves attention and spends a lot of her time looking for that white man who is going to validate her. Her salvation, however, is in her girlfriends. They accept her for who she is: wounds and all. As soon as she realizes that for herself, everything in her world will change.

Portia Taylor-Adams, the big, beautiful flashy woman who appears outwardly to be the most secure, is desperately worried about losing everything. You wouldn't know it because she covers it up by being busy. She is a woman who loves to eat, shop, party and have sex. Everything that she does, she does big: big hair, heavy makeup, long nails, fancy wardrobe. She is just a Vegas showgirl on the inside, and it spills over into her life.

Portia was fortunate enough to meet and marry Chuck Adams, the handsome hunk, several years younger, who loves her deeply. She has a job she loves. Basically, she's got a great life. On the surface, she's happy and satisfied, but Portia has trust issues. Deep down she's insecure and hides it by using other people's problems as a way of feeling superior. She grew up feeling secure in her body, but was betrayed by the men in her life, who always abandoned her for thinner girls, while keeping her on the side for sex. She learned to use sex as a means to keep the men in her life, even when she knew they didn't love her. Now that she found Chuck, a man who truly loves her exactly the way she is, she sometimes treats him as though she expects him to walk away any day. She's the one that others look up to, but she's a perfect bubble about to burst.

Melissa was able to see her friends clearly. Now it was her turn. She had to look at her life from the outside in. Melissa Murdock, bi-racial, but looks white. In love with her blackness, and wishes she was darker. She hates being mistaken for being white, even though it's half of who she is. She goes out of her way to prove that she is just as black inside as she is white outside. She has never fit well in either camp, but tried so hard that it hurt. She's a talented singer who believes in herself but always feels that she has to prove something. She dates black men, has a black soul, and uses sex as a means to calm her demons and make her feel good about herself. It rarely works.

It's time for Melissa to accept herself and what she's done to contribute to the position she's in now. Shot and almost dead at the hands of someone who she should have held dear. Once again Melissa clearly replayed the scene in her apartment as a woman she loved aimed a gun directly at her.

"You think this is about some nigga you fucked?" the woman laughed. "Oh, wait a minute. That's right." She was eerily nonchalant as she slowly moved closer to Melissa. "That nigga was mine."

Melissa saw herself scream as her beloved cousin, Eleanor Foster, pulled the trigger, shot her in the head and left her for dead. How desperate her cousin must have felt to think that her only choice was to eliminate Melissa from the face of the Earth. How much Eleanor must have held hatred in her shattered heart over the many times that Lester Buckingham was thrown in her face, and then even when Melissa was nowhere around, Lester didn't give her the time of day. Seeing the two of them together in Atlanta was more than poor Eleanor's pride could take. She had snapped.

Melissa never went to see Eleanor after she was arrested, never even tried to reach out. She had basically put her entirely out of her mind. Mention of Eleanor had become a short blurb in a conversation with her family, to be quickly moved away from, replaced by more relevant and pleasant topics. Talking about Eleanor upset her grandmother. Susie Murdock's health had been on a decline ever since her granddaughter Eleanor went to prison. However, after serving her sentence with no problems and passing her psych evaluation, Eleanor had been released. No one even knew that she was coming home, much less that she still had intentions to harm Melissa.

There are so many things that could have been done differently. Melissa should have gone to see Eleanor because she was the only one in the family who knew the full story as to why Eleanor really set that motel fire, the only one who could piece together the events that led up to her cousin trying to kill her and Lester Buckingham years ago. Melissa should have told the truth. She should have told Mama Susie everything, instead of only saying that she couldn't find Eleanor in Atlanta. The family had no idea that Eleanor wanted her dead, but Melissa had always known it in her soul. She knew that she had given her cousin a reason to be pissed, but this was on a whole other level. Something was wrong with Eleanor, something that no one could have been prepared for.

After all this time, Eleanor still wanted Melissa dead and was willing to go back to prison to ensure that it happened.

Melissa saw that history was repeating itself with Krome. She didn't really love him, but wanted him because he wanted her, just like Lester. It was almost a game, one that she had no right to play. She also saw something that shocked her more than anything else. She created such hurt that Aurora wanted her dead, too. She realized that in order for her to be free, for all of them to be free, they had to face their individual truths, and pray it wasn't too late.

Together, six beautiful women from different backgrounds, different lifestyles, and different experiences all ended up together in Los Angeles as friends. They each had something in them that the others needed. None of them understood how important their existence was to their collective survival. How could they? They were only human.

Melissa saw the big picture of their life's purpose as it was agreed to before they came to the world. She remembered them as spirits together before they were born. Remembered why they individually chose the parents that they chose. She watched them find families who would provide the challenges that they would require in order to fulfill the needs of their souls. She saw how their pasts had worked to bring them all together, and the reasons that they had agreed to embark on this journey to help each other to heal, and therefore evolve spiritually.

In her realization, she found peace. There was no reason for her to fear anything. Her life was exactly as it should be, based on the choices that she had made. The five other women in her life were in the same boat. She instantly saw their mistakes as well as their triumphs. There were rare times when their unconditional love for others allowed them to rise above their challenges and experience real spiritual growth. Most of the time, however, they made choices out of fear and not out of love.

"Wow!" she exclaimed. "We've really made a mess of things, haven't we?"

"Yes, you have," replied the guide. "You all have moved away from the light of your friendship and dabbled within the darkness, but you can still come back together. Your spiritual connection as a group is much stronger than any of the individual human frailties that you may possess. However, it's up to you, as the leader of your soul group, to go back and pull the others back into the light. Time is of the essence."

"What's the rush?" she asked.

"That isn't something that you need to know."

"This doesn't mean I have to go back and be a preacher or anything, right?"

"Melissa Murdock, as interesting as that might be for the world to experience, it isn't necessary. All that is required of you is to go back and give Aurora Duncan, Candy Martin, Debbie Marshall, Portia Taylor-Adams and Snookie Watson the insights you have gained about each of them. They will hear you, not all of them will listen. And that's okay. The information is to remind them of who they are, and it's not going to be easy. That's life. However, the sooner they get it, the happier they will be."

"So, I can continue to have my music career?"

"You still have free will, Melissa," the guide said with no judgment. "If that's how you see your contribution to the world, knowing what you know, then proceed."

"Why do you say it like that?" she asked. "You said that I could still be myself."

"You will be yourself, but you will also feel changed," the guide continued. "How you effect that change is up to you."

"Okay. It's a riddle. I get it."

Laughing again, the spirit looked at Melissa with such love and understanding, Melissa felt it pouring into her.

"You are so precious," said her spiritual guide.

"I guess my human side is pretty strong, huh?"

"The Earth school is a powerful way to bring the soul into a pure state of love. But it doesn't happen without struggle. Most spiritual evolution comes from human challenges, and happens over many lifetimes. The knowledge that your soul has chosen to go through these challenges, makes it all divine."

"I always like a good challenge," she said.

"If you are successful, you will all find your spiritual paths easier the next time."

"What do you mean, next time?"

"Next lifetime."

"Let me just get through this one first." Melissa laughed. "When do I go back?"

"You're already there," replied the guide.

CHAPTER 71

Melissa

Junior Murdock and the rest of the clan were gathered in the waiting room at Cedars Sinai Medical Center, praying and waiting for word from Melissa's doctors. She had been admitted in critical condition with a gunshot wound to the face. The bullet had hit her in the right cheek and missed parts of her head that could have been fatal. She lost a lot of blood and fell into a coma. The surgeons were able to stabilize her and now they could only pray that she would wake up soon. Also waiting for Melissa to wake up were Snookie, Portia, Debbie, and Candy. Aurora was rushing to join the other women. She had finally checked her messages after an hour of mind-blowing sex with Mark Sullivan.

In the back of the limousine, all Aurora could think about was how she had wanted Melissa dead a few hours before. Now all she could do was pray that she made it to the hospital in time. So much had happened in one night, she could barely wrap her mind around it. Aurora felt free and knew that she needed to tell Melissa that she forgave her. It was extremely important to her. So, she urged Mark to drive a little faster.

"I'm just a phone call away if you need me," Mark said, hugging Aurora before she ran into Cedars Sinai to join her friends.

When she stepped into the lobby waiting area where the ladies were gathered, they rushed to embrace her. After a long, emotional moment, they separated.

"How is she?" Aurora asked.

"It's a miracle that she's alive," Portia responded.

"Thank God," Aurora said, almost weak with relief.

"Her family's with her," Candy said.

"Where the hell have *you* been?" Snookie added.

For the next thirty minutes, Aurora told her friends the story of her temporary insanity, nervous breakdown, or whatever it was that she had experienced. They were shocked and appalled. There were moments when they were sure that she was about to confess that she was the person who tried to kill Melissa, but they all remained silent until she was finished. Snookie finally blurted out what everyone was thinking.

"So, if you didn't do it, then who did?"

Just then, Junior Murdock, who was even better looking as he got older, stepped off the elevator and walked into the lobby. The ladies held their collective breath as he approached them.

"She's awake and asking for all of you," he said.

When Melissa woke up from her coma, her family was by her side and she was thrilled to see them. Junior Murdock broke into tears and told her that her mother was on a plane from Dallas. Mama Susie, who had continuously prayed and refused to go home, finally gave in to her exhaustion now that God had seen Melissa through the storm. Other than the pain that was being controlled with drugs, Melissa's condition was good, vital signs were strong and the doctors considered her a minor miracle.

Police officers took a statement, and then Melissa explained to her family what happened. There was an APB issued for the arrest of Eleanor Foster. Even though the doctors wanted to limit visitors after that, Melissa insisted that her friends be allowed to see her, especially after she heard that they were waiting in the lobby.

As the doctors explained to her family how miraculous it was that she was in such great shape considering the trauma that she went through, Melissa asked to talk to each woman separately, beginning with Aurora, who was once again afraid. But Melissa already knew her deepest fears and as soon as Aurora walked into Melissa's hospital room and saw her reach out to her with a big smile on her swollen, bandaged face, she felt a wave of love and forgiveness and complete understanding. No words were necessary. Aurora rushed to Melissa's side, laid her head on Melissa's chest and broke down, her tears cleansing her and washing away a lifetime of hurt. Melissa caressed Aurora's face as both of their prayers had been answered.

Nurses had to come in and check on Melissa as each of the ladies came and went. The medical staff was still puzzled by her accelerating recovery. As each of her friends took turns at her bedside, Melissa revealed how the spirit visited her and told her what they all have to do better. There were so many things to tell them, and as each one of them came to sit with her, she was able to bring them the information that would change their lives for the better. They listened to her because she was able to tell them things that came from the well of their souls and they instinctively knew them to be true.

CHAPTER 72

Lawrence

Anita Desmond never had to settle for anything in her life. She wasn't going to start now. She was a proud, beautiful woman who was well educated and had owned her own consulting business for several years before she met her husband, Lawrence. Unlike other men she had dated, Lawrence was intelligent, sophisticated and strong, and also had an exciting life as a designer of classic men's suits. She liked his style. He was very levelheaded, worked hard, but also knew how to relax. He wasn't easily rattled. She previously attracted the same neurotic, corporate types who were workaholics. When they did have a little down time, they still couldn't stop working. Anita got bored very quickly. She knew business. She wasn't interested in talking about it all the time.

Meeting Lawrence was a breath of fresh air. He had the serious, business side, but then had creative talent as well. He wanted to settle down and have a family. He had strong values and that's what attracted her to him. Anita gave up a lot of her own ambitions to be his wife and help him run his business. Her story was nothing new. How many women had let go of their own dreams so that their families could flourish? It was a sacrifice well worth making. Lawrence turned out to be a good provider and was an involved father with his two kids, so Anita was able to enjoy a good life. They raised their son and daughter together and had a solid marriage that took them through good times and bad. Luckily, it was mostly good and the entire family seemed happy.

For years, Lawrence and Anita had been looking forward to this time in their lives when the kids were out of the house and they could be a couple again. For the last few months, he had been spending a lot of time at his studio, especially the past six weeks, because of the top secret new clothing line. Anita understood his need to be focused during his creative periods, so she respected his privacy and supported him. His business was doing better than ever. This was their time. They had two healthy children in college, and were in the prime of their lives. Anita had waited patiently and she knew that her husband was getting close to revealing his new collection.

It was time for her to plan some trips and weekend getaways for them. She loved to travel and really missed the freedom to do more of that. And she wanted to begin throwing parties again. She was once known as the hostess with the parties that you didn't want to miss. Instead, she was a cliché. The wife: the last to know.

What Anita heard while outside of Lawrence's studio made her sick. She was devastated by the fact that her husband had cheated on her, especially with a woman almost half her age. But now she had to do what needed to be done in a situation like this. Anita packed a small bag and left a note saying that she was going to visit her sister in Fresno for a few days. She did that often enough that Lawrence didn't think anything of it when he returned home late that night, but he was a little disappointed that he couldn't surprise her with the news that his collection was finished. For a split second he felt guilty for sharing it with Debbie first.

Three days later, when Lawrence came home from the studio, he saw that Anita's car was in the driveway. He was happy to see that she was back. He entered the house and when he didn't see her right away, poured himself a glass of wine and went to check the mail that was on the counter. As Lawrence stood sipping his wine, he heard movement behind him. He turned around and saw Anita walking towards him. He smiled, and before he even knew what hit him, Anita slapped his face with one hand, and then slapped divorce papers onto the counter with the other hand.

"I was at the studio the other night," she said calmly. "I saw the two of you together. I heard what you said and I know all I need to know."

Before the sting of Anita's hand had worn off his face, she was gone. It took him a long time to absorb the reality of the situation. He had to replay every moment with Debbie to realize how much trouble he was in with his wife. He had to fix it somehow. He heard her moving around upstairs, so he slowly made his way to their bedroom. Anita was busying herself with the task of removing Lawrence's clothes from the closet.

"Anita, what are you doing?" he asked as she moved purposefully around the room as if he wasn't even there.

"Let's talk," he said softly.

Lawrence needed for her to stop and have a conversation with him. He wasn't going to insult her by denying anything or saying she was crazy. He just felt the need to explain the whole truth. Grabbing her arm, he intercepted her.

"Please listen to me," Lawrence said. "I've always loved you, Anita, and I've been totally faithful to you all these years."

"Let go of me." She wrestled out of his grasp. "How can I believe anything that you say now?" asked Anita.

"I swear to you," he said. "I only slept with her one time."

"You may have only given her your body once, but you pursued her with your heart and soul for a whole lot longer than that," Anita said. "That's what I can't forgive. You swore to me that she was just a friend. How good was your word, Lawrence?"

"I love you, Anita. You know that. I love you." Lawrence kept his voice calm.

Anita wasn't tolerating his sweet talk. "You can't love me, because apparently you don't even know me."

"What?" he said, confusion all over his face. "How can you say that?"

"You can't love me unless you know what breaks my heart," Anita said, sadly. "Because if you knew it would break my heart, you wouldn't do it. Not if you knew me. Not if you loved me."

"Sweetheart," he said, getting close to her. "Please, let's calm down and talk."

Anita walked away, and then turned back to face him. "When we got married, that was one of the few things that I asked of you, Lawrence. One of the few things that I've *ever* asked of you. Always keep our love between us. Always keep us, just us. So, stop looking so shocked. You know exactly how I feel about infidelity. I told you that cheating would be a heartbreaker for me. Now it's the deal breaker."

"Why can't you forgive me for this one indiscretion?" he asked, his voice trembling. "I made a mistake."

"You made more than a mistake, Lawrence," she said. "You showed me what kind of man you really are now, and it's not the kind of man that I want."

"Dammit, Anita. We've gone through too much to just throw it all away," he said, his voice pleading.

"You should have been thinking about that when you came out of your pants."

"You're not a cold woman. I know that you have the capacity to forgive."

"I might have the capacity, but I can't think of a good reason why I should."

"Can you give me one good reason why you *shouldn't* give me another chance?"

"Grow up," she said, barely able to look at him. "You know how it works, Lawrence. You make your choices in life. Then, no matter how difficult, you live with the consequences of those choices. Allow me to draw you a picture."

Anita spread her arms apart and began to gesture passionately.

"You have me on one side, with everything that represents. Complete love and devotion for over twenty years. Then you have the other side. A quick piece of ass from a woman you barely know, and who will never, ever do for you what I've done." Anita's voice was full of emotion. "I cooked for you, kept a clean house and took care of our children. We even had great sex. We had a great life. We had fun together."

"We still do, my darling. I agree with all of that," he said. "You're the best. That's why I want you to forgive me and don't do this."

Anita couldn't believe her husband's arrogance. "Let me get this straight," she said, annoyed. "You had what you say was 'the best', right here with me."

She picked up a framed picture from her nightstand. It was the two of them on their honeymoon. "But you sacrificed 'the best' for what was over there, behind door number two?"

Lawrence tried to speak, but every time he opened his mouth, nothing came out. Anita thought that he looked pitiful, standing there thinking that there was anything he could say to make it better. She also knew that he would try, so she waited. He finally found his voice.

"You're right, Anita," he said, "I'm an idiot."

"Exactly," she said with confidence. "And I'm way too smart to saddle myself with a man that stupid."

Anita flung the picture against the wall next to him, shards of glass spraying over the floor.

"Now, sign the fucking divorce papers and get out."

Lawrence was shocked. Anita had never even spoken to him like that before. He searched her eyes for the compassion that was always there. What he saw was something cold and unrecognizable. That was the moment when he realized how deeply he had hurt her. He couldn't believe that he was about to lose everything. It hadn't been worth it.

Epilogue

CHAPTER 73

Popi's Place, July 2007

It had been a whole year since the tragedy that nearly took Melissa Murdock's life. With her new insights and guidance, the ladies have slowly repaired the damage done to their friendships and have also grown tremendously in every aspect of their lives. These days they spent a lot more time together outside of Popi's Place, and a lot less time partying, however, tonight was special. They were having a big party to celebrate their love for each other.

Snookie Watson realized that her hardcore attitude and random sex life wasn't going to get her anywhere. While spending the Christmas holidays in Alabama with her family, she had a heart-to-heart conversation with her sister, Shawna, who told Snookie how amazing her little boy was, how big and smart he was, and how her ex-husband, Fernando Watson, had never stopped loving her. Shawna told her what a great father he was to her little boy. And how he always told their son how much his mother loved him, even though she couldn't be there every day.

Snookie really enjoyed spending time with her siblings and all of their children. Unlike other visits with her family since moving to Los Angeles, this time it seemed that they filled some of the void in her life that she never admitted was there. Snookie didn't want to leave them, and for several months she was overcome with remorse over so much time wasted. She knew that she didn't want to spend the rest of her life alone, and then she realized that she wasn't alone. She had a family of her own. All she had to do was reach out. Snookie made a courageous move: one phone call that changed her life. Fernando Watson insisted that she come back home to him and their son where she belonged, so tonight was also Snookie's farewell party.

Aurora Duncan had resigned from Tazora Records and started her own music consulting business. She was doing very well and had discovered several new artists who were making waves. She received a lot of accolades for that, but tonight she was celebrating a very personal victory with her girlfriends. She was showing off a huge diamond engagement ring, but this time she vowed to keep it forever, along with the man who gave it to her. For once, she was truly happy.

Mark Sullivan had spent the past year showing Aurora, in word and deed, that she could trust him to love her and always put her first. The freedom that allowed her to forgive the people who hurt her, also gave her the freedom to love from the depth of her soul and not from the pain of her past.

Three weeks before, Aurora even took Mark to Chicago to meet her family, something that she could never do with Krome. That's when Mark asked Baxter and Camille Duncan for permission to marry their daughter. Her parents were still doing their thing together and were happy to give their blessing. They had been tired of reading about her awful love life in the tabloids.

Mark's limo company had been expanded since his brother retired from football and took over the day to day business, and that gave Mark the freedom to travel with his lady love, which he did often. He still rode Aurora around in a limousine stocked with her favorite champagne, but someone else did the driving and he stayed by her side.

Debbie Marshall had to keep a low profile after Lawrence Desmond's wife filed for divorce. He was crushed and confided in her as a friend, but she was adamant about not being seen together. She let him off the hook about trying to help her get into school and got her letters of recommendation from Juan Figueroa and John Becker. She was accepted to Prescott Lane, a prestigious fashion school, which she began attending that fall. She was having a wonderful time, but she was also anxious to begin making her own dress designs again. Going to school was like starting over for her. All these years of feeling unworthy were for no good reason. She had already made dresses that were worn by the rich and famous, but she never felt that she was good enough to compete in the "real world" of fashion.

Well, Debbie needn't have worried about that. During the Christmas holiday, she took time off to make some formal gowns for the awards season in Los Angeles. Debbie and her designs became an overnight sensation at the Grammy Awards which were held at the Staples Center in February. Among the beautiful women wearing her one-of-a-kind fashions on the red carpet were Kyria, who won Best New Artist, and Debbie's good friends Aurora Duncan and Melissa Murdock. Debbie made a fashion stir of her own two weeks later when she was escorted to the Academy Awards by Lawrence Desmond. It was the first time the two of them had been seen out in public since Anita Desmond filed for divorce. They were still just friends, but at least the divorce became final just in time for him to enjoy the night with Debbie, guilt-free.

Candy Martin gave up drugs and alcohol for the sake of her pregnancy and for the remaining seven months spent most of her time being pampered by her friends. She gave birth at the end of February to a healthy boy who she named Morocco Martin Adams. He was not the little mulatto baby she had always imagined as a result of her fear. Instead, he was the most beautiful brown baby in the world. By giving him the name of an African country, she was displaying her acceptance of who she was. By also giving him her surname, she vowed to be connected to him for life. However, she would not be raising the child as a single mother. She was breaking the cycle of her own family.

Portia Taylor-Adams had agreed early on that she would adopt Candy Martin's baby, and that she and Chuck would raise the child together. Portia had chosen to forgive them for their mistake and Chuck had suggested they tell people that Candy was a surrogate. They had planned to announce it to the other ladies the night Melissa was shot, but after speaking with Melissa in the hospital, Portia realized that telling the truth was the only way to live, just like she and Chuck had always done, even if it wasn't easy.

It was announced to everyone close to them that Morocco had "two mothers and several loving aunties." Candy was free to participate in his life as much as she chose to. She had already set up a college fund for the baby. Chuck and Portia would not have to worry about that. She was happy to be available to help out, but she knew that Portia and Chuck would be good parents. It was a blessing all the way around, despite what the situation looked like.

After Morocco was born, Candy felt great. She decided that she didn't need the artificial highs anymore. Feeling good about herself and her life was giving her all the high she required. Happy to have her figure back, Candy began dating black men, who suddenly found her irresistible. Loving herself gave her a different attitude. She didn't give up the white men, but her criteria had more to do with who they were as people rather than how much money or prestige they had.

"Thanks to 'ol Chucky boy," Snookie proclaimed in her irreverent way, "Candy finally got the white man stank off of her. Welcome to the dark side."

Candy waited until the baby was in the legal hands of his new parents before telling her mother and grandmother. Katie was doing fine, but Gwen's hard living had finally caught up with her. Candy decided to give them a new home, so she went to South Carolina recently and hired a team of movers to help them pack what they needed. Within record time, she had moved them into a cute three-bedroom house in West LA, not far from her Westwood condo. She even hired a live-in nurse to help Gwen with her health issues. They were excited to be part of Candy and Morocco's life.

Portia Taylor-Adams was the happiest woman on the planet. Once Morocco arrived, she immediately became a working mom. She toned down a little bit on the hair, makeup and nails, but she was still big and beautiful. Chuck was thrilled to have a son that he could bond with. He became Mr. Mom. His uncle passed away and left him a few of the properties that he owned, including a big house that they were in the process of renovating. They would be moving in at the end of the month. Chuck used his inheritance to hire a lot of the work out so that he could take care of his family in every way. He still did most of the cooking and Portia was still grateful. She was also able to cut back on her hours at work to make sure that she wasn't too tired to help out with the baby. She had lots of help from her friends. Life was good.

Melissa Murdock was proud of her girlfriends and they were proud of her. They had all come a long way in the past year and things were only getting better. True to form in the entertainment world, the news of Melissa's shooting on the night of her scheduled debut at Popi's Place propelled her first single, *"Pale Chocolate,"* to a top ten hit. Her recovery was even greater news and she became an inspiration to a lot of people. "*Forgive Me Now*," a song she wrote after her ordeal, debuted at number one.

On Grammy night, Melissa got a standing ovation from the audience when she won for Best R&B Album. She gave a beautiful speech and proudly displayed the scar that she declined to have removed when she had her face reconstructed from the shooting. Portia's boss, Dr. Clayton, did the beautiful work for her, pro bono.

"Every life has purpose and value," Melissa said, accepting her reward. "Our job as human beings is to find those things for ourselves and share it with others. Love survives when the mind and body can't, and inspires us to move beyond any limitations which are self-inflicted. Love is what seals the deal."

So here they were at Popi's Place, their favorite spot, where so many memories were made. They were all friends because they served a purpose in each other's lives. Even the bad things that happened were predestined so that they could learn forgiveness and elevate beyond their petty disagreements and see the spiritual growth possible by learning from their mistakes. For the most part, they were really trying and Melissa was using her newfound fame to spread the word.

They took only a moment to discuss the people who created havoc in their lives. Krome was still in jail after he got drunk at the Grammys, left early and got into a fight outside. When he was arrested, there was a seventeen-year-old teenage girl in his limo drinking and smoking with him. She was a blond.

Two days after Melissa was shot, the police found Eleanor Foster in East Los Angeles trying to get on a bus to Tijuana. She resisted arrest and bit a cop. As a result, five cops beat her with batons, creating a new LAPD scandal. A homeless man had captured it all on videotape.

Holding up their glasses of champagne and sparkling cider, the ladies celebrated each other with a toast.

"Snookie Watson in the house."

"Aurora Duncan in the house."

"Debbie Marshall in the house."

"Candy Martin in the house."

"Portia Taylor-Adams in the house."

"Melissa Murdock in the house."

They clinked their glasses, happy to be together as the band played Al Green's *For the Good Times*.

THE END

About Rainelle

A true renaissance woman, Rainelle Saunders has spread her wings beyond her birthplace in Connecticut to reach for the stars that filled her childhood dreams. By age six, she was recognized as a creative writer and placed in a group of gifted children. Throughout her school years, she wrote plays, stories, poetry and songs, and eventually went on to study drama at NYU. Rainelle began her professional artistic career in NYC. After a few years, destiny brought her to Hollywood, where she became a writer/actor on a show for BET. With KARTI Productions, she and four friends wrote, produced and acted in several stage productions, and sold their first screenplay. Rainelle completed several other screenplays and stage plays over the years. She's also published several songs, and recorded a spoken word CD. In 2005, Rainelle completed her first independent feature, *I Dance in Jasmine*, which she wrote, produced and starred in. Expanding into directing, she produced and directed *It Makes Sense*, a documentary short, and is directing and co-producing a documentary feature. *Popi's Place* is her first novel, and there are more to come. Rainelle brings her loving spirit to every project and continues to be blessed with opportunities to use her many gifts. These gifts and their expressions are a great part of who she is: a creative being…being creative.

Visit Rainelle Saunders:

Twitter @RainelleS

www.facebook.com/rainelle.saunders

Email: rainellesaunders@gmail.com

About Glover Lane Press

Azaan Kamau started Glover Lane Press in the summer of 2000 to give aspiring writers, journalists, photographers and passionate poets a platform to be seen and heard.

The company's catalogue features reference, fiction, non-fiction, spiritual/ metaphysical, epic novels, poetry, memoir, custom journals, full color coffee table books, and much more.

Visit Glover Lane Press:

Twitter @azaankamau

www.gloverlanepress.webs.com

www.facebook.com/gloverlanepress

www.ingramcontent.com/pod-product-compliance
Lightning Source LLC
LaVergne TN
LVHW021506260826
846436LV00056B/361